*Winter Kill: The Complete Cases
of MacBride & Kennedy, Volume 4*

Frederick Nebel

Frederick Nebel

WINTER KILL: THE COMPLETE CASES OF

MacBRIDE & KENNEDY

VOLUME 4, FROM THE PAGES OF BLACK MASK

FREDERICK NEBEL

Illustrations by
ARTHUR RODMAN BOWKER

Introduction by
EVAN LEWIS

With an Article by
ED HULSE

Series Editor
KEITH ALAN DEUTSCH

Another Volume in the BLACK MASK LIBRARY

Boston • Philadelphia • New York
2013

© 2013 Altus Press • First Edition—2013

DESIGNED AND PUBLISHED BY
Matthew Moring

BLACK MASK SERIES EDITOR
Keith Alan Deutsch

PUBLISHING HISTORY
"Introduction" appears here for the first time. Copyright © 2013 Evan Lewis. All Rights Reserved.

"Frederick Nebel Reaches the Screen" is a revised and expanded version of an article that originally appeared as "Pulp Page to Silver Screen: *Smart Blonde* (1937, Warner Brothers)" in *Blood 'n' Thunder* #16 (Fall 2006). Copyright © 2006, 2013 Ed Hulse. All Rights Reserved.

Owing to limitations of space, permissions to reprint previously published material appear on pages 371-372.

Published by arrangement with Black Mask Press/Keith Alan Deutsch (keithdeutsch@mac.com).

THANKS TO
Ed Hulse, Evan Lewis, Ken McDaniel, Rob Preston & Ray Riethmeier.

Visit altuspress.com for more books like this.

Printed in the United States of America.

Another volume in the BLACK MASK LIBRARY.

Table of

CONTENTS

Introduction

EVAN LEWIS

THIS has been a long time coming.

Nebel fans like me have been waiting not just years—but *decades*—for this series to be reprinted.

In the heyday of *Black Mask*, two series stood head and shoulders above the rest: Dashiell Hammett's adventures of the Continental Op, and Frederick Nebel's saga of Richmond City. Both authors excelled in their mastery of the hard-boiled style, the depth and humor of their characters, the richness of their settings and the varied scope of their stories. But while Hammett is now a household name, Nebel has been largely relegated to the shadows.

The reason is simple. While Hammett and many of his contemporaries went on to write mystery novels, Nebel stuck to novelettes. As the pulps gave way to paperbacks in the 1950s, the novel became the dominant fictional form, rendering the novelette almost defunct. *Black Mask* writers like Erle Stanley Gardner, George Harmon Coxe, W.T. Ballard—and a guy named Raymond Chandler—remained in the public consciousness thanks to their books, while Nebel was remembered only by pulp collectors.

Nebel was a skilled craftsman who put his own stamp on the hard-boiled school of writing. His prose, packed with crackling dialogue and keen characterization, is as fresh today as it was in the 1930s. Altus Press has brought the bulk of his detective writing back into print. Now, at long last, they introduce new legions of readers to his most important body of work—the adventures of Captain Steve MacBride and his pal, reporter Kennedy of the *Free Press*.

When this series debuted in the September 1928 *Black Mask*, it was called "The Crimes of Richmond City." The title was appropriate because while this is the story of MacBride and Kennedy, it's also the story of a city. The series lasted nine years, and from first to last, Richmond City was portrayed as a living, breathing and growing metropolis—almost a character in itself.

Nebel's secret was simple. In writing about Richmond City, he was writing about his home town. The borough of Staten Island, New York, where he was born, was then known as Richmond. It comprised most of Richmond County, with Richmond Valley at one end, Richmond Terrace at the other, Richmond Creek in the middle, and joined by Richmond Avenue and Richmond Road. He took the harbor and residential areas of Staten Island and combined them with elements of the Bronx and Manhattan to create his own scaled-down version of New York. Richmond City seemed very real—because to Nebel, it was.

In the first volume of this series, comprised of stories published between September 1928 and February 1930, we saw Richmond City at its most violent. As the series began, crooked politicians and racketeers had such a stranglehold on the city that MacBride was powerless to act. It was only when his best detective quit the Force to fight fire with fire, that the grip is broken, and MacBride could start cleaning up. He did this with a vengeance. We saw pitched battles in the streets, usually with MacBride himself leading the charge, and the death toll was high on both sides of the law. While the worst offenders were weeded out, the corruption ran deep, keeping MacBride on the defensive. Things were so bad that the precinct house sometimes seemed the last bastion of law and order.

Now late in its second year, the Richmond City series was entering a new phase. In the second Altus Press volume, featuring stories published between April 1930 and February 1933, we saw MacBride on the lookout for new rackets and new forms of corruption, hell-bent to nip them in the bud. Though he took heat from other cops—and the commissioner himself—for overstepping his bounds, MacBride was on a crusade. And when his efforts finally earned him a spot at Headquarters, he faced the reality that some of his fellow officers were on the take.

The stories published between March 1933 and February 1935, collected in the third Altus Press volume, took on a more personal note. Rather than combating large scale corruption, MacBride and Kennedy often applied their talents to murder cases, and sometimes involved old friends. That group also includes "Bad News" (March 1934), in which MacBride is away on vacation and Kennedy took the lead for the first time. That story, as you might expect, was the most comedic of the entire series.

With the series in its fifth year, MacBride is beginning to feel his age. He gets more and more frustrated with the job, particularly when men he considers friends don't support his actions. "It just breaks my heart with gratitude," he says. "Some fine day I'm going to start out and systematically change the shapes of a lot of schnozzles in this man's town." In "Rough Reform" (March 1933), he remarks, "The longer I work at this job, the more I think I should have taken up farming." He's tired of the long, irregular hours, and sick of "the blood and intrigue" that goes with police work.

In this fourth and final volume, featuring stories published between May 1935 and August 1936, we'll see secondary characters assume larger roles, and the introduction of two new regulars. By this time Nebel had come to think of himself as a novelist and wanted to delve deeper into his characters. This results in longer scenes, and sometimes longer stories.

MacBride's two best detectives, Ike Cohen and "Mory" Moriarity, were introduced early in the series, but in the final years their personalities grew stronger, providing more comic relief. They're often found sneaking drinks in the station or matching quarters in the back of the police car, and both spend a lot of time in speakeasies. The medical examiner calls them MacBride's cowboys. Kennedy calls them his stooges. MacBride calls them apes or tramps, but trusts them implicitly. "I've got two palookas working for me," he sums them up, "who think of me first and then the department."

The new regulars also add to the comedy. One of these is Kennedy's wacky bartender pal, Paderoofski. He's always ready to lend Kennedy an ear, and sometimes other essentials, like money or a gun. The other is MacBride's driver, Gahagan. He's an all-around dimwit and pays not the slightest notice to safety or traffic laws, but has an uncanny ability to get places in a hurry, and always delivers MacBride in one piece.

At this point in the series, the humor is welcome, because MacBride's moods have grown increasingly dark. He reaches the lowpoint of his career in "Fan Dance" (January 1936), when he finds himself suspended. "I ought to have been kicked in the head," he says, "the first day I ever put on a uniform." Kennedy's scenes are darker, too. Both the author and his characters seem to realize that Kennedy's drinking is out of control, posing a threat to his health and life.

Though Nebel had a long and varied career (a detailed biography appeared in Volume 1), his greatest legacy was the saga of Richmond

City. To you who are about to enter the city limits and fight crime with MacBride and Kennedy, I offer a word of advice:

Hold onto your seat. It's going to be a wild ride.

That's Kennedy

A man worldly wise to human frailties, unafraid to drive a murderer into the open— that's Kennedy.

IT was the night of the big Charity Ball. They threw it once a year, in the dead of winter, in the grand ballroom of the *Hotel Ambassador*. It was always quite an affair. Political big shots, publishers, merchant princes, showed up with their wives or sweethearts, the women laden with jewels and trying to outdo one another in décolleté gowns. The cast-your-bread-upon-the-waters theme was lost in a competitive spirit that had nothing to do with charity. Contributions were made with intense gravity, long-winded speeches, a nauseous air of self-deprivation. The sporting men who tossed their money to the alleyway bums did it with far more grace. The longest, juiciest, most elegant speech was made by Tate Hildebrand, publisher of the Hildebrand News Chain; locally, of the Richmond City *Evening Telegraph*.

There were three bars located in the *Ambassador*: the Cocktail Lounge, the Tap Room, the Alcove. The Alcove was in the basement, near the men's washrooms; it was the smallest—its shape and size almost paralleled what its name implied—and by far the coziest. Sand-colored lights shed a warm glow on dark panels and on Marcus, bald as a new-born babe and fat as Falstaff; impressive in a white starched monkey-jacket.

Everybody was listening to the Mayor's speech. Everybody but Kennedy. Kennedy was in the Alcove: a slender man in a rented evening suit, his pale hair slightly windblown above a student's forehead, his usually keen eyes now deceptively slumberous. His face wore the expression of a benign and philosophical satyr.

He said: "Marcus, how many drinks have I had?"

"Seven, Mr. Kennedy."

"I'll have another. Seven's an odd number. An odd number of drinks is apt to unbalance a man."

Marcus looked concerned. "Mr. Kennedy, excuse me if I suggest along these lines: I suggest you go upstairs and get a kind of a sort of a general idea about the Ball, on account of that is what you said you came here for, on account of you ain't been up there once tonight."

"Marcus, you're a friend. Do you think I ought to go up?"

"I truly think so, Mr. Kennedy, inasmuch."

Kennedy considered this with a melancholy air, then shrugged. "I suppose I'll have to. Hate to, Marcus. But I guess one has to eat, sleep, work for his living."

Marcus sighed. "Ain't it true? Look at me." He placed his hands on his chest. "Just look at me. All my life, ever since I was a kid in Uniontown, Pennsylvania, I wanted to be a horse doctor. And I love horses. I kind of get it from my old man, who for years played the rear end of a horse on the stage. And look at me: a bartender."

Kennedy hiccoughed. " 'S tough, my fraand." He paid his bill. "I'll see you anon."

"Anon," bowed Marcus.

Kennedy meandered into the marble corridor, made a right turn twenty yards farther on and followed a wider corridor towards a lighted glass sign lettered *Men*. The corridor was deserted, its emptiness pulsing dully with the sound of some nearby compressor. The explosion that came to Kennedy's ears was muffled. He stopped,

wondering in a hazy way if it had anything to do with the pulsing sound that impregnated the corridor. He looked back in the direction whence he had come, tilted one ear. He wasn't intensely interested, he was merely curious. And presently he shrugged and continued towards the white enameled swing-door ahead.

It swung open before he reached it. The man who came out was tall, slender, in tails. A lock of yellow hair hung down over his left temple. His face was angular, young; it was pallid but there were small feverish splotches on it. His jaw was set. In his eyes, burning with a cold white fire, there was a straight-ahead look. He strode resolutely past Kennedy without apparently seeing him.

Kennedy caught the door before it had stopped swinging and floated into the tiled lavatory. Tony Price was washing his hands at one of the basins. Price looked up into the mirror, saw Kennedy's reflection there and said crisply:

"Hello, kid."

"Hello, Tony."

Price went on washing his hands vigorously, then stood erect, flung the wet from them and yanked a towel from the shelf above the basin. He was a tall man with a good wiry build, black crinkly hair close against his scalp, a bitter mouth, dark, intelligent eyes. He was not over thirty. A high-priced feature writer on Tate Hildebrand's *Evening Telegraph*. He smiled now—a tight, hard smile.

"Well, kid, what do you think of the Charity Ball?"

Kennedy said: "Has it changed any—from last year, or the year before?"

Price finished drying his hands, slapped the towel into a metal hamper, spread his legs before a mirror and adjusted the wings of his white tie. "I didn't see you around upstairs, old pal."

"I wasn't around. Marcus and I were doing a bit of whimsy. How's Belle?"

"Upstairs. Didn't you see her?"

Price was going over his tie again, pressing and tugging at the wings with strong, nimble fingers. A small muscle at the left side of his mouth twitched spasmodically; seen in the mirror, it was like a twitching shadow.

"How's tricks?" Kennedy asked sleepily.

"Swell. By you?"

"Okie-doke."

Price finished with his tie, turned and tugged at his stiff shirt-cuffs; grinned with hard, taut good humor. "My old pal Kennedy. My mentor. You know, you haven't changed a bit in ten years. You taught me a lot."

"A guy that never changes, Tony, never gets anywhere."

"Hell, you're the best known newspaperman in town."

"I mean financially."

Price frowned, said in a low voice: "That a crack?"

"Would I make cracks at you?"

"I know you hate my guts," Price muttered.

"Skip it, Tony. Give Belle my best."

He looked down at the floor drowsily as Price strode past him.

When the cushioned door had closed, making a small compressed sound, Kennedy raised his head. His eyes opened and moved round the walls. He was older than Price. He had broken Price in on the old *Daily Standard,* shared a furnished room with him for two years. Things had changed since then. No two men remain for long on the same level. Price had gone up, swiftly, surely—a moody man, impatient, headlong.

Kennedy strolled across the tiled floor, bent and picked up from beneath one of the basins an empty cartridge shell. A thirty-two. He pursed his lips, moved his lips reflectively back and forth across his teeth. His eyes strayed again, went round and round the walls; up to the ceiling; down to the floor and round and round again. In one corner was a chipped tile baseboard. He picked up bits of flaky tile. There was no hole. He found the slug in one of the closets behind a door.

BELLE PRICE was smoking a cigarette by herself in one of the lounges off the main ballroom. She was a brunette, her hair pancaked over the ears and parted in the middle. Her eyes were brown, full of a tired intelligence. She was good-looking, with the drawn look of a woman who thinks too much about things which it is futile to think about. The slant of her eyebrows, high cheekbones, a wide, full mouth, made her appear exotic; the lines of her body amply supplemented this impression. She would be devoted to a man, but there would be nothing doglike about it.

Kennedy, who had not seen her in over a year, sat down beside her as though he'd seen her but a minute before. "You're looking well, Belle."

"Someone said you were around. I was looking for you."

"What's up?"

"Oh, nothing. I just wanted to say hello. I've often wondered why you never came around the house. Tony said he never ran into you."

"Probably right." It wasn't, of course. Price had seen him any number of times at the *Press Club,* at another table, or on his way; but Price had always avoided being with him. "Tate very happy these days?"

"Why?"

Kennedy shrugged. "Looks tight around the mouth. Tense. Too much work, I guess."

She looked straight ahead. For an instant her mouth hardened, then relaxed, and she said: "You know Tony. He's his worst enemy."

"I wouldn't say that."

"Well, you know what I mean."

"I know what you mean," Kennedy nodded absently.

She looked sidewise at him, uncertain. Suddenly she put a hand on his arm. "Kennedy, when Tony and I were married, you remember you and I were talking one night. Just the two of us. No, you probably don't remember; you were tight. But you told me you could name on the fingers of one hand the fellows you cared a damn about. One of them was Tony. Has it changed?"

"I don't change much, Belle."

Her voice dropped lower. "There's a change come over Tony. Just in the past few months." She shook her head at his upward sidelong look. "No, not me. He loves me, Kennedy. Something else. He's begun to shun friends. He goes out alone at night quite often and never comes back until after midnight. No; it's not another woman. I'd know if it was another woman It's something else—something I can't fight."

"Maybe you're morbid."

"If I am, there's your reason." She paused for a moment and stared morosely at the rings on her hand. "I thought maybe you might be able to talk with him."

"I'm punk at that, Belle."

"Wouldn't you try, Kennedy?"

He looked at his palms. "Oh, I guess so. Sure. Day or so be all right?"

"Any time it's convenient."

"Oke."

Kennedy went down to the Alcove and said to Marcus: "Rye straight, Marcus."

"Mr. Price was in here a minute ago looking for you, Mr. Kennedy."

"I'll probably run into him again."

"Hey," said a redheaded, lean-jawed woman at the end of the bar, "do you know Tony Price?"

"I do, Madam," Kennedy yawned.

She hiccoughed. "Don't brag about it."

"Double rye, Marcus."

"I said, don't brag about it," the red-head growled.

"And a little water."

"Yes, Mr. Kennedy."

"Nerts," said the woman.

"Marcus, pass the almonds to the lady."

The woman's mouth drooped sullenly. "Making a fool out of me, huh? Making a fool out of me. Smart guy. Wise guy. Stuck up. What have you got to be stuck up about? So you're a pal of this louse Price! Well, you look like the kind of a guy that'd be a pal of a louse like Price. To hell with you."

Kennedy lit a cigarette amiably, said to Marcus, "Did you say your father was the front end or the rear end of that horse?"

"The rear end, Mr. Kennedy. Gustav Stolz was the front end."

"You can just tell that louse Price that I know one guy in this town that's aching to meet him in a dark alley some night. And when he does, fella, something will go boom-boom in the night. Go ahead, be stuck up. If I wasn't a lady I'd tell you just what I thought of you."

Marcus rolled his eyes.

Kennedy paid up, said, "Be seeing you, Marcus," and drifted out of the bar.

He ran into Price on the mezzanine and Price grabbed him by the arm, said in a low, tense voice, "What'd you see downstairs before, Kennedy?"

"Where?"

"In the lavatory?"

"You, pal. I saw you."

"What else?"

"Nothing."

Price's lips slapped shut hard, then parted meagerly. "No one went in there after you left. I was the first one in after you left. I went in to look for something. I didn't find it."

"You're busting my arm, fella."

Price let go, saying: "Now don't affect the well-known dead pan, Kennedy. You're not fooling me. You found something."

"If a man loses something, Tony, and then wants to claim it, he usually tells what he lost."

"You know what I'm talking about."

"Now you presume."

"A slug and a spent shell," Price muttered thoughtfully.

Kennedy stared absently at the floor. "Meet me for lunch at the *Press Club* tomorrow."

"Listen, Kennedy. I want those. Now."

"Meet me at the *Press Club*, half-past twelve."

Price squinted down at him. "What the hell are you trying to pull on me?"

"I just want to have a long talk with you, Tony."

Price gripped his arm again, ground out: "As one newspaperman to another—"

"You stopped being a newspaperman, fella, when you left the old *Standard.* That's what I want to talk to you about."

Price flushed. He released Kennedy's arm, folded his fingers into his palms, took a deep breath. "I know you think I'm a rat, Kennedy. I've known it all along. I didn't dodge you these past years because I didn't like you. I did it because I knew what you thought of me—what any number of guys think of me. Okey—tomorrow at the *Press Club.* Maybe I'll tell you something that'll stand your hair on end!"

He turned on his heel, strode off, his arms close to his sides, the back of his neck red.

The clock on the mezzanine pointed to three minutes past twelve o'clock.

STURDEVANT PARK is a rectangular oasis of shrubbery and evergreens in the heart of Richmond City's best residential center. It is one block long, enclosed by a high iron fence and with gates which are locked at nine every night. Fine houses face it on four sides; none of these houses is more than four stories and all are private residences of brick or stone, very formal.

At three in the morning Patrolman George Hafferkampf was moving his big feet up Westminster Street, three blocks from Sturdevant Park. He was a huge man whose enormous belly marched solidly before him. The stars were bright in a cloudless sky. Earlier there had been a moon, but it had gone away over the housetops and down. It was cold, windless, but Hafferkampf, with woolen socks on his feet, two sweaters beneath his blue overcoat and plush earmuffs on his ears, was comfortable. Ten minutes before, he had poured a pint of hot coffee down his throat. He whistled placidly to himself. The thong of his nightstick was looped round his mittened wrist and the stick itself dangled alongside his thigh. He was fifty-five years old, red-faced, slow, a plodder but a good cop.

The three shots that exploded in the starlit silence, each on the other's heels with deadly rhythm, brought Hafferkampf to a halt. He put his head on one shoulder, listening, moving his body slightly from side to side. He was not going to go barging off in any direction. The echoes hammered away through the streets. Hafferkampf still listened—for running feet, or the sound of a motor suddenly accelerated. He heard neither.

He broke into a cross between a hobble and a run, his head back and his belly thrust forward, his big feet hitting the pavement hard. Up Westminster and into Tremont by the Park. Here he stopped, again to listen. But he saw an auto's tail-light, up Westminster. He went along in the shadow of the Park, cautiously: rashness had long ago been knocked out of this man. Drawing up the skirt of his overcoat, he took his gun from its hip-holster.

The car, he decided, was parked. But he proceeded cautiously, still hugging the shadow of the iron fence. The car was parked in front of a three-storied graystone house and now Hafferkampf saw a light spring on within the house. This encouraged him. He crossed and came up back of the car, his gun leveled. But when he saw the shape lying on the sidewalk he let his gun droop. Another light sprang on within the house. Then suddenly the vestibule was lighted.

Hafferkampf got down on one knee with more effort than the average man uses to get up. He tore open the man's overcoat, his inner coat. He saw, felt, that the man's chest was smashed. Removing his mitten, he tried for a heart beat. Wagged his head slowly. Then he tried the wrist. Wagged his head again.

"Officer."

Hafferkampf looked up at the lighted vestibule. Its door was open and a man clad in a bathrobe was standing there.

"Was this guy comin' here?" Hafferkampf asked.

"Not that I know of. Who is he?"

"How do I know? I just got here."

The man in the bathrobe came down the steps. He was short, burly, with a small mustache. He said:

"Let me look at him."

"Look," said Hafferkampf.

The burly man bent over as Hafferkampf snapped on his flashlight. "Know him?"

The burly man's brows came together, then sprang apart and upward.

"Good cripes!" he exclaimed.

"So you know him," said Hafferkampf.

"Know him! Hell, man, he's Tony Price."

"The hell you say! Wait'll I get my spectacles on." Hafferkampf put on his spectacles, leaned way over. "Damned if he ain't!"

"Wait'll the boss hears this!"

Hafferkampf looked at him. "What's your name?"

"Ed Stone. I'm the boss' chauffeur-valet."

"What boss?"

"Mr. Hildebrand! Mr. Tate Hildebrand!"

"Yes?" said Hildebrand, standing in the doorway.

Hafferkampf and Stone turned. Stone jumped up and said, "Gee, Mr. Hildebrand, it's Mr. Price!"

Now Hafferkampf was on his feet.

Hildebrand, wrapped in a heavy velvet robe, came down the steps slowly, impressively. "Badly hurt?" he asked.

"Dead, I'm afraid, sir," Hafferkampf said.

Hildebrand dropped to one knee, felt heart and pulse. He remained kneeling for a long minute, pursing his chiseled lips. At last he stood up, chopped at Hafferkampf:

"Where were you when it happened, officer?"

"Three blocks away. I was—"

"You fellows always manage to be somewhere safely distant whenever there is trouble. Did you see the gun flashes?"

"No, sir. I was down beyond the bend in Westminster."

"Carry him inside," Hildebrand clipped bitterly.

"I can't," Hafferkampf said. "He's dead. I got to leave him here till the sergeant gets over. Can I use your phone?"

"In the hall. Show him, Stone."

Hafferkampf had seen something. "Just a minute!" He charged up the street, stopped and turned on his flashlight. On a small patch of winter-blanched grass lay an automatic pistol. He picked it up carefully by the muzzle, called back: "I think I got the gun."

Other house lights had begun to flash on and one by one heads appeared at windows.

Hafferkampf carried the gun almost daintily. "Fingerprints. Got to watch out for fingerprints. Where's the phone, now, if you don't mind?"

Stone said: "This way. Right this way."

"Wait," said Hildebrand. "Tell them he was killed in front of Tate Hildebrand's house. Tell them I said I don't want any crackpots on this case; I want the best brains they've got. If they send any half-wits over here, I'll kick them out."

"Yes, sir."

Hildebrand gestured briefly. "That's all."

BELLE PRICE was having her third cup of black coffee. She told the colored houseboy to take away the tray. The morning sun shone through the casement window and laid bright bars on the floor of her living-room. The houseboy, his eyes wide, nodded and moved his lips without saying anything; took the tray away into the kitchen. Belle saw nothing but the thoughts that went round and round inside her head. Her hair was disheveled, her face drained to shiny gray color; she hadn't bothered about make-up. Her eyes wore the dumb, blank look of the stricken.

Homer, the colored boy, let in MacBride and Kennedy at ten past nine. Kennedy was sober, but he looked the same: drunk or sober, he always looked the same—slightly windblown, un-pressed, and droopy-eyed. MacBride, lean-boned and freshly shaved, laid his derby on the table in the foyer, retained his overcoat. His chin and cheekbones were prominently red, whipped to that color by the brisk morning cold. He blew his nose, making a sound like a trumpet.

They went into the living-room and Belle Price looked up at them dully.

The gentleness of Kennedy, whenever on those rare occasions it came to the surface, was a touching thing. It was never obvious in the way that gentleness is usually obvious. It came out mostly in his dusty, slightly grotesque smile, his hazy eyes, a certain obliqueness in his movements. He almost circled the room before he reached Belle. He did not take her hand in his, did not pat her shoulder. Sitting down opposite her, he stared at the spot on the floor at which she was staring, the dusty half-smile drawing at one corner of his mouth. Until at last he said:

"Well, Belle...." A garrulous man by nature, given at times too much to persiflage and horseplay, he could say no more. Not that there was a lump in his throat: there was not.

MacBride cleared his throat. "Mrs. Price."

"Yes," her flat voice said.

"This is a terrible thing, Mrs. Price, and I don't want to go all over it if I can help it. That is, I don't want to—"

"That's all right, Captain MacBride."

The breath which he had been holding now flowed out. He sat down, bending his wiry brows, looking down for an instant at the polished tips of his old shoes. "Has anyone talked to you about this?"

"You're the first. The police notified me—a Patrolman Bonno came over to tell me, but he didn't question me; he said someone else would be over later. Then Mr. Hildebrand telephoned to say how sorry he was."

The skipper leaned back in his chair, folded his arms, stared down the length of his bony nose. "Now about what time was it when your husband left?"

"Between two and three. I don't know exactly. Homer woke us up."

"Homer?"

"Our colored boy."

"And who wanted to see your husband?"

"It was a phone call. We got in the habit of cutting out our bedroom phone at night, because so many people used to phone Tony when he was asleep. Homer received all the incoming calls and if they were important he'd wake Tony. This one was from Mr. Hildebrand. Homer woke Tony and told him Mr. Hildebrand had phoned and wanted him to come over to his house immediately on urgent business. So Tony dressed and went out."

"Of course he took his car."

"Yes. It's hard to get a taxi out this way at that hour."

"Where's Homer?"

Homer came into the room, his black hands folded, his eyes wide.

MacBride said: "What time did you get that phone call from Mr. Hildebrand?"

"You mean d' one—"

"I mean the one early this morning."

" 'Bout ha' past two, must ha' been, Cap'n boss."

"What did Mr. Hildebrand say?"

"Well, he say, 'Mistuh Price. Lemme talk t' Mistuh Price.' Ah say, 'Mistuh Price asleep, suh.' Then he say, 'This 's Mistuh Hildebrand. Tell 'Mistuh Price to come oveh ma house right away.' An' den he hang up."

"You're sure it was Mr. Hildebrand?"

"Must ha' been, Cap'n boss. He says he's Mistuh Hildebrand. Was a very bad connection an' Ah shuah had to listen hahd."

"All right, Homer."

"Yassuh, Cap'n boss."

The Negro left the room.

MacBride said: "Mrs. Price, when Mr. Hildebrand phoned you—I mean, the second time—did he say anything about that earlier call?"

"Well, he asked me if I knew why Tony'd come there to his house at that hour. I said, 'Because you phoned him to.' He exclaimed, '*I* phoned him?'... Well, it seems Mr. Hildebrand didn't phone him. It must have been a trap."

MacBride's voice dropped: "Was your husband any different last night than other times?"

She looked at Kennedy. "Only—well, a little upset."

"What about?" the skipper asked.

"I don't know," she said wearily. "I didn't ask."

"He traveled armed, didn't he, quite a bit?"

"I think so. I believe he had a permit."

MacBride nodded. "I know. He was armed when the patrolman on the beat found him dead. His gun was still in his pocket. Did he ever talk to you about people he feared?"

She shook her head. "I really knew very little about his business, Captain MacBride. He shut his business behind him, as a rule, when he was with me."

"Did it ever occur to you, Mrs. Price, that the kind of work he was doing, the kind of writing, was very dangerous?"

"Always."

"Did you tell him?"

"Once. I think I—hurt him. So I never mentioned it again."

"Kennedy tells me he was a pretty sensitive lad."

She nodded bleakly. "Very. Outwardly he appeared blunt, bluff. Under it—well, that was a defense mechanism. Do you mind if I say I feel a little ill and should like to lie down?"

MacBride was on his feet. "By all means, Mrs. Price. I really didn't mean to go into all this song and dance. Excuse an old copper."

"You're kind," she murmured; and to Kennedy: "Come around and see me very soon, Kennedy."

His voice was hardly above a whisper: "Oke, Belle."

MacBride and Kennedy left the house and walked down the flagstone path to the boulevard, where the police phaeton was parked at the curb. Gahagan was across the street playing duck-on-the-rock with a gang of kids.

"Gahagan!" barked MacBride.

Gahagan came striding back to the car and MacBride said:

"I'd like to once leave you at the wheel of this car and find you at it when I come back."

"Jeese, I was only playing with the kids."

"I saw you!"

"Well, jeese, it's Children Week, ain't it?"

"Get in, get in. You and your screwy alibis!... And listen to me, Gahagan," he went on, climbing into the tonneau. "If I catch you, or hear of you, shooting any more insulators off the telegraph poles—"

"Cap'n, I told you now a dozen times it was a stray shot."

"Oh, so one stray shot knocks off seven insulators on three different poles. If you don't respect my position, Gahagan, at least respect my intelligence. Shut up! Drive downtown and cut out waving to all the janes you know on the way."

Gahagan crashed into gear, muttered under his breath, "Am I humiliated!" and drove smack through the first red light he came to.

"There's another waste of taxpayers' money," the skipper ruminated ruefully. "Traffic lights. Nobody pays any attention to them any more."

Kennedy was lounging on the small of his back. "I am going to get the guy the chair," he said placidly. "The guy who killed Tony Price."

MacBride looked down darkly at him. "Liked him, didn't you, bo?"

"I liked him."

"If you liked him so much, why the hell didn't you tell him long ago to bail out of that smut and do a white man's job?"

Kennedy smiled. "Some fellows like people one way; some, another. You don't really like a guy for what he is or does; there's no reason at all for liking a guy you like. Besides, I mind my own business."

"Price ripped the lid off more people's private lives than any other two guys put together. And why?"

"He was paid to do it. The *Evening Telegraph* found it couldn't print feelthy peectures, so it printed the next best. Tony did it up brown.

Wherever he got his information, I don't know. But he got it—and it was true—the real goods."

"Suppose it was? It still wasn't news."

"You don't have to tell me, old tomato. And I'll bet this: I'll bet Tony didn't like it. He had it up to his throat. It was getting him. I know it was getting him."

"Why didn't he bail out?"

"Money. He was born with a silver spoon in his mouth. He liked to live well. He was used to living well.... Drop me off somewhere on the main drag—near Jockey Street."

"I hear Hildebrand's offering a reward of ten thousand for information leading to, and so forth."

"Why not? Tony was his right-hand man. He was the guy that built Tony up, groomed him, taught him the way to promotion and pay.... Are you checking up on that gun was found?"

"Ike Cohen's working on it now."

"Drop me off at the next block. I want to see a man about a thing."

HILDEBRAND was a large man, with heavy shoulders, a thick torso and long, slender legs. His face was big, stern, with a bold nose, large ears, imperious eyes and wide, forceful mouth. He had in his youth been an amateur heavyweight boxer, and now, at fifty-five, he carried himself with a physical sureness which, combined with a direct manner of speech, often withered lesser men who came to him with complaints. He dressed elegantly, as a rule in dark clothes, and there were only a few strands of gray in his thick, brushed-back brown hair. He was a bachelor.

MacBride entered the sumptuous suite of offices as naturally as he would have walked into a Little Italy saloon. By devious ways he was led finally into the inner sanctum, where Hildebrand, smoking a large pale cigar, was gazing out across the city. The secretary closed the door, leaving MacBride in the office; and Hildebrand turned, came across to his vast carved desk and sat down in his high-backed Spanish chair. He said gravely, grimly:

"It's a pleasure to make your acquaintance, Captain MacBride. Though I regret the circumstances which bring it about. Please sit down." He did not offer his hand. He was a great man, a powerful one in a vast domain.

MacBride, unimpressed, remained standing, one hand in his overcoat pocket, the other holding his derby against his thigh.

"I've just come from Mrs. Price's," he said.

Hildebrand frowned. "I should deeply appreciate it, Captain, if you would spare Mrs. Price as much unpleasantness as possible. I'd have gone over myself, but condolences, so soon after the event, are awkward manifestations at best. I plan to see her in a day or so. I plan also to create a trust fund for her. Tony Price, as you may know, was a very valuable man."

"I don't intend to run her ragged, Mr. Hildebrand," the skipper said in his burry voice. "We have to check up, though. She told me about that phone call."

"The one I was supposed to have made, yes. She mentioned it over the wire when I talked with her this morning."

"Of course you didn't call him to come over to your house."

"Certainly not."

"Did you ever get him out of bed during the night."

"Any number of times."

"So that he wasn't surprised when he got that call to come over to your house."

Hildebrand leaned forward on his elbows and looked MacBride straight in the eye. "That is the essence of the trap."

"You think it was a trap?"

"Don't you?"

"It'd seem so," MacBride nodded. He went on: "Now we all know the kind of work Price did for you. We know that his stuff, the stuff he published in your paper, must have made him a lot of enemies. Do you know of anyone recently who threatened him?"

"No one. I know, by inference more than anything else, that he received all kinds of threats. But Tony usually kept his own counsel. He had a job, and he did it—remarkably well."

"I suppose it occurred to you, Mr. Hildebrand, that you were constantly putting him in a dangerous spot."

"I don't like the way you phrase that. Humanity is news, Captain; weak humanity is big news. We hear a lot about man thrilling at his neighbor's success. The truth of the matter is, he goes into ecstasy over his neighbor's transgressions and the results thereof. I am called by many a vendor of smut. I am, really, a purveyor of drama—human drama, the weaknesses of humanity: truth stranger than fiction. The extent of my audience may be judged by the audits of my circulation department. I trained Tony Price for his job. He had the talent, the ability to root out half-forgotten details. I paid him well. I question your criticism of me."

MacBride shrugged. "I'm not criticizing you. That's not my business. I want the entire list of names Price wrote about since he began doing this work. Send them over to Headquarters as soon as possible."

"Gladly. You'll probably find them of great value."

"It'll be necessary, Mr. Hildebrand, just as a matter of routine, to find out if any telephone calls went out from your house last night between two and three."

"There were none. I arrived home at about one, from the Charity Ball. I have a housekeeper during the day—Mrs. Storr—who goes home at nine, as does my cook, her sister-in-law. Storr, who drives and valets for me, lives at my house. If he made any call between two and three, I don't know of it. You'd better ask him. But I know I made none. I was awakened by the shots. You'll find Stone at home."

"Has he worked for you long?"

"Seven years. I can vouch for him."

"Good."

"My entire organization, Captain, is at your disposal. I'll send that dame over to you directly. And, again, please—go easy with Mrs. Price." He picked up some papers, attached pince-nez smartly to his nose, clipped: "Good day to you, sir."

MacBride returned to Headquarters.

"Ike back?" he said to Bettdecken, who was at the central-room desk.

"He just went up, I think."

MacBride climbed to his office and found Ike Cohen regarding a bowl of goldfish which stood on the radiator. The skipper went over and stood beside Ike and also regarded the bowl of goldfish. After a moment he turned to regard Cohen.

"Is this yours?" he asked.

"Yup."

"Is it by any chance a present for me?"

Cohen brightened. "D'you want it?"

"I do not!"

Cohen shrugged. "D'you know of anybody who might like it?"

"Where—now, where the hell did you pick it up?"

"I won it. You know, down in the Honkytonk Museum. Ten cents. First time I played, I won the outfit. I just put it on the radiator there because I thought the fish might get cold."

MacBride groaned and sat down on his desk. Instantly he erupted, "I thought I sent you out with a gun, to try to—"

"Oh sure; oh, sure. I did that. First I phoned the people that make the brand, gave 'em the number, and they said it was sold to the Sportsman's Bazaar two years ago. So I just went over to the Sportsman's Bazaar. They looked up the number in their books. On Friday, April 7, 1933, they sold the gun to a BMW named Cook Addison, 234 Rambler Street, this city."

"Swell!"

"Don't jump at conclusions, Cap. On Saturday, 13 May of 1933, number 234 Rambler Street, an apartment house, burned to the ground. I went around to the district post office and asked the postmaster to look up his change-of-address book. He did and we found that after the fire Addison left instructions for his mail to be sent to the *Hotel Fisk,* this city. He remained at the *Fisk* a week, then moved into a five-room apartment at the *Montblanc Towers.* On July 2, 1934—it was a Monday—he moved from the *Montblanc Towers.* I'll correct that. He *left* the *Montblanc Towers,* owing three months' rent. Left his baggage behind and note to the manager, saying he figured they'd be able to get what he owed them out of the stuff he left behind. There it ends. Then I stopped in and won the goldfish."

"What'd the manager say about him?"

"This was another manager. He never knew him. I got this from their records—they had the letter Addison wrote, too, on file. I took that. Here," he said, tossing it to the desk. "The manager who was there when Addison skipped left for Switzerland a couple of months ago, to run a hotel. He's a Swiss."

MacBride read the letter, which ran to six apologetic lines. Then he said: "Hildebrand at the *Evening Telegraph's* getting me some data about the people Price chucked mud at in his paper. Run over there and ask 'em quick if they've got anything on this bird Addison. News items too. And pictures, if any. And on your way stop off at the phone company and see if there were any outgoing calls from Sturdevant 1001 after midnight last night and before, say, four this morning. That's Hildebrand's home number. Shake a leg, fella."

When Cohen had gone the skipper got up, crammed coarse brown tobacco into his battered brier and stared abstractedly at the bowl of goldfish. He lit up, strolled over and wrinkled the surface of the water with his finger. The fish—two of them—circled the bowl swiftly. After a moment the skipper crossed to his desk, picked up the phone; changed his mind and put the instrument down. He took down his hat and overcoat, went out, walked four blocks and entered a general store.

"Got any goldfish food?" he asked.

WHEN the red-head opened the door, her hair a shambles, a green silk dressing-gown drawn haphazardly about her hefty body, Kennedy said:

"Good morning."

"That's what *you* say. What do you want?"

"I'd like to come in."

"Listen, mister, I can't take a joke so early in the morning. What bill collector are you? I'll pay you next week."

"Come on; let me in. I want to talk to you."

She could hardly keep her eyes open. "That's funny. I don't want talk to you—or anybody. Go 'way. I got most frightful hangover." She fell against the door, trying to close it.

Kennedy's foot was in the way.

She opened the door wide again and glared red-eyed at him, her lower lip pouting. "Hah?"

"Don't you remember me?"

"No."

"Last night. The Alcove at the *Ambassador.*"

"My gawd! Was I at the *Ambassador?*"

"Plenty. You were carried out at one by a couple of bellboys and the house dick got your name and address out of your bag and took you home. I got the story from the house dick by way of Marcus, the Alcove barman. You were shooting off your mouth at the Alcove last night. I'd like to talk to you about that."

She looked confused, harried. "Declared myself, huh?" she gulped.

Kennedy wormed his way through the doorway, closed the door. The woman ran her hand up through her shock of red hair and licked her parched lips.

"Listen," she implored, "don't kid me. Give me the straight of it: was I at the *Ambassador* last night?" He nodded and she tugged at her hair; she said hoarsely: "What'd I do? Did I invite people to fight me? Listen"—she pointed a finger at him—"I didn't have a goat with me, did I?"

Kennedy was smiling drowsily. "My name's Kennedy," he drawled. "I was a close friend of Tony Price."

Her eyes seemed to bounce—once—in their sockets. "That guy," she said in a dull voice that hardened. "I'd like to see that guy hang!"

"You can't hang a dead man, Miss Brannigan."

"I'd like to see him strung up and—" She stopped short, her eyes hanging motionless, her lower lip drooping. Then she said in a very quiet voice: "What was that about a dead man?"

Kennedy's voice was almost gentle: "Tony Price was killed about three a.m. this morning. Shot. Three times."

Her eyes slid sidewise in their sockets, the lids shuttering a bit. Her voice was quick, doubting. "Who says so?"

"Would you like to go over to Police Headquarters and check up on me?"

She began to shake. "But what—what've I got to do with it?"

He was placid, unhurried. "You were in your buckets last night, Mae Brannigan. Shooting your jaw off for all you were worth. You cracked about knowing a guy that'd like to do Tony Price up brown."

She took two jerky backward steps, shaking her head. "No. No. I didn't."

"I've got a witness if I want him. The barman Marcus."

She clutched at her dressing-gown with one hand, used the other hand to slap the hair out of her eyes. "If I did, I didn't mean it. I didn't, I tell you—I didn't mean it. I was tight. I don't even remember being at the *Ambassador*."

"Who's the lad you referred to? Who's the lad was aching to take a fall out of Tony Price?"

"Listen, please. On a hangover, how can I know anything? I've got an awful hangover."

He was patient. "I know just how you feel. I get 'em myself, plenty. But drunk as you were last night, you knew what you were talking about. You know a guy that hates Price's insides and Price was murdered at three this morning and he was a pal of mine and I intend, Mae, to find out who did it."

She seemed to make an effort to pull herself together. "I must have been just talking through my hat last night. I never saw Tony Price. I don't know anyone who knows him well enough to want to knock him off."

"That's your story, eh, and you'll stick to it?" he smiled.

She said: "You're a kind of a rat yourself, Mr. Kennedy, for taking advantage of a woman when she's tight. A body that's tight is liable to say anything."

"All right; I'm a rat." He shrugged amiably. "If you want to get dressed, go ahead. Meantime I'll phone for a cop."

"So you are a rat, huh?"

"Didn't I admit it?"

He slouched across the room toward the telephone.

"Wait a minute!" she cried.

He turned, still amiable, still patient.

"So help me, I don't know a thing," she croaked. "That's Gawd's honest, Mr. Kennedy. I get tight like that and I tell the wildest stories. I'm always getting myself in Dutch. Sometimes I want to fight people and sometimes I tell those wild stories and once I stole a trolley car and wrecked it—that was two years ago. But listen, now: this thing you said I said last night, it can't be true. I mean, hell, I just spouted."

He sighed tranquilly and picked up the telephone. She tumbled towards him and gripped it, shaking her head desperately. "Don't, please. Please, don't. Those cops are fed up with me. Only last month I got gay and ran off with a milk wagon, lickety-split down Jockey Street, and the wagon turned over and busted about ten dozen bottles of milk."

He said: "I'll tell the cops to treat you nice, Mae."

"Ah, Gawd, please don't, Mr. Kennedy. You're a nice fellow."

"I'm a rat, Mae. You said so."

"I didn't mean that. I apologize."

He said: "Who was the guy that wanted to take a crack at Tony Price, Mae?"

She looked hopelessly at him, a bitter grimace on her face; and she said bitterly: "You're an awful hard guy, Mr. Kennedy. You got no heart at all."

"I'm not hard. I just want a little information."

"I swear to you, those cops told me that if ever I was dragged in again I'd get sent to the workhouse."

Kennedy put down the telephone. "Be sensible, Mae."

She snuffled, found a handkerchief and blew her nose. "I haven't seen the fellow in almost a year. I didn't know him well. He picked me up in a cafe one night, I was singing there, and he was pretty tight and he told me his troubles, all about how this guy Price had ruined him. He told me that some night he was going to get damned good and tight and shoot Price down the minute he set eyes on him. Well, I tried to talk him out of that. I can't remember what it was all about, but it seems like this fellow was in some business and married and Price found out he was two-timing on his wife and it got in the papers: something like that. Anyhow, the wife divorced him, it was quite a scandal, and his business backers pulled out on him and he was broke and stranded. When I met him, he was a clerk in a soda fountain. I never saw him again after that night. Of course, for a while I was out West. I only got back a month or so ago."

"What's his name?"

"Cook Addison."

"What does he look like?"

"Well, black curly hair. About as tall as I am and kind of stocky and dark. I guess he's about thirty-seven."

"Where'd he live when you knew him?"

"I don't know. I just knew him that night."

"You must have liked him, to be so touchy about telling me this."

She scowled. "He was a nice guy, as I remember. But it ain't that, I just hate being a snitch. And if I didn't have a hangover and if I wasn't broke and afraid of being sent to the workhouse, I'd never snitch." She shuddered. "I ain't even got a bit of the hair of the dog around—"

Kennedy dragged a pint flask from his inside overcoat pocket, uncorked it, said: "From the neck, or have you jiggers?"

"I got some water glasses."

She went into the bathroom and returned with two water glasses, set them down on the table where Kennedy had placed the flask.

He said: "Measure your limit."

She poured half a water glass.

Kennedy equaled it.

"Taking it straight this way," he said, "is supposed to shrivel your stomach."

"It's a lie. Look at me."

"Well, bottoms up."

"Upsydaisy."

They drained their glasses and for an instant each looked petrified. Then Mae blew out a breath.

"What is it?" she asked.

"I haven't the slightest idea."

They tried it again. Kennedy went into the bathroom and when he returned Mae had taken a third drink and looked pretty well set-up. Kennedy emptied the flask.

"You're an awful glutton," Mae said.

"I just remembered," Kennedy said.

"What?"

"I haven't eaten since five last night."

"How do you make your head jig up and down like that?"

"My dear Mae, I'm perfectly motionless. Well, I've got to float along. Toodle-oo."

"Happy days. And listen: if you see a goat, it's mine. I lost a goat. Gee, I didn't know you could jig!"

Kennedy meandered out of the apartment.

THE SKIPPER came back from luncheon smoking a long nickel cigar, trailing banners of rank smoke over his shoulder. His heels kicked his overcoat tails as he drummed up the stairway and when he cracked into his office Ike Cohen, who was sitting on the desk, said:

"Cook Addison's dead."

"Suicide? How long ago?"

"Three months ago. And not suicide."

MacBride stopped half out of his overcoat, looked suspiciously at Cohen for an instant, then took off the coat and hung it on a three-pronged costumer. He chafed his hands vigorously, bent a hard glance on Cohen.

"Go ahead, spit the rest of it out," he said.

"He was knocked down by an auto and died on his way to the hospital. There was a four-line item about it in the *Telegraph*."

"So that's that."

"Yup. Suspect number one eliminated. Back during last spring

Price published a juicy bit about Addison." He tossed a clipping onto the desk. "Addison got tangled up with some gold-digger and Price hooked onto it and cut loose in the paper. It's rich. Read it. Addison's wife got wise and divorced him. Here's a little item about that. It all leads up—but it don't go off. Dead men don't kill. We've got to start from scratch again."

"Addison must have pawned his gun or sold it to some hot spot.... I see the time of his death he was living at 905 Skiff Street." His lips moved as he read. Without looking up, he said: "Did you go to the phone company?"

"Yup. There was no call out of Hildebrand's house from ten p.m. until eight a.m., except that one of Hafferkampf's to Headquarters at three."

"Well, I didn't expect any. That phone call to Price was a trap, the guy that made it figuring it'd be kind of poetic justice, as Kennedy'd say, to bop Price off in front of Hildebrand's house. I want you to take that gun, Ike, and fan the pawnshops. Some of those guys get absent-minded about reporting guns they sell. Also fan the second-hand stores. You know the ones that pull fast turnovers in firearms. Hildebrand ought to have the data over that I want pretty soon, and I'll run through that."

Cohen went out and the skipper relit his cigar, sat down at his desk and waded into a mass of correspondence. He was almost finished, half an hour later, when the door opened slowly and Kennedy wandered in.

MacBride said: "Ike found out who bought that gun, Kennedy, but the guy that bought it died three months ago. He was smacked down by an automobile."

Kennedy hiccoughed.

MacBride went on: "It was a guy named Cook Addison. We thought we had something ripe there, because Addison was a guy that your pal Price laid into. Addison's wife kicked him out and—"

"Sh—sh, tomato. I know all about it."

MacBride looked up sharply.

Kennedy's eyes were almost shut. "Did you also find out that Addison was in business with a fellow named Donald Garth?"

"No."

"Well, he was, he was. Let me elaborate. Garth and Addison were expanding a small building and loan association, backed by a number of solid citizens. I believe Addison was the brains of the partnership. The two were old friends, very close. Addison unfortunately got mixed up with some floozy and there was a row in her apartment one night. A cop by the name of Samuels busted it up and Addison gave him fifty dollars to keep his mouth shut. A month later the cop got canned off the Force. You yourself canned him for breaking a woman's jaw. The cop got a job as night watchman in the Hildebrand building. Hildebrand himself got a lot of stories out of Samuels, the Addison brawl being one of them. He set Tony out to dig it up. He dug it up. The gag was: 'Should a man like Addison, who squanders his money in nightclubs on light-o'-loves, be allowed to manage a building and loan association?'"

"Where'd you find out this stuff about Samuels?"

"He later got canned by Hildebrand for sleeping on the job. After that I met him in a pub one night and he was plastered and feeling sorry for himself and he told me his life story.... But to go on: The Garth-Addison partnership busted, because the men who backed them pulled out. Addison, after his wife tossed him over, took to drink. I didn't get that from Samuels, I got it from another source. I know about his death—I just came over from the *Free Press*. Then I got the idea of trying to locate this fellow Garth and I looked in the telephone directory and found his name, with an address at 905 Skiff Street."

"What was the idea of looking for Garth?"

"Well, I have an informer, Stevie, whose identity, in case you want to know, is none of your business. From this useful person, a drunk like myself, I got a general idea of what Addison looked like."

"Now wait," MacBride cut in, waving a newspaper clipping. "It says here that Addison at the time of his death was living at 905 Skiff Street. That's the address—"

"I know, I know," Kennedy nodded. He took his hand from his pocket and placed an empty cartridge and a bashed slug on the desk. "I picked these up in a washroom at the *Ambassador* last night."

The skipper's eyes were round with confusion.

Kennedy went on: "Tony Price was there last night. I left the Alcove bar to go to the lavatory and while I was in the corridor I thought I heard a shot, but I wasn't sure. Then a fellow came stalking blank-eyed out of the lavatory and went past me as though I didn't exist. When I went into the lavatory, Tony was there. Well, we talked about this and that and I said nothing about the shot. Tony went out and I found the slug and the shell—"

MacBride cut in: "And why the hell didn't you bring these in to me before this?"

"I kept my mouth shut. I knew a shot'd been fired but I didn't know who fired it—Tony or the other guy. In any event, at the time it wasn't any of my business. I half-believed that Tony'd fired it. So now that you've traced the gun to Addison, that clears that much up."

"But you don't know if the gun we have fired that shot."

"True. I also know that the gun couldn't have been fired by Addison. I know that the gun that killed Tony was a thirty-two. You have a thirty-two shell on your desk. The guy I saw coming out of the lavatory was Donald Garth."

MacBride slumped back in his chair, raised his hands and let them slap down limply upon the desk. "I give up. Go on."

"It's easy. I went around 905 Skiff Street, which is a rooming-house. I asked for Donald Garth. The woman who runs it tried his door and it was locked and she didn't have an extra key. I asked her what he looked like. She described him. He was the lad I saw barge out of the lavatory in the *Ambassador*. If you want to be technical, have your ballistics man check what I gave you with the gun you've got."

"Did you tell the rooming-house woman to keep her mouth shut about you being around?"

"I did. Nice, motherly old soul, and very upset at my interrogating her in *re* Donald Garth. She likes him."

"Did you ask her about when Addison lived there?"

"Addison and Garth shared a two-room apartment."

"Where does Garth work?"

"He's a floorwalker at Godfrey's Department Store."

MacBride stood up. "Let's go get him."

"Save your shoe-leather. He's not there. Hasn't been all day. Hasn't phoned in."

The skipper pressed his lips together. "Any time you want my job, Kennedy, say so. I'm absolutely useless here, with you clowning your way through all the clinches."

"Oh, you have your uses, old tomato. It was in my mind to, well, tipple a short one—rye, if you have it—and then you and I toddle over to 905 Skiff Street and summarily bust down Garth's door. Have you seen a goat around?"

"A—*what?*"

"Let it pass. I got my lines mixed up. I have a feeling that when Addison died he left all his effects to Donald Garth— among them one .32-caliber automatic pistol…. Where the hell did you get the goldfish?"

"Ike won them."

"I understand a certain charitable organization recommends revolving bowls for tired goldfish."

THE SKIPPER did not break down Garth's door. He used a master key, opened the door with little difficulty and noticed instantly that all the shades were drawn. He said briefly:

"Don't pull 'em up."

He switched on all the lights.

The bedroom and the living-room were high-ceilinged, old-fashioned; the bath was two steps up from the living-room and looked as though once it might have been a spacious clothes closet. The rooms were furnished with odds and ends, old, substantial, in good repair. They were on the second floor, rear.

MacBride said: "Ten to one he wasn't here this morning."

"Why?"

"The shades. You pull shades up in the morning, don't you?"

"Check," murmured Kennedy. He picked up a photograph, said: "This is the chap barged out of the men's room last night. Garth. I knew it, I knew it, tra-la, tra-la. See: 'To my great good friend Cook, from Don.'"

MacBride studied the picture. "Not a bad-looking guy."

"Then what do we assume, Skipperino: he didn't come home last night?"

"No. We allow, Kennedy, that he might have come home last night, and early this morning, and left again. We assume that he didn't return—"

"After he shot and killed Tony Price."

"Please, for crying out loud, let me win some of these clinches! I like to feel that the taxpayers are getting their money's worth in supporting this Police Department…. There's a dress shirt he started to put on and changed his mind. Spot on it." He picked up another photograph. "Who's this? Oh-oh, I see. This is a picture of Addison. 'Don—always your loyal friend Cook.' These guys must have been real buddies." The skipper sighed. "Well, that's life, that's life."

Kennedy came out of a closet, said: "As far as I can make out, Garth didn't take a hell of a lot with him, if anything. Clothes in the closet. Shoes, slippers, ties."

MacBride was looking at a slip of paper he had taken from his pocket. He went to the telephone and called Headquarters. "Otto," he said, "this is Steve. Call the phone company and ask if there were any outgoing calls between three and four this morning from Southern 2213. Especially, Otto, if there was a call from this number to Western 3567.... That's right. Call me back here, Southern 2213. If there's no answer, it'll mean I'm on my way over."

He hung up and held out a dollar. "Bet you a buck, Kennedy, there was a call from here to Tony Price's place between three and four this morning."

"What a daredevil, what a daredevil! Go chase yourself."

The woman who ran the building appeared timorously in the doorway. "Is there anything I can do, Captain MacBride?"

"I don't know, Mrs. Anderson," the skipper said. "Seems as though this lad Garth vanished. Mr. Kennedy said you kind of liked him."

She was shy. "Yes, I do. He's a very fine young man. When his friend, Mr. Addison, died he took it so hard. You know, everybody said it was an accident, but Mr. Garth always believed that Mr. Addison deliberately threw himself in front of that auto. Oh, it was awful, awful."

"When'd you last see Mr. Garth?"

"Only yesterday morning. It wasn't the end of the month yet, it's five days yet to the end of the month, but Mr. Garth gave me the rent. 'I may be away,' he said, 'at the end of the month, so you better take this now.' Then he sat and talked with me for a while, about how long he'd been here, about Mr. Addison. I've had a queer feeling ever since."

The skipper regarded her gravely. "Of course you wouldn't know if Mr. Garth came home around midnight, or later."

"No. I last saw him when he went out, at about nine last night. He was wearing evening clothes. It was the first time I ever saw him in evening clothes. He didn't make much, you know."

"Did you talk to him then?"

"No. The last time I talked to him was yesterday morning. Last night I just saw him from my window as he went down the outside steps."

The skipper pursed his lips thoughtfully over this. Then he said:

"I'll have to keep a policeman in this apartment for a day or so, Mrs. Anderson. I hope you don't mind."

"If you have to, you have to," she said philosophically. "Will you gentlemen please tell me if you find him, poor man?"

When she had gone, MacBride turned to Kennedy. "Then it looks as though Garth got all dolled up for a fare-thee-well. He must have known Price would be at the Charity Ball. He tried to kill Price in that washroom and failed, but he tried again and succeeded."

"Reasonably, yes."

"Any doubt in your mind?"

Kennedy was musing, swaying gently from side to side. He started a little. "Huh? Doubt? No, no."

The telephone rang and MacBride scooped it up. "Hello.... Yeah, Otto.... I see, I get you. That's swell, Otto.... And listen. Send a cop over right away to 905 Skiff Street."

He hung up, slapped his hands together.

"So?" said Kennedy.

The skipper nodded grimly. "The call was from here to Tony Price's. Donald Garth, fella, is wanted. I got a feeling I'm going to hate to pinch this lad."

"Don't feel so downhearted, my fraand, until you find him."

BELLE PRICE was dressed when Kennedy walked into her living-room. She had put on some make-up, but there still were circles beneath her eyes, her face looked drawn.

Kennedy said: "The skipper found where that fake phone call came from."

She was listless. "Did he?"

"It was the buddy of a lad Tony'd cracked down on. These lads were partners and the cracking down busted their business and apparently their lives."

She moved her hand. "Don't, Kennedy. Don't."

"I catch on, Belle."

A bleak smile came to her face. "Tony was not the rotter so many people claim he was. He couldn't have been, he was so wonderful to me."

"Did he ever tell you why he stuck at it?"

"Oh, he said he wanted the money. I know he was always used to nice things, much more so than I ever was. But he didn't spend an awful lot of money. He left quite a bit in the bank. In fact, I handled all the money, all the checks. He'd ask me for cash when he needed it. It was never very much. The stuff he was doing must have held an unholy fascination for him. I know, I know he was trying to break away from it."

"Lately," Kennedy mused aloud, "he always looked like a man fighting an idea."

"I used to tell him, 'No one's perfect, Tony.' Whenever I read those awful revelations of people's weaknesses, it tore at my heart. Everyone has secrets, Kennedy...."

He looked at her, dropped his eyes. Her lips were shaking but in an instant she compressed them and stared hard at the floor. Her voice was very low when she spoke again:

"I was never really in Tony's class—"

"Skip it, Belle. I've known you five years. You'd be an ace in the hole for any guy. You're the top, Belle."

Her voice drifted on: "It was like a dream when he asked me to marry him. I was so happy—except for one thing."

"Belle."

"One thing. A secret." She looked a little groggy now. "I made a slip when I was a kid—"

Kennedy shook his head ruefully. "Belle, Belle."

"I tell you—"

"Who cares, Belle? You're the top, I say."

She was shaking. "And to read all that mud-slinging against people—" She clapped her hands to her face.

He did not touch her. He was not a back-slapper. "Pull out of it," he said. "Pull out of it, Belle."

She wanted to cry and he let her, saying nothing. On the table were odds and ends of Price's belongings which the police had brought over: wallet, pen, watch, two rings, money, a keyring containing six keys.

After a while Kennedy said: "Do you know if he had a safe deposit box?"

She murmured: "We had a joint one, just for our valuable papers. We had two keys. One is on his ring, but he never used the box. The car key's there and the key to the garage and the key to his office desk.

I don't know what the other two keys are for—the new ones you see there."

Kennedy picked up the keyring. "They're different," he said.

"Are they? I hadn't noticed."

Kennedy's eyes were drowsing over his thoughts. He said: "You told me that lately Tony used to go out a lot at night and stay late."

She nodded. "But I know it wasn't another woman, Kennedy. He spent so little money. I think he used to take long walks."

"Did he ever go out in stormy weather?"

"Yes. Yes, he did."

"Come home soaked?"

Her eyes steadied, then looked up at him. "As I remember"—she swallowed—"no."

He jangled the keys. "I'd like to borrow these, Belle."

WHERE Rayburn Street meets Pike at a sharp angle, south of Center Square, there is a large hardware store.

Kennedy, crossing Rayburn, was knocked about by the stiff wind. The wind flattened his overcoat against his frail back, tore at his faded fedora, made his eyes water, found its way up his trousers' legs and down his neck. It blew him through the doorway of the hardware store. He fought the door until it was closed and stood for a moment getting his wind. It did not take very much to knock the wind out of him.

"Yes, sir?" said a tall, button-nosed man, moving his palms against each other.

Kennedy handed him a key. "I see your name's on this. Did you make it?"

"Obviously."

"Obviously, of course," Kennedy said. "I'm from the *Free Press*. My card.... I see the key has a serial number on it. Can you tell me when you made the key, and for what address?"

"Certainly."

"Please."

The man took the key and walked off. Kennedy blew his nose. The man turned, raised his eyebrows.

"Beg pardon?"

"Uh-uhn. Just my nose."

The man bowed, went upstairs to a mezzanine office. He came down five minutes later, returned the key to Kennedy and said:

"It was made for Mr. Anthony Cash. Our man was called to measure a lock at Room 21, the Onyx Building, exactly two months ago today."

"Thank you very much," said Kennedy. He held up a smaller key, very slender, which bore merely the number 140. He said: "What do you make of this key?"

"It looks, sir, like a safe deposit key. Some banks put no other form of identification on their keys—for obvious reasons."

"I understand. Thank you again. And good-day."

"Good-day, sir."

The Onyx Building was only four blocks distant. Kennedy made his way through the hard-handed wind, holding the collar of his threadbare topcoat tight about his throat. The wind got in the way of his legs like stubborn weeds. No one ever looked more like a scarecrow. But he got to the Onyx Building, skidding by way of a revolving door into the lobby. He took an elevator to the second floor, went down the second-floor corridor eyeing the ground-glass door panels, each with its legend lettered in black. Until he came to 21, which bore no lettering. He fitted the key, opened the door, entered and closed the door swiftly behind him.

A desk and a chair: nothing more, except the old typewriter which stood upon the desk. He ran his gloved hand over the typewriter, his eyes suddenly sly, wily, behind their lazy lids. He opened a drawer, saw sheets of foolscap, carbon paper. He ran through the sheets of foolscap, found no writing. He opened the other drawers: they were empty; but one of them held his eye. Small shavings of wood, fresh shavings, in the drawer. The lock had been forced with a knife or a screwdriver. The bottom of the drawer was dusty except for a space about nine by twelve inches. He closed the drawer. Closed all the drawers.

He went downstairs and found the superintendent. "Is office twenty-one occupied?" he asked.

"Yes, but I understand from the night watchman that it's been used only at night, and at infrequent intervals. A Mr. Anthony Cash; a writer, I believe."

Kennedy took a cab to *Enrico's,* in Flamingo Street. He was chilled to the bone and he liked Paderoofski's hot toddies.

"Hal-lo, Meester Kennedy!" cried Paderoofski. "Long time I no see. Hahss treeks?"

"Brightening, Paderoofski. Make me a very hot one."

"Shoo t'ing, I guess so. 'S good for whata hails you, I'm say so! Musta be very cold hout, by damn."

"How's tricks by you?"

"Ukkey, t'ank you so much. My keed he's a-gotta wan 'nother tooth. Axcuse me, it was tod hottie you want?"

"A very hot one."

"Shoo t'ing!"

Kennedy drank three hot toddies and felt warmth lay mellowly in his body.

"You are an artist, Paderoofski," he said, paying up.

"I'm not care, hell's bells, Meester Kennedy."

"Okey-doke."

"Ukkey-duck!" boomed Paderoofski; and then he lunged around to the front of the bar, trailing a large woolen muffler done in orange and green. "Now looka here, Meester Kennedy. You no drassed hop warm liking you should. Leta me puta dis around de neck... so... like dees."

"Paderoofski, you're magnanimous."

"Ah, no, no. My old man's de Italian, my old woman's de Joosh."

"Auf Wiedersehen!"

"Happy tays!"

When Kennedy walked into MacBride's office twenty minutes later the skipper looked up, brought his brows together. He said:

"Where in cripes' name did you find that thing you're wearing around your neck?"

"No cracks against Paderoofski's contribution to the lame and the halt." He tossed a small flat key on the desk. "You might send some of your boy scouts around town to the various banks and find out what bank has a safe deposit box it fits. The box will be Tony Price's."

MacBride laughed. "I'm just after looking in the box he and his wife kept at the First National. Nothing there."

"This is one his wife didn't know about." He threw another key on the desk. "This one fits an office he was using under the name of Anthony Cash. Room twenty-one, the Onyx Building. You might want to case it."

"Why was he using an office under an assumed name?"

"After all, Skip, there's a limit to what I can know."

"Does his wife know about it?"

"No."

MacBride scowled. "This makes another angle."

"Better see about that safe-deposit-box key. Find the bank and then get a court order to examine the box. And, if I may say so, send a fingerprint man to that office in the Onyx Building."

"We may find out, Kennedy," MacBride said darkly, "that this pal of yours may have been a heel at heart."

"He could be a heel, kid: he was still my pal."

MacBride shrugged, reached for the phone, saying, "By the way, that empty shell you left with me checks with the gun that killed your pal."

"What'd you expect?"

THERE was a box at the Citizens' Bank and Trust in Anthony Price's name. The manager brought it into a small, private office and set it down upon a desk there. He bowed, said:

"Shall I remain or would you rather be alone?"

"Alone," MacBride said, "if you don't mind."

The manager went out.

Kennedy wandered around the office looking at some etchings.

"Come here," the skipper said, "and we'll go through it."

Kennedy yawned, patting the yawn with his fingertips. He came over and leaned on the desk, propping his chin in a cupped hand.

The skipper removed a thick sheaf of foolscap, flattened it on the desk.

"Typewriting on it," he said.

"Carbon copy," Kennedy muttered.

"Let's see—the last page is numbered 186."

"Skip that and see what it says."

Both began reading. The skipper frowned, saying: "This is funny: wherever there should be a name, there's a blank."

"Anyhow, it's Tony's writing. He always put an 'e' in the middle of judgment."

"Ain't that right?"

"Well, it's all right, yes, but the habit nowadays is to leave it out. Go on, keep reading; I'm ahead of you."

They read twenty pages.

MacBride said: "Well, this Mr. Blank or Mr. Dash was born June 5, 1881, in Cleveland, Ohio: we know that much."

"Just for fun, skip now to about page one hundred."

MacBride skipped and they read fifteen pages.

"Boy, this is rich!" the skipper said. "He had the goods on this fellow—and how!"

"Nice research there. He was a bear for research."

"But why no names?"

"Tony was being cagey, maybe."

MacBride looked at him. "You know, you smell like a damned distillery."

"Turn the page—"

The door opened and the manager looked in. "Excuse me, Captain MacBride. Your office wants you on the telephone."

"Thanks. Be right with you."

The skipper followed the manager out of the office and Kennedy bent over the manuscript, read rapidly; drew a piece of paper from his pocket and from time to time jotted down notes. He skipped several pages, read bits here and there, skipped some more and continued to make brief notes. Five minutes later the skipper barged back into the office.

"They didn't find any fingerprints in that office but Price's," he said. "But they found a mark left by a wet rubber heel on the floor. Moriarity found it, and he gave me a long spiel that it's just as good as a fingerprint, the same way the marking of a tire tread is: no two tires wear down just the same, neither do two rubber heels wear down the same."

"Maybe it's Tony's."

"Don't butt in. They looked over all Price's shoes. Rubbers too, though Mory says it's not a tread from a rubber, it's from the rubber heel of a shoe. He cut out the linoleum where the tread was left and took it along. I sent him around to Garth's place to pick up Garth's shoes."

"How about the shoes Garth is wearing?"

"I knew you'd spring that. Evening shoes, or pumps, or whatever you call them, don't usually have rubber heels, account of you dance in them."

"Check."

"I'll take that manuscript along with me."

"Okey. Let's go."

They parted outside and Kennedy rode a street car to the *Free Press* Building, went upstairs and took down a copy of *Who's Who*. He left the building five minutes later and took a taxi-cab to Police Headquarters and when he entered MacBride's office the skipper and Moriarity were looking over several pairs of shoes. On the desk lay a piece of linoleum, with a heel print clearly defined. Kennedy bent over it.

"A Trojan brand rubber heel," he mused aloud. "The 'n' worn almost completely away, the 'a' worn half away, the 'j' chipped in three places. Would you say the imprint was made recently, Mory?"

"Not very. I tell you, Kennedy—it looks like a guy that left that print stepped in oil somewhere before he went in that office. You know, like you'd step in oil in the street or something. It might be weeks or days or hours old, but I don't think it was made very recently. On the other hand, I wouldn't swear to it."

MacBride tossed down a shoe, said: "I'm damned, Mory, if I'm going to get all worked up about that heel mark. It could have been made by, say, a janitor."

"Nobody was allowed in that office," Moriarity shouted. "The guy Price had a special lock made for it of his own."

"All right, then. He could have had a visitor."

"Sure he could have. But you sent me down there to see what I could see and I'm telling you what I saw." He threw up his hands, said to Kennedy: "This is a hell of a police department. They tell you to do this or that and when you do it—"

"Forget it, forget it," MacBride grumbled. "All I say is, I'm not going to get myself all worked up over every screwy angle that crops up here. We know who we want: we want Garth." He knuckled the desk. "I go over the bank with Kennedy and we read some dirt and I let myself get all worked up over that. Then you go into the heebeejeebies over this heel print. Garth is the guy we want. We want him for murder! I'm sending out a general alarm and—"

The telephone rang and Moriarity, frowning irritably, picked it up and growled into the mouthpiece: "Yeah?... Hang on." He handed the instrument over to the skipper, saying, "You."

"Captain MacBride speaking," the skipper said. "Ike?... What?" His eyes steadied. "When?... Where are you now?... What does he say?... Okey. I'll be right down."

He hung up, spread his palms. "School's out, fellows. That was Ike. A guy hunting rabbits out along Gunstock Road thought he saw the top of a car just below the surface of the river. He told a passing motorist to report it to the first cop he came to. The motorist stopped at the Hillside Avenue booth. Ike happened to be there talking to the guy on duty. Ike went out to the spot, met the hunter. He phoned for a steam lighter and the lighter came up the river and hoisted up the car with its derrick. It was a car stolen in Elm Street sometime after midnight. Garth was in the car—dead, of course. There's no guard rail there by the river. A scallion to your heel print, Mory."

"Okey, okey; a scallion to it. I done my best."

MacBride got into his overcoat, slapped on his derby. "Come on. We'll take a look."

Moriarity and the skipper went to the door but Kennedy remained leaning on the desk.

MacBride said: "Coming, Kennedy?"

"I don't like to look at drowned people, old tomato. Give me the details when you get back."

Alone, Kennedy meandered around the office, staring dreamily at the floor, pursing and unpursing lips. He stopped to stare at the goldfish for a moment, scratched his jaw, sighed, wandered over to the desk and sat down. Then he picked up the telephone and called the owner of the rooming-house where Garth had lived.

"Mrs. Anderson," he said, "this is Kennedy, the fellow who was around there with Captain MacBride.... Well, it's not good news, Mrs. Anderson. He was found dead in a stolen car which he must have driven off the road into the river.... Yes, he stole the car and drove it into the river.... What's that?... How do you know?... I see. That's very interesting. Thanks for telling me.... Of course, Mrs. Anderson."

He eased the receiver back into the prong, kept his hands on the instrument and stared meditatively straight before him. Presently a thin half-smile came to his lips, a look that was both wily and wise crept into his eyes.

IT WAS dusk when Kennedy rang the doorbell of Hildebrand's Sturdevant Park house. Stone, the burly valet-chauffeur, opened the door, grinned amiably.

"My name is Kennedy," Kennedy said, "I'd like to see Mr. Hildebrand and get a statement for the *Free Press*. He doubtless knows that the police found the owner of the gun that killed Mr. Price."

Stone's face fell. "Yes, we heard about that. Step in and I'll see if Mr. Hildebrand's busy."

Hildebrand was not busy.

"Hello, Kennedy," he said, when Stone showed Kennedy into the library. "I've heard a lot about you. I suppose every newspaperman has." His voice was firm. He was tamping tobacco into a pipe, his back to the fireplace, where red coals glowed warmly in the warm room.

Stone left the room.

"Sit down," Hildebrand said crisply, taking a match from the mantel. "I received the news about five minutes ago. Rather a miserable ending to a bad bit of business." He lit up, rolling the flame across the tobacco; tossed the match into the fireplace. "Offhand I can't seem to remember Garth, connect him with anything."

"Tony wrote a piece about him and his friend by the name of Addison."

Hildebrand looked at the ceiling. "Addison. Garth. No. I can't seem to recall what Tony wrote in connection with them. Of course"—he brought his eyes down—"you couldn't expect me to."

Kennedy was rolling an unlit cigarette round and round in his fingers. He said quietly: "The police found out that Tony was renting a small office in the Onyx Building. I suppose you knew of that office, didn't you? He used the name of Cash there."

Hildebrand looked puzzled. "Office? Why, no. What possible reason could he have had for renting an office under an assumed name? Or for renting an office at all?"

"There was a typewriter in the office. I guess he wanted a place where he could work without being disturbed. Not even his wife knew about it."

Hildebrand still looked incredulous, bending his brows sharply above his strong nose. "That's possible. Though certainly if he wanted peace and quiet he could have had it in any one of our offices. Are you positive it was his office?"

"Positive."

"Well, you must know, I daresay. Tony did have a few odd streaks in him. I suppose I should not be surprised."

Kennedy was nodding. "I knew him well, you know. I broke him in on his first newspaper job."

"I know. He often mentioned you."

Kennedy looked down at his cigarette. "I ran into him at the *Ambassador* last night. You know he had a little trouble there, don't you?"

"I know that at one time he appeared to be in a high state of excitement. I questioned him but he said it was nothing, that he'd had a stupid petty argument with some drunk."

Kennedy shook his head, said slowly: "It wasn't petty."

"I only know what Tony told me."

"The argument he had was with Garth."

Hildebrand took his pipe from his mouth, looked levelly at Kennedy. "Why haven't I heard of this before?"

"It was a great deal more than just an argument," Kennedy went on. "A shot was fired. Garth fired a shot at Tony. In the downstairs washroom."

"But my dear man, why do I hear of this only now? Do the police know of it?"

Kennedy nodded. He lit his cigarette, choked on a puff of smoke, went on choking until he was red in the face. He said: "Could I have a drink of water?"

"Of course." Hildebrand pressed a button and Stone appeared. "Bring Mr. Kennedy a glass of water, Stone."

Kennedy sat with a handkerchief pressed to his mouth. Stone returned with a glass of water on a tray and as Kennedy reached for the glass he coughed again, bumped the tray, sent the glass of water tumbling. It fell on Stone's feet, spread out on the hardwood floor.

"I would do a thing like that," Kennedy said. "So sorry."

Stone rushed out, returned with a mop and another glass of water. When he had mopped up the floor and left, Kennedy said:

"Are you sure, Mr. Hildebrand, that Tony didn't mention to you the incident in the *Ambassador* washroom?"

"Don't be absurd. If he had, I should have had Garth arrested instantly. If you knew it, why didn't you take some action of that sort?"

"I didn't know, at the time, who fired the shot—Tony or Garth." He stood up, took a few languid steps. His cigarette fell from his fingers and he bent to pick it up, used his fingertips to brush up the ashes. Rising, he said: "Will you ask Stone to come in?"

"Stone?"

"Yes. Stone."

Hildebrand stared curiously at Kennedy, who was staring lazily at the floor. But Hildebrand rang for Stone.

The burly man appeared promptly, came to a stop, heels together, and dipped his head towards Hildebrand. Hildebrand said:

"Mr. Kennedy wishes to speak to you."

Stone dipped his head towards Kennedy, smiled cheerfully.

"Mr. Stone," Kennedy said, "were you ever in an office in the Onyx Building?"

Stone's forehead wrinkled. "The Onyx Building, sir?"

"Yes. More precisely, room twenty-one in the Onyx Building. Mr. Price used it."

"But I thought Mr. Price's office was at the newspaper building."

"You *knew* Mr. Price's office was at the newspaper building. You also found out, somehow, that he had another office, a place where he worked nights, in the Onyx Building."

Stone's round squat face looked blank. "You must have me mixed up with someone else," his heavy voice said.

"I don't think so."

Hildebrand said brusquely: "Now look here, my dear Kennedy. Stone has been with me a long time. I deny you the right to hold an inquiry here: it's hardly in your province.... You may leave the room, Stone."

Stone dipped his squat head. "Yes, sir."

"Stay here, Stone," Kennedy said tranquilly.

And Hildebrand said: "Stone, you may leave the room."

"Excuse me, sir," Stone said in his heavy voice, "but I'd like to hear what this man has to say about me."

KENNEDY ambled across the room, lay down on a leather couch, on his side. "How old are you, Mr. Stone?" he asked.

"I'm forty-nine."

"Aren't you fifty-five? Weren't you born on June 5, 1885?"

Stone smiled, shook his head. "No, I wasn't."

"In Cleveland?"

"No, sir."

"Didn't you become obsessed with the idea that Mr. Price knew more about your past than your employer did?"

Stone's smile was almost a smirk. "My past is an open book, to anyone who wants to look it up." He stood comfortably now, at ease.

Kennedy said: "You don't think that if certain research work of Mr. Price's appeared in the newspapers, it would harm you? Suppose for instance it appeared in the paper that a Mr. Dash, who was born in Cleveland, June 5, 1885, and in his tenth year moved to Buffalo with his family, where two years later his father forged a check for $5,000 and was saved from public exposure only by the kindness of his employer.

"Suppose it carried on with Mr. Dash's boyhood, his young manhood, the death of his father by suicide—not accident—and revealed the young man as secretary to a wealthy steel magnate. Suppose it showed how the secretary gradually, bit by bit, turned the old man against his son and his daughter, even his wife, and was rewarded with a legacy. If these and a hundred other hitherto unknown incidents in the life of Mr. Dash were to appear in the papers, wouldn't they by any chance embarrass you, Mr. Stone?"

Faint bewilderment stirred in Stone's eyes. He shook his head. "No, sir."

"What kind of a fantastic story is this!" exclaimed Hildebrand. "Are you drunk, man?"

"A little. The story of this fantastic Mr. Dash ends on a tragic note: he kills the only man who knows his past. That is the part that Tony Price didn't know about. But he knew about a lot of other things connected with our Mr. Dash: the ruined waitress in Utica; the innocent auto salesman in Hartford who took a first degree murder rap because of Mr. Dash's perjured testimony; innumerable other little sidelights. Honest, Mr. Stone, don't you feel uneasy?"

"I just don't know what you're talking about, if that's what you mean?"

"Is Stone your real name?"

"Of course it's my real name."

"Can you prove it?"

"Of course I can prove it!"

Kennedy sat up. "Can you also prove where you were, every minute of the time, from midnight last night until, say, the present moment?"

"I—of course."

"Between, say, the hours of midnight and three a.m., Mr. Stone?"

"Here. In bed, from one on. I drove Mr. Hildebrand home—"

"Who can prove you were here—in bed?"

"Mr. Hildebrand—"

"Would not know if you were actually in bed, or even actually in the house."

Stone's face colored. "I tell you he knows it!" his heavy voice cried out.

Kennedy stood up, a wasted figure of a man. "Do you know he was in the house, in bed, Mr. Hildebrand?"

"Of course he was in the house, in bed!"

"Where's his bedroom?"

"In the rear, left."

"Yours?"

"Directly above this room."

Kennedy smiled dreamily. "What you doubtless mean is that you *supposed* he was in the house, in bed. You didn't actually see him in bed, did you?"

"My dear fellow, hardly. After all, I don't put my valet to bed."

"So then no one can prove that your valet was actually in the house and actually in bed."

"In that sense, no. But—"

"You know I was here!" shouted Stone, his eyes blazing.

"Of course," said Hildebrand.

"You *saw* me here—all night—"

"Of course, of course."

Kennedy smiled. "But you just said, Mr. Hildebrand, that you didn't actually see him in bed, in the house."

"He did so!" yelled Stone. "He did so see me!"

"Do you think, Mr. Stone, that any jury will believe that a servant's master actually saw him in bed every minute of the night?"

"Jury? What do you mean, jury?" Stone cried in his heavy hoarse voice.

"Why, don't you know that I suspect you of murdering Mr. Anthony Price?" Kennedy asked gently.

Stone roared: "It's a lie!"

"Mr. Hildebrand," Kennedy said, "may I use your phone? I think the police ought to know about this. It's tough that you won't be able to prove that your servant was *actually* in the house, *actually* in bed. I imagine you're very fond of him."

Hildebrand's eyes bored into Kennedy's. "Don't be an idiot. You know blamed well the police have the man who killed Tony."

Kennedy pointed to the floor. "I spilled that drink before on purpose. You can see the print of a rubber heel there. Mr. Stone's rubber heel. He also left the same heel print in Tony Price's office when he went there to swipe a manuscript. I later saw the manuscript he stole."

"That's a lie!" shouted Stone, his face sweaty. "And I was in bed last night. The shots woke me up. Mr. Hildebrand can prove I was right here in the house."

Kennedy shook his head. "Mr. Hildebrand couldn't afford to perjure himself by swearing that he actually saw you in bed all that time, when he didn't. I don't think you ought to expect that of Mr. Hildebrand."

"I do! I do expect it! You're off your head, damn it! You say I stole a manuscript and then right on top of that you say you saw it later!"

"Let me revise a bit. For some reason no one will probably ever understand, Tony Price made a duplicate. He kept the duplicate in a safe deposit box. I got the duplicate. You swiped the original—the one was locked in his desk. . . . Where's the telephone, Mr. Hildebrand?"

Hildebrand said in a cold voice: "Wait." There was a gun in his hand, steady as a rock imbedded in earth.

Kennedy looked dreamily at the gun. "You believe in standing by your servant, don't you? Well, that's a swell idea."

Hildebrand's face was white, his jaw was set, there was a pale, unwavering fire in his eyes. "I don't think you are going to make that phone call, Kennedy."

Stone came across the room, tapped Kennedy's pockets. "No gun," he said.

Hildebrand said: "First, Kennedy, I want that manuscript."

"Second, you want to bump me off," Kennedy drawled.

"I happen to be dealing the cards. You'll have to take a chance on the turn of your particular card."

Kennedy looked at Stone. "Your master certainly sticks by you, doesn't he?"

"Enough of that!" Hildebrand said in a low, taut voice. "I want that manuscript."

Kennedy shrugged. "I'll have to take a chance on the turn of that card. Will you take your car?"

"Get the car out," Hildebrand said to Stone.

IT WAS dark in the street. Hildebrand prodded Kennedy into the rear of the limousine, followed and sat down beside him, drawing the window curtains. Stone climbed in behind the wheel, said over his shoulder:

"Where to?"

"Tuft Street."

"Tuft? Where is that?"

"Well, go over and hit Main, turn left on Main. I'll direct you from there."

The car moved off, clicked smoothly into high, left the Park behind. Hildebrand sat stiffly, his gun pressed against Kennedy's side, a frozen gray look on his face. Kennedy was gazing absent-mindedly at the back of Stone's squat neck. River fog was rolling through the streets, dampening the pavement, clinging to the windows of the limousine like cold sweat. Stone set his windshield wiper to working, leaned forward a bit over the wheel, to see better.

"An excellent night for a dark deed," Kennedy mused aloud. He turned his wasted face towards Hildebrand, regarded him with an expression that was almost sad. "Think of it: A man like you, a great man, a great publisher, suddenly become like unto any desperate man with a gun."

Hildebrand said coldly: "I should prefer you to omit the philosophizing."

"Haven't you any qualms?"

"None. You have become suddenly an obstacle in my way. You are smart, but not smart enough. Your penchant for playing a single-handed dramatic role represents your undoing. You should have told the police first."

Kennedy sighed, nodded. "We live and learn."

"And sometimes die."

Kennedy said to Stone: "Next right."

Stone wheeled into the next cross street and drove along between rows of misted street lights.

"Make a left into Eve Street," Kennedy said.

"Eve? Where's that?" Stone asked.

"Two blocks beyond…. Your chauffeur, Mr. Hildebrand, doesn't know his city very well."

Hildebrand asked: "What, by the way, is your destination?"

"I have a small room in an apartment house."

Stone made a left turn into Eve Street and rolled along past garages. Neon signs made red smears in the foggy darkness.

"Your next right will be Tuft Street," Kennedy explained. "It's really an alley, one of the oldest in the city."

"This it?"

"Yes. Turn right."

The big limousine swung from Eve into a dark cobbled alley and Kennedy said:

"That white light ahead is the apartment-house garage, in the basement. Turn into the garage and take it easy, it's quite a little grade."

Stone shifted back into second as he came up to the white light and heaved on his wheel to make the turn into the garage, whose wide double doors were open. He tooled the car down a sharp cement grade, into a large basement garage where a few lights glowed dimly and several cars were parked, several motorcycles.

"This'll be all right," Kennedy said, as he leaned over and opened the door.

Two men in blue flannel shirts came strolling out of the shadows towards the car. Another car came down into the garage, pulled up behind the limousine.

Hildebrand said: "I am now going to place my gun in my pocket. You will walk on my right side and we will go up to your apartment…. Stone, what's the matter?"

Stone was stiffening in his seat.

Hildebrand's low voice snapped: "Stone!"

A couple of men who had got out of the other car now swung past the limousine on their way towards an inner door.

Kennedy yelled: "Hey, old tomato!"

MacBride stopped a few feet short of the inner door, turned and made a face. "That sounds like—"

"Kennedy," Moriarity muttered.

Stone was opening the front door of the limousine, his face dead white, his jaw shaking. He stepped out, his shoulders hunched, and suddenly made a dash towards the ramp down which he had driven.

He crashed into Gahagan and fired his gun as he crashed. The bullet whanged into a metal light shade hanging from the ceiling.

Kennedy fell upon Hildebrand, whose gun was in his overcoat pocket. Kennedy put all his feeble strength on Hildebrand's right hand, trying to prevent Hildebrand from withdrawing the gun. Hildebrand surged against him, a hard-bodied strong man.

"Be sensible," Kennedy panted. "You should have known your town better. Stone too."

"What is this place?" Hildebrand muttered, still struggling.

"Police Headquarters garage. We came in one of the blind entrances—"

Interlocked, they tumbled from the car, across the running-board, on to the cement floor.

Gahagan hit Stone on the jaw and drove him tumbling backward and Stone crashed into the luggage rack on the rear of the limousine. Hildebrand kicked himself free of Kennedy, jumped up and ran towards the ramp.

"Hey!" MacBride yelled.

Hildebrand ran on.

The skipper put a shot a few inches above Hildebrand's head, yelled again: "Hey! Stop!"

Hildebrand half-turned, fired. His bullet ripped through the hood of his limousine. Kennedy pressed flat against the floor.

MacBride was muttering: "This ain't very clear to me but—"

Moriarity's gun blazed. "I know this: we're being shot at." His bullet staggered Hildebrand, threw him against a steel pillar; but Hildebrand swerved away instantly, plunged on towards the ramp, reached it and began to toil upward.

Gahagan's gun exploded three times and Stone crumpled backward against the luggage rack.

Hildebrand reached the top of the ramp, emptied his gun into the garage before dashing into the glare of the light outside. MacBride was standing spread-legged, his gun raised and at arm's length. He could see only Hildebrand's legs now. He took four deliberate shots, saw the legs crumple, saw Hildebrand's trunk come down, then his head. The echoes fled away out of the garage and a hollow silence followed.

Kennedy was still pressed against the floor, but gradually he began to lift his head, peer cautiously around. He said:

"Is it safe now?"

MacBride walked over to him, bent down and hauled him to his feet. "You hurt, kid?"

"Uh-huh. Just a little, you might say, jittery. What's the score?"

"I think there were two put-outs."

"Our side won, huh?"

MacBride nodded, narrowed one eye. "I suppose you think it's a great joke to start a ballgame in Headquarters."

Kennedy was still shaking. "The joke's not on you, pally."

"What the hell are you shaking so for?"

"I was scared, you dope! I was scared stiff. For tears in your eyes, what do you expect? I bring in the bacon and you expect me to slice it too!... Quick, a drink—rye—before I faint. If you have no glasses, just give me the bottle."

THE SKIPPER got back from the hospital at eight. He entered the central room carrying a paper sack and a milk bottle filled with hot black coffee. Fog lay wet upon his face, beaded his derby. He went up to his office and found Kennedy playing solitaire. At Kennedy's elbow was a quart bottle which two hours before had been full of rye; now it was empty.

"Well, I got back," MacBride clipped, placing the paper sack and the bottle of coffee on the desk. He hung up his overcoat, his derby; returned to the desk, tore open the paper sack and produced four hamburgers. "I brought two for you," he said.

Kennedy studied his cards. "Thanks so much, old fellow, old chap."

"Now don't start talking that way. Here, shove this food in your face and listen to me. Both Stone and Hildebrand talked and the more I stick around in this business the more I find out that human nature's about as screwy as the stock market.

"Price in that washroom scene took the gun away from Garth and chased him out. Then he went upstairs and got hold of Hildebrand and they went into a private room and Price pulled the gun and gave it to Hildebrand and said, 'There's a souvenir for you.' And he told Hildebrand what'd taken place down in the washroom, and said, 'one more thing like this, Hildebrand, and hell knows what I may do.' Deadly enemies, Hildebrand and Tony Price.

"It goes back a couple of years, according to Hildebrand. Price was getting fed up on the work, he wanted to leave, but Hildebrand had him tied up on a contract that had about three months to run. When Hildebrand held him to the contract, Price went off his nut and they had a fight and Price threatened to expose him as a heel and a fraud. It must have been pretty hot. Hildebrand got scared and then what did he do but hire a private detective to get the lowdown on Price's wife. It was a chance, a chance in the dark, but it turned up something that had happened when she was a kid of seventeen or so. Hildebrand locked his information in a safe.

"But a month later he was shocked out of his shoes when Price walked in, sat down, and said, 'You're going to let me break that contract, Hildebrand. Or else. I've spent a month looking up your history.' And he told Hildebrand the whole story of Hildebrand's life. Then Hildebrand pulled his own ace. 'You'll not only stick with the contract, Tony, but you'll sign another one. You're a genius at this sort of thing. The minute you break a contract with me, I know what you'll do—you'll publish what you know. But you'll stay with me, Tony, and like it. Here's the reason why.' He showed Tony the lowdown on his wife. Tony said, 'I know about that, though Belle doesn't know I know it.' And Hildebrand said, 'How would you like everybody to know it?' So there you are, a deadlock.

"They began to hate each other to hell from then on, and Tony Price began to lose weight and go into long trances. Hildebrand began to worry and he sent Stone, who was actually his bodyguard, to keep tabs on Price. Stone knew all about Hildebrand too, from years back. And it was Stone who tailed Tony to that office, saw him go there night after night. He master-keyed his way in one day, saw the script in the drawer which he forced open. That day, fella, was yesterday. He swiped the script and took it to Hildebrand. Hildebrand read it and said to Stone, 'Tony's losing his head. He may lose it completely and publish this. Could you use ten thousand, Stone?'

"Something like that was bound to happen. Hildebrand or Price—one was bound sooner or later to kill the other. A deadlock like that can't go on forever. The Garth business at the *Ambassador* gave Hildebrand a swell chance. After Tony gave him the gun, with the souvenir crack, Hildebrand spotted Garth, who was pretty drunk by that time. He saw Garth at one of the bars trying to charge a drink and the way things were happening, he knew Garth would be led out pretty soon. Hildebrand went outside for a smoke, crossed the street to where his limousine was parked and Stone was standing. When Hildebrand saw Garth come out of the hotel and stagger down the street, he said to Stone, 'Follow that fellow in the car. When he crosses an intersection—pick a dark one—brush the car against him, just enough to knock him down. Then take him to my house. Wait there for me. Keep him there. Feed him liquor.' Stone did that.

"Hildebrand came home at a little past one, found Garth dead drunk and sound asleep. He told Stone to go out and try to steal a car and Stone came back half an hour later, with a small sedan. They piled Garth in the sedan and took his key, found his address in his wallet. Stone drove the sedan and Hildebrand followed with the limousine. Out on Gunstock Road, Stone ran the sedan slow, headed it for the river and jumped. The sedan and Garth sank. Hildebrand picked Stone up and they drove to the neighborhood of Skiff Street. Hildebrand went up to the door in the rooming-house that had Garth's name on it on a white card. He went in the room and telephoned Price's place and told the Negro to tell Price to come over to the house. Then he went back to the house with Stone.

"As Price stepped out of his car in front of Hildebrand's house, Hildebrand fired three times from the living-room window, tossed the gun out to the grass. Garth's gun—the gun Price gave to Hildebrand as a souvenir. Tie that!"

Kennedy was picking up his cards. "We should have figured nearer those lines in the first place, tomato. We should have realized that whoever phoned Tony at that hour in the morning must have known that he was in the habit of going on those calls in his own machine. If he was in the habit of using a taxi, the scheme would have been not so good. Then we should have known that whoever made that call knew that Tony never answered the phone, that the Negro had a bad ear for voices. If Tony had answered, he'd have known definitely if it was Hildebrand's voice and would have said as much to his wife.

"When we read that script at the bank, I began to visualize Mr. Dash as Hildebrand. Tony gave the date of his subject's birth. So I went over to the office, looked Hildebrand up in *Who's Who*, found the date of his birth was the same. Even so, that still didn't incriminate Hildebrand. Though when I chided Tony at the *Ambassador*, he said he'd have something to tell me next day that would knock me over. I wasn't positive until I found that Stone's heel print matched the one Mory took out of the office in the Onyx Building. I began to lay into Stone, to gradually impress upon him that he was the killer, the only one, and that Hildebrand couldn't possibly prove he was in the house, in bed, during those hours. I had to break Stone down in order to get at Hildebrand. I was positive that Garth never drove that car into the river."

"Why were you so positive about that?"

Kennedy put the cards away. "Because when I phoned Mrs. Anderson, to tell her the bad news, she said Garth didn't know how to drive a car, he'd never driven one in his life."

MacBride took a long drink of coffee. "It's a little thing like that, Kennedy, that will always trip a guy up. They take too much for granted. Hildebrand planned a swell murder, but he took it for granted that Garth was able to drive. Eat your hamburgers before they get cold."

"He was a bum newspaperman too."

"Well, I don't know about that."

Kennedy shrugged. "He should have known his city. He didn't know that Tuft Street was one of the back entrances to Headquarters."

"If he had—"

"I would not now be eating hamburgers."

Die-Hard

Cap. MacBride finds a mystery hard to solve until hot lead begins to sing.

Chapter I

Mᴀᴄ**BRIDE** pushed the receiver back onto the hook, and for a moment left his hand on top of the instrument. His brows bent downward and inward, creasing the flesh between. His eyes fixed themselves on his memo pad with a narrow, preoccupied stare. He rose abruptly, ripping the top sheet off the pad, and crossed the office to a large wall map of Richmond City. The street index on the left helped him. Evergreen Place. He squared off a small area with the assistance of marginal numbers and letters and vertical and horizontal lines. Evergreen Place: one block long.

He jammed his arms into the sleeves of his four-year-old overcoat—worn but neat as a pin—and slapped a faded brown fedora on his bony head. His big black shoes, polished to an onyx luster, drummed out of the office and down the wide wooden corridor. He poked his head into a room near the head of the staircase.

"Mory and Ike"—his chin jerked backward—"come on."

Moriarity woke up and stretched, yawning, "Where?"

"Down the basement, to begin with."

The skipper pounded his heels down the stairway to the main floor, pushed open a heavy metal swing-door that closed slowly behind him against pneumatic pressure. He followed cement steps downward, pushed open a similar door and entered the basement garage.

"Gahagan!" he barked. The echoes of his voice banged around the garage. He made a beeline for a long black sedan, pulled open the rear door and climbed in; settled down and lit a two-cent cigar which smelled like old rubbish being burned in the spring.

Heavy footfalls sounded and Gahagan, his uniform cap on the back of his head, appeared and climbed in front behind the wheel. Moriarity and Cohen showed up at a stroll and the skipper snapped:

"Come on, come on."

They climbed leisurely into the back of the sedan and sat down beside him. Moriarity yawned, said:

"I must have spring fever."

MacBride snorted. "In the middle of winter, yeah."

"I always get it ahead of time."

"Gahagan," the skipper said, "drive to fifteen Evergreen Place."

"Where's that?"

"Go to the fourteen-hundred block of Tremont. It's around there."

Cold winter rain hit the sedan as it rolled out into the street. Gahagan turned on both windshield wipers. A strong, boisterous wind clapped and howled, drove the rain in thick, noisy sheets. It streaked and beaded the windows of the sedan. Gahagan drove truculently, bullied other cars out of the way. He sirened his way through red traffic lights and cut corners on the inside and from time to time used his gloved hand to wipe cloudy vapor off the inside of the windshield.

"I should have worn my rubbers," MacBride growled.

Tremont Avenue was wide and rackety with the sound of trolley cars, buses, taxi-cabs, and people hurrying in the rain beneath an undulating field of umbrellas. The wind boomed in soaked awnings and tussled with the bulky rubber raincoats of traffic cops. Gahagan turned right into a narrow street with a dead end and pulled up back of a couple of parked cars.

Ike Cohen said, "This can't be Evergreen Street. I don't see any evergreen trees."

"It said it on the sign," Gahagan replied defensively.

MacBride opened the door, saying, "If that ain't an ambulance. I'll have it pinched for impersonating one," and stepped out into the blowing rain. He ducked between a sedan and an ambulance and shot up three wooden steps to the dismal gray porch of a clapboard bungalow. Moriarity and Cohen arrived precipitately, their heads lowered, and almost bowled the skipper over. A uniformed cop appeared in the doorway and said:

"Hi, Cap'n."

There was no hallway inside. The door opened directly on a small, shabby living-room, and the room was cluttered up with several policemen, their rubber coats dripping, and several men in civilian clothes. In a back corner of the room stood a small pot-bellied stove and on a chair beside it sat Kennedy, twiddling his wet stockinged feet near its warmth. His face was wet with rain and it had darkened the shoulders of his threadbare topcoat. His air was one of good-natured indifference.

"Skipperino," he smiled drolly.

The dead man lay on the floor in front of a small divan. His shirt and undershirt had been torn away and there was a dark hole a little to the left of his breastbone. By the look of him, he was an Italian or a Spaniard; young, with thick dark hair and a lean, muscular face. The ambulance doctor had gone over him and was now standing and wiping his hands on a limp towel. Lieutenant Shacklin, plain-clothed, attached to the District Attorney's office, was taking notes on the back of an envelope. He was a tall, thin man in his late thirties, dressed in a belted gray mackintosh. His face was hawkish, dark, and stamped with a kind of brutal, hard intelligence. His lips were thin, bloodless, and hardly moved when he said casually:

"Know the stiff, MacBride?"

"No."

Shacklin went on making notes. "His name's Edward Lebanco and he was instantly killed by a shot through the heart by"—he motioned negligently—"the gun on that table."

"Who fired the gun?"

Shacklin sighed as though infinitely bored and said, "She's in the next room."

SHE WAS in the bedroom, a small room made dismal by the dark day. She sat in a wicker armchair and stared at the floor. When

MacBride turned on a floorlamp she started a trifle, not much, but did not lift her eyes. Her brown hair was disheveled and her face had a dead-white, lifeless look. She was about twenty-five. The utter listlessness of her did something to MacBride—checked him, and for a minute he looked sourly about the room.

Shacklin came and leaned darkly in the doorway. "Her name's Lottie Gravesand and she's twenty-four and unmarried. She lives here. She shot Lebanco through the heart."

MacBride muttered, "Why?"

"She said he attacked her. She said she'd told him time and time again to stay away, that she didn't want to see him. She said he forced his way in today, half an hour ago, and after an argument he attacked her and she pulled the gun out of her bureau drawer and shot him dead."

"Who phoned the police?"

"She did."

MacBride looked at her. "How long did you know Lebanco?"

"Three years," she said in a dull, sapped voice.

"What was the argument about?"

Her eyes remained glued to the floor. "The same thing. I told him I didn't want to see him any more. I told him to stay away. I told him to get out. He got mad. Then things happened and I ran in here and got the gun. He was coming through this doorway when I shot him and he backed up and fell down by the divan."

"Do you work?"

Shacklin chuckled dryly. "She's out of a job. She used to work for Demorest up until three months ago."

"The Commissioner of Public Works?"

"It's the only Demorest I know."

"Was she canned?"

"She said she left because of her health. We can easily check that up." His thin lips drew sidewise in a dry, humorless smile. "She's lied once already."

Her hands moved on the arms of the chair and her eyes flicked nervously upward, her lips pressed together. "I didn't," she said in a low, clogged whisper.

Shacklin continued to wear his humorless smile. "She insists that Lebanco came here of his own accord. She insists that she didn't want to see him." He drew a folded piece of paper from his pocket and said, "Read that, MacBride."

It was a square of personal stationery with her initials, L.G. embossed in the upper left-hand corner. The letter read:

> *Dear Edward,*
> *I've got to see you immediately. Please come as soon as you receive this.*
> *I'll be in all day, waiting. For God's sake, don't fail me!*
> *Lottie.*

MacBride scowled over the letter, lifted his eyes and set them on the girl. She was looking at him, a pulse beating in her throat and a strained look round her mouth. Her shoulders were hunched, as though she feared a blow. In her eyes was a look of mixed fear and challenge; but they wavered beneath the skipper's grim, searching stare.

MacBride said to Shacklin, "Where'd you get this?"

"One of the boys saw it beneath the divan. Lebanco must have brought it with him and dropped it."

The girl said in a shaking voice, "That note was written six months ago, when I thought I loved him."

"And it's been under the divan that long," mocked Shacklin.

"No," she choked. "I was cleaning my desk out the other day and I must have dropped it then."

Shacklin took a couple of stiff strides and snatched hold of her wrist. "You're lying like hell!" he ripped out.

She cringed. "I'm not. I—"

"Remember," said Kennedy, coming to the doorway in his shoeless feet, "that anything you may say will be held against you."

Shacklin spun. "You keep your mouth out of this!"

"Well, I thought she ought to know. After all, it's no more than right."

"You keep your damned mouth shut or I'll—" He strode to the doorway and shoved Kennedy roughly back into the other room.

Kennedy teetered back to the doorway and said complacently, "I still think she ought to know."

Shacklin swung at him but MacBride caught the blow in mid-career. "Take it easy," he muttered.

"And you mind your own business too!" Shacklin snapped, jerking his arms free.

"All right, but take it easy. If you hit him you might kill him. He's only a shell."

The front door opened and a man breezed in, took off his wet hat and scaled it on to the table. "Where's Miss Gravesand?" he asked good-naturedly. He was a little man, roly-poly, with short restless arms, a shiny bald head and small, sharp eyes set in a fat red face. He pushed a policeman out of the way and headed for the bedroom. He pushed Kennedy out of the way and bobbed into the bedroom.

"Okey, Miss Gravesand," he said. "Just keep your mouth shut. Don't let these wiseacres talk you into saying anything."

Shacklin reared back on his heels, demanded, "Rosbeck, how the hell did you get here?"

"Cab. Why?"

"Who phoned you?"

"The little girl there. Why?"

Shacklin turned and glowered at her. "When did you phone for him?"

She dropped her eyes. "Just before you came."

Shacklin glared at MacBride. "She's no dummy. Look"—he pointed to the roly-poly man—"she gets the best criminal lawyer in the city."

Rosbeck smirked and made a formal bow and MacBride looked suddenly disgusted and muttered "Nuts." Rosbeck leered good-temperedly at him, saying, "I hear you hate my insides, Skip. Say it isn't so."

"I hate more than your insides," MacBride growled dully.

Rosbeck chuckled lightly, airily, and winked at Kennedy with vast good humor.

MacBride turned bluntly to the girl. "Get your things on. You're pinched, in case you don't know it."

The girl rose listlessly, and with empty, dull eyes looked at the men. Rosbeck nodded affably at her.

Chapter II

THE RAIN kept on, sweeping wind-driven over the housetops, smothering the streets. It spumed high above the city, billowing in huge wet clouds. Gutters roared with water. Drains jammed and the water bubbled like hot springs. The sound of the rain and the wind was incessant.

MacBride stood in his office, one foot raised and planted on the windowsill; elbow on knee and chin in hand. He stared morosely at the whipping skeins and pennants of rain.

Kennedy had his shoes off and was drying his feet by the steam radiator. His pale hair was damp and unkempt and on his washed-out face was a dreamy, whimsical smile. "You sure look down-hearted, old tomato. And why not? Aye, why not? On the one hand you have your bitter departmental enemy, Niles Shacklin; on the other, your pet Nemesis, Morry Rosbeck. You are, so to speak, in a quandary, tra-la."

MacBride flung his foot on the windowsill and took a turn up and down the room, his big fists resting heavily in his coat pockets. "Those guys don't worry me," he grunted.

"No, not much. Morry Rosbeck, f'r instance. In the past three years you nailed, if I remember correctly, six outstanding public enemies: Mike Truber, Sancho Morales, Luke Grant and his brother Sax, Polack Joe Tomulski, and White Boy Borensen. Morry Rosbeck was counsel for the defense in each case—and none of the six named is, I believe, behind prison bars today."

MacBride went back to the window and stared grimly at the rain.

"And," Kennedy smiled on, "Niles Shacklin would like to be head of the Homicide Bureau. The present head, they tell me, is a chap named Stephen J. MacBride. Some claim the J stands for Joke, but I doubt that myself. Niles is out to burn this gal Lottie Gravesand, and because you hate Morry Rosbeck so much, you become Shacklin's running mate. What a curious situation." He felt his socks to see if they were dry. "Oh, no; you're not worried—not a bit."

MacBride turned and looked steadily at him. "Kennedy, I'm getting tired of gals that bump off guys on the spur of the moment. I know Shacklin's after my job and though I don't like the guy I'm not going to get in his way. I'm a softy where dames are concerned—but this time I'm going to be a mugg. I'm going to collect every bit of evidence I can against this gal. I'm going to prove to myself that she's guilty. I'm going to leave no stone unturned and—"

"You're going to trump Morry Rosbeck," Kennedy broke in with a droll smile. "He's been in your hair for three years and you're going to comb him out. You're going to hang the gal in order to get even with Rosbeck."

MacBride's jaw set. "My job's to bring criminals to justice. This time—I'm not going to pull my punches because a gal's involved. I don't hang innocent people and I don't let guilty ones go free. And as for Rosbeck—there ought to be a distinction between criminal lawyers and lawyer criminals. This crime smacks of premeditation. The minute the guy's killed, she calls up Rosbeck. It stamps her as being in the know. Any other gal, if she was innocent, would never have thought of phoning him—of phoning any lawyer."

"Did you get Lebanco's address?"

MacBride frowned. "No. She wouldn't tell it. She's scared stiff that we'll find more letters there. Rosbeck's kind of given her confidence. She keeps her mouth shut. I thought I might be able to get his address from the telephone people, but they have no record of him. I sent Ike and Moriarity out to dust the hotels. Meantime—"

There was a knock on the door and Bogardus looked in and said, "T.E. Demorest wants to see you. Cap'n."

"Send him in. Kennedy, out."

Kennedy had put his shoes on. He picked up his hat and coat and meandered to the door and a moment later Demorest, the Public Works Commissioner, strode in. He was a tall, burly man in a tan raincoat that crackled with his movements. His hair was cupped, neat, and his face was good-looking, rugged, with a strong nose and gray, curious eyes.

"They said at the office you wanted to see me, Captain."

"Yes. About—"

"I heard."

MacBride shrugged, sat down and told Demorest to sit down. The Commissioner took off his raincoat, laid it over one chair and seated himself in another. He blew his nose. His eyes were grave, concerned, and he said:

"What chance has she?"

"With her openers, none. She said she'd told Lebanco to stay away and we find a letter written and signed by her and begging him to come to see her."

Demorest looked at his hands. "She worked for me for two years, you know. She was a good worker, very competent."

"She leave or was she fired?"

"She left."

"Why?"

"Well, she complained about headaches and nervous spells, and my office is a busy one and she said she couldn't stand it. I told her to take a month off but she said she felt it would take longer than that. She seemed determined to leave. I asked her if she had any money and she said she'd saved enough to live on a while. I told her that when she decided to work again, I'd see what I could do for her."

"Know anything about this Lebanco?"

"Lebanco?"

"Yeah—Lebanco, the guy she knocked off."

"Oh, is that his name?... No, I don't."

MacBride lit a two-cent cigar. His face was grim, relentless; his voice low and blunt. "I want to be sure you're telling the truth, Mr. Demorest. I want to be sure that this girl left her job and that you didn't fire her."

"I told you she resigned."

"I know what you told me. I'm just wondering if you're not saying that to help her. You've got to realize that a man's been killed and that this woman killed him and before his body was cold she phoned Morris Rosbeck."

"What's wrong with phoning Morris Rosbeck?"

MacBride's face turned sour. "Only desperate criminals go to Morris Rosbeck."

"I think your attitude's wrong. His name's well known. It's always in the papers. She probably thought of it instantly, for that reason," Demorest's look of concern deepened. "I can't see Lottie as a criminal, MacBride. She was such a damned good worker. It seems to me you're jumping at conclusions."

"Jumping?" MacBride gave a short scornful laugh. "I haven't budged yet. I haven't done a thing. What conclusions I've come to I based on what laid cold before me. I haven't started yet to build up on that evidence."

Demorest's jaw jutted. "It seems to me," he said warmly, "that you're already bent on railroading this girl."

MacBride's fist hit the desk hard and he barked, "I never railroaded anybody in my life!" His fiery look did not quench the disdainful expression on Demorest's face.

"I happen to know," Demorest said quietly, "that Shacklin is in strong with the political crowd and that he has eyes on your job and that both of you are breaking your necks to make the headlines: you to hold the job and Shacklin to get it."

MacBride stood up, an angry man. "I didn't invite you here to criticize my methods."

"I don't care what you invited me here for," Demorest shot back, rising also. "This girl worked for me faithfully for a number of years. She's alone in this city. She has no close friends, or had none when she worked for me. I refuse to stand by and see her bullied by a thick-headed police captain."

MacBride lifted his chin. "So what do you think you can do about it?"

Demorest sighed and relaxed. "I don't suppose," he said bitterly, "there is anything I can do about it I only hoped to bring you to reason."

The skipper was tart: "My advice to you, Mr. Demorest, is to mind your own business."

Demorest snatched up his hat and coat and stalked to the door. He turned and placed steely eyes on MacBride. "My advice to you, Captain, is to watch your step—or you may land out in the sticks."

"If you think you can scare me off this case by a crack like that, you don't know me. Keep your mouth shut, because the more cracks you make, the solider I'll stay in this case."

Demorest snorted contemptuously and slammed out.

The skipper relit his cigar, jammed his hands deep into his coat pockets and strode hard-heeled round the office, his face red, his brows bent angrily. The door opened slowly and Kennedy leaned indolently in the doorway and said:

"Ike and Moriarity call up yet?"

"No. No. Stay out. I'm thinking."

"I just wanted to tell you that I found out where Lebanco lived."

MacBride stopped short and glared over his shoulder.

"I just took a chance and called up our circulation department. He's a subscriber to the *Free Press* and lives, suh, at number ninety-eight Mughetto Street. My tenses are balled up, but my heart's in the right place."

MacBride said grudgingly, "So is your head, kid," and put on his hat and overcoat. "Every time I begin to think you're excess baggage around the place, you surprise me." He picked up his rubbers. "Here, put these on before you catch a death of cold and croak on me."

"What am I going to put in 'em besides my feet, so they won't fall off? I wear only a seven, Cap'n boss. Besides, I never wear rubbers. They make my feet sweat."

MacBride put them on his own feet and marched out. Kennedy went with him down to the basement garage and they climbed into the sedan and Gahagan wheeled it out into the downpour.

"Turn left," MacBride said.

Gahagan did not turn left but sailed complacently straight ahead.

MacBride growled, "Dummy, I said turn left! Okey. Turn left at the next block and get around to Center Street."

Gahagan drove straight ahead.

MacBride smacked him on the back and Gahagan pulled up promptly alongside the curb and turned about, screwing up his face and baying, "Hah?"

"You deaf?" MacBride yelled.

Gahagan seemed to remember something. He poked at his ears and pulled out a ball of cotton from each. "I git cold in the ears easy," he explained, "and hangin' around that draughty basement the way I do—"

MacBride groaned. "My Gawd!"

"I forgot," admitted Gahagan sheepishly.

"All right, all right," MacBride said patiently. "Get going, get going. Ninety-eight Mughetto Street. Back around to Center and down Center. Shoo! Get going."

"Funny, how I forgot," said Gahagan, wagging his head and shifting into gear.

"I ought to fire you, only ten to one you'd forget you were fired and turn up next day for duty."

Kennedy drowsed.

Chapter III

MUGHETTO STREET lies on the south flank of Richmond City and is a narrow, straggling thoroughfare five short blocks in length. In many places its pavement is cracked and the sidewalks are uneven. The buildings for the most part are frame, with small stone stoops and iron handrails. They run to three and four and sometimes five stories: rooming-houses, flats, poolrooms, lunch-rooms, grocery stores and butcher shops. On clear days the street is jam-packed with kids. The tough Irish a couple of blocks north call it Wop Alley.

The police sedan stopped in front of a faded yellow frame house and Kennedy said, "Mughetto is dago for lily of the valley. Pertinence was not one of the qualities of the guy that named it."

MacBride, paying no attention to him, shoved open the sedan door and took a good look at the yellow house. A board bearing the word Rooms in faded letters hung alongside the door.

"You wait here," MacBride said.

"I didn't come just for the ride," Kennedy told him, and followed him out into the rain.

MacBride tried the front door and it opened at his touch and he stepped into a narrow hall that smelled strongly of cooking. On the left were half a dozen black tin mailboxes nailed to the wall and from one of them jutted a folded newspaper. MacBride yanked it out and found Lebanco's name on a yellow slip pasted on the margin. There was nothing else in the box. He crossed the hall and knocked on the first door he came to. It was opened by a short big-bellied man in an undershirt.

"Where's Lebanco's room?"

"Whassa dat boss?"

"Lebanco. Edward Lebanco. Where's his room?"

"Oh, shu. Dassa opstairs. Toppa floor, boss. Way in back, toppa floor. Onna de right, way back, toppa floor."

"You run this rooming-house?"

"Me? Ha! Nossir, boss. She's run by Sam Milio. He's gotta da delicates' store oppa da block."

MacBride turned away and went up the narrow staircase and Kennedy dawdled along behind. When the skipper reached the top floor, the sound the rain made on the tin roof hummed in his ears. There was a window at the back of the corridor and he could see the rain pouring against it, splashing, falling in thick streams down the pane. He strode to the rear, palmed the knob and gave it a twist and the door opened.

A man standing in the middle of the room whipped around in surprise and without a moment's hesitation jumped and took a vicious swing at MacBride's jaw. The skipper's jaw stopped the swing but the swing didn't stop him; his right fist grooved upward along the man's chest, took him on the point of the jaw and sent him smashing against the farther wall. A small picture fell from the wall and crashed on the floor. The man made a frenzied rush along the wall and clawed at his pocket and MacBride, not budging an inch, pulled his gun and said:

"That'll do."

The man choked and his gun, half-drawn, fell to the floor. He backed against the wall, pressing against it, his hands raised, and his heavy breathing making his lips blubber. He wore a brown slicker and a rain-smudged gray felt hat. His face was sallow, with pale knobby cheekbones and a long jaw, red shapeless lips and a flabby nose. He looked to be in his early twenties.

"Ah," said Kennedy, arriving in the doorway. "I didn't expect a host."

MacBride snapped, "Stop clowning, Kennedy," and crossed the room, picked up the man's gun and stowed it away in his pocket. His hard eyes clamped on the sallow face before him and he said, "Well, I suppose you live here."

The man shook his head, his eyes very round and scared. "No, no, I don't live here."

"Then what are you doing here?"

"I—I was looking for Ed."

"Ed who?"

"The—the fella that lives here. Ed. Ed Labanco."

MacBride said, "Why were you looking for him?"

"Well—well, I know him, I come up to see him. His door was open and I come in and he ain't here."

"So what?"

"Well—so he ain't here."

"And so the minute I shove my puss in the door you take a sock at me."

"Well, who wouldn't? There you bust in, you bust in Ed's place, and I'm here, I know him, and the way you bust in—Jeese, I thought you was going to smack me. How do I know who you are?"

"Well, if it'll take a load off your mind, I'm head of the Homicide Squad."

The man's eyes widened in not unpleasant surprise. He placed a forefinger on MacBride's chest. "No! Jeese, are you Captain MacBride? Well, well! Boy, I heard a lot about you. Now how did I know you was Captain MacBride?" He held his jaw and grinned. "Say, you sure can sock, mister."

MacBride fixed him with a beady eye. "So you just came here looking for Ed Lebanco, did you?"

"Me? Sure."

The eye got beadier. "Close friend of his?"

"Well, it's like this. I met him in a bar a couple months ago—you know how you will. We was standing at the bar and got to chinning and we walked out together, you know how you will, and walked down the street, not friends or anything, but just walking along. And a couple of gals stroll along and give us the big eye and we pick 'em up and take 'em to the movies. So that's how it was I met Ed, and after that, well, I'd drop in here, or we'd run into each other at a bar."

"Where do you work?"

The man was eager to explain. "I'm getting three days a week on the emergency relief."

"What's your name?"

"Arthur Henderson's my name."

"What about Lebanco? Where'd he work?"

Henderson shook his head. "I don't know that, boss. I never asked him."

"Did he have much money?"

"No, boss, he didn't. He couldn't afford anything else than beer and he didn't go out with gals because he said he couldn't afford to. He was a funny guy, kind of quiet, boss. Kind of mooning around all the time. Did he get hurt or something?"

"He got himself shot dead."

"Jeese—no!"

MacBride said, "Sit down."

His eyes wide with shock, Henderson sat down.

MacBride crossed to a bureau and pulled open the drawers. Over his shoulder he said, "Did he ever mention a girl named Lottie Gravesand?"

Henderson put a forefinger thoughtfully alongside his temple. "Lemme think. Lemme think…. Oh. No, not to me, boss. But we was in a bar one night and I heard him make a telephone call and call somebody Lottie. But he was close-mouthed, boss. He never told me about her. See, I was just what you might call an acquaintance of his, though we got on good and I guess"—his voice dropped—"we would ha'e been good friends if he lived."

"There's nothing in here," MacBride muttered to himself, and closed the bureau drawers.

"Whatcha looking for?" Henderson asked earnestly.

"Letters—papers—personal things."

"Oh," said Henderson, getting up. "I know. I seen him put things in this"—he gangled across to the bed table—"little drawer here."

"I'll get 'em."

"I was just—"

Henderson's hand came out of the drawer with an automatic pistol and he spun and there was the sound of his sharp, indrawn breath.

"Reach, Skipper. And you too, scarecrow."

MacBride's face got very sour and his hands rose. Kennedy, leaning indolently against the wall, raised his hands wearily.

Henderson's eyes bulged with a glazed expression and his flabby mouth shot over to one side. "You're easy, flatfoot," he told MacBride. "I guess you sit on your brains."

"I sure did this time," MacBride said grimly.

"Get over and stand alongside your pal."

MacBride walked over and stood beside Kennedy and Henderson squared off in front of them, his flabby lips stretched out in a loose leer. "Just for fun," he said, "I ought to bash both your mugs in."

Kennedy's eyes rolled and a sickly expression came to his mouth, his knees began to give away.

Henderson laughed. "Jeese, the little guy's fainting like he was a dame!"

Kennedy's body slumped against MacBride and the skipper, to prevent him from falling, grabbed hold of him. One of Kennedy's legs buckled completely and MacBride, saying, "Kennedy, Kennedy!" tried to haul him to his feet.

Henderson snarled, "Leggo him! Drop the sissy!"

MacBride, his face suddenly grave, let go of Kennedy. Kennedy fell to his knees, hunched over. He groaned and fell suddenly sidewise and as he did his right hand shot upward gripping a gun. The gun boomed and Henderson screamed and wheeled backward and crashed to the floor.

MacBride jumped over and disarmed him.

Kennedy sat on the floor and wiped cold sweat from his forehead.

MacBride barked, "Where'd you get that gun, Kennedy?"

"Out of your overcoat pocket, dearie. It was the one you took from our host. Did I hurt him?"

There was a significant hole in Henderson's slicker. The skipper opened the slicker and tore away the clothing underneath. He felt Henderson's pulse. He looked at the hole in Henderson's chest.

"You nailed him, Kennedy."

"Hell, I just wanted to—"

"Dead center."

MacBride noticed some papers protruding from Henderson's inside pocket. He withdrew them. There were five letters held together with a rubber band. Each began with "Dear David" and was signed "Lottie." They were love letters. One of them was dated a week before. Some bore no dates and since none of them was in an envelope, no date could be approximated.

The skipper held them up. "These are what he came here for, Kennedy—and got. He'd searched the place. He knew there was a gun in that bed-table drawer. He got scared I might search him later."

"Are they all from the girl?"

"Yes."

"Oh-oh."

"I suppose," the skipper said, "you still think I'm picking on her." He thrust the letters into his pocket. "I've got a hunch I'll find more against her. She lied—she lied. I'm sick and tired of dames that think they can get temperamental and knock a guy off. She lied—lied—lied!"

"Apparently," drawled Kennedy, "she lied."

Chapter IV

SHE SAT on the cot in her cell, her hands clasped between her knees. The orderliness of her hair mellowed the lines of her face. There was no expression in her face. Her eyes were downcast, the lids almost shut, and her lips, quite colorless now, were motionless—not set, or grim, or fixed, but merely motionless.

MacBride said, "How well do you know a man named Arthur Henderson?"

"I don't know him."

"That may not be his name. A tall fellow, about twenty-two or three. Pale. Big eyes. Big nose."

"I don't know him."

"You wrote a letter on the twenty-second to Edward Lebanco in which you said life was not worth living without him. You wrote a letter on the sixteenth saying that if he didn't come and see you, you'd go nuts—crazy was your word. You wrote other letters, undated, along lines like that."

She remained silent.

His face was in shadow. "Didn't you?"

She remained silent.

"You lied," he went on in a hard, level voice, "when you said that the letter we found in your bungalow was written six months ago. We found out the type of lettering on it, your initials, weren't introduced on the market until a month ago."

Her face remained expressionless.

He said, "This fellow I mentioned, this fellow Henderson, tried to get out of Lebanco's room with letters you'd written Lebanco. You say you don't know him. He must have known you well enough, to try to get rid of evidence that'll weigh heavy against you."

"I don't know him," she said simply.

"What about the letters? Do you mean to sit there and deny that you wrote them?"

Her lips closed and she said nothing.

He demanded: "Do you?"

She looked up at him. "I have nothing to say. You'll have to see my lawyer. You're wasting your time here." She dropped her eyes and stared at the floor.

He said: "Henderson's dead."

She made no comment.

He went to his office and loaded a pipe. Reports came in from a dozen of his men and he pieced them together in a patchwork of information concerning Lebanco. An express agency had, four months ago, delivered a trunk to Edward Lebanco at 98 Mughetto Street. The trunk had been billed from Des Moines, Iowa. It had remained in storage in Richmond City for a week and then been delivered to the Mughetto Street address. Lebanco had been in the habit of buying bread, cold cuts and milk at Sam Milio's delicatessen store. Milio also owned the rooming-house where Lebanco had lived. Milio said of him that he was quiet, nice, and paid cash for everything.

Two months ago Lebanco had been treated by a dentist named Highland. Three months ago he had registered at a local Y.M.C.A., especially for the use of its gymnasium; he had not mingled with any of the members. A book found in his room had led the police to a lending library in Spender Street: the man who ran it remembered Lebanco as being quiet, studious. Other odds and ends of information were all favorable to Lebanco. The only thing that might be held against him was the apparent fact that he had not worked. Money found in his room and on his person amounted to fifty-eight dollars and sixty cents and there was no indication that he had opened a bank account. MacBride sent a long wire to the Des Moines police....

The phone rang and he picked it up and a woman's voice said, "Captain MacBride?"

"Yes."

"This is Geraldine Garey. I wish you'd come over to my apartment immediately."

"Why?"

"I wish to speak with you about a very personal matter."

"You can do it over the phone, ma'am."

"I'm afraid I can't."

"But—"

"Please. It is very important."

He scowled at the desk, muttered, "What's your address?"

"I'm in apartment ten at four-o-four Kingsland Avenue. Will you come immediately?"

"Okey."

Still scowling, he hung up and did not move for a full minute. He had been bitten before by crank calls and was reluctant to go. But after another minute's deliberation he rose, put on his hat and overcoat, and his rubbers, and left the office. He was so dubious about his wisdom in having agreed to go that instead of taking along Moriarity and Cohen, and Gahagan, he went out into the rain and nagged a taxi. At Center and Bridge Streets the taxi skidded into another cab and he lost ten minutes settling the argument as to who was at fault. The rain still fell in great blowing torrents, traffic was heavy, congested, and it took the skipper half an hour to get to 404 Kingsland.

The apartment house was five stories tall, it was built of light tan brick and had shrubbery and a few plain trees in front of it. The lobby was square, neat, and contained a rectangular marble table and two large earthenware urns. Beside the single elevator were a small switch-board and a number of pigeon holes. Elevator, pigeon holes and switchboard appeared to be presided over by a vague-eyed negro in a faded mulberry suit.

MacBride said, "Apartment ten."

"Yassuh," droned the negro, and followed him into the elevator.

"Who lives in that apartment?" asked MacBride.

"Mis' Geraldine Garey."

The car stopped at the next floor and MacBride strode out into the corridor and asked, "Which way?"

The negro yawned and pointed, "Tha' way."

The skipper proceeded towards the rear of the corridor. The last door on the right was numbered ten and he jiggled a small iron knocker, took out his handkerchief and wiped the raindrops off his face. Then he set his face preparatory to being very stern and matter-of-fact. But no one came to the door and he knocked again, very hard this time, and paced impatiently up and down over a small area of mouse-colored carpet. Then he tried the knob but the door was locked, and after again knocking, and waiting a minute, he growled under his breath and took the fire-stairway to the lobby.

He snapped at the negro, "Did Miss Garey go out?"

"Ah'll ring an' see did she."

"Never mind. I—"

"Ah just a minute ago took a man up was goin' to see her," the negro yawned.

MacBride snorted, "That was *me* you took up!"

The negro scratched his head. "Were it? Hully gee, boss. Ah reck'n—"

"Break it up, break it up," MacBride interrupted tartly. "Get me a key that'll open her door."

"No can do, boss. Orders is—"

MacBride held his badge up close to the negro's sleepy eyes.

The negro said. "Dat's different, mistuh boss man."

WHEN the skipper keyed his way into the apartment, two minutes later, he saw that, due doubtless to the dim day, several lights burned in the small living-room. Three in all. There was a light in the bathroom. There was also a light in the bedroom. But the apartment was empty.

On a small occasional table just inside the door there was a key. He tried the key in the lock on the door. It fitted. He dropped the key back to the table.

On the divan lay an extra on the murder. Several columns had been clipped out and lay on the floor, and there was a pair of shears nearby. A clothes-closet door stood wide open. The skipper returned to the bedroom and saw on the dressing table there a photograph of a woman about thirty years old. Her hair was black, thick, and her skin looked tawny. He turned. His eyes moved sharply round the room and he crossed to a chest of drawers and looked at the photograph of a man that stood on top. The face was familiar. He gave a start. It was the face of Edward Lebanco.

He wheeled about as though half-expecting to find someone in the room. There was no one.

He took both photographs and went down to the lobby. First he held up the photograph of the woman and said to the negro:

"Is this Miss Garey?"

The negro squinted near-sightedly, then scratched his head. "Ah reck'n it is."

"Now this one," MacBride said, holding up the photograph of Lebanco. "Did you ever see this man come in here?"

Again the negro squinted, bringing his nose almost against the picture. He shook his head. "No, suh."

MacBride looked exasperated. "Did you see this woman leave within the past hour?"

The negro stared, mystified. "No suh."

"Did anyone come in here besides me in the past hour?"

"Oh, folks comin' 'n' goin' all the time, boss man."

"Did anyone besides me ask for Miss Garey?"

"No, suh."

"Do you mean that Miss Garey didn't go out or that you don't remember if she went out?"

The negro looked pained and scratched his head. "Boss man, Ah don't know. Sometimes folks on de next floor jest walk down, maybe if when Ah'm in de elevator way upstairs."

MacBride said aloud to the wall. "I can see where this guy is going to be a great help." And to the negro: "Plug in to Police Headquarters. I'll take the call in Miss Garey's apartment."

He went upstairs and as he entered the apartment the phone rang. "Otto," he said into the transmitter. "Put Ike Cohen on the wire." He waited, drumming with his fingers on the table. Then he barked, "Ike?... Ike, shoot over to four-o-four Kingsland and come up to apartment ten.... Well, something stinks around here.... Snap on it, fella."

He whanged the receiver into the hook and stood for a minute biting his lip in perplexity, staring hard at the rain-drenched window panes. Then he turned to a small secretary and began rifling it, but found that it contained very little—and nothing into which he could sink his teeth. He went into the bedroom and pulled out the drawers of the dressing table, finding various creams, lotions, manicuring implements, rouges and powders. In another drawer he found heaps of novelty jewelry, vanity cases, cigarette cases, two wrist-watches, several small purses. On the back of one of the wrist-watches he found engraved *From Edward to Geraldine with love.* He sat back and his face fell into grave, grim lines.

Ike Cohen came in and said, "Penny for your thoughts."

"They're worth more than that, Ike."

"Who calls this home?"

"A woman named Geraldine Garey."

"Nice name."

MacBride stood up and said, "She phoned me to come over and when I arrived there's nobody here."

"If it was April first, I'd say—"

"Skip it. She wouldn't say on the phone what she wanted to talk to me about. When I got here, I found the story about the Lebanco kill clipped out of the paper. I found Lebanco's photograph here."

"Whew!"

"Ike," the skipper said, dead in earnest, "I'm beginning to get all mixed up. Every bit of information that comes in shows that Lebanco was a white guy, temperate, quiet. We know that Henderson—the bird Kennedy plugged—swiped letters from Lebanco's room and would have got away with 'em if we hadn't nailed him. We know that those letters incriminate the Gravesand gal and for that reason were stolen from Lebanco's room. We know the Gravesand gal lied about when she wrote the letter we found under her divan. Now we find that a gal who was going to tell me something about this case—I know she was, by the clippings I found here—we find that she's vanished. There's somebody trying to prevent further incriminating evidence against Lottie Gravesand from being brought to light. Now on top of that, here I find a woman's wrist-watch—take a look at the back of it."

Ike Cohen looked, said: "H'm."

"It gets me all mixed up," MacBride growled.

"Oh, no," said Ike Cohen. "A telegram came back from the Des Moines police. I brought it along," He drew a folded yellow form from his pocket and handed it to MacBride.

The message read:

> *In* re *Edward Lebanco he left Des Moines four months prior to above date stop has no police record stop occupation until time he left this city accountant in firm of Riordan and Gammella general contractors record there excellent stop no living relatives here stop had a sister Geraldine who left Des Moines approximately five years ago.*

MacBride lowered the telegram. "The watch, then, was from her brother—Lebanco. So that unmixes me a bit. I was beginning to think that maybe Lebanco was a playboy." He crushed the telegram into his pocket. His eyes flashed, bright and hard. "Somebody didn't want us to see those letters in Lebanco's room. That same somebody doesn't want us to know what Geraldine Garey knows. I've got an idea who." He changed his tone, spoke crisply: "Ike, you stay here till you hear from me."

Chapter V

MORRIS ROSBECK was barricaded behind a mound of tumbled books, file boxes and dead cigar butts. His private office was big, barnlike, with a massive desk, scarred and battered and covered with amateur carvings. The floor was bare. The walls were covered with pictures of prizefighters, wrestlers, burlesque strippers. Books lay piled all over the place, on chairs, the floor, and plain wooden shelves. The private office contrasted strangely with the general offices in front.

Rosbeck was working furiously over a sheaf of papers when Mac-Bride walked in. The skipper had a big cigar in his mouth and a bad look in his eye. The fat, hammered-down bald head of the attorney popped up from behind the tumbled books. "Hi, Mac!" The head disappeared abruptly, and there was the sound of a pen scratching swiftly across paper. "Sit down. Find a chair."

"Ever hear of Geraldine Garey?" the skipper asked, stopping at the desk and picking up a book, which he thumbed.

Rosbeck wrote furiously, spoke rapidly, cheerfully: "No. Should I know her?"

"Ever know a guy named Henderson who was bumped off in the late Lebanco's room today?"

"No. Well, I don't think so. Hell, how should I know? Go out and ask Miss O'Monahan—the big dame with the part in the middle—and she'll look it up in the files."

"I got a hunch, Rosbeck, it wouldn't be in your files."

"Oh," said Rosbeck, diving into a reference book, "you mean do I know him socially. Henderson. Henderson. Yes, once I knew a fellow named Henderson. A judge. Judge Something Henderson, from Detroit."

"This guy I'm talking about is no judge. He was a young punk that we collared in Lebanco's room. He was there swiping letters that the Gravesand gal'd written to Lebanco."

"Why d'you suppose he did a fool thing like that?" Rosbeck asked, galloping his pen across paper.

"The letters don't help Lottie Gravesand any."

Rosbeck sat back suddenly and looked serious. "Were they hot?"

"Plenty."

Rosbeck jumped up and ranged round the vast, bare room in a highly nervous state. He rasped, "These dames and the letters they write. Henderson, Henderson," he repeated, stopping and scowling petulantly at the floor. "Did he say he was a friend of Lottie's?"

"We never got that far."

"And this—this—what's her name? The dame you said—"

"Geraldine Garey. She wanted to tell me something. When I got over to her apartment she was gone. Lights on all over the place make it look like she left in a hurry."

"Where does she fit in?"

"Lebanco's sister."

Rosbeck's face looked very angry. "Sister? Why the hell wasn't I told he had a sister?"

MacBride looked dourly at him. "Rosbeck," he said, "the act is swell but you ain't rolling me in the aisle with it. The Gravesand woman's in the can. She can't use a phone, she can't phone and tell people what moves to make. There's somebody who can—and who would, under the circumstances. Rosbeck, you've got a lot of brains. You've got about a million more than I have—but I make up for it by a lot of footwork. You know about the Garey woman. You know about Henderson."

Rosbeck grinned from ear to ear, whooped: "Hot stuff, Mac! Go ahead, kid me some more!"

"I'm not kidding," the skipper said dully. "I've no right to expect you to divulge any of your professional secrets, but this time a woman's disappeared. That's police work. It's up my alley. You can't pull stuff like that, Rosbeck."

Rosbeck stopped grinning and came over, put his hands on his round hips and stuck his bulbous chin up at the skipper's chest. "Listen, baby. If you know where your alley is, stay up it—don't come in here and try to get tough with me. I don't know who the Garey woman is. I never knew Lebanco had a sister. As for this Henderson guy—if a friend of the Gravesand dame wants to give her a hand, that's his affair. If he boobs it up, that's his affair too—and her bad luck. It might make it a little harder for me in court, but I like hard things. Now pick up your tail, monkey, and get out."

Rosbeck turned angrily on his heel, sat down at his desk and plunged into further research.

"You still don't roll me in the aisle," MacBride muttered.

"Oh, go on and take the air. I'm busy, I've got no time to listen to you bleating all over the place."

MacBride went out. His face was red and there was a dull humid look in his eyes. He banged into a taxi-cab and told the driver to go to Police Headquarters. He crowded back into a corner of the cab and gnawed on his cigar. A thing like this angered him because he knew he could do nothing about it. He might have all the suspicion in the world against Rosbeck, but it was useless unless he had evidence behind it. In his heart he knew that either Lottie Gravesand or Rosbeck was behind the Henderson angle and the disappearance of Geraldine Garey. And since Lottie Gravesand was in jail, the scales swung towards Rosbeck. That was common sense; there was nothing fantastic about such reasoning. But even common sense is worthless without substantial evidence. It doesn't matter what you believe; you have to produce evidence.

When he strode into his office Niles Shacklin was sitting on the desk swinging his feet. In MacBride's chair sat a skinny youth in a tight, striped collar, a cigarette perched in one corner of his mouth and his feet on the desk.

MacBride growled. "Take your feet the hell off my desk."

The youth was slow about it and MacBride picked up both feet and swung them to the floor.

"And sit somewhere else," he added. The youth got up and MacBride, still in his wet overcoat and hat, sat down.

Shacklin swiveled on the desk and said, "This is Jake Gillon, MacBride. I think he cinches the case."

MacBride took a good look at Gillon, then shifted his eyes to Shacklin. "Go ahead."

Shacklin said, "He knew Henderson. Henderson came to him and propositioned him—asked Gillon if he'd like to make a little quick money. Gillon told him, well, it all depended. So Henderson said it was a soft snap, all he had to do was go to a room and find some letters. He told Gillon a girl friend was on the spot and that ten to one the cops would hit the room and it'd be tough for the girl if they found the letters. Gillon asked him why he didn't do it himself and Henderson told him he'd had a scrap with a guy that lived in the same house and the guy threatened to bust his nose if he ever came in the place again. Well, Gillon asked how much was in it, and Henderson told him fifty bucks. Gillon said it was small change and that, anyhow, he was keeping to the straight and narrow. Henderson tried to win him over by telling him that the gal was hot stuff and that maybe he wouldn't regret doing her a turn. Gillon asked who the girl was and Henderson hedged, but said, 'Oh, she used to hold down a job in the Public Works office but she got tired of working and took the primrose path.' Right, Gillon."

"That's right," nodded Gillon. "But I told Henderson I guess he'd have to find somebody else, I was keeping my nose clean these days."

Shacklin said casually, "I haven't told this story elsewhere yet, MacBride. I came to you first."

"Why?"

"Well, Gillon was in trouble a couple of times and I don't want you to hold that against him."

"I get it. You want me to back up you and Gillon."

Shacklin lit a cigarette. "That's about it."

MacBride said, "Gillon your stool pigeon?"

"He—er—has helped the course of justice a number of times. He's good onions."

MacBride leaned back, tipped his wet hat to the back of his head, and stared squint-eyed at Gillon for a long moment. "Now I remember you," he said. "You ran with the Monnigan boys four years ago when they were mopping up the small-time merchants in Little Italy. You were in the taxi-cab strike and opened a driver's head with a rock. You carried a shotgun on one of Murphy Smith's beer trucks. You ran down a cop on a motorcycle two years ago. You turned State's evidence on the Dwyer boys. You beat up a gal in a dance-hall last winter. You socked your mother in the jaw. You never did an honest bit of work in your life." He waved to the door. "Beat it."

"Now wait!" snapped Shacklin, leveling a long imperious arm at the skipper. "That has nothing to do with the case at hand. This lad has testimony that'll cinch the case and—"

"You heard what I said about him, didn't you?" MacBride broke in. "I mentioned only the things I can remember offhand. If I go downstairs in the files—"

"But this man's testimony will hang the dame!" Shacklin yelled.

"I'll hang her without his testimony. I won't back him and I won't back you. I don't like the guy's puss, I don't like his record, and I don't trust him. You're out of your mind to bring him in here."

"You're cutting your own throat, MacBride."

"Well, I'd rather cut it myself than have somebody else cut it for me. Get out. Take him out of here!"

When he was alone, the skipper took his wet, ragged cigar from his mouth and slammed it into the metal waste-basket. Then he rang for Moriarity, and in a minute Moriarity appeared.

MacBride slid the wrist-watch he had taken from the Garey apartment across the desk. "Mory, take that and see if you can find out where it was bought. See when. I want to see if Lebanco bought it in this city, when he bought it, and how much he paid for it."

"Oke."

Moriarity went out and MacBride called the Garey apartment. "Ike?... This is Mac. Anything turn up?... I see. Well, keep hanging around."

Chapter VI

IT WAS six o'clock—and dark and wet— when the skipper turned up at Demorest's apartment. He left his rubbers in the hall and was admitted by a jap houseboy in a white jacket. The boy showed him into a large, luxurious living-room, and in a minute Demorest, in dinner clothes, entered.

"Sorry to keep you waiting, MacBride."

The skipper was lounging disheartened in a big wing chair and said: "Forget it. I'm here about the Gravesand gal again."

Demorest made a hopeless gesture. "I wish to hell I could do something for her."

"A guy turned up, a lug, with some damaging bits of news. The guy is a heel, a rat, he's run with various mobs in the past few years, and he knew Henderson, the guy we shot. Well, this lug said that Henderson tried to get him to steal those letters and said it was for a gal that used to work in the Public Works office."

"You don't want to believe everything you hear, Captain."

"I don't. But this bird is just the kind of rat that would pull a squeal like that. Now look here, Mr. Demorest. I want to know the real reason why she left—or was fired. It's admirable as hell for you to try to shield her, but this is serious. We've reconstructed Lebanco's life, and there's not a blot on it. If that guy got a dirty deal, damn it to hell, this woman must pay for it—and we want enough conclusive evidence to make sure that she does pay for it."

Demorest put thumb and forefinger on his chin and took a slow ruminative stroll up and down the room, wagged his head gravely. "MacBride, I've told you the truth. She wasn't fired. She left. And the reason she gave for leaving was that she was ill and needed a rest. Good God, man, I can't say more than that. That's all I know."

MacBride stood up, got his hat and left the apartment. He rode back to Headquarters through the driving rain. When he slammed into his office Kennedy was leaning against the wall. Kennedy said:

"There was only one outgoing phone call made from Lottie Gravesand's bungalow this morning."

"Well, what of it?"

"Well, she made one call to Police Headquarters. That checked okey. She said she phoned Rosbeck right afterwards. She did not. There's no record of it."

"How'd you find that out?"

"I got Bettdecken downstairs to call the phone people."

MacBride's voice dropped. "Another lie, eh? Lies, lies, lies—all the time, lies." He stared at Kennedy. "It was premeditated then. She'd got in touch with Rosbeck beforehand."

The phone rang and MacBride made a pass at it. "Hello.... Yes, Ike? What's up?... Sure I can.... Okey, right away, kid."

Gahagan drove him through the rain to the apartment house at 404 Kingsland. And when MacBride swung into the Garey apartment, Cohen was having a drink, a uniformed cop was standing by the window, and the negro was shaking in a chair.

MacBride said, "What's eating you, Ike?"

"The dinge," Cohen said, wiping his mouth. "To kill time up here, I was phoning friends of mine, and every time I phoned I had a hunch the switchboard key was open. It seemed black boy here was damned interested in my phone calls. So I took a stroll downstairs, went out and got Keegan here, who was up at the corner. I told Keegan to go back to the apartment and that I would phone him in about fifteen minutes. There's a drug-store halfway down the block and I went in there and in fifteen minutes I phoned him and said: 'Listen, Keegan. I'm down in mid-town and I got a hot tip that the boy in the lobby is mixed up in this case. Run down and grab him.' I hung up and ran out and as I reached the front door downstairs black boy came out hell-bent for election. I nailed him and me and Keegan had our hands full getting him up here."

MacBride looked at the quaking negro. "Black boy," he said, "you don't look comfortable."

"Boss man, Ah ain't."

"What did you run for?"

"Ah was scared."

"Why?"

"Boss man, two fellers come around dis mawnin' and say to me, 'Dahky, you is goin' to git hurt if you don't do like you're told.' They has guns, suh—yassuh, guns. They tell me dat Mis' Garey ain't sup-posed to leave de buildin'. Ah got an idea dey phoned her before dat. Dey hold dem guns under mah nose, suh, boss man, and say dat dey will be watchin' outside. Dey say dat if Mis' Garey makes any phone calls Ah sho' got to tell 'em what dey is or dey shoot me daid. So when she phones de police station, boss—"

"You told them. Then what?"

"Dey went up and got her and took her out, boss. And when dey is takin' her out dey wave dem guns under mah nose and say dat if Ah peeps to de police Ah'm a daid man already. Boss man, Ah'm de most scared guy dat ever was scared."

"Did they have a car?"

"No, suh."

MacBride snapped, "Don't lie, boy!"

"Ah ain't lyin', suh. Dey went down de corner and got in a taxi-cab. Ah seen 'em get in dat cab wit' Mis' Garey."

Moriarity said, "It's a regular hackstand. Cap. That ought to be easy."

"Keegan," MacBride said, "you stay here. Ike, take the boy to Headquarters. Go in the car with Gahagan."

THE TAXI rolled down the long cobbled grade to the foot of Gates Street, turned right into Faber and rolled along through the beating rain. Red and green, blue and white lights winked or glowed steadily. It was a narrow street, jammed with cafes, third-rate movie houses, bars, second-hand stores, a bowling alley, a shooting gallery. The cab stopped across the street from the shooting gallery and the driver said:

"I brought 'em this far and they went in that shootin' gallery—not in the front, but in that hall door there."

"What'd they look like?" MacBride asked.

"The one guy was about as tall as you, maybe heavier, and he had a yeller mustache. The other guy was about as tall, but thinner, darker, and I think he had a nose that was busted once. Anyways, his nose looked dented in. I didn't get a look at the woman."

"Okey. You stay here in the cab."

MacBride climbed out, turned up his coat collar, yanked his hat down over his eyes and crossed the street. The windows of the shooting gallery were steamed up and when he opened the door he could hear the flat, staccato racket of a dozen twenty-two's, firing at the same time. The gallery was in the rear and between it and the door were machines; machines in which you dropped a penny or a nickel and peered through magnifying glasses; machines to test the strength of your grip and machines to test the strength of your pull. The place was crowded with a lot of hangers on. MacBride, from the combined shadow of his hat and his coat collar, looked them over. Then he turned and went outside, stepped across to the hall door and opened it.

Inside, it was dark and the rackety-bang of the gunfire in the shooting gallery was deafening. He climbed a dark stairway, feeling along the banister with his hand. There was no use trying to listen, for the sound of the gunfire rattled violently in the hall, pulsed in the walls, in the slender rungs of the banister. But he stood motionless in the dark upstairs hallway for a long minute. He had no flashlight along and the hallway was so dark that he couldn't see beyond his nose. He began to feel his way along the wall and presently he could tell that he had come to a door. He groped for the knob, found it, turned it slowly and with extreme caution. The door was locked. He moved on, found another door which opened easily. He stood with his gun trained on the darkness beyond. Closing the door behind him, he found the light switch with his left hand; his right hand held his gun gingerly, the hammer cocked. He turned on the light.

The room was sparsely furnished, and empty. He turned out the light and made his way into the corridor again. A minute later he found a third door and this too opened at his touch. When he turned the light on, his gun held ready to fire, he saw a room similar to the other one—drab and empty. Back in the dark corridor again, with the echoes of the twenty-two's hammering in his head, he continued his search but found no more doors. In a little while he was back at the door he had first tried—the locked one.

He stood in the darkness for a long minute, deliberating, reasoning that if two doors, unlocked, had nothing to conceal, a locked one might have a lot to conceal. He stepped back, gauged his distance in the darkness, and drove hard with his left shoulder against the locked door. The door tore open under the impact and a dimly lighted room sprang out of the darkness.

A man sitting at a table slapped his hand down on a gun that lay on the table and another man, sitting on a chair with a drink in his hand, dropped the drink. The racket of the twenty-twos was loud here.

MacBride barked, "Hold everything!"

The man at the table was half out of his seat and his hand was on the gun and he fired the gun without removing it from the table. The bullet shattered a beer bottle standing near the edge of the table and glass burst apart and a big chunk of it ripped across MacBride's left eyebrow. It shocked him and he drove his left knee against the table, upsetting it into the man's lap. The other fellow had cleared his gun when MacBride turned on him and fired point-blank. The loud explosion mingled with the hammering echoes from the gunfire downstairs. The man fell sidewise off the chair and the other fellow, heaving off the table, found MacBride crashing into him. The table rolled over on its side, teetered for an instant, and then fell on the man whom the skipper had shot off the chair. MacBride carried the other fellow up to the wall and cracked him over the head with the barrel of his gun. The man yelped, dropped his own gun—then tried instantly to retrieve it. MacBride punched him in the ear and drove him back against the wall again and the man flattened there, out of breath.

"Where is she?" the skipper growled.

"Wait. Can't—breathe—"

MacBride lashed out, "You can breathe enough to say that! Where is she?"

"I don't—know—I—"

MacBride, bitter-mouthed, cracked him on the head again and the man slid down to the floor, then sprawled after the gun he had lost. MacBride stepped on his hand, grabbed a handful of his hair and yanked him back and over, so that he fell flat on his back. The skipper glared down at him.

"It's like this," he said. "If you don't know, that's okey. But you fired on a cop a minute ago, you stumblebum, and I'll finish you for that."

The man raised a hand. "Listen—don't."

"Where is she?"

The man pointed to a curtain.

MacBride stepped to the curtain and tore it down with one violent yank. A woman, with adhesive tape over her mouth, was strapped upright against the wall. Her head hung downward. Her waist, of some thin white material, was growing darker at the left shoulder. MacBride knew instantly that she had been struck by one of the shots.

His head moved to the right and he saw the man who had been beneath the table now leveling a gun across it. The skipper shot offhand and got him in the face and grimaced and then took a long stride towards the other man, who was crawling towards the door, and knocked him out with a blow on the head.

"You asked for it," he muttered.

He crossed to the shallow closet, took out his pocket-knife, cut away the straps and took the woman in his arms. She was a dead weight. He carried her downstairs and out into the street and he pulled out his whistle and blew it. A cop came around the corner on the double and another came hurtling out of a saloon across the street.

"Take her," he said, "to the hospital. Then send an ambulance around. One of you guys stay at the hospital and see that no smart guys get to her."

HE WENT upstairs again and found that the man he had shot in the face was dead. He sighed heavily, wagged his head, and went over to look at the other. Then he crossed to a sink, poured water into a pitcher and threw the water in the man's face. He pulled up a chair, lit a cigar and sat down. In a few minutes the man on the floor opened his eyes, looked at the gun trained on him across MacBride's knees.

"Spill it," said MacBride grimly. "I don't know whether the Garey woman'll live or not. So spill it."

The man licked his lips. "We only was keeping her here till we got orders."

"You scared hell out of the dinge, didn't you?"

"We had to."

"Why'd you snatch the Garey women? Who gave you the orders in the first place? I'm going to plug you right where you lay if you pull any comedy. Who gave you the orders?"

"Morris Rosbeck."

MacBride took a drag on his cigar. "You're doing fine. Go ahead."

"Well, Artie—you guys got Artie—"

"Artie who?"

"Henderson—the guy you got in Lebanco's place."

"Was Gillon in with you?"

"No. But Artie seen Gillon and handed him a gag. He was supposed to ask Gillon to swipe some letters out o' Lebanco's place and then make the ante so low that Gillon'd turn him down. We knew Gillon was a stool and that's why Artie told him—so Gillon would go to Shacklin and tell him some guy wanted to steal letters out o' Lebanco's place to help a dame."

MacBride frowned. "There's some-thing cockeyed about that."

"No. That was just to fool Shacklin. Artie wasn't going to steal no letters, he was goin' to *plant* some letters in Lebanco's place."

MacBride sat back, his eyes opening wide.

The man went on: "Then when that went sour on us, Rosbeck told us to cover the Garey woman. I phoned her this mornin' and told her not to leave her place or make any phone calls. I told her that if she tried to leave we'd cut her down."

"Why?"

"Them was just Rosbeck's orders. The Garey woman knew too much, I guess. I guess Rosbeck was afraid she'd tell things that'd clear the Gravesand woman."

MacBride leaned forward. "What the hell are you talking about? Rosbeck is Lottie Gravesand's attorney!"

"You figure it out. I was just workin' for Rosbeck."

Chapter VII

LOTTIE GRAVESAND sat in the swivel chair in MacBride's office, her hands in her lap, her face calm, expressionless, her eyes lowered. MacBride stood behind her, back against the wall, his arms folded and a stony look on his face, a touch of thin steel in his eyes.

Rosbeck, followed by two uniformed cops, came in through the doorway. He paused, looked at the girl, raised his eyes and looked at MacBride. His fat face broke into a loose, beaming smile.

"Cut it out," said MacBride, "before I take a stroll across the room and punch that smile down your throat."

Rosbeck stopped smiling and scowled. "Don't get tough with me, Skipper."

"Sit down."

"I'll stand."

"Sit him down, boys—right there, opposite the girl."

The two cops picked up Rosbeck and bounced him into a worn armchair.

MacBride did not move. He said: "We nailed Artie Henderson first. Twenty minutes ago we nailed Grabel and Drucker. We killed Grabel. In the fight, Geraldine Garey was wounded. She's in the hospital now—and may die."

"That's too tough."

MacBride said: "Ain't it? You're supposed to be Lottie Gravesand's attorney. It's the first time I ever heard of a thing like it. You're her attorney and yet you plant evidence that will build up against her."

Rosbeck's eyes narrowed, shimmered. "What are you trying to pull on me?" he demanded.

MacBride came over and stood beside him. "Drucker talked his head off. You hired him and Grabel and Artie Henderson to plant letters in Lebanco's apartment—letters to him signed by her—and you hired them to stop the Garey woman from opening her mouth in Lottie Gravesand's behalf."

Rosbeck jumped up and MacBride slammed him right back into the chair.

Lottie Gravesand had raised her eyes and placed them strangely on Rosbeck. Color was rising slowly in her cheeks. Rosbeck's hands gripped the arms of the chair.

"What was the idea?" MacBride asked somberly.

Rosbeck snapped, "You're crazy! Drucker's a liar—a coke and a liar. She has no dough. I took the case out of the goodness of my heart—so where is there any sense in this fantastic yarn you're spinning?"

"Who phoned you, Rosbeck, to come over to the scene of the murder this morning?"

"She did—Miss Gravesand."

"You're a liar. There was only one phone call made from that bungalow and that was the one to the police."

Rosbeck struck the arms of the chair. "I tell you she phoned me!" He jumped up and glared at MacBride. "I can't make head or tail of what you're talking about. I'm not going to sit here and be insulted by a crackbrained flatfoot. I'm—"

He stopped short as Demorest strode into the office. Demorest placed hard, unwavering eyes on him. Moriarity came in, closed the door and leaned back against it. He cracked chewing gum with his tongue and teeth and said:

"Well, Cap, I tailed down that wrist-watch."

"Don't bother me with that," MacBride growled. "There's a more important angle here right now."

"The hell there is," said Moriarity good-naturedly. "That wrist-watch wasn't given to Geraldine Garey by Lebanco. It was given to her by Demorest here, four years ago."

"You're crazy," said MacBride.

"I'm not. He gave it to her. I checked up with the shop where it was bought. It says on the watch *From Edward to Geraldine with love.*"

MacBride's face went blank as he turned it toward Demorest. "By God—your name is Edward Demorest!"

Demorest was still looking fixedly at Rosbeck, but his eyes seemed to be out of focus. He swayed slightly, and there was sweat on his face, his hands were clenched at his sides.

Lottie stood up slowly and put a hand to her cheek. Her eyes were wide with horror. Suddenly she gave a small cry and collapsed.

Demorest turned and looked vaguely at her.

KENNEDY sat in MacBride's office at ten that night, warming his feet against the radiator; warming his insides with a rye highball. He said:

"Well, his name—the way he signed it—was T.E. Demorest, but they usually used his middle name."

MacBride stared at the wall. "Geraldine Garey worked for him up to two years ago and was in love with him. He tossed her over and she hit the skids—drank, ran around, and was on her way to the dogs. She stopped writing to her brother and he came on four months ago, to look for her. She'd never written him telling where she worked, but once she happened to mention a girl she had seen now and then in the office, although they were in entirely different departments and only casual acquaintances—Geraldine merely wrote that Lottie looked like the sort of girl Edward should fall for—Lottie Gravesand.

"You see, Geraldine had taken the name of Garey to hide her identity. So he was licked at the start. But he finally tracked down Lottie—this was a week ago—and Lottie told him that she'd seen his sister on the street only a week before, carrying groceries. Lottie was in a cab at the time hurrying to make a train and couldn't stop. But she remembered the street and Lebanco went around and haunted that street. He had a picture of his sister with him and he showed it in the neighborhood grocery stores. One of the guys recognized it as a picture of Geraldine Garey. So Lebanco found her at last.

"She looked pretty bad, I guess. At least, when I was over the hospital an hour ago, that's what she said. When he found her, she cried. He suspected man trouble and saw a picture of Demorest on her bureau. He remembered that he'd seen the same face on a picture in Lottie Gravesand's bungalow. Geraldine refused to tell him Demorest's name, but he worked out of her that the guy in the picture had done her wrong. He went to Lottie's, taking the picture with him. Lottie wouldn't tell him the name, either. But he kept after her, not giving her the real reason but telling her that Demorest had swindled him through his sister out of a large amount of money. The letter we found under her divan was one of three she'd sent Demorest about Lebanco. In the others she'd mentioned Lebanco's name. Well, Lottie was in love with Demorest. He was fed up on her, but she didn't have the slightest inkling of that. He went to see her this morning, however, and while he was there Lebanco walked in.

"They started to fight and Demorest ran into the bedroom, where he knew Lottie kept a gun, and pulled it. He shot Lebanco. Then he began wailing about his career, scandal, and junk like that, and the gal, still mad in love with him, and not believing the swindle angle, told him to beat it—she'd handle it herself. He said he'd get her a good lawyer. He went over and told Rosbeck the truth and offered him thirty grand to take the case, make a big show, but fix it so that he'd lose and Lottie would go to the pen. Demorest figured it'd be a swell way to be free of her and he figured that she loved him enough to take the rap and keep her mouth shut.

"Some of the letters which she'd written him—well, you know, he tried to plant them in Lebanco's room. They were all addressed to Edward and naturally the cops would take it for granted that that meant Edward Lebanco. And he knew he had to keep Geraldine out of it. The woman scorned, you know, for if Lottie had got wise to the other gal there would have been no further dice on her loving sacrifice. He was wise enough, too, after he shot Lebanco, to take along the two pictures of himself—the one Lebanco had and the one Lottie had. It was all deliberate. And when he confessed, he told it right off, like a guy that knew his time was up."

Kennedy put on his shoes. "Well, old horse, for a time there you sure were determined to hang Lottie."

"Hell, I thought she was guilty. I just wanted to make the case air-tight." He dropped his voice. "The poor gal sure took it on the chin, Kennedy. Why she ever fell for a bum like that is more than I can figure out."

"I hear Shacklin got sore because you wouldn't play ball with him."

MacBride snorted. "He didn't want to play my kind of ball, Kennedy."

"You're just an old die-hard, Skippery-whippery. You go right on year after year banging your head against a stone wall and damn me if sometimes you don't actually bust the wall down. You're a great guy."

MacBride passed across the bottle. "You don't have to hand me a lot of hearts and flowers to get a drink, Kennedy."

The door opened and Bogardus said breathlessly, "Jeese, Cap. Gahagan just got wrecked with the car. Down at Davidson Square. He was sitting in the car at the west intersection there, waiting for a traffic light, when a fire engine came hell-bent up behind, siren going. Well, the other cars pulled over but Gahagan didn't, and the fire engine sideswiped him and turned him over. The car's wrecked but Gahagan only got a split lip. They say he didn't hear the fire engine because he had cotton stuffed in his ears."

MacBride put his left hand over his eves, groaned, reached out with his right hand and said: "Kennedy—the bottle."

Winter Kill

*Kennedy and MacBride team
on a two-way killing.*

Chapter I

RHUMBA music rose pleasantly muffled from below.

Tom Shack leaned back in the mahogany desk chair, took his cigar from his mouth and watched Testro manhandle the blond boy in through the doorway and across the carpeted floor to a blue leather divan. The blond boy hit the divan on the small of his back, bounced once, then tried to get up. Testro slapped his face flat-handed; first one cheek, then the other. The blond boy stopped trying to get up.

"Take it easy, Jerry," Shack said placidly.

Jerry Testro snapped, "I'll slap him silly."

The blond boy lay back on the divan now, holding a hand to his cheek. He breathed heavily. His eyes were bloodshot and brimming with impotent fury.

Testro went over and closed the door and the rhumba music was more muffled. He stood with his fists clenched against his lean thighs and his dark eyes bent threateningly on the blond boy.

Shack moved his heavy-boned, loose-jointed body in the mahogany chair. He scratched his lantern jaw with a thumbnail and peered from beneath a slab of sandy hair with amused eyes. He was an old man, with young eyes.

"What's eating you, Jerry?" he asked.

Testro said angrily, "He's stinko and wants to drive. I won't let him."

The blond boy choked, "You can't do this to me! If I want to leave, I guess I've got a right to leave! I don't have to—"

"Mr. Parcell," said Tom Shack amiably.

Parcell looked at him rebelliously.

Shack said, "Suppose you just curl up there and sleep for a couple of hours. Sleep it off."

Parcell pursed his lips, then spat out, "No! There's no fresh dago

can rough-house me around—" He stopped as Testro came over and stood in front of him.

Testro said, "You owe us exactly eight thousand five hundred dollars, sonny boy."

Shack took a book out of his desk, turned to the Ps, shook his head. "Eight thousand five hundred and fifty, Jerry."

Testro paid no attention. His savage dark eyes were locked on the blond boy's face. He said, "We're trying to protect what you owe us. I'm not going to let you drive a car when you're stinko and maybe get yourself killed."

"When, by the way, Mr. Parcell, are you going to pay us?" asked Tom Shack.

Parcell's bloodshot eyes were also harassed. He cried out, "Damn it, I'll pay you, I'll pay you!"

"When?" smiled Tom Shack.

Parcell groaned, grimaced. "As soon as I get it."

"I've been waiting," Tom Shack said, "for exactly a year. I told you last week that I wanted the dough and no more excuses."

Testro muttered, "If you ever get it, Tom, tell me."

"Oh, I'll get it," sighed Tom Shack.

Testro snapped, "Like hell you will! The guy is a heel and a gyp! He's got no more intention of paying it than—"

The blond boy cut in, "You're sore, dago! That's all! You're sore because Mae—"

"Shut up."

"Ha! See? You're sore! Because Mae—"

Testro struck him and flattened him on the divan. Parcell rolled over on his face and groaned and blubbered.

"Tsk, tsk," said Tom Shack.

The door opened and Kennedy of the *Free Press* meandered in, stopped and looked faintly surprised. "Bless my soul," he said, "why do you keep changing the men's room around all the time, Tom? The last time I was here this was the men's room and now I find it your sanctum sanctorum."

Testro chopped off, "This was never the men's room, Kennedy. It's two doors down the hall."

"So sorry, so sorry," said Kennedy. "Have you a match?"

Testro gave him a packet.

"A cigarette?" asked Kennedy.

Testro flexed his lips impatiently and gave him one.

Kennedy said, "Thank you. Match. Cigarette." He lit up. "Result, a smoke." He was not drunk, but drunk or sober he was always much the same: slightly whimsical, sleepy-eyed, harmless-looking. His clothes were always haphazard, badly pressed; his yellow hair was rarely orderly and he always looked as if a stiff wind would blow him over.

Parcell cried, "Kennedy, they won't let me go! They won't let me go!"

"Why, Russ," said Kennedy, "fancy seeing you here."

"He's tight," muttered Testro. "He wants to drive that chariot of his and I won't let him. He couldn't tell a street from the side of a building."

Kennedy said, "Better take a cab, Russ."

"No!" shouted Parcell. "I'm going to take my car! They can't do this to me, Kennedy. You're a reporter. You know a man's rights. They can't keep me here against my will." He was panting and there was a break in his voice.

Tom Shack sighed, shrugged. "Mr. Parcell, Kennedy, is indeed in his cups. What would you suggest?"

Kennedy looked at his watch. It was half-past midnight. "It's half-past twelve," he said. "I was just about to leave anyhow. Suppose I drive him?"

Parcell staggered to his feet. "Come on, Kennedy."

Testro nibbled his lip in indecision, but Tom Shack said, "That will be fine, Kennedy. We wouldn't want to see Mr. Parcell hurt himself."

Testro turned on his heel and walked out of the office. Parcell stumbled around the room while straightening his tie and his clothes. He glared wet-eyed at Tom Shack.

"I won't forget this," he said bitterly. "I won't forget this, Tom Shack."

Tom Shack's smile was lopsided. "If we both remember what we talked about, Mr. Parcell, everybody ought to be happy. Good-night. Take care of him, Kennedy." He reached out, tore *Wednesday, January 2* from the padlike desk calendar. "Well, here it's the third of January," he mused aloud. He picked up the phone and called a number. "Hello, my wife," he chuckled. "Happy birthday, honey. I'll be home in an hour."

IT WAS two flights down to the main floor. Kennedy had his hands full getting Parcell down, for Parcell was easily six inches taller than he and had played tackle at college the year before. There was a big center hall fitted with mirrors and high-backed heavy chairs. Off one side was the dining- and dancing-room and off the other the chrome and black marble bar. The *Mansion House* was the swankiest place in town.

Parcell hiccoughed. "I gotta find Mae."

"Suppose," said Kennedy, "we keep this a twosome."

"Listen. I gotta find Mae. She— There she is."

She was sitting on one of the high-backed chairs, watching him. Her hair was the color of raw copper. It was parted in the middle, rolled in a braided mat over each ear. Her evening gown was white and fitted her slender body like a white silk glove. Her eyes were dark; there was a storm held in check in their depths. Her lips, full and pink, were set.

As Parcell staggered towards her Testro stepped in his path and muttered, "Out."

"I'm taking Mae. I'm taking Mae."

"You're not taking Mae."

Parcell called out, "Mae—"

Testro twisted his lean dark head and stared levelly at her. She dropped her eyes, drew in her breath, remained motionless. Parcell began to be bewildered.

Testro said, "Kennedy, take it before I go native."

Mae was biting her lip.

In the few moments that Parcell remained soddenly bewildered

Kennedy was able to get their hats and overcoats on. He took Parcell out, led him through an alley alongside the *Mansion House* to a parking lot in the rear. The attendant knew Parcell's car. It was a Chrysler brougham. Parcell fell into it and Kennedy took the wheel.

The sound of the rhumba music drifted out into the cold night as they drove off. For an instant Kennedy saw the lighted *Mansion House* sign reflected in the rear-view mirror.

"That dago," mumbled Parcell in a drunken stupor. "He's got an evil eye. It does things to Mae."

"How's your wife, Russ?"

"She left me. She don't understand me. Let's stop somewhere and get a drink and a steak sandwich."

Kennedy said, "Only one drink, though."

"Sure."

They went to *Enrico's* in Flamingo Street. Paderoofski was behind the bar getting his accounts in order.

"A couple of steak sandwiches," said Kennedy.

"And don't forget the drinks," said Parcell.

Paderoofski looked crestfallen. "Ah, de cook he's a go home, gentlemens. No cook, no steak sanweeches. I'm so sorry, yes."

"Drinks, then," mumbled Parcell in a surly voice.

They had one apiece and were starting on another when a broad man wearing a Chesterfield and a derby came slowly into the barroom, put his elbows on the far end of the bar and said, "Scotch, Paderoofski." He had a ruddy, heavy face and brown, somber eyes. He placed the eyes on Parcell; got his drink and downed it without removing his eyes from Parcell. Then he paid up and headed slowly for the door.

Parcell, who had turned his back to the bar at about the same time, saw the man's back, hiccoughed, muttered under his breath, then called out, "Nuts to you, Sam!"

The broad man did not turn until he reached the door. His somber brown eyes lay on Parcell and a dark shadow hung between his smooth brows.

Parcell laughed. "Okey, I said nuts to you."

The broad man's expression did not change.

"Stuck up, eh?" cackled Parcell. "Like Rena. Just like your sister Rena! Stuck up, and why? I'm a Parcell, damn you! Am I stuck up? No! But I got a right to be. But am I? No!" He laughed again, a touch of drunken madness in his voice. "Look, Kennedy. Meet my brother-in-law Sam Church. He's just like his sister—just like—"

Church came slowly towards him, taking his hand out of his overcoat pocket, making of it a fist.

He said simply, "You yellow-bellied skunk!"

Paderoofski hopped up and down. "Please, Meester Church, dun't make de fight! Gentlemens, please! By me it's ukkey, it's zhake, but de cops—"

"Okey, Paderoofski," Church said. His face was dull red. He gave a small, embarrassed smile, turned on his heel and strode out.

Paderoofski was indignant. "Meester Kennedy, I'm t'ink your frand Meester Parcell wants to going home. Good-night, please to meet you, Meester Parcell, I'm dun't t'ink so."

Parcell glared at him. "I'm not going home. Give me another drink."

"I dun't t'ink so."

"Listen, you stinking half-breed!"

"Cut it, Russ," said Kennedy. "We're going home."

"You go to hell too! I'll go out. Okey, I'll go out. But I won't go home. You're all against me." He began weeping. "All of you! You and Paderoofski and Sam Church and Testro and Shack and everybody!" He lunged for the door, sobbing, and banged out.

Kennedy sighed. "They say God watches over drunks and fools. I place him, Paderoofski, in God's keeping."

Paderoofski was still smarting under Parcell's insult. He said in a thick, shaking voice, "Some day I'm not surprise if Meester Parcell be deader dan de doorknob."

"Door nail, Paderoofski."

"Axcuse me, please. I am excitement. Noor dail, yassir. Having a night hat before you going, Meester Kennedy."

Chapter II

FRIDAY, January fourth. Richmond City lay in a welter of snow that had begun falling on the night before. It stopped on Friday afternoon and the thermometer went down to zero. Telephone and power lines looked like fat white cables. The streets were choked with snow. Trolleys and motorcars were stalled. Plows were out by the dozen. The stars came out at night and at eleven Patrolman August Schnurll, passing a lone drug-store on Flemming Street, saw by the thermometer out front that it was three below.

He was a fat man but fat men feel the cold too. He plodded on, the soles of his overshoes crunching dryly on the snow. His peg-post was an outlying district; scattered dwellings, fields, a few storage houses, a woolen mill, a dowel factory, counted on his vigilance. There were some fields and then, up near the end of Flemming Street, stood the dowel factory—a two-storied frame building fifty feet square. The plow had been through and August Schnurll walked in the middle of the street past the fields. He went as far as the dowel factory, looked it over, grunted complacently to himself, and turned to head back down Flemming. He saw a dark object lying on a mound of snow and picking it up found it to be a dark fedora. He shrugged and was about to toss it away when he saw another object lying where the hat had lain. He tried to pick it up but it resisted. He pulled a little harder and this dislodged some of the snow and then he found that he had hold of an arm. He was a plain, everyday man, and he shuddered. He let go and the arm dropped back to the snow like a rigid stick. He dropped to his knees and began pawing at the snow with mittened hands. In a few minutes he knew that a man lay buried in the snow. He knew that the man was dead.

"God 'n Heaven!" mumbled Patrolman Schnurll.

He ran heavily on the packed snow to the drug-store, his breath spouting in white clouds.

The druggist said, "Hello, August. Cold night out."

Patrolman Schnurll bellied his way into the phone booth. In all his years as a policeman he had never found a dead man on his post. He phoned and then pushed out of the booth and the druggist said:

"What's up, August?"

"Frozen stiff... a fella...."

He barged out and loped ungracefully up Flemming Street and dropped to his knees again and dug more snow away with his mittened hands. In fifteen minutes the cars came. The police ambulance with its red-tinted headlights, clanging skid-chains. A precinct flivver. A big Buick sedan from Headquarters.

MacBride got out of the sedan and said, "Hello, August." He had a charred old pipe between his teeth, rubbers on his feet. His overcoat collar was turned up and his bony face was red with the cold. He strode across the snow to where the body lay in the glare of the Buick's headlights. "H'm," he said.

"He was practically buried in it," said Schnurll.

Moriarity and Cohen came up and Cohen said, "Cold storage, eh?"

"Well," said Moriarity philosophically, "in the summer people die of the heat and in the winter they die of the cold. If it ain't one thing it's another. And in the springtime they die of busted hearts—or get married."

MacBride said tartly, "I don't think either one of you guys are very funny." And then out loud, but to himself: "I wonder how long he's been here."

"The plow," said Schnurll, "went through this street at five this afternoon. Musta been after five."

The ambulance doctor was lighting a cigarette. "Any need to look it over here, Skipper?"

"He's past that long ago," said MacBride ruefully. "But look him over and see what you can see. Put him in the ambulance first. You can work better there.... Who is he, August, do you know?"

"I went through his pockets, Cap'n. All I found was five dollars and fifty cents and—this." He held up a pint whiskey flask that was two-thirds empty.

"That's all, huh?"

"That's all, Cap'n."

MacBride turned about, squinting. "Get Kennedy. Maybe he'll know him."

"Kennedy won't get out of the car," Moriarity said. "He told me to get what news there is and bring it to him. He's under the blankets in the car."

"Help get the stiff in the ambulance."

They moved the dead man into the ambulance and crowded at the rear while the doctor went over the body. In a little while the doctor said, "Not a mark on him. He was probably one of these walking drunks. The drunker they get the more they walk and then after a while they decide to lie down, regardless." He turned. "Nope. Not a mark on him."

MacBride clipped, "Get Kennedy, Ike."

Cohen went back to the Buick and returned a minute later shaking his head. "Nope," he said. "Kennedy won't get from under the blankets. He says if you get him a pair of snowshoes, yes; but otherwise, no."

The skipper's jaw clamped and a bad light glinted in his eyes. He strode to the Buick, reached in with both hands and hauled Kennedy and the blanket out into the snow.

Kennedy said, "That's battery and assault."

"You're drunk. Get up."

Kennedy got slowly to his feet, wrapped the blanket around his frail body. Moving toward the ambulance, he looked like a dilapidated tent that had decided to get up and walk. MacBride practically lifted him up into the back of the ambulance, where Kennedy promptly sat down on the seat. He was only half-awake and had come along from Headquarters only by force of habit.

He said, "There ought to be several pairs of snowshoes in each police vehicle. And this blanket, by the way, is of inferior material. We taxpayers—"

"Shut up," barked MacBride. "You never paid a tax in your life except the tax on liquor. Do you know the dead man?"

Kennedy blinked, rubbed his eyes, yawned. He stopped halfway through the yawn and stared wide-eyed. He was suddenly wide awake.

MacBride said, "I knew he'd know him. Drunks of a feather probably. I'll find him some cold night the same way. Who is he, Kennedy?"

"Russel Parcell," said Kennedy; and to himself, reflectively: "Russel… Parcell."

The doctor asked, "Hector Parcell's kid?"

Kennedy nodded.

MacBride asked, "How well'd you know him, Kennedy?"

"Oh, not very well. I used to run into him at bars now and then. Was he shot?"

"If you mean drunk, yes," said the doctor.

"I don't mean drunk."

The doctor shook his head. "Not a mark on him."

"What'd you have in mind, Kennedy?" MacBride asked suspiciously.

Kennedy pulled the ends of his blanket together and climbed down out of the ambulance. He said, "Nothing much. I just thought he might have been shot."

"Why?"

"He was an impetuous guy. He had an absent-minded way of calling people names."

"Who, for instance?"

"Oh, hell, I don't recall. Anybody. Me even."

The doctor said, "The guy was soused. He just fell down and went to sleep and froze."

Kennedy was heading for the Buick. But he paused and turned about. "Did you master minds notice anything funny about his clothes?"

"What's funny about a dead guy's clothes?" asked the doctor. "There's not a mark on him. No blood on his clothes. Nothing."

Kennedy sighed and continued on his way to the Buick. He climbed in and curled up with the blanket on the rear seat.

MacBride appeared in the doorway. "What's funny, Kennedy?"

"His clothes are wrinkled," Kennedy yawned.

"So what?"

"Wrinkled, as if they'd been wet."

"I'm dull-witted, bozo. Go on."

Kennedy pulled the blanket closer about his chin. "If you pour water over a guy and take him outside when it's zero, ten to one the guy will freeze in a hurry. Wake me up when you get back to Headquarters. Bettdecken said some of the boys were going to have hot toddies at twelve-thirty."

Chapter III

HECTOR PARCELL would have been distinguished-looking in any group of distinguished-looking men. He was tall, well-built, with a fine head of white hair, frosty eyebrows, carved lips. It was obvious that in his daily intercourse with men he was used to demanding respect. It was equally obvious, when MacBride walked into his library, that he was upset.

"I'm Captain MacBride from Police Headquarters. You have my deepest sympathy, Mr. Parcell. This," he added, "is Mr. Kennedy, of the *Free Press*. He knew your son slightly."

The frosty, uneasy eyes moved back and forth from the skipper to Kennedy. The carved lips were having trouble framing words. But finally—"Thank you, Captain MacBride. Russel's death is a great blow to me, even though you doubtless know that he was in many respects not all a son of mine might have been."

The skipper's face was grave. "I understand, Mr. Parcell. There's a chance that he may have come by foul play. That's what I came to talk about this morning."

Parcell tightened his lips, crossed the room to let in a little more of the bright morning sunlight. A younger man came in from the adjoining room. He was about forty; not quite as tall as Parcell but heavier. Speckled gray was at his temples. His eyes were gray, level, his mouth firm but not hard.

Parcell said, "My son-in-law, Mr. Ringers. Marshal, this is Captain MacBride, from the police. This gentleman is a Mr. Kennedy, from the *Free Press.*"

Ringers stopped and said, "How do you do." He glanced sidewise at Parcell, curiously.

Parcell looked like a man preparing himself for an ordeal. "Captain," he said at length, "you mentioned the possibility of foul play. You may omit the word 'possible.' There was," he said, lifting his fine chin, "foul play."

MacBride squinted.

"Yes," said Parcell, "there was foul play. There must have been. My son was kidnaped."

MacBride started.

"I know, I know," Parcell went on, "you've had no report of it. I chose not to report it. On Thursday evening I received a special delivery letter, signed Triple X. It explained that my son was being held for ransom. It demanded thirty thousand dollars within twenty-four hours. It instructed me to immediately call the *Free Press* and have inserted in their Personal Column on Friday the words 'Please come home, Jane.' And sign it simply 'Charley.' I was to have the money by three Friday afternoon. I was told that at half-past three I would receive a telephone call. I was warned against telling the police. I put in the notice, I got the money. At exactly half-past three a woman telephoned and said, 'Have you got the money?' I said, 'Yes.' She said, 'Send a man, only one man, with the money to the northeast corner of Charlton and Bessinger Streets, at eight o'clock tonight. Wrap the money in newspapers. At the corner is a regular city refuse can. Drop the package in it and walk away.' I followed all instructions. Mr. Ringers was good enough to deliver the money."

Ringers shrugged. "It was quite a job getting there, with the snow."

"Were you there on time?" the skipper asked.

"A few minutes ahead of time. I left here early. But I waited until exactly eight to put the money in the receptacle."

"Did you see anyone take it out?"

Ringers frowned, shook his head. "Mr. Parcell told me definitely not to wait around. I walked up Bessinger to the *Avalon* movie house and went in for about twenty minutes and then I left and strolled back to where I'd left the money. I looked in the receptacle and it was gone."

"The other junk in there look the same?"

"Yes."

The skipper spoke to Parcell, "Did they say when they'd release your son?"

"The woman said he would be released an hour after the money was delivered. She said the time was important. She explained that Russel would be killed without delay if the money were not delivered at eight."

MacBride frowned thoughtfully. "Usually they don't kill 'em when the money's paid."

Parcell shrugged bleakly. "Usually. But these people who kidnap are degenerates anyhow, and you know yourself that records prove contrary to what you've just said. I know that in the majority of cases the victim is let go. I realized that of course when I chose not to notify the police."

"Have you seen your son's wife yet?"

"She telephoned me this morning after she'd read the extra." He looked very unhappy. "She is a good girl. Russel never quite realized that."

MacBride said, "Were you and your son on speaking terms?"

Parcell shook his head slowly. "Not for the past six months. I told him not to come near me again until he learned a decent way of living. Perhaps I was a little harsh. But I thought it was for his own good. I really cared a lot for him."

"I'd like to see the letter you got from the kidnapers."

Parcell got it out of a desk drawer. It was printed in pencil on plain white paper that showed no watermark. The envelope was the kind you buy at a post office, already stamped; the special delivery stamp had been added.

Kennedy was absent-mindedly helping himself to almonds from a bowl on a console and apparently paying no attention to what was going on. After a moment he drifted into a kind of den where skins lay on the floor. Antlers, a deer's head, a bear's head, a pair of snowshoes, adorned the walls. He went back into the living-room.

"Mr. Parcell," he said, "I like your den very much. Would you care to sell the snowshoes?"

Parcell looked dumfounded. "Certainly not," he said. "I used them in the Klondike when I was a boy. Haven't you read my book?"

Kennedy shrugged and munched some more almonds. MacBride shot him a sidelong exasperated glance, then turned to Parcell saying:

"Did you keep a record of the numbers of the ransom money?"

Parcell said, "I didn't, but Mr. Ringers did."

Ringers was terse: "It's over at my apartment. We can pick it up whenever you want, Captain."

"Swell," MacBride said. "Let's."

Ringers got his hat and overcoat and went out with MacBride and Kennedy. Gahagan was throwing snowballs at a group of kids across the street.

"Gahagan!" barked the skipper.

Gahagan came over to the Buick looking very red-faced and indignant. "Them brats," he complained, "yelled at me 'Brass buttons, blue coat, couldn't catch a nanny goat.'"

"What of it?" MacBride bit off. "Where's your dignity? Ignore those things. Get in behind the wheel."

One of the kids yelled, "Cops are flops, cops are flops!"

MacBride stiffened, glared. "Hey, you!" he yelled back. "I'll turn you upside down and fan you so hard—" He stopped, swallowed, reddened, then stepped into the sedan.

RINGERS lived in a modest apartment in a modest house on Westervelt Avenue. He had let himself in with a key, explaining, "My wife said she was going to see Rena. That's Russel's wife. This way, gentlemen."

He led them into a small alcove fitted with a desk and bookcases. The whole apartment was neat, orderly, substantial. It had not the elegance of Hector Parcell's home but to MacBride it seemed a great deal more comfortable, though shabby.

Ringers selected a key from his ring, bent towards the desk and then frowned. A drawer was part-way open. With a short oath he yanked it open and plunged his hand into it, shuffling a mass of papers.

"It's gone," he said. He pointed. "The drawer's been forced open."

MacBride could see scars which a chisel or a knife had left. He growled, "Did the kidnapers know you were going to carry the money?"

"Mr. Parcell told them, yes."

Kennedy, who was already lounging in the most comfortable chair in the place, asked, "Mr. Ringers, do you know Rena's brother, Sam Church?"

Ringers turned with a puzzled frown. "Why, yes."

"Well?"

"Fairly."

"He ever visit you here?"

"A number of times."

"What does he do?" Kennedy asked.

Ringers shrugged. "Why, I believe he works in a cigar store. He used to make good money cutting diamonds, until his eyes went back on him."

MacBride said, "What kind of a puzzle are you trying to put together?" to Kennedy.

"None," said Kennedy dreamily. "I knew Rena had a brother and I just wondered what he did. Skip it."

There was the sound of a door closing and a small, plain-looking girl in a dark cloth coat came in. She stopped at sight of the men and looked confused.

Ringers grinned. "Hello, Lucy. These men are from the police and the newspaper. Captain MacBride and Mr. Kennedy."

"How do you do," she said gravely.

Ringers' face clouded. "Somebody rifled my desk, Lucy, and stole the numbers of the ransom money."

"Who could have done that?" she asked flatly. "I locked the door when I went out."

MacBride said, "Skeleton keys often get doors open, but not desk drawers. When did you go out, Mrs. Ringers?"

"About two hours ago. About nine-thirty. I went over to see Rena, Russel's wife." She took her hat off and looked almost drab; but she had a firm little chin, direct blue eyes. "Who would have the nerve to come into this apartment after getting the money and killing Russel?"

"Kidnapers," said MacBride, "exist by nerve, Mrs. Ringers." He asked, "Is your phone here connected with the switchboard downstairs?"

"Why, yes," said Lucy Ringers promptly.

The skipper and Kennedy went downstairs and MacBride, showing his shield, asked the telephone operator, "Were there any calls for the Ringers apartment after nine-thirty this morning?"

"Yes, one. There was no one in."

"What time?"

"Just a few minutes after Mrs. Ringers went out."

"Man or woman?"

"Man."

"What's your number?"

"Westervelt nine-eight-eight and nine-eight-nine."

"Get me Police Headquarters," the skipper said; and when he was connected: "Hello, Otto. This is Steve.... Put a tracer on calls made to Westervelt nine-eight-eight or nine-eight-nine between nine-thirty and ten this morning. I'll ring back."

Outside, he paused before the Buick and said to Kennedy, "Listen, bright eyes. Are you telling all that's on your mind or are you giving me the run-around?"

"Why fill your mind with a lot of chaff, Skipperino?"

"Why not let me decide what's chaff and what isn't?"

"I like everything about you, Stevie, but your suspicious nature. Who am I to offer suggestions to the head of the detective bureau? It would be presumptuous."

MacBride growled, "Go to hell!" and climbed into the sedan.

The skid-chains dug into the snow as Gahagan lurched the car off.

Kennedy bummed a cigarette off the cop on the corner and meandered up the street. He was a scarecrow of a figure in a threadbare topcoat that could not possibly have kept him warm. He wore no rubbers, no gloves. Though the sun shone, the wind was raw, rowdy. Kennedy shivered, but good-temperedly.

Chapter IV

*T*HE *ACME* was a social-political club at the foot of Barrack Street, not far from City Hall. It was a square, dull building of sandstone with thick brass rails flanking its six stone steps. The interior was paneled in old, dark oak and the chandeliers were ancient. You could run into anyone there from the Mayor to a Skiff Street ward-heeler or certain hard-faced men whose means of earning a living could be questioned.

Tom Shack was sitting in a leather sofa in the vast reading-room having a pre-luncheon cocktail with his constant shadow, Jerry Testro. Tom Shack liked tweeds and wore them summer and winter. Testro went in for dark clothes, always.

Kennedy ambled up and dropped wearily into a chair facing the leather sofa. "Florida must be nice," he sighed. "No snow. I dislike snow."

Tom Shack's eyes were merry, inscrutable. "Would a drink cheer you up?"

"It would. Rye, straight. What do you think about Russ Parcell?"

"Rye straight for the gentleman," Tom Shack said to one of the ancient waiters; and to Kennedy, "I was afraid he'd get drunk and pass out some cold night."

"That report is obsolete," Kennedy said drowsily.

"Have an anchovy. Is it?"

"He was kidnaped."

Tom Shack sat back and exclaimed, "No!"

Kennedy ate an anchovy. "Kidnaped, yes. The dough was paid—thirty grand—but Parcell was killed anyhow."

"The paper said he was found frozen to death."

"Sure. Some enterprising guy probably poured water over him and took him for a walk."

Testro said, "Some enterprising guy should have thought of that a long time ago."

"Now, now, Jerry," said Tom Shack.

Testro snapped, "He was a heel."

"Who owed Shack," Kennedy said, "eight thousand five hundred and fifty dollars."

Tom Shack grinned. His battered old face folded into a hundred wrinkles and he began to shake with silent laughter. Testro did not laugh. He stared very hard at Kennedy. Then he ripped out:

"Watch those cracks, Kennedy. If Parcell told you that—"

"Parcell didn't. The transom over your office door was open Tuesday night. I never carry cotton around for my ears."

Testro had a dark, cold smile. "So it was a gag, that one about the men's room."

"Admittedly. The curiosity of the newspaperman is well known. You said you didn't want Parcell to drive home because he might crack himself up and you fellows would be out some dinero. You want to know the real reason?"

"I'm dying to hear it."

"Mae Bannon."

"Rabbits out of your hat, eh?"

"My head, Jerry. You're nuts about Mae and she was nuts about Russ Parcell. You figured it was a good excuse, the one about Russ being too drunk to drive, to keep him from taking her home."

Testro's dark jaw was set. "Rabbits, and they're still out of your hat, and they're blind. Mae Bannon's a chiseler and I knew Parcell was a sap for dames and at the *Mansion House* we watch out for that, even though the guy's a sap. So your two and two makes what?"

Kennedy grinned. "Maybe you add differently than I do."

"Maybe I add with my head."

Kennedy turned to Tom Shack. "How do you add, Tom?"

"Well, I could always add pretty good."

"Come clean, then. Wasn't Jerry gone on Mae?"

Tom Shack looked wistfully into his cocktail, then shrugged. "Whatever Jerry told you, it goes. I never took any interest in his love life."

"This might be a good time to begin," Kennedy said. "The cops don't know that Russ Parcell owed you eighty-five hundred and fifty dollars. They don't know that you need the money. You need it bad. The overhead at the *Mansion House* is big. You dropped twenty thousand on the Rigo-Lamont fight before Christmas. Your wife just came out of the hospital and that cost you six thousand. You couldn't meet a note due on January first for five thousand. The thirty-thousand ransom money would just about clear up what you've dropped and what you owe."

Tom Shack set down his drink and smiled with his lips, not his eyes. "So you're a rat, too, huh?"

"A rat would have told the cops what I know long ago. I'm a horse trader. Just an old hoss trader."

Tom Shack picked up his glass. "It's tough I haven't got anything to trade, Kennedy. As far as I know, Jerry hated Mae Bannon's guts."

Kennedy stood up, wearing a vague, dreamy smile. "Thanks for the drink, Tom."

Testro growled, "Pedal your dogs, little man."

"Mae wasn't home," Kennedy said amiably. "I probably won't be able to locate her for a day or so."

"I wish you luck," snapped Testro.

Tom Shack was staring fixedly at the floor.

Kennedy left *The Acme* and made his way between walls of snow taller than he was tall. Traffic still moved slowly. He boarded a street-car and sat mooning in the back of it until it reached Baxter Street. Then he got out, huddled in his coat, and walked down Baxter to Chevron. There was a combination cigar store and barber shop on the corner. He went in.

"Hello, Sam," he said to the broad man back of the cigar counter. "Sorry to hear about your brother-in-law's death."

"Thanks, whoever you are."

"Kennedy's the name. I met you at *Enrico's* Tuesday night. I was with Russ."

Church took a cigar out of his mouth. "Now I know you," he said, after a long squint. "I didn't recognize you. My eyes are not so good."

"I'm from the *Free Press*. Anything you'd like to say about your brother-in-law?"

Church looked levelly at him for a moment, then put his cigar back in his mouth, shook his head and went about rearranging his showcase.

The door opened and MacBride came in hard-heeled, red-nosed. "Well, what are you doing here, Kennedy?"

"I have a lot of cigarette coupons. I thought I might be able to trade for a pair of snowshoes. No luck, though. Did you want to see me?"

"I never want to see you. Church—I want to see Church."

"What can I do for you?" asked the man behind the counter.

"You Church?"

"Yeah."

"I'm MacBride from Headquarters."

"Glad to know you."

"Yeah?" the skipper said. "What's the number of that phone alongside your cash register?"

"South two-one-three-two."

"Okey. You rang Marshal Ringers' apartment at nine-forty this morning. There was no answer."

"I know there wasn't. Smoke?"

"I buy my own. Why'd you make the call?"

Church leaned on the showcase. "Marshal orders his pipe tobacco through me. I wanted to tell him I'd just got some in."

"You sure you didn't want to find out if the apartment was empty so you could go there and swipe the numbers of the ransom bills?"

Church stared for a long moment. Then he smiled. "So I'm a kidnaper, eh?"

"I asked you a question."

"The answer's no. How the hell could I go to the apartment when I hold down a job here from eight till five. And if you want to know if I was here all morning, ask the barbers. There's four of them."

MacBride shot back, "I don't think you'd be dummy enough to leave your job. You could've sent someone there."

"Who?"

"If I knew, do you suppose I'd be wasting my time here? Close up and put your duds on. I've got your sister Rena over at Headquarters."

Church's mouth snapped shut.

MacBride chuckled. "She can't explain how three hundred bucks got in her handbag. Suppose you come over and try."

RENA PARCELL was a brunette. She was small, slight, with olive skin, small feet, small hands. She had about her that competent air which is often found in small women. Her eyes were brown, wide-open. She was no clinging vine.

Sam Church entered MacBride's office followed by the skipper and Kennedy.

Rena said, "Hello, Sam."

"Hello, Rena," Church said. "Have they been pushing you around?"

Moriarity, who had been sitting in the office with Rena, said, "We thought we'd push you around instead."

MacBride sat down at his desk, filled his pipe and lit up. "The thing is," he said bluntly, "that three hundred dollars can't get up, take a walk and sit down in a woman's handbag. You," he said, pointing his pipe-stem at the woman, "left your husband, Russel Parcell, a month ago. You took a room in a rooming-house at 710 Cassland. It's a place where you pay by the week. The owner wanted two weeks' rent in advance but you said you didn't have it, so she took one week's. Then you hunted for work and got a job as hostess in the *Hotel Raphael* coffee shop at twenty-eight bucks a week. So far you've drawn three weeks' salary, or eighty-four dollars. I'm not making this stuff up in my head. You told me this an hour and a half ago and I checked up with the rooming-house owner and with the hotel people. You also told me that you were practically broke. A minute later, while you're getting me a drink of water, I pick up your pocketbook, open it and find three hundred dollars. My God, madam, what do you take me for!"

"I haven't decided yet," she flipped back at him. "You asked me how the money got there and I told you I don't know. I still don't know."

"Listen, listen," the skipper said sadly. "You leave your husband. While you were married to him—or rather, lived with him during your marriage to him—he never supported you. You lived with him for two years. When you married him, you had ten thousand dollars which your aunt'd left you. He bled you of that, bit by bit. I know because a bank teller friend of mine was good enough to tip me off that he used to cash checks for your husband. The checks were signed by you. Do you deny that?"

Her lips worked. "No! No, of course I don't!"

"Okey. He bled you, he ran up bills, and on top of that he chased other women. He was a drunkard. He didn't support you. He didn't even come home for two and three nights at a time. So you left him. You got to hate him and you left him."

"I got to hate him," she said, "and I left him. All right. Now what else?"

Church said, "Don't let him rattle you, Sis. He's trying to pin the ransom money on you. He's screwy. They haven't got the bill numbers. He's a bag of wind. You don't have to talk."

MacBride got up and came over and said to Church, "How would you like to get a bust in the puss, Mr. Church?"

"Kick him in the shins," Moriarity said. "It hurts more."

Church said with a mocking smile, "If it'd give you a lot of pleasure to bust me in the puss, Captain, bust me. You cops must have your fun."

MacBride sat down on the desk, looked reflectively at his pipe for a minute. Then he sighed and said to Moriarity, "Take the woman downstairs and lock her up."

Moriarity bowed. "Mrs. Parcell, if you please."

Church growled, "You can't lock her up!"

"Can't I?" MacBride asked. "I can lock her up and I can lock you up. Now ain't that surprising?"

Church's voice rose: "You're trying to pin something on her! Damn you, she's not mixed up in this kidnaping and murder! She wouldn't have dirtied her hands on that yellow-bellied slob! He stunk! He was a lousy skunk at heart and for two cents I'd have bashed his kisser in!"

MacBride said, "So for thirty grand you made a smoother job of it."

Moriarity was taking hold of Rena's arm. Church, his face dull red, took one step and one swing. Moriarity plowed through odds and ends of furniture before he hit the floor. MacBride clipped Church on the side of the jaw and Rena headed for MacBride and as the skipper turned she kicked him in the shins.

"Ouch!" he said. "You little—"

"Never in my life!" roared Moriarity. "Never in my life have I been struck inside Headquarters! This is the end!"

Church said, "Well, this makes it twice," and knocked him down again. Moriarity's gun flew from his hand and Church caught it and turned on the skipper. "You started this, big boy. Come on, Rena." He grabbed his sister by the hand.

"You forgot the visiting Press," said Kennedy, leaning against the wall with a small automatic in his hand.

Rena exclaimed, "Say, I never noticed him!"

"I'm really part of the wall paper," said Kennedy, "except I shoot. Drop it, Church, or I drop little sister."

Church grunted and slid the revolver on to the desk.

The skipper picked it up. His eyes were hard, his mouth a grim line. He said quietly in a low, heavy voice, "Maybe you'll talk now."

"I'll give you two guesses," Church said.

Rena cried, "You people can't handle us this way! What have we done? Nothing! Talk? I wouldn't talk to you if you were the last man on earth!"

MacBride pressed a button and two uniformed officers came in.

He said, "Take these two down and lock 'em up. If the guy gets wise, crown him."

The two officers took Church and his sister out.

MacBride dropped to his chair and looked suddenly haggard. "Parcell wasn't worth a hell of a lot, Kennedy. It's tough I got to go to work on the wife. The funny thing about justice is, you don't know just where it begins and where it ends."

Kennedy said, "Still the old softie, eh?"

"You got to admit Parcell was a heel. There ought to be some distinction between when you kill a heel and when you kill a guy."

"I know," said Kennedy. "You're going to take the lady, pat her on the head, and send her home."

MacBride stood up, frowned. "That's the hell of it, bozo. I'm going to hang her."

Moriarity sat up, groaned.

MacBride looked down at him. "What the hell's the matter with you? Were you muscle-bound?"

Moriarity stood up, white fire in his eyes. "Just give me five minutes alone in a room with that guy."

"Don't be a dope, kid," the skipper said. "We got enough cops on the sick list."

Chapter V

KENNEDY went to *Enrico's* for dinner. It was a cold, black, windless night. The snow in front of *Enrico's* was piled shoulder high and shovelers were still at work.

"I'll eat at the bar," Kennedy told Enrico. "Steak sandwich, French fries, and an artichoke with butter sauce."

He went into the bar and climbed on to a stool. "Paderoofski, my friend, a double Martini. Chuck the olive out the window."

"Meester Kennedy, howza av'ry leetle t'ing? Isn't it so bad Meester Parcell wazza bomp off?"

"Yeah. D'you do it, Paderoofski?"

Paderoofski leaned intimately across the bar. "Meester Kennedy, between us axtremely, I am not bosted up weeth griff. Meester Parcell wazza potickelly nasty man, I'm dun't t'ink not. I wazza not be crazy 'bout his gots."

"Paderoofski, your French is improving. How about the double Martini?" He added, "And the olive out the window."

Paderoofski made the Martini with a flourish, served it with a piratical grin. Kennedy took the olive out and popped it into a spittoon. He finished another Martini before his meal arrived; had a rye highball with the meal. He hung around for another hour and drank five brandies. Before he left he said:

"No kidding, Paderoofski. You didn't kill him, did you?"

Paderoofski's eyebrows spread upward and outward. "Meester Kennedy, I'm never bomp off a man in my life! Never! Only once. No, it wazza twice. Well, maybe t'ree times. I'm dun't know too sure."

"Where was that?"

"In de war," sighed Paderoofski.

Kennedy left.

He killed another hour in the *Stokehold* drinking brandy and then grabbed a cab, to go home and get some more money. He lived in a not-too-run-down rooming-house in Hallam Street, a quiet, dull corner of the city. The snow had been shoveled off the stone stoop and ashes had been spread on them. Humming contentedly to himself, he climbed to his room, switched on the light and blinked.

Two big men were sitting in chairs and one of them said in a hard, lazy voice, "We been waitin' for you, sweetheart. Ain't you nice to come home early?" He wore a rough brown cap and had a jaw like the bow of a tugboat.

His companion said, "Oh, he ain't a bad guy, Bat. Ah still claims he ain't a bad guy a-tall."

"Jazz, ain't I told you never to mention no names?"

"Lawzy, has Ah, Bat?"

They stood up. The white man was angular, rocky-boned. The Negro was burly, with a mouthful of gold teeth. The white man came over, put his left hand on Kennedy's shoulder and said:

"Can you take it?"

"No," said Kennedy.

"Then that's just too bad," the white man said and knocked him cold.

Kennedy woke up in a ramshackle room where a single light bulb hung from the center of a ceiling whose plaster was cracked in many places. The light bulb had no shade. He lay on a pile of rags in a corner.

Bat sat on a chair with his legs outstretched. He was munching popcorn which he drew from a large paper sack. The Negro squatted on the floor strumming a banjo.

Bat said, "Play me de 'Prisoner's Song,' Jazz."

"Ah don't like t' play dat song, Bat."

"Play it. I likes it. It's got class."

Jazz strummed it and sang the words in a husky whisper. When he finished he reached for a drink.

"Lousy," said Kennedy.

Bat stared. "De noive o' some people! De noive!" He leaned forward, his eyes glaring. "Jazz," he commanded, "go over and kick his teeth in."

The Negro whined: "Bat, Ah tol' yo' dat song ain't no good."

"Listen, Jazz, you gonna make me get up and do it?"

Kennedy said, "I wasn't referring to the song. I was dreaming about something."

Bat relaxed and dug his hand into the paper sack. "It's lucky you was, sweetheart."

Kennedy sat up and pawed feebly at his face. He stared dismally around the room, his stringy hair hanging over his eyes, his face pale and emaciated. He coughed a little, rubbed his hand against his chest.

The Negro grinned. "Any song you-all'd like t' hear, Mistuh Kennedy?"

"Listen, Jazz," Bat remonstrated. "Dis mugg ain't a guest here, he's a prisoner. Play 'Mammy'. If he don't like dat I'll knock him in two so's I kin kill some time tryin' to put him together again. Go ahead. Don't argue. Play 'Mammy'."

"Ah wisht," pouted the Negro, "Ah could jest once play what Ah want. Jest once."

Kennedy said, "I think there's something funny about my neck. You better get a doctor." He grimaced as he tried to straighten his head.

The Negro said, "Ah told you, Bat, you should nevah hit dat man de way you-all did."

"Shut up!" growled the white man. He got up and swaggered across the room. He reached down and cuffed Kennedy on the ear. Kennedy said, "Oooo!" and flopped around on his face, lay there quite motionless except for his jerky breathing.

The Negro looked scared. "Bat—"

"Shut up!" the white man barked. He sat down again, picked up the sack of popcorn and said, "Play 'Mammy'."

"Ah know, Bat, but you-all take care. Dat man ain't no more 'an a shadder an' if you-all kills him—"

"I said, Jazz, play 'Mammy'."

Kennedy remained lying on his face. After a while he moved his hands up and seemed to be resting his head on them. Little twitchings coursed over his body. In about half an hour he rolled over, stumbled to his knees, his head still way over to one side.

"Glory be!" wailed the Negro. "Look!"

"Hah?" said Bat.

"Oh, Lawd, Bat! Look!"

Bat squinted.

Kennedy was crawling feebly across the floor. There were ghostly blue patches beneath his eyes, on his cheekbones. His lips and the flesh around his lips were also blue. There was a glassy stare in his eyes.

The Negro jumped to his feet, his big lips shaking. He cried, "Bat, you done it!"

"Lay off!" snarled the white man, standing spread-legged. "This guy thinks he's gonna waltz outta here, eh? I'll waltz him! I'll kick his ear off!"

The Negro's eyes bulged. "Bat, man, you-all listen to me! He's goin' blue, Bat! Ah tell you, you busted his neck. *Bat!*"

Bat drove his foot at Kennedy's head but the Negro, blind with fear, threw himself on the big man and crashed with him to the floor. Bat roared.

The Negro cried, "Bat, Ah'm tellin' you-all—"

The white man heaved and struck the Negro between the eyes. The Negro looked shocked, then angry. His teeth bared. He jumped up as Bat jumped up and hit the white man in the belly. Bat grunted and closed with him and their big bodies crashed against the wall. They separated. The Negro took a wild overhand swing, smashed the lightbulb and plunged the room into darkness.

Kennedy was on his way. He reached the hall outside, raced down the staircase, followed another staircase to the street level and stumbled to the front door. He unlatched it, hauled it open and fell down a flight of four wooden steps to the snowy sidewalk. He could hear heavy footsteps pounding down the inside stairway. He got up and ran down the street on the rutty snow, his legs unsteady, his frail arms flying. The street ended at a railroad abutment. He could see two figures in swift pursuit.

The drop to the yards below was a dozen feet, but he took off and landed broadside in a snowbank. He rolled out of it and tottered across tracks and switches. He crawled beneath a motionless string of box cars. On the other side, a yard engine was hauling a string of empty gondolas slowly and he swung aboard and rode crouched between two gondolas. He was so exhausted that it hurt him to breathe. The wheels creaked monotonously in the cold night air. The pungent smell of soft coal smoke boiled in Kennedy's nostrils. When the cars jerked to a stop he half-climbed, half-fell to the ground. Frozen clinkers joggled his feet.

He got out of the yards beneath the West Viaduct and went around to the passenger terminal and into the toilets. When he had run hot water into a basin he scrubbed the light-blue ink from beneath his eyes, his cheeks, and from around his mouth. There was some on his hands too, for he had used his fingers to spread the ink after having squirted it from his fountain pen. He got his hands clean also.

There was a booth outside the toilet door and he entered it and called MacBride. He said, "Turn two-o-six Liversey Street inside out and see what happens. Two guys took me there when I wasn't looking and a colored man's fear of ghosties got me out.... Kennedy, of course.... How do I know. Pull your own chestnuts out of the fire. I'm going out and get a drink."

He went around to *Enrico's* and said to Enrico, "I'm broke. I want to borrow twenty bucks, a gun, and two drinks of rye."

Enrico took twenty dollars from the cash register, a .32 automatic out of a jar labeled *Peppermint.* Then he looked very severe. "Kennedy, it's the troot, you weel have to pay for de drinks. Strictly cash iss my motto."

Kennedy grinned. "You're an old meany, Enrico."

Chapter VI

HE COULD not have looked formidable had he tried. He was naturally round-shouldered, hollow-chested, and his clothes were always haphazard and ill-assembled. Color schemes meant nothing in his life. He wore a tie till it was worn out and a hat until someone stole it or until, on one of his benders, he lost it.

When he entered the *Mansion House* at eleven-fifteen the hat-check girl said, "Good evening, Mr. Kennedy," and reached for his hat and coat. "How is everything?"

"Fine, Toots," he said and gave her his things.

His yellow hair was tousled and one corner of his collar stood upward. The rhumba music was very catchy. Men and women in evening clothes drifted languidly from the bar across the central hall into the dining-room. Mirrors flashed light back and forth sharply, like beacons.

Kennedy went through the central hall and climbed the stairway. The carpeting felt almost pneumatic beneath his feet. He did not hurry and he did not look particularly wide-awake. When he reached the door to Tom Shack's office he did not knock; and when he opened it and drifted in, Tom Shack said:

"Hello, Kennedy. Wrong door again?"

Kennedy smiled whimsically, closed the door and said, "Right door this time, Tom." He crossed the room to the blue leather divan, sat down, put his feet upon the divan and leaned back comfortably on the rolled armrest.

Tom Shack chuckled, clipped the tip off a cigar and said, "All the comforts of home, eh? Well, why not? Thanks for not telling the police." He lit up.

Kennedy began cleaning his fingernails with a penknife. "Where's Jerry?" he asked.

"Jerry? Oh, night off."

"And where does he go on his nights off?"

Shack shrugged. "Don't ask me, Kennedy."

"I'll bet he stays home reading the Encyclopaedia Brittanica or writing letters to his mother."

"No. I guess he goes to a show or a movie or something."

"That's the boy. Be cagey, Tom. Or something."

Tom Shack sat back with an impatient gesture. "What the hell's in your hair now, Kennedy?"

"Jerry Testro."

"Jerry? Hell, man, Jerry's a fine boy. Honest as the day is long."

"Days get pretty short in winter." Kennedy put his knife away and his feet on the floor. "Where does he live?"

"Who?"

"If we've been talking about two people, stop me."

Tom Shack's eyes narrowed. "Look here, Kennedy. Jerry's a white guy, he's the tops. Lay off him."

"Where does he live?"

"That boy's worked for me for six years. He's straight as a straight line. He cut his own salary to help me out."

"I'm not asking for that kind of groceries. Where does he live?"

Tom Shack turned up his palms, dropped his shoulders. "The Green Towers." He made a sour, unhappy face, saying, "I wish you'd leave Jerry alone."

Kennedy went to the Green Towers in a cab. The cab jolted over snow ruts and ice hummocks and Kennedy huddled in the rear seat, his teeth chattering with the cold. The Green Towers was a Norman structure on Cloverdale Boulevard—an apartment-hotel, mostly residential. Its lobby had a huge fireplace, wrought-iron lighting fixtures. Its desk-clerk was an amiable gray man.

"Mr. Testro," Kennedy said.

"Why, he's not in, sir. There was a phone call for him five minutes ago. He hasn't been in all day. In fact, he wasn't in last night."

"How sure of that are you?"

"Oh, quite sure. You see, last night he phoned me from Letzville. It was about this time. He wanted to know if there were any important messages for him. I said there was not. Then he told me he wouldn't be in tonight and asked me to please feed his macaw. He said if there was any important message— By the way, is yours important?"

"Very."

The clerk handed him a slip of paper. "There's the phone number he left. The snow, of course, must have detained him in Letzville last night but I know the tram was running this morning."

Kennedy thanked him and crossing the lobby entered a telephone booth. He called police headquarters and got Otto Bettdecken on the wire. "This is Kennedy, Otto.... Do me a favor, will you?... Okey. Here's a phone number: Letzville one-five. Get me the address and find out what kind of a place it is.... Call me back at West one-four-four-one."

He hung up and sat down in a chair outside the booth. Bettdecken rang back in fifteen minutes and Kennedy said, "Thanks a million, Otto," and left the Green Towers. He walked three blocks south and caught a high-speed trolley to Letzville. It took him half an hour to reach the sleepy suburb; five minutes to walk from the car stop to the Letzville House, a two-storied frame hotel. A gaunt man was drowsing behind the desk.

Kennedy said good-naturedly, "Hello. Did a man named Testro stop here last night? Or am I bothering you?"

The gaunt man yawned, motioned. "Look in the register."

Kennedy looked and found Jerry Testro's name. "What time did he check in?"

"What did he look like?"

Kennedy said, "Tall, dark and handsome. About thirty."

"Oh, I remember, sure. Well, he first came in around six and asked to look at the register, and I guess he didn't find what he wanted, so he went out. Then he came in again about eleven and said the tram wasn't running and he'd have to spend the night. So he spent the night. He checked out at about nine this morning, when I told him the tram was running again."

"He have any visitors?"

"Nope."

Kennedy trudged back through the snow to the car stop, shivered in the cold for twenty minutes. Then a car came along and he rode back to Richmond City. He got off at the point where he had boarded it outbound and returned to the Green Towers. He grinned sleepily at the clerk, saying:

"There's probably no truth in this, but we got a call that there was a dead man in Testro's apartment. I'm from the *Free Press*," he added, showing his press card.

The gray clerk stared. "Surely, I can't believe—"

"We might take a look. I think it's a gag myself."

"By all means, we'll take a look."

The apartment was on the third floor. There was a large living-room with a gallery. There was a macaw in a huge cage. The clerk went up to the gallery and Kennedy went into the pantry, looked in the kitchen. There was a service door in the pantry fitted with a heavy brass snaplock. He turned back the snaplock and set it, then returned into the living-room. The clerk was coming down from the gallery, saying:

"Nothing to it. I looked in both bedrooms."

Kennedy said, "Nothing in the kitchen, either. I thought it was a gag."

They went down in the elevator and Kennedy left by the main door. He walked around to the side entrance, slipped in through the single swing-door and took the fire stairway up to the third floor. He entered Testro's apartment by the service door, snapped shut the lock and then strolled casually into the living-room. Switching on only one floor lamp, he relaxed wearily into a huge divan beside which stood a decanter of whiskey, a rack filled with glasses. He helped himself liberally to Testro's whiskey and Testro's cigarettes. The macaw made low clucking sounds.

Kennedy yawned, "Polly want a cracker?"

"Nuts to youse, pal," the macaw said.

Kennedy polished off four drinks and lay back full length on the divan. It was half-past one by the banjo clock on the wall. Then it was a quarter of two. Then it was two. At two the buzzer sounded. Kennedy sat up.

"Nobody home!" squawked the macaw. "Nobody home!"

Kennedy ambled to the door, taking his gun out of his pocket and holding it negligently in the palm of his hand. He opened the door and saw Mae Bannon standing in front of him. His smile was gentle, dreamy.

He drawled, "Fancy seeing you here, Mae."

Chapter VII

SHE BEGAN to back away. Pain welled up in her eyes and a grimace rolled down her under lip.

"Come in, Mae," Kennedy said tranquilly.

She swallowed and made a sound doing it. Her eyes staggered from his dreamy face to the gun in his hand. The corners of her mouth became wet. He reached out gently with his left hand, took hold of her arm, drew her slowly but firmly into the small foyer. He closed, locked the door. He prodded her gently in the small of the back and she moved wooden-legged into the living-room. Her eyes wandered dazedly around the room. He put the gun back into his pocket.

"Been places, Mae?"

She turned and stared at him for a long minute, a hunted look in her eyes, her lips quivering against her teeth. She let out a small, hoarse sob and bolted for the door. He caught her in the foyer and pulled her back into the living-room; shoved her into the divan. He showed no especial anger.

"Drink?" he asked.

She shook her head.

"Smoke?"

She shook her head.

He took a drink himself. "Talk?"

She pressed back into the divan and stared up at him with terrified eyes. He stood slouching on his feet, mild, quiet, whimsical. There was nothing formidable about him, nothing terrifying.

"Where've you been since Russ Parcell died?" he asked.

She swallowed hard and looked away with wide, straining eyes. Her breathing began to be very audible and her fingers crawled tightly, aimlessly on the cushions of the divan.

He said, "Was it nice for you and Testro to gang on Russ?"

She sobbed tautly.

"I know Russ was a heel," Kennedy went on, "but you should have given him a break."

She shook her head and her lips burst apart and she cried passionately, "I didn't, I didn't! I don't know what you're talking about!" She jumped up wildly. "Let me out of here! Let me go!"

He stepped in front of her and she turned and ran toward the gallery. He pulled her back down off the steps. She broke away and headed for the door. He caught hold of her arm and spun her about and she reeled and then struck out for the kitchen. He reached the kitchen door a jump ahead of her and blocked her and she swiveled and ran towards the gallery again. He went up the steps after her. She screamed, "Let me go!"

The macaw squawked, "Hey, Bat! Hey, Bat!"

Kennedy stopped in his tracks and stared at the bird.

"That's far enough," Testro said. He was standing in the foyer entrance with a gun in his hand. He looked very dark and worn and grim.

Mae had reached the gallery and she stood with both arms braced on the railing, gasping for breath.

Kennedy looked at Testro, shrugged and came leisurely down to the living-room. He said, "You'll never get to be President doing this, Jerry."

"You will clown, won't you?"

"When did Bat give you the bird?"

There was no humor in Testro's voice when he said, "For a little guy, Kennedy, you sure take chances."

"When a couple of gorillas named Bat and Jazz bounce me around, I sure do."

Mae ran down from the gallery, ran across to Testro crying, "Jerry, I shouldn't have come here. But I—I—"

"Quiet, Mae."

"I just didn't know what—"

"Quiet, baby."

"Oh, Jerry, Jerry!" she sobbed hoarsely.

Testro said. "How long you been here, Mae?"

"Only about ten or fifteen minutes."

"Was the squirt rough?"

"No—no!"

"What'd you tell him?"

"Nothing, Jerry! Nothing!"

Testro's lips clamped. His jaw was a hard dark knot, his eyes two black coals.

She panted, "Jerry—look out. He's got a gun in his pocket."

Testro's smile was hard, wolfish. "It won't do him any good, baby. Kennedy, you pulled one wisecrack too many. You ought to stick to your pencils and stay out of man-sized company."

Kennedy's smile was dusty, dreamy. "For a little guy, I seem to be giving you and the girl a hell of a big headache."

Testro said, "Mae, go over to the *Panama* and wait for me in one of the booths."

"Jerry, what are you going to do?" she begged.

"Get, Mae. The *Panama.* I'll join you in an hour."

"Jerry—"

"Beat it, Mae. I'll take care of Kennedy. Beat it, will you?"

Wide-eyed, grimacing, she stumbled from the living-room, into the foyer. Testro came over and took away Kennedy's gun. He socked Kennedy on the jaw and drove him flying into the divan, saying, "Now I'll find out what your habits look like." Kennedy hit the divan so hard that he bounced right back to his feet, and with a silly, crooked smile on his face he walked up to Testro and hit him in the mouth. Then he staggered around, chuckled loosely to himself, picked up a bronze and marble ashtray and flung it at Testro. Testro ducked. Kennedy floundered across the room, picked up a bronze statuette, hefted it and went staggering straight at Testro. Testro eyed him in amazement. Kennedy took a roundhouse swing and Testro ducked easily, hit Kennedy on the jaw and sent him crashing to the floor. Kennedy began crawling towards other heavy objects and MacBride appeared in the doorway leading from the foyer and said:

"Drop it, Testro."

Testro whirled and MacBride fired, saying, "I didn't say turn. I said drop it."

The gun fell from Testro's bloody hand.

MacBride came into the room and Moriarity was at his heels. Ike Cohen came in with Mae Bannon.

MacBride said, "Thanks for the tip about the Liversey Street place, Kennedy. We picked up two lugs named Bat Muller and Jazz Shannaway and they got around to telling us that Testro hired them to keep you salted down indefinite. What have you been doing, messing around again?"

Kennedy lay on his belly on the floor, his chin braced on his hands. "Jerry Testro and the girl kidnaped Parcell."

"Okey," MacBride said. "Wrap something around your hand, Testro. We'll get it fixed at Headquarters."

"No—no!" the girl shrieked. "Jerry had nothing to do with it! You can't arrest him!"

"She's the loyal type," said Kennedy, getting to his feet.

Testro snapped at her, "Keep your mouth shut, Mae!"

She was tugging at Ike Cohen, trying to free herself. "Oh, Jerry, why, why?" she groaned, sobbed. She looked at MacBride, shaking her head. "Not Jerry, not Jerry! He had nothing to do with it! I wrote the ransom note! I—I made the phone call to old Parcell!"

"Sure," said Kennedy, pouring himself a drink. "And Jerry picked up the dough and finished Parcell."

She screamed, "No—no! I tell you he didn't know anything about it! He didn't! He wasn't in on it all. It was Russ—it was Russ! It was Russel's idea! He told me what to write, he told me what to say on the phone! Russ! Russ! Not Jerry!"

Kennedy did a strange thing: he put down his drink without touching it. He stared stupidly at Mae Bannon.

She whimpered, "When Russ didn't show up, I—I got scared. I ran away, hid out. I—I came here tonight looking for Jerry because I needed help. He was always good to me. He warned me against Russ. But I was screwy. I—I went for Russ in a big way. I—I—"

Kennedy said, "What were you doing out around Letzville, Jerry?"

Testro scowled at the floor. "Looking for Mae. I knew she used to go out there sometimes. I've been looking for her all over."

MacBride found his tongue. "But who," his blunt voice said, "killed Russel Parcell?"

Mae was sobbing. "I don't know. I don't know."

MacBride looked at Testro. "I don't know, either, but I got a swell idea," he said. "Take him, Mory. Ike, you take the gal."

Kennedy was musing out loud, "Parcell was like a young tree, bent a little and not very strong. Young trees sometimes die in the winter-time. I think it's called winter kill."

MacBride growled, "What the hell are you rambling on about?"

Kennedy's eyes were filled with dreamy thoughts. He picked up the gun which Testro had taken from him and slipped it into his pocket. He did not, as they went out, overlook the drink.

Chapter VIII

WHEN Kennedy let himself in through an unlatched window of Hector Parcell's house the warmth was balm to his chilled bones. Once inside, he did not close the window. He stood for a few minutes in the darkened room pressing his hands and his body against a steam radiator. Then he moved. He knew he was in the living-room and he had an idea where Hector Parcell's den lay. It took him a couple of minutes to find it. He pulled down the shades and turned on a light. Bookshelves surrounded him. The only sound was the leisurely ticking of a clock.

He moved to the bookshelves and after a brief survey of the volumes found that they were arranged alphabetically according to authors. He moved down to the Ps, found a volume entitled *My Youth in the Klondike,* by Hector Parcell. He carried the book to the desk and sat down and turned to the contents page. There were forty-one chapters, each with a sub-division describing its content. He read rapidly down the contents page until he came to Chapter Sixteen:

> The food problem—The liquor problem—The first bank—A false alarm—My lead-dog Jeff—The mails—John Tinkard: his strange death—

Kennedy turned to Chapter Sixteen, skimmed down the first page, the second, slowed down on the third. He read the third page over several times, then closed the book and put it into his overcoat pocket. He climbed out through the window, pulled it down quietly and toiled away through the snow. When he reached his Hallam Street room he set the alarm clock for eight-thirty.

He was out by nine next morning, shivering in the cold, only half-awake. Three cups of black coffee wakened him a bit. He phoned Police Headquarters and found that those still being held in connection with the kidnaping and death of Russel Parcell were his wife Rena and her brother Sam Church; Bat Muller and Jazz Shannaway; Testro and Mae Bannon. Mae Bannon had confessed half a dozen times. Testro had not uttered a word.

Kennedy, who was not fond of leg work, spent an hour making telephone calls, jotting down memoranda. But he had to do a little leg work. He visited a movie theater, a bank teller, a dozen filling stations, the Richardson Dowel Factory's manager, at his home. It was, of course, Sunday. Kennedy lunched at a bar and then went into a telegraph office.

He took a cab out to Westervelt Avenue, humming abstractedly to himself. When he knocked on Marshal Ringers' door someone inside shut off a radio and in a moment Lucy Ringers opened the door. She looked drab as ever and a little fretful.

"Yes?" she said.

"Perhaps you don't remember me," he said. "I'm Kennedy from the *Free Press.* Is your husband in?"

She shrugged. "Yes. Come in."

Ringers got up from a neat but shabby armchair and laid aside the Sunday papers.

"Hello, Mr. Kennedy," he said bluntly. "I see you're giving it quite a spread in the papers."

Kennedy said, "I suppose you've heard the latest from Headquarters?"

Ringers looked moody, nodded his head slowly. "I never thought Russel would do a thing like that. He was pretty hopeless, but a thing like that…. Well, sit down."

Kennedy sat down and Lucy Ringers went into another room. Kennedy said, "Are you sure your father-in-law, Mr. Parcell, remained at home while you went to deliver the ransom money?"

Ringers looked up. "Yes. As far as I know."

"You're not sure, though."

"I'm as sure as I can be. He told me he did. There was no reason for him not to."

Kennedy said, "When he was a young man, you know, he lived in the Klondike. Lived a rough life. Men took a lot of things in their own hands up there in those days. They had plain ideas about justice."

"I imagine they did," Ringers nodded, "from what I've read."

"Have you read much about the Klondike?"

"Not an awful lot."

Kennedy switched: "That was funny, the cops finding three hundred dollars in Rena's pocketbook when she said she was broke."

"It was strange indeed."

"How long have you worked for the Milbeck Furniture Company?"

"Ten years."

"And your salary, as accountant there is sixty a week. Not much, is it?"

Ringers smiled. "You seem to know a lot about me, Mr. Kennedy."

"Ask your wife, will you, if when she went over to see Rena she didn't slip three hundred dollars into Rena's pocketbook?"

Lucy Ringers stepped into the room, said sternly, "I did not. If I had three hundred dollars all at one time, I'd put it in the bank. Is this man drunk, Marshal?"

Ringers shrugged. "He's pointed, anyhow. What else, Mr. Kennedy? Sundays are usually dull but you brighten this one."

The door-bell rang and Lucy Ringers went to the door. A telegraph messenger gave her a small package and she closed the door and said, "Something for you, Marshal."

Ringers took it, cut the cord with a penknife and pulled off the heavy brown wrapper, revealing a book which had been recently covered with similar brown paper. Printed on the paper in large letters, in ink, were the words, TURN TO PAGE 156. Puzzled, Ringers thumbed the pages, stopped at 156. Around the margin of page 156 was drawn a line in red ink. Ringers read a word or two, then started. His lips closed hard, tight, and the book fell from his hands.

Kennedy said tranquilly, "I sent you that book, Mr. Ringers."

"Marshal!" cried Lucy Ringers. "Marshal, goodness, what is wrong?"

Ringers' jaw shook, his eyes jigged. He sucked breath in through his teeth and whirled ferociously on Kennedy. Kennedy had his gun in his hand.

"Look out, buddy," Kennedy said.

Ringers charged blindly and Kennedy fired but Ringers did not stop. The full force of his body struck Kennedy and a chair splintered to pieces as they went down. Ringers' eyes were crazed, his teeth were bared, and inarticulate sounds rasped from his throat. He must have weighed about a hundred and ninety. Kennedy weighed about a hundred and thirty-seven and none of it was tough. But Ringers' crazed haste made him miss the clubbing blow he sent towards Kennedy's head and in that split-instant Kennedy flung himself aside. But as he did so Ringers' flying fist struck the gun from his hand and it flew across the room.

Kennedy jumped up and Ringers jumped up, blood on his arm but still an able-bodied man. Kennedy jumped behind a victrola and Ringers came at him, hurled the victrola aside. Kennedy, his eyes not sleepy now, yanked down a portière and flung it into Ringers' arms.

Lucy Ringers was spellbound, her hands pressed to her cheeks, her throat sobbing.

She cried, "Marshal! Marshal!"

Ringers did not hear. His eyes were glazed with terror and a fierce singleness of purpose. He flung off the portière, stalked Kennedy, suddenly slapped aside a chair and leaped for him. Kennedy scrambled out of the way and Ringers crashed against the wall. Two pictures fell down, smashed. Ringers spun, his chest heaving, froth at his mouth. He lunged across the room, the broken chair again crackling beneath his feet. He hit Kennedy and plastered him against the wall, and a mirror came down past Kennedy's head and crashed against Ringers' skull. Glass showered down over Ringers' shoulders as he staggered backward.

Lucy Ringers had picked up the gun. Her jaw was set.

"Marshal," she said sternly, "what's got into you?"

Kennedy said, "Lady, he killed your brother."

Her face turned gray. "Marshal, it's a lie. Marshal, tell me it's a lie! Russel was reckless, he was weak, but you wouldn't—"

Ringers stumbled to the door, clawed at the knob.

"Marshal," the woman groaned, "tell me it's not true. Tell me he lies. Marshal, you—you didn't kill Russel!"

Ringers, unsteady on his feet, got the door open. Lucy ran across the room, grabbed him by the arm, cried, "Marshal, speak to me!" But he tried to move on, tried to get through the doorway. She dropped the gun and gripped him with both hands, tugging, holding him back, crying, "Marshal! Marshal!" in a choked, panic-stricken voice. He turned groggily, awkwardly, and tried to pry her loose. His eyes were blank, unseeing. She suddenly released him and shrank back, her knuckles pressed to her lips. She sobbed, "You did, then… you did…" and fainted.

Kennedy had picked up the gun which she had dropped. Ringers stared at it for a minute. Grimaced. Sat down.

Chapter IX

MacBRIDE leaned back in his office chair and pushed tobacco deep into the charred bowl of his pipe. He took his time about it, getting the tobacco nicely packed. Then he lit up, rolling the match's flame slowly back and forth across the bowl, to get an even light. He waved the match out.

"How did you guess, Kennedy?" he asked.

Kennedy was huddled on a chair next to the radiator. "I had to guess at something, Skipperino. I thought sure as hell it was Mae and Testro, but it became evident that Testro was running his dogs off trying to find Mae. Then when Mae confessed in his apartment, I had a hunch she was right. She cleared up the kidnaping but not the murder.

"Then I began to really reason things out. Take a lad like Jerry Testro. Hot-headed, eh? Why should he do away with Parcell in a manner like that? He'd have busted Parcell's neck or shot him. I thought of old Parcell, but threw that out too. Then I thought of Ringers. A cool, calculating fellow. I checked up on him. He's an underpaid accountant living in a shabby flat with the daughter of a guy worth thousands. All right. He was the one sent to deliver the ransom money.

"He said he delivered it at eight p.m. and then killed about twenty minutes in the *Avalon* movie theater. I went around to the *Avalon* and found that from eight to nine they were not letting people in because the motion picture machine was temporarily broken down. I went to a bank teller and found that Ringers' account was low, about a hundred and fifty dollars. I found out he had often visited the dowel factory in the street where Parcell was found. Now take this book of memoirs that old Parcell wrote.

"In the first place, it's a strange thing to find a guy frozen stiff from having had water poured over him. I'd read about it somewhere, but I couldn't remember where—and it was long ago. But I thought I'd read it in a book about the North. So I raided Parcell's library and sure enough it was in his book. He recounted how a fellow had been found frozen to death in the Klondike and that another guy later confessed he had poured hot water over him while he was drunk and taken him for a walk.

"Again I thought of Parcell but again I chucked it out. I had Ringers on my mind. And where would Ringers get hot water? Well, I fooled around some gas stations in the neighborhood and one guy said, yes, a fellow had stopped by at about ten o'clock with his radiator damned near empty. He remembered because the guy stopped for gas but the tank was almost full. I then sent the book by telegraph messenger to Ringers and hurried to get there ahead of it. When the book arrived—"

MacBride nodded. "Yes, I know that from his confession. He delivered the money all right but he hung around and watched and saw Parcell take it from the ashcan. He followed the kid and caught up with him and Parcell damned near fainted. He got weak in the knees. Ringers took him back to where he'd parked the car and they got in and Parcell immediately began taking swigs from a bottle and begging Ringers not to tell. Ringers claims he said nothing, he just let Parcell talk and guzzle. Then he said, 'We'll drive for a while and think it over.' Parcell drank and drank, trying to steady himself, but he got pie-eyed.

"Ringers drove up that street by the dowel mill and stopped. Parcell was so drunk he couldn't move. Ringers pulled him out, shoved him beneath the car and opened the petcock on the bottom of the radiator, drenching Parcell. Then he lugged him up the road a bit. Parcell was struggling a bit but kind of feeble. Ringers wrapped his woolen scarf around his fist, so he'd leave no mark, and hit Parcell a terrific wallop on the chin. Parcell passed out and Ringers pushed him down into the snowbank and piled snow over him. It's a dead-end street at the mill and there's no traffic, not even a mill watchman. He left Parcell there and drove off.

"He hid the money next day in his safe-deposit box. He destroyed the list of numbers of the ransom bills but made it look like somebody had rifled his desk. He'd always hated Parcell because the old man'd got Russ out of scrapes for years but never put any money in the Ringers' household. Not a cent. Ringers was a drudge, he knew he'd never get anywhere, and when he saw a chance of getting thirty grand he took it."

Kennedy nodded. "What about the three hundred Rena had?"

"Her brother Sam had put it in her purse the night before. He knew she was broke and owed bills and that the bills worried her. He was giving her a little surprise. She didn't know the dough was there till I found it. Only thing is, the guy lifted it from his boss in order to help her. That's why he kept his mouth shut until we kidded him into confessing by telling him Rena had confessed to the kidnaping and it was ransom money."

"Where's Testro?"

MacBride didn't look happy when he grumbled, "In the lock-up. I got to hold him because he sent Bat and Jazz to take you to that house and hold you for a couple of days. Jazz told me when we picked them up that Testro's warned Bat not to do anything rough but Bat got drunk in the meantime and socked you and that scared the life out of Jazz. Testro's in love with Mae; been for a couple of years. He had an idea she was mixed up in the trouble but he didn't know just where. He knew you were getting pretty close and he was so gone on that girl that he wanted to keep you out of the way for a couple of days, until he could locate her and find out what was what. When he found you and Mae in the apartment, he was pretty desperate. He sent her to the *Panama* because he wanted to beat out of you just how much you knew. He says he's sorry about that, but nothing mattered to him but Mae. It's up to you whether you want to press any charges."

"How about Mae?"

The skipper said ruefully, "Tough. I got to charge her with extortion, though there'll be lots of extenuating circumstances. I told her to get the best lawyer in town—Danny Meckelwitz. Testro'll pay the fee. Kennedy, he'd die for that gal."

Kennedy stood up. "I'm not going to prefer any charges against Testro. Best thing to do, charge him and Bat and Jazz with disturbing the peace and give 'em a suspended sentence." He went to the door. "Toodle-oo, Skipperino. I feel like a wreck, as if my joints were all knocked loose. I think I will have to fuse them together again with some balm of Bacchus."

Late that night, while he was cleaning up his desk, the skipper looked up and saw Bettdecken standing in the doorway, wearing a fat, worried expression.

"What's got you down, Otto?"

"Kennedy," said Bettdecken. "Patrolman Hauserkranz just called up to say he had to grab Kennedy for obstructin' traffic and asked me what he should do with him. I asked him was Kennedy tight and he said, yes, indeed, Kennedy was plastered. So I said, well, chuck him in the lock-up overnight so he don't get lost and freeze to death, poor fella. I was wondering did I do right."

MacBride said, "You did right, Otto. The guy is screwier than a staircase in a lighthouse. But how the hell could he be holding up traffic?"

"Well, it seems he got a pair of snow-shoes somewhere and was tryin' to snowshoe down Jockey Street. Hauserkranz said he can't snowshoe worth a damn."

MacBride leaned back in his chair, groaned, and closed his eyes.

Fan Dance

Kennedy, like a stick of dynamite, is all right if left alone; but when they start throwing him around—bango!

THE *SUMMIT ARMS* stands on the northeast corner of Summit Avenue and Pencil Street, in the West End of Richmond City. This intersection is the highest point in the city and from the top, the tenth floor of the *Arms,* you can on clear nights see the harbor lights or the Night Express crossing the Eastmarsh Bridge.

It was a clear night and Osborne, gazing through the casement window on the tenth floor, saw the Night Express cross the bridge. He checked his watch with it. Ten-ten. Right. His butler, who had left him a moment before, returned now ushering in Kennedy of the *Free Press,* and then departed.

Osborne said, "Hello, Kennedy," without removing his eyes from the moving lights of the Night Express.

Kennedy, rubbing his chilled hands together, came over to stand beside Osborne. The reporter looked pale and faded in his rumpled suit. The Special Prosecutor was a big man, with amiable shaggy brows, hard padded cheeks, big hands with square-ended fingers. He was in slippers and velvet housecoat and pulled on a triangular cigar. He was fifty, but his eyes were youthful and blue and shrewd.

"Help yourself to a drink, Kennedy."

Kennedy watched the Night Express vanish back of the packing houses, then crossed to a table and poured out some rye. He said, "Flannery'd like a statement before he puts the edition to bed," and downed the drink.

"On what?" Osborne said casually, turning and going to a wing-chair, where he sat down and propped his heels on a footstool.

Kennedy shrugged. "You know as well as I do, Dan. The *Carioca Club.*"

"H'm," mused Osborne.

"The bad news has reached a climax. We're running a statement by Howard Gilcrist, Chairman of the Chamber of Commerce. He wonders why you closed down sixteen night spots in the past two

weeks and omitted to close down the *Carioca Club*. He doesn't think it's an oversight, because you've been prodded on this twice before. He found out that you and Marty Sullivan, the owner of the *Carioca*, went to school together out in Detroit. He claims you're not closing the *Carioca* because Marty Sullivan knows things about you that you wouldn't want publicly known. Would you like to read his statement?"

"Yeah."

Kennedy handed him a typewritten sheet of foolscap. Osborne read it from beginning to end in silence, without a move, without any change of expression. When he had finished he folded the sheet of paper neatly and returned it.

"Thanks," he said. He rose and went to the window and put one hand against the wall and leaned there straight-armed. He nibbled on his lip, his eyelids widening and narrowing. "You're going to print that, of course," he said.

"Have to," said Kennedy.

"Of course," nodded Osborne.

Kennedy said reasonably, "Gilcrist's right. And he's a damned sight more polite about it than a lot of other people. Down in Jockey Street they're saying it's just plain lack of insides—you're afraid of Marty Sullivan."

"Yeah?" said Osborne, squinting at the harbor lights. He turned to Kennedy and smiled and said again, "Yeah?" There was a certain glitter in his smile that was puzzling. "Let's see; tonight's Friday. Isn't it some kind of 'big night' there?"

Kennedy nodded. "Visiting Salesmen's Night. Every Friday night it's something else."

Osborne went to the phone, picked it up. "Yes, Kennedy; I went to school with Marty Sullivan, in a little town outside of Detroit. I used to be a kind of big brother to Marty. Used to fight his fights—well, he was a little guy. I used to lend him pennies, then nickels; and as I grew older, dollars. I saved his life twice as a boy. When I was admitted to the bar. I hung out my shingle in Detroit. He was my first case. I won it. He'd been driving a milk route then and had got

tight and blown in all the money he collected on his route. I got him out of that.... Operator, give me Police Headquarters.... Yes, Kennedy, I've known Marty a long, long time. There was always something about the little runt you couldn't help liking.... Headquarters? This is Dan Osborne. Give me MacBride.... Steve, this is Dan Osborne. Run around and close up the *Carioca*.... Tonight. Make it at about eleven, when his show's on, just for fun."

He hung up, sighed bitterly. "There's your statement, Kennedy."

"Which picture would you like us to use?"

"Better use Marty's. He was always nuts about publicity." Osborne knocked the ash from his cigar. He looked morose, preoccupied. He kept flicking the cigar long after the ash had fallen.

THE police sedan was hiking down Center Avenue at a lively clip. It passed a trolley car on the wrong side, ran through a safety zone, jumped a red light, and cut the inside of the corner going into North Jockey Street.

MacBride, sitting in the back with Moriarity and Cohen, said, "Gahagan, if you got to bust every traffic law that was ever made, why don't you at least use the siren? I haven't heard a peep out of it."

"Ah," yawned Cohen, "he don't like to wake people up."

Moriarity said, "No, Ike; he's just bashful. He don't want everybody to know it's a police car."

"Youse is all wrong," laughed Gahagan coarsely. "I ain't blowing the siren because there *ain't* no siren."

"There ain't no *siren?*" echoed MacBride.

Gahagan said, "Didn't Sergeant Bettdecken tell youse? Ha," chortled Gahagan, "somebody stole the siren this evening while the car was parked in front of Headquarters. Ha, ha!"

MacBride growled, "If you weren't at the wheel of this car, you jackass, I'd kick you in the ear. Last week no lights. The week before no spare tire. This week no siren—"

"Next week, maybe," said Cohen, "no Gahagan."

Gahagan sulked and gunned the car hard down Jockey Street. The animated lights of the *Carioca* bloomed at the bottom of the hill. Cars were parked for blocks around and there were a couple of cops on duty out front. The captain's sedan stopped. The skipper got out and watched the squad car draw up behind. Sergeant Holtzmann climbed out with a flock of uniformed policemen.

The big Negro doorman of the *Carioca* craned his neck and began to look worried. The taxi-cab drivers hanging around began talking among themselves.

The skipper said to Sergeant Holtzmann, "Okey, Rudy. Send a man up to Lark Street and another down to Vickers. Cut traffic out of Jockey between those streets, so we can clean these cars out in a hurry. Detail three men to move these cars quick. You run things outside, and don't let anybody go in the *Carioca*," He looked up. "Here come the two wagons. If anybody gets nasty, pile 'em in and we'll dump 'em later."

"Right, Cap'n."

MacBride raised his voice: "Ike... Mory!"

"Yowssuh."

"Come with me," he said, and picked six more cops.

He picked up the two cops who were standing in front of the entrance. "We're clamping down, boys. You come in with us."

Plain-clothed Sergeant Doake, from the local precinct, touched MacBride on the arm and said, "What kind of a run-around is this?"

"What's eating you, Bennie?"

"Slamming down on Sullivan, I mean. What's the idea? I mean, on a Friday night. Marty'll be sore as a boil."

"I told that little Mick a week ago to go slow. I told him to yank off this fan dancer, or put some clothes on her. I warned him. I warned him that Dan Osborne might put the finger on him any minute."

"But, hell, Cap'n, why didn't you phone him?"

"Bennie, I warned him that when I came around it'd be with bells on."

The skipper opened his overcoat, looked at his watch. It was exactly eleven. "Let's go," he said. He was the first through the door.

The *Carioca* was jammed. There must have been five hundred persons there. The lights were dimmed in the vast room and there was a milky blue spotlight trained on the small, semi-circular stage. This fan dancer had taken the town by storm, not only because of her ability as a dancer and a shocker but also because she had succeeded in keeping her identity hidden. Her slender body was covered with a kind of platinum grease paint. Her face was like a Benda mask—unsmiling, immobile. The traps were rolling, the knocking sound of the gourds was electrifying. The dance was pagan, voluptuous. It was spellbinding. There was not a sound among the five hundred persons seated at the hundred-odd tables.

MacBride tapped the hat-check girl on the shoulder. She turned. He held up his hand and in its palm his badge shone.

"Where's the master switch?" he said.

She stared at him. He gripped her arm, shook her. Frightened, she led him to a door that opened on a small corridor. The switches were in the corridor.

"Bright lights," he said.

She hesitated, her hand resting on one of the levers. He reached up and pulled the lever and he could see a white glare spring into the lobby. He heard the music falter. He heard small, scattered sounds of astonishment. The music dribbled away. There were running footsteps and these culminated in the appearance of Jaeger, the headwaiter—an angry, purpling man.

MacBride blocked him at the corridor entrance, pushed him back into the lobby. "Padlock, Jaeger. Go make your little speech. Tell 'em all to leave quietly."

Jaeger looked incredulous. He spouted, "What's the meaning of this? You can't do this!"

"I know, I know, Jaeger. You're surprised. I didn't warn Marty a week ago. I know, I know—"

"This—this is our biggest night!" choked Jaeger.

"Tough. Go make your speech."

Jaeger's fat jaw shook. "I've got to see Marty first."

MacBride gripped his arm. "Skip that. Do as I tell you, Jaeger, and don't be a dummy."

The sounds of confusion were growing. The waiters were skittering around. Some of the people had risen and were shouting questions. The fan dancer had vanished. There was an air of frustration, of anger. Some began to clap hands, to stamp feet. Chairs scraped.

Jaeger's jaw still shook. He refused to move.

Moriarity walked into the ornate bar and said to the head barman, "Close it up, pal. Lights out."

"Yeah?" said the head barman.

"Honest," said Moriarity.

"I take orders from Mr. Sullivan."

Ike Cohen came in and said, "What's the matter, Mory?"

"Big boy says he takes orders only from Mr. Sullivan."

Ike said, "One, two—"

"Three," said Moriarity, and they dragged the barman across the bar, slapped manacles on him.

"I'll turn the lights out," said the assistant barman.

"You catch on, brother," Cohen grinned.

The uniformed cops began to circulate in the main room. MacBride, his hands in his overcoat pockets, walked hard-heeled down the center of the room, crossed the dance-floor and climbed to the stage.

He said in a loud voice, "Everybody clear out. The place is closed by order of the police. Please go quietly."

"Nuts to the police!" somebody yelled.

Angry voices hummed, surged, broke in a wave. The uniformed cops stood motionless, scattered, saying, "Clear out, clear out."

Somebody threw a bottle. It bounced off the head of Patrolman Mariano, who promptly sat down on the floor. The other cops did not move; their hands tightened on their nightsticks but they did not move. Mariano got up slowly.

"Take it easy, Tony," another cop said.

The women were querulous, insulting. MacBride stood on the stage, his hands on his hips, his nose in the air, his eyes flicking the vast room. Bread, meat, potatoes were thrown at the policemen. Oaths rose. The cops remained motionless; they kept throwing glances at the skipper. He watched. He yelled:

"Come on, come on; clear out!"

Moriarity came up to him. "I can't find Sullivan."

"Look again."

Dan Osborne, in overcoat and derby, walked out on the stage, smiled. "Hello, Steve," he said to MacBride. "Having trouble?"

"Where'd you come from?"

"Oh, I came in the back way."

"Did you see Marty?"

Osborne was still smiling. "No," he said.

Somebody was squirting a siphon at Patrolman Shotz. Patrolman Shotz, cursing under his breath, took it, while his eyes strayed hopefully to MacBride.

A man yelled. "There he is! There's Osborne! Let him have it!"

"Duck, Dan!" MacBride rasped.

"Not me, Skipper."

A flung bottle brought him down.

MacBride, who had seen the thrower, jumped from the stage, barked, "Okey, boys—the mop!" and made a beeline for a tall, blond man who was crowing to his companions, "Did you see me crown him?"

MacBride kicked three chairs out of the way, said, "Yeah, we saw you, sweety pie," and hit him a terrific blow on the chin. The man folded up like a folding chair and lay down. MacBride rapped out, "You other guys bail out! Beat it!"

The nightsticks were chopping. The women were yelping, screaming. One of the cops cut loose with the tear gas. Tables spun over, crockery crashed.

Kennedy was strolling about idly, wandering magically among blows and flung objects that never touched him. MacBride ran into him.

"How'd you get in?" the skipper barked.

"With Dan Osborne. Lively, isn't it?"

"Go up and see if Dan's hurt. He's on the stage." A glass crashed against his shoulder. He looked disgusted. He reached up and stopped in mid-career a water carafe that otherwise would have knocked Kennedy flat. "Go on, Kennedy; get out of this before you get killed."

Ike Cohen appeared saying, "I'm damned if I can find Marty Sullivan."

The tear gas was a great persuader. The crowd began streaming towards the door, leaving behind it a wasteland of broken chairs, crockery, glass, foodstuff. The cops bunched together and herded the crowd out into the street and in a little while only MacBride, Moriarity and Cohen, Kennedy and Dan Osborne remained. Jaeger appeared in a moment, white with rage.

"Look what you done, look what you done!" he choked. "Just look at the place. A wreck!"

"Where's Marty?" the skipper asked.

"How do I know? He was here when the show started. Look, just look at the place! This is an outrage—"

"Yoo-hoo," called Kennedy from the opposite side of the room. "Come over and see what I found."

MacBride strode across the littered dance-floor to where Kennedy was standing. A man lay on the floor against the wall, his body twisted awkwardly, his hard white collar rumpled. His face was discolored.

Near him was a narrow doorway, open.

The skipper muttered, "Good cripes!" and dropped to his knees. When he rose he lifted his chin and called out, "Hey, Dan!"

Osborne came slowly across the floor, holding a handkerchief to a cut on his forehead.

MacBride was pointing. "Marty Sullivan."

"Passed out?" Osborne asked negligently.

"Passed out complete," the skipper said. "Dead."

Osborne stopped. He stared down at Sullivan with blue, expressionless eyes. He patted the cut on his forehead absent-mindedly.

"Choked to death," the skipper said.

"H'm," Osborne mused.

"He must have been choked before the fighting started." Cohen said. "Because I never saw him—not once."

"Me neither," Moriarity said.

MacBride stared towards the door. "Something like this would have to happen," he growled. "And everybody that was sitting around here is now gone out—including the guy that choked him. As sure as we're standing here the opposition press will claim a cop did it. Mark me, fellas; mark me."

Jaeger was shaking all over. His fat hand rose to his lips, his eyes bulged as he stared down at Sullivan.

MacBride went backstage, where half a dozen girls and as many men were sitting around under the uncompromising eye of a policeman.

"Where's the fan dancer?" the skipper asked.

"She musta breezed," the policeman said. He pointed. "That there is her room. The door was locked and I busted it down but she wasn't in there."

MacBride entered the room. A rear window was open and he stuck his head out and saw an alleyway. He returned to the group outside the door.

"Who is this fan dancer?"

One of the girls said, "Ask Mr. Sullivan. He's the only one who knows."

MacBride chuckled ironically, bit the end off a three-cent cigar, lit up.

THE REPERCUSSION was greater than anyone expected. The opposition press, egged on by the Liberal League and insurgent political cliques, exploded; and the backwash was pretty devastating. The Mayor came in for a drubbing for having appointed Dan Osborne to the post of Special Prosecutor in the Chief Executive's vice drive. Osborne himself came in for a merciless hammering. The police were roundly criticized, from the Commissioner down. It came out in the newspapers that Marty Sullivan had been beaten and strangled to death by brutal policemen....

MacBride himself issued a statement denying this charge. He stated that his men had endured all kinds of insults and been at the mercy of the mob for ten minutes before a nightstick was wielded or tear gas unleashed. The opposition press was full of statements of persons who had been in the *Carioca* when the police raided it. Every statement was a hot indictment of the police and of the way the raid was handled. Some threatened court action. No one had actually seen a policeman choke Marty Sullivan to death but since all the statements enumerated acts of brutality on the part of the officers the opposition press felt free to assume that Sullivan had died as a result of an act of police brutality.

City Hall was in an uproar. Committee after committee called on the Mayor. Naturally there had to be lambs for the slaughter. The buck had to be passed. Some palliative had to be given to the outraged opposition press, to the Liberal League, to the political insurgents.

MacBride was suspended for thirty days without pay. The order stated that when he returned to duty it would be as acting captain in some outlying precinct. Moriarity and Cohen were removed from Headquarters to the Ninth Precinct. Every policeman who had taken part in the raid was farmed out to various precincts. The shake-up jarred the whole Department. Captain George Danno, formerly of the Alien Squad, moved into MacBride's office.

"I'm not going to like this job, Steve," he said.

MacBride was bitter, hard-jawed. "I've been taken for a ride, George! I'm the goat! There's an awful boner somewhere and Marty Sullivan was murdered and those crackpots are so anxious to fry me that they forget all about that—they forget that Marty Sullivan was murdered! Okey. I'm suspended. I've been a cop almost thirty years and I'm suspended. I ought to've been kicked in the head the first day I ever put on a uniform. I'm suspended. Okey, I'm suspended. Almost thirty years a cop and because a lot of lousy drunks in a honkytonk start throwing things so fast that a cop has to defend himself—" He threw up his arms and glared at George Danno. "What the hell are cops supposed to be anyhow—part of a daisy chain? This city reeks to high heaven, George!"

Danno looked gloomy. "I know just how you feel, Steve. I only hope I can do half as well here as you've done."

MacBride punched him in the ribs. "Hell, George, you're the tops."

FLANNERY of the *Free Press* said, "This is funny, it's really screwy. Here a guy is ostensibly murdered and all the yelling seems to be about something else. About City Hall and the Special Prosecutor and Steve MacBride, with a generous history, not complimentary, of City Hall and the Police Department thrown in. If it makes sense, if it even makes news—then I'm a punk editor."

"I would never argue with you," Kennedy said dreamily.

"I wasn't talking to you. I was thinking out loud. I told you years ago that one day MacBride would go a step too far and get himself a Bronx cheer, with trimmings."

Kennedy yawned. "The skipper is a big bull-headed mutt. He's got a one-track mind and he thinks that shield he wears is another kind of bible. It never occurs to him to walk around a tree, he's got to batter his head against it. To him the law, my friend, is the law: good, bad, or indifferent, it's the law. He carries it out as strictly on himself as on any heel that he picks up. Sometimes I think he's goofy. I don't approve of his outlook on life, his foolhardy honesty, his blind loyalty to his shield. But I like him. He's probably the best friend I've got. That being the case"—he rose wearily, a spare shadow of a man, frail, emaciated—"something's got to be done about conditions in Denmark. They seem to be particularly dirty. Would you have a drink in that desk of yours?"

"I would not."

"You would not, of course. If I ever saw a bottle come out of that desk I'd swear it was a mirage. Toodle-oo."

"Where you going?"

"To investigate conditions in Denmark."

Flannery barked, "Be sure to keep your name and address on you, in case you pass out drunk somewhere, so they'll know where to take you."

Kennedy shivered as he stepped into the bitter wind that slammed down Hill Street. The threadbare light topcoat he wore was hardly adequate for midwinter weather. His shoes were low, thin; his socks silk. His suit had been intended for spring. It wasn't that he didn't have the money; he just never got around to buying things for himself.

When he reached Dan Osborne's office, in the Municipal Building, he was jittery with the cold and his skinny hands were almost blue. The office was warm. Dan Osborne looked warm and comfortable in a gray herringbone suit. He was leaning on his elbows on the desk—a neat, well-groomed, healthy-looking man, amiable as always, even when he was worried. He puffed a triangular cigar.

Kennedy sat down on a radiator. Osborne had not spoken; he had evidently been following a line of thought, and though his eyes greeted Kennedy familiarly, he did not utter a word for several minutes. Finally he sat back, shrugged, smiled ruefully.

"I got Steve MacBride in a nice jam, didn't I, Kennedy?"

"I don't think he figures you did."

Osborne's large, well-packed face looked grave. He said, "I did all I could, Kennedy. I talked with the Mayor, with the Commissioner. I offered to resign if they'd keep the ax off Steve's head." He shook his head. "They wouldn't hear of it."

Kennedy smiled. "The Mayor couldn't afford to do that. He appointed you. He couldn't lose face by kicking you out. He didn't appoint MacBride. Hence… MacBride."

"I suppose so," Osborne sighed. "You don't think Sullivan was accidentally killed by a cop, do you?"

Kennedy said, "Sullivan wasn't accidentally killed and he wasn't killed by Steve's flying squad. I was there about a minute before the cops cut loose. I didn't see Marty anywhere. If Marty was alive then he'd have been on his feet. He wasn't alive. He was dead then. Up till then, up until the time Steve turned the bright lights on, the place was practically in darkness, except for the stage. Everybody's eyes were glued on the fan dancer.

"We know now that Marty Sullivan was alone at the table. The table was against the wall, the chair he was sitting on was next to that door that leads back to his office and the men's lavatory. Somebody could have stepped through the door. The drums and the gourds were pretty loud. Somebody could have stepped through that door and throttled him then, while the music was loud, while everybody was watching the fan dancer."

Osborne's blue eyes were fixed intently on Kennedy; they remained so fixed for a moment after Kennedy had finished talking.

Kennedy went on: "You and I went in the back way. We got in about five minutes before Steve turned the bright lights on. I left you and went up front to see the thing break. You said you wanted to stay back to get a close-up of the fan dancer when she came off the stage."

He said no more. He got off the radiator and rubbed his hands together and stared dreamily at the floor. Osborne never took his eyes off him. There was a peculiar quality to the silence that ensued for a long minute. Then Kennedy took a rumpled packet of cigarettes from his pocket and lit one.

He said. "Why, Dan, did you really hold off raiding the *Carioca* until you absolutely had to?"

Osborne sat back and seemed depressed. "Marty," he said. "I told him several times to cut out the undressed shows and especially the fan dancer. He laughed at me. He never took me seriously. I was trying to give him a break. He thought it was fun to goad me, I guess. He was that kind of a guy."

"No other reason, huh?"

Osborne looked up, smiled blandly. "Of course not."

Kennedy inhaled. "This thing might break Steve's heart," he said. "As far as I know, he's never had a mark against him. He's a proud guy. So proud that sometimes he's funny. I don't approve of a guy being as proud as he is, but he's that way, and that's that. Sullivan was murdered. The fan dancer disappears. She doesn't show up. There's a connection. Got to be. Between her and the murder of Marty Sullivan. If the opposition press keeps hammering long enough, everybody'll believe that the cops actually killed Sullivan. They didn't. I know they didn't. I hate to have to prove it, it entails too much work, but I guess I'll have to. Not because I want any glory. Hell, I hate guys who want glory. I hate work. I hate to have to prove things. But I've got to. They've railroaded the skipper and—"

The door opened and Lakeman, one of Osborne's field men, appeared red-nosed from the cold outdoors, and excited.

"Later, Sam," Osborne clipped. "I'm in conference."

Lakeman was breathless: "But I—"

"Later, I said!"

Lakeman looked confused, injured. He shrugged and backed out, closing the door.

Osborne said, "Lakeman's enthusiasm sometimes runs away with him. I'm inclined to believe with you, Kennedy, that Marty was murdered. If you can prove it, they'll have to reinstate MacBride—because they suspended him on the premise that Marty was accidentally killed when MacBride let his men get out of hand. Good luck. And on your way out tell Lakeman to come in."

Kennedy took a cab to the South Side. He rode huddled in the back seat, half-asleep, his body jolting as the cab jolted. When he got out of the cab in Trumpet Street he fumbled sleepily in his pockets, brought a couple of bills out and gave one to the driver. He tipped a dime and, yawning and shivering, climbed the steps of the old brownstone and was let in by the superintendent.

"Where's Mr. Jaeger's apartment?"

"On the second floor. Number Six."

Kennedy climbed slowly, his head between his huddled shoulders, and knocked on the door of Number Six. It was opened after a couple of minutes by the headwaiter of the *Carioca*. Jaeger was in a bathrobe. His eyes were bloodshot, his fat face pasty, his stringy hair uncombed.

"What do you want, what do you want?" he asked irritably.

"I'm Kennedy from the *Free Press*. I want to talk to you."

"Listen, I don't want to talk to anybody. I'm sick. I got a headache and a bellyache and I'm sick. Go 'way."

"What you need is a drink. I need one, too."

"What do you want?"

"Talk to you."

"Listen, I told you I don't want to talk to you. Why should I have to talk to people when I got a headache and a bellyache? Go 'way."

Kennedy stepped on his slippered foot and Jaeger yelped and teetered and Kennedy walked in saying, "And don't strike me, because I'm undernourished and you might kill me."

Jaeger, bulky and ungainly in his bathrobe, looked angry and vexed. Kennedy strolled past him into a large, clean, shabby living-room and saw a woman sitting on a straight-backed chair smoking a cigarette. She was stout, fifty-odd, with a swell head of red hair, painted lips, and she wore a mink coat, open and thrown back.

She said to Jaeger, "Who's the nasty man, Hermie?"

"He's one of those damned newspaper guys," Jaeger crabbed.

"The name, madam, is Kennedy. And yours?"

"Lady Godiva."

"I thought she was a blonde and rode a horse, or maybe the horse was blond."

"He's a wise guy, too," observed the woman, steely-eyed.

Kennedy said, "I'm just a poor scrivener."

"If scrivener means scarecrow, you're it, except that I've seen more attractive scarecrows in my time. So sorry to have you go. You must drop by again sometime when nobody's home, laddy."

Kennedy calmly turned his back on her and addressed Jaeger: "Where was the last place you saw Marty Sullivan before the cops arrived?"

Jaeger looked miserable. "Now listen, buddy. I got a headache, see? My head is near to bust, see? I got a bellyache, too. I feel lousy."

"Where was Marty?"

Jaeger held his head between his hands and groaned. "Where he always was, I guess. At the table he was always at. How do I know? I was busy."

"The table where we found him dead?"

"Sure. Sure. Listen, buddy—"

"Then he always sat at the table, eh?"

Jaeger rocked his head in his hands. "Sure—sure he did, when he wasn't nowhere else. How do I know? Can I be ten places at the one time? Oh, my head—what a head I got—Ooo, what a head I got! Listen—please do me a favor—go somewheres else."

Kennedy sat down.

Jaeger shook a finger at him. "If you don't, I—I will! I can't stand to be annoyed this morning. Not with this head I got."

Kennedy said, "Calm yourself. I'm trying to find out who killed Marty Sullivan."

"Ah, *you're* trying to find out! Now ain't that something!"

"You," said the woman to Kennedy, "don't look as if you could find your way home, even with a map. Why don't you throw him out, Hermie?"

Jaeger sobbed, "Me—with my head—I should throw anybody out? No. No. No! It'd jar my head right off, Emmy." He groaned and fled into another room, slamming the door.

Emmy said, "See here, half-pint, why don't you take the air? They say fresh air is healthy and you don't look as if a little fresh air would hurt you. Hermie's got a hangover."

"And I've got a yen to ask him things," Kennedy said, rising and drifting towards the closed door.

Emmy jumped up and got in his way. She was a big woman. In her day, she must have been handsome, with that head of hair. But her eyes were too much like steel now, her mouth too hard.

"Get out," she said.

"Sit down and tend to your knitting."

"I never knit. Get out. Hermie's got a hangover."

"Please—"

"You don't have to be polite, laddy. Pick up your dogs and shuffle."

He started to brush her negligently aside. She doubled her fist and let him have it flush on the jaw. He reeled backward, tripped and fell flat on his back. She jumped after him, grabbed him by the back of the collar, dragged him across the floor, opened the corridor door and then dragged him to the head of the staircase. Saying, "This is called the shoot-the-chute," she started him headlong down the staircase, turned and went back into the apartment.

He lay for minutes in the hallway below, thinking things over. Then he got painfully to his feet, opened the hall door and went outside. He stood for a minute in the wind, shivering, his teeth knocking. A cab came along and he flagged it and said, "Go to the *Carioca Club.*"

THEY had closed, padlocked the *Carioca*. By daylight its façade looked tarnished, drab, and the street itself was no beauty spot. The shutters had been closed, the canvas marquee removed.

Kennedy leaned against a pole across the street, eyeing the building as though he hoped to wring some secret from its yellow brick walls. There was no evidence of anyone being about. The building yawned with desertion. After a while he turned up his collar, crossed the street and followed the service alleyway to the rear of the building, to a square cindered yard. There were a dozen garbage drums lined up, waiting to be removed. He tried a couple of windows but they were locked. He tried a couple of doors. They were locked also. He blew his breath into his cold hands, drummed his cold feet. He tried a third door and almost fell down when it swung inward at his touch. Instead of entering immediately, he remained on the threshold, pondering. Then he stepped in, closed the door quietly.

He was in a small room and there were half a dozen battered easy chairs standing around. There was a phone on the wall and against the wall a table littered with magazines. A door leading from this room was ajar. He sauntered through it and into a narrower room fitted with rods and coat hangers and on some of these hangers there were ballet dresses. There was daylight, but it was dim, feeble.

Suddenly he found himself on the small stage, with the vast sweep of the main dining-room before him. A rectangular skylight admitted light but could not dispel the gloom of the place. Wreckage was still scattered all over the dance-floor. Nothing apparently had been removed, or even straightened. The inside of the building was, without the aid of incandescents, more drab than the outside.

Taking his time, he crossed the dance-floor to the table at which Marty Sullivan had died. He stepped into the narrow doorway there, reached out to the point where the chair on which Sullivan had sat still stood. He nodded to himself, then entered the corridor which gave off the doorway. He followed this rearward to a point outside the dressing-room, where he remembered he had left Dan Osborne.

There was an L in the corridor and he took it, feeling his way now, for no daylight penetrated here. He stopped short when small sounds came to his ears. He did not move for a full two minutes. The sounds were nearby, small, unsteady, erratic. With his fingertips feeling along the wall, he proceeded. Suddenly he was in front of an open doorway and saw beyond, in a small room, a glowing flashlight aimed downward on a littered desk. A small hand, white-gloved, was scattering papers to left and right.

A woman's hand. He could tell that she was slender. Vagrant offshoots of the flashlight's glow showed him, intermittently, a young woman's face, lean, desperate-lipped. A cloth coat of some dark red material with a thick fur collar. On her head, cocked over one eye, a moderated shako. She was, he thought, very good-looking in a strange, black-eyed, desperate way.

He did not enter the room. He did not make his presence known. Slowly, step by step, he backed up, then turned and made his way cautiously back to the main corridor. He left by the door through which he had entered the building, walked to the street and entered a bar a few doors away. He ordered rye and stood at the front end of the bar, where he could see the alleyway of the *Carioca*.

"The cops sure mopped that place up across the street," the bartender said.

"Yeah," said Kennedy.

"The bums."

"Yeah."

"But I see they got theirs. That flatfoot MacBride, too."

"Yeah."

"Ever since I'm a kid I have got no use for cops. They're bums."

Kennedy threw a half-dollar on the bar, picked up the fifteen cents in change and watched the girl in the black shako walk past. She looked lean, lithe, muscular. He opened the door and drifted into the street and followed her, though you would never have guessed he was following anybody. Though she walked rapidly he could tell that she was watching for a cab. One came along, but he was nearer, so he grabbed it. There were not many cabs afield in this neighborhood.

Kennedy said to the driver, "I'm going to get off at the next block. Make a right turn and stop. The girl in the funny hat we just passed is looking for a cab. She'll see you parked there and probably want to get in. When she gives you the address, say you're hired."

"Nix. It ain't legal."

Kennedy showed him his press card. "How'd you like to get your picture in the paper and a notice saying you're the most polite driver in the city?"

"Was that the dame we just passed?"

There was a cigar store on the corner and Kennedy, leaving the cab, went in to get a deck of cigarettes. Through the glass door he saw the girl approach the cab, pull open the cab's door and say something to the driver. The driver shrugged. The girl made an impatient gesture and walked on. Kennedy went out.

The driver said, "Six-fourteen Westland."

"Let's go."

"Where?"

"Six-fourteen Westland."

The cab swung around in the middle of the street and headed westward through the city, skirting the untidy hem of Little Italy. Fifteen minutes later it wheeled into Westland, in the two-hundred block. As it pulled up, four blocks beyond, in front of the *Somerset House,* Kennedy saw Dan Osborne come out of the doorway, cross the sidewalk and climb into a Ford coupé, which he drove off.

The *Somerset* was an old hotel that had been refurbished during the past year. It was second-rate, showy, with a popular coffee shop and a rowdy bar. A lot of traveling men stopped there. The rates were low, the hotel was convenient to the trolley lines, buses, and the shopping center, and it had a lot of sample rooms. It did a thriving business.

"Well, this must be six-fourteen," the driver said, squinting. "I wonder why the hell she didn't just say the *Somerset.*"

"You sure you got the number right?"

"Sure I got the number. I pride meself on gettin' numbers right."

Kennedy climbed out, paid up and meandered into the garish lobby. He was still puzzled about Osborne. Not that Osborne didn't have a right to come in or go out of the *Somerset;* but under the circumstances....

Kennedy shrugged. He considered the possibility of snatching a drink, but the bar was downstairs, at the other end of the lobby, and he gave up the idea. He placed himself just inside the main entrance, and when, five minutes later, he saw the girl alight from a cab he crossed to the desk, showed his press card and said:

"Is Benedictine Krause, the actress, stopping here?"

"Benedictine Krause?" the clerk asked, puzzled.

"She's that new Alsatian actress. I heard she was in town. I'm trying to find out where she's staying."

"I never heard of Benedictine Krause."

"Sorry," said Kennedy, and turning leisurely, broke open a packet of cigarettes.

The girl in the black shako came up to the panel beside the desk and picked up one of three house phones. Kennedy heard her say:

"Mr. Webb, please." And in a moment: "Joel?... Inez. Listen, Joel," she said in a taut, fearful voice, "I didn't find it.... Yes, everywhere.... Everywhere, I tell you!... I'm down here in the lobby... I just came from there.... No, no, Joel! I tell you I looked everywhere! There's no use talking over the phone this way. I'll come up.... But I must see you!... Well, all right.... All right.... But make sure you call me."

Kennedy walked out to the sidewalk, drew a cigarette out of the packet he had opened and stood on the curb lighting up in the wind. The girl almost brushed his shoulder.

"Go to nine-ten Waterford," she said to the driver of the cab parked there.

Kennedy tossed away the match and re-entered the lobby and strolled up to the desk.

The clerk said, "I just asked one of the operators if she ever heard of Benedictine Krause and she said no."

"Well, look," said Kennedy. "You have a Joel Webb stopping here, haven't you?"

The clerk referred to his card index, said, "Yes."

"Ah," said Kennedy, rubbing his hands. "That's the man was supposed to have brought her to America. I knew him when I was covering the shows in New York. I'll surprise him. What room's he in?"

The clerk grinned. "Five-o-five."

Kennedy winked. "Mum's the word."

"Mum's the word," nodded the clerk, also winking.

MR. JOEL WEBB was a long-legged young man with crisp brown hair, impetuous blue eyes, and a small but determined mouth. He looked upset, harried, but by no means abject. His neck was lean, wiry, his chin aggressive.

"Well?" he demanded of Kennedy, who drowsed in the doorway.

"I've got something very important to tell you, Mr. Webb,"

"Okey. Tell it."

"It will take time and I wouldn't want passersby to hear it."

"Well," snapped Webb, "come in then."

Kennedy sighed pleasurably and drifted into the small bedroom and Webb closed the door, barged across the room, found a pipe and piled tobacco into the bowl. He was still upset, still harassed, and apparently more preoccupied with his own thoughts than he was interested in the presence of Kennedy. But in a minute he seemed to remember that Kennedy was in the room. He snapped:

"Well, well, come on, come on. You've got something to tell me. Spill it, spill it."

Kennedy was half-reclining on the bed. "My name is Kennedy."

"All right, your name is Kennedy. So what?"

"So this, Mr. Webb. What was Inez looking for at the *Carioca* about half an hour ago?"

Webb, who had struck a match and was about to light his pipe, dropped the pipe and the match.

"Better step on the match," Kennedy recommended placidly.

Webb slapped his foot down on the burning match, put it out. His eyes bounced on Kennedy, his lips tightened, his lean jaw grew hard. He turned and strode to the window, rubbed the back of his neck. He swiveled. He leveled an arm at Kennedy and seemed all set to unleash a torrent of invective. But instantly he appeared to change his mind. He did change his mind. He came over and sat on the bed and said rapidly and in a low, earnest voice:

"Now be reasonable, Mr. Kennedy. Inez and I were at the *Carioca* the night the police raided it. We had to get out in a hurry. In the rush, Inez lost her handbag—a little bag—oh, you know, one of those small mesh bags." He eyed Kennedy steadily. "You're a broad-minded man, aren't you?"

"Very."

"Well, look now," Webb went on confidentially. "Inez and I went to school together. We're old friends. I've been away, oh, for years, and when I came back, why, Inez was married. She's been married for three years. To a nice guy, but"—he wagged his finger—"a very jealous guy. He'll never let Inez see anybody, even her old friends. You understand, things between Inez and me are strictly on the level. But we went out that night.

"We went to the *Carioca*. She lost this handbag, with some of her cards in it. She was afraid it would be found and her husband would find out that she was there. She said she was going to try to get in the *Carioca* and see if she could find it. I told her not to. I told her that if the worse went to the worst, I'd explain everything to her husband. But she wouldn't listen. She went to the *Carioca* to see if she could find the bag. For God's sake, mister, don't tell her husband. He's a nice guy, a swell guy, only he's jealous—and if I thought I'd make trouble for Inez, why, I'd never forgive myself."

Kennedy sat up, scratched his ear, smiled dreamily. He rose from the bed, chuckled reflectively, and wandered to the door.

"Okey, Mr. Webb," he said. "I believe you implicitly."

"Gee, that's swell of you."

"Don't mention it. I was just keeping an eye out on the *Carioca* and I saw Inez come out. No harm done. If I run across the bag, I'll return it to you."

Webb actually beamed. "Will you! Say, you're a regular guy, Mr. Kennedy!"

Kennedy went down to the lobby, entered a phone booth and called Flannery at the office. "Listen," he said, "I've run into something that's worth fooling around with but I can't be sixty-eight places at one time, so I'll need some help.... Well, I want a guy to tail a guy.... Is Tucker around?... Well, send him over to the *Somerset House*. Pronto, baby."

Tucker arrived ten minutes later. He was a small, slight, middle-aged man, who wore spectacles. A derby was perched high on the top of his head. He looked innocuous, simple-minded, but he was a good man on spot news and a good all-around newshawk. You would expect him to speak softly, precisely, apologetically.

He said, "Is this on the level, bozo, or is it just one of your practical jokes?"

Kennedy said, "Level as a mill pond, Tucks. I want you to tail a guy. Don't let him out of your sight. Check every place he visits. If he tries to take a train, a plane, a boat, or a bus—have him pinched."

"On what charge?"

"Any charge. Rough-house him, stick your watch in his pocket and then tell a cop he stole it. Anything to hold him. His name is Joel Webb. He's stopping here. In five-o-five. Go up to the fifth corridor and float up and down. If he leaves, tail him. If he comes down while you're on the way up, I'll tail him and send up a bellhop to tell you. If a hop doesn't come in five minutes, you'll know Webb's still in his room. Got it?"

"Sure," said Tucker, and took an elevator up.

Kennedy waited five minutes, then left.

The cab he rode in had a broken window and before it had gone six blocks Kennedy was chilled to the bone. He called out:

"Stop at *Enrico's*." And when the cab stopped in front of *Enrico's*, in Flamingo Street: "Wait for me."

MacBride was sitting at the bar eating ham and baked beans and drinking beer. Paderoofski, the barman, was paring his fingernails. His huge eyebrows shot halfway up his forehead and he grinned, greeted:

"Hah, Meester Kennedy, no seeing for a long time, mebbe t'ree days. Huss afry leetle t'ing?"

"Jake, Paderoofski. You're looking tip-top."

"Shoo, I'm alwuz top-tip. M' wife she's say, 'Honey-bun, youzza top-tip, youzza da berries, youzza da coffee in m' crim.' Honey-bun she's call me."

MacBride looked sour. He muttered, "Honey-bun!"

"Shoo, Honey-bun. She's swal nackneem, no?"

MacBride glared at him, swallowed, went on eating.

"Rye," said Kennedy. "And don't mind the skipper. Somebody hit him in the face with a bottle of sour cream. Well, well, Captain MacBride! Fancy meeting you here!"

"Nuts," said MacBride.

"How is everything at Headquarters, Stevie?"

"Nuts."

"Still working as hard as ever?"

"Nuts."

"Ha—nots!" laughed Paderoofski.

MacBride stabbed him with a violent stare, picked up his food and his drink and moved to the other end of the bar.

Paderoofski scratched the top of his head with the middle finger of his left hand, and wondered what he had done.

Kennedy picked up his drink and made his way amiably to the end of the bar where the skipper had gone. The skipper pointed with his fork, growled:

"Lay off, Kennedy. I feel meaner than a mad dog. I feel so mean I can't even be civil to my wife. Now I don't have to be civil in a public bar and I don't intend to be. The reason why I came here was because I wouldn't have to be civil. And I don't want any suggestions, any sympathy, or any razzberry. In fact, I don't want anything—from you or anybody else. I want to be left alone. If people don't leave me alone I'm going to punch them in the nose."

Kennedy chuckled, downed his drink and skated the empty glass down the bar. From the doorway he saluted, saying gaily:

"Tally-ho, Skippery-wippery."

MacBride glared at him.

NUMBER 910 WATERFORD was a greystone apartment house of six stories built around a small circular court which had a circular driveway. The lobby was at the back of the circle. There was no desk but there was a rack for letters and a small switchboard and a mopey negro in plum-colored livery. His eyes were only one-third open and he sat on a high stool, droop-shoulder, with his lower lip hanging down to his chin.

"Hello, George," Kennedy said.

"Cunningham is m' name."

"I'm looking for an attractive young lady who wears a hat that looks something like a coal scuttle."

The negro suddenly burst into a guffaw and slapped himself on the knee. "Boss man, you took de words right outen ma mowf! It sho' do look like unto a coal scuttle! Yassuh, boss man cap'n, it sho' do!" Then suddenly he was morose again and seemed on the point of falling asleep.

"Cunningham—"

"Folks don't call me Cunningham, boss. Dey call me Oscar."

"Well, Oscar, I'd like to see Miss Inez. She's in two-five, isn't she?"

"No, suh. She's in four-eight."

You operated the elevator yourself.

There was a white button alongside the door numbered 48 and Kennedy, looking tranquilly pleased with himself, pressed it. He heard prompt footsteps. The door opened and he was face to face with the girl. Even without the shako she looked striking. Her throat was slender but strong, her face was angular, handsome, with wide full lips. Her eyes were like two jets of black fire—full of passion and, he thought, couched with tragedy.

"I bring important news from Joel Webb," said Kennedy.

She started. Her eyes leaped, then settled. "Come in," she said in a low, curious voice.

He entered blithely and strolled through a small foyer and into a living-room. As he tossed his hat on to the divan a shape bulked in the bedroom doorway. The woman Emmy, who had thrown him out of Jaeger's place. She scowled. Her eyes darkened and hardened and she snapped at the girl:

"Who let him in?"

"Why—I did. He said—"

"He said!" snarled Emmy, striding into the room. "You," she commanded the girl, "get in the bedroom. Get!"

The girl ran into the bedroom and Emmy closed the door after her, locked it.

Kennedy sighed, "Well, it's a small world after all."

The woman pivoted. "It's probably going to be smaller than you ever thought it was before, smart guy," she growled. "How did you find out she lived here?"

"I heard her give the address to a taxi driver."

"You stinking liar!"

He shrugged philosophically. "Okey, Emmy. No matter how I got here, I'm here. I don't want to talk to you, Godiva. I want to talk to the girl."

Emmy laughed harshly, dangerously. "And why, laddie?"

"I want to find out what she was looking for in the *Carioca* this morning."

Emmy put her hands on her hips. She grinned broadly, showing all her teeth; but there was no mirth in that grin. Her eyes shimmered. "Now ain't that just wonderful!" she mocked. "The little newspaperman wants to find out what she was looking for in the *Carioca!*"

"Emmy," said Kennedy, "let us have done with this repartee. It is written in the stars that I must meet the girl." His voice was tranquil, there was the barest shadow of a smile on his lips. He was genial and good-natured, but even so a man can be purposeful. Kennedy was purposeful without being dramatically high-flown about it. He said in his gentle, almost coaxing voice:

"Open the door, Emmy."

He had never seen a woman tower the way Emmy towered. The rage which had started burning within her was whipped to white heat by his casual, easygoing manner; harsh words could not have enraged her more. Hatred and fury lashed out from her eyes. Her lips tightened and worked against each other and her jaw hardened and seemed to grow larger. She seemed to expand, to swell all over, and Kennedy expected to hear an unleashed torrent of abuse and invective.

But Emmy turned suddenly and walked hard-heeled into a small pantry, her elbows out from her side, her arms swinging. She reappeared instantly with a twelve-inch heavy carving knife gripped in her hand. Her voice was thick, rasping:

"So you'll shove your nose into my business, will you!"

She bore down on him and there was no doubt in his mind about what she intended doing. He scooped up a pillow and flung it and she was so primed to strike that instantly the blade wheeled. Its point pierced the pillow and when she saw this she cried out hoarsely, ripped the pillow free and hurled it away.

Kennedy was at the other end of the room. He said dryly, watchfully, "If you've got a head, Emmy, use it now. Put that cleaver away."

She made no reply. Her broad nostrils twitched. With her left hand she swept a chair out of the way. She headed across the room and on the way she used her left hand to pick up a vase. She hurled the vase at him and then charged with the knife. He was watching both, but the vase caught him; it shattered against his head, brought blood to his forehead. The pain was so sharp that he flung himself halfway across the room on the reflex. He would have gone farther, but the open pantry door stopped him. It stopped him abruptly, jarred his whole body. In trying to steady himself, he reached out a hand blindly. It caught the top of a light chair and closed on it.

His eyes danced and he saw two or three Emmies coming at him, two or three knives sweeping towards him. Even in this split second he must have realized that it would be just as fatal to remain motionless as to take a swing. He gripped the chair with both hands, took a swing and connected and instead of feeling the swift incision of a knife he felt the hard bulk of the woman crash awkwardly against him, then fall away and crash to the floor. The knife was out of her hand. He did not see it anywhere. Then he saw it imbedded in the pantry door, its handle still quivering. Emmy lay in a heap, quite senseless.

Kennedy staggered to the bedroom door, unlocked it and tripped on his way into the bedroom. Rising, he looked around. Things still danced before his eyes and his head, having stopped the vase and been stopped by the pantry door, seemed to be jogging up and down on his shoulders. But he could see that the girl was not in the room. He looked under the twin beds. The bathroom was empty. So was a closet. Then he saw an open window and bowled across to it, thrust out his head. There was a fire-escape leading to a rear alleyway. The cold air felt good. He saw drops of blood falling on the windowsill and remembered his head. As he pulled his head in he heard a door slam.

Turning unsteadily, breathing heavily, he saw that the connecting door, through which he had entered, was closed. He fell on it, fought the knob. It was locked. Then he saw a door which he had overlooked before and stumbled towards it, yanked it open. But it was only another closet. He did not close it instantly, however. Reaching in, he withdrew an immense white fan. He made a small, rueful sound. Then he noticed that drops of blood were falling on the fan. His head felt like a huge red-hot clinker. He dropped the fan and went into the bathroom.

He washed the blood from his face and painted three cuts with iodine. His stomach felt a little shaky too by this time, so he took some bicarbonate of soda. Then he returned to the bedroom, picked up a chair and broke down the connecting door. The living-room was empty but on the floor next to the rim of the carpet the stub of a cigar smoldered. It was triangular in shape.

THE BEATING-UP called for a drink. After a ten-minute talk with the plum-liveried negro, Kennedy hopped a cab and returned to *Enrico's*, hoping to catch MacBride. But MacBride had left.

"Did he say where?"

Paderoofski shook his head. "He's say he was take his car and go f'r a long ride, suzz he's not pastered by pipple. It's to me a great mysterium, the skipper he's so axcitement."

Kennedy sighed, "The lug would do something like that," and turned to go. But he saw Jaeger sitting at a corner table, obviously plastered to the eyebrows. Jaeger's eyes wore that dizzy expression of a drunk who sees nothing, hears nothing. Kennedy strolled over and sat down opposite him, saying, "Trying a bit of the hair of the dog, eh?"

Jaeger's fat brown eyes revolved, his big head wobbled. It took him a minute to place Kennedy. "Yeah," he said, "I'm having a li'l' pick-me-up."

"How long have you known Emmy Canfield?"

"Lishen. When I'm on the job, and I'm a damn' goodsh head-waisher, I"—he waved his index finger—"never tush drop likker. Never! Likker 'n' work don't mix, hah? Nope. But no job, no work—so drink likker. Hah? Sure."

"How long have you known Emmy Canfield?"

"Never, never mixsh work 'n' likker, my friend. Don't pay. Lookit me—besh headwaisher in business. Why? Never mixsh work 'n' likker."

"Does Emmy Canfield come from Detroit?"

"Emmy? Sure. Everybody cumsh from Detroit. Ever know that? Hah? Sure. Lots 'n' lots people cumsh from Detroit."

"When did Emmy come from Detroit?"

"Shanksgibbin Day."

"Thanksgiving Day?"

Jaeger banged the table petulantly. "Damn it, di'n't I shay Shanks-gibbin Day!"

"Did she kill Marty Sullivan?"

Jaeger's eyes bounced. He stared stupidly at Kennedy for a full minute, then began to chuckle. His chuckle grew and grew until it became a laugh and then he was roaring, shaking with laughter, the tears streaming down his face. He put his head on the table and laughed and laughed and slapped the table uproariously with his hands. Then suddenly he sat up and looked grave in the manner that only drunks can look grave.

"Me," he said, touching his chest, "I killed Marty."

"Why?"

"Sh!" whispered Jaeger, leaning forward. "Becaush hish left eyebrow wash yeller an' hish right wash black. Time an' time again I ashked him, please, Marty, either bleach black one 'r dye yeller one. He laughs at me. Laughs at me! Sho I kill him. Ha, ha, ha! Pretty good, hah!" He hiccoughed. "Well, think I'll git drunk. *Ober!* Rye!" He giggled and pawed his face and shook with silent mirth.

Kennedy gave it up. He rose, turned up the collar of his topcoat and went out. He took a cab to the *Free Press* and had a talk with Flannery and then he made a long distance call and spent twenty minutes on the wire.

IT WAS three o'clock when he drifted into Dan Osborne's office. Osborne, busy with a sheaf of papers, looked up, frowned, and sat back. He said with real concern:

"What the hell happened to your face?"

Kennedy was tranquil. "When are you going to put your cards on the table, Dan?"

"What are we playing," Osborne grinned, "poker?"

"I don't know what you're playing, Dan."

Osborne chuckled good-naturedly.

"What's troubling you, kid? Let's have it."

"What were you doing at the *Somerset* this morning?"

"Telling the manager that his cocktail-hour entertainment was not funny, it was smutty. He was reasonable. He said he'd cut it out. Why?"

Kennedy went over and stood by the window, his hands in his pockets. He gazed drowsily down at the street traffic for a minute, then turned and sat on the broad windowsill, his feet dangling.

He said, "I always thought you were a bachelor."

"I am."

"You weren't always."

Osborne sat back, clasped his hands behind his head and smiled jovially. "Been checking up?"

"Where's the wife?"

"Kennedy, I married twenty-four years ago. A girl named Sally McLean. She ran away from me three months after we were married. I never heard of her again."

"Ever hear of Emmy Canfield?"

"No."

"Inez Canfield?"

"No."

"Ever been in apartment forty-eight at nine-ten Waterford?"

"No." Osborne leaned forward. "Why?"

Kennedy crossed to the desk, opened the humidor and lifted out a triangular cigar. "I found one of these in that apartment."

"I suppose other men smoke them, too."

"I suppose so." Kennedy dropped the cigar into the box. "It happens to be the place where I got beaten up. I found the fan dancer there."

Osborne's eyes were steady. "Where is she?"

"She skipped. Her name's Inez Canfield. Her mother's name is Emmy Canfield. Emmy's an Amazon. She came at me with a knife and while she was doing it Inez left by a fire-escape, from another room. I knocked Emmy out with a chair and went in the other room to get Inez. But she was gone and while I was looking out a window the connecting door slammed and I was locked in. When I broke it down, Emmy was gone, too. There was this triangular cigar, still burning, on the floor."

"You figure that somebody came in and took Emmy out, eh?"

Kennedy looked at him. "Yeah."

Osborne knit his brows thoughtfully. His eyes stared at the surface of the desk, glazed with thought, and his fingers drummed lightly on the square blotter. After a couple of minutes he shook his head, said, "I can't make it out, Kennedy."

"You wouldn't happen to know a young fellow named Joel Webb, would you?"

"No." He looked up. "Who is he?"

"He's in the puzzle, too. He's stopping at the *Somerset*."

Osborne sat back. "Oh, so that's who you thought I went to see. Did you grab him?"

"No. I put a tail on him. I didn't want to grab anybody until I had a talk with you."

Osborne eyed him speculatively. "I can't make you out, kid. But you needn't worry about me. Grab anybody you like."

Kennedy dropped his eyes, gazed curiously at the floor. Then he turned and went out slowly, his head still lowered. He was still in a kind of day-dream when he reached the street, but the sharp wind roused him and he looked up as if surprised to find himself there. He walked around to the *Free Press* office and found Tucker sitting gloomily in the office.

Kennedy said, "Don't tell me you lost him."

"He checked out of the *Somerset* with a bag and took a cab and I took another cab. The cab I took got a flat and before I could get another your special oyster was among the missing. I shot right down to the railroad station, got in a booth where I could watch people come in and phoned Bob Angler at the airport. I told him to watch and see if Webb took a plane—gave him a description of the guy. Well, he didn't show up at the railroad station and according to Bob Angler he didn't show up at the airport."

"When did you lose him?"

"Two hours ago. What happened to your face?"

"It's a rash. I get it every winter."

Kennedy killed a couple of hours floating from bar to bar. He felt he was up against a stone wall for the time being and saw no sense in running his head against it. It was much pleasanter to browse over a drink, to idly chase thoughts here and there in the hope of running to ground one that was useful.

Soon it was dark, and time to eat, and he took a cab to *Enrico's*. He had paid the driver and was ambling to the door when he heard the driver scream:

"Look out!"

Kennedy threw himself flat on the sidewalk as three shots blasted the silence of the street and dug into *Enrico's* heavy door. The cab-driver blew his horn wildly. Kennedy lay tense, motionless, the sound of the horn braying in his ears. Then the horn stopped and he was being lifted to his feet by the driver, who gasped:

"You hurt? You hurt?"

"I—I d-don't think so," stammered Kennedy.

"I scared him wit' me horn. D'ja hear me scare him?"

Kennedy was trembling like a leaf. "Wuh-where is he?"

"He beat it. Up that way. Out o' sight now."

"What'd he look like?"

"Damned if I know. Only thing I seen, I seen this shape run out in the street and lift his arm out level and I yelled."

"Thanks, pal."

Enrico was standing in the doorway, his hands on his hips. "So what is this, so what?"

"I arrive," said Kennedy, "under a salute of guns." He tottered through the doorway. "A drink, before I pass out."

He took three in quick succession, under the concerned eye of Paderoofski. All he could eat was a ham sandwich. His appetite had been blown away. An hour and a half later Paderoofski said:

"Please to axcuse you, Meester Kennedy. On de telephone is a poddy was wishing he should spik wit' you horry-op."

"Paderoofski, your French gets better and better," Kennedy said and went to the phone; and on the phone, "Yes?... When?... Okey, Tucks, grab a car and pick me up here. In the lower left-hand drawer of my desk is a pair of manacles I stole from MacBride a year ago. Bring those, too. Can you get a gun?... Swell. Snap on it, Tucks."

He returned to the bar, said, "Paderoofski, lend me Susie."

Paderoofski took an automatic from beneath the bar and said, "Please, Meester Kennedy, being too careful," and handed across the gun. Kennedy shoved it into his pocket and, entering the restaurant, stood by the front window waiting. In a little while a black sedan yanked to a stop outside and Kennedy went out and found Tucker at the wheel. Kennedy climbed in, slammed the door, said, "What's that in back?"

"A gun. You said bring a gun. The cuffs weren't there."

"I didn't tell you to bring a twelve-gauge shotgun. You can't go walking around the streets with that thing."

"It was the only one in the office. Flannery bought it once, about five years ago, when he thought he might go duck hunting. He never went. Well, don't worry; I don't think it works anyhow."

He slammed the car into gear and drove off and as they boomed up the street Kennedy heard his name being yelled. He looked around. Tucker put on the brakes.

"Keep going. It's only Paderoofski. Probably Flannery phoning to give orders. Step on it. What time does the plane leave?"

"In half an hour."

TUCKER parked the car in the parking lot at the airport and climbed out, saying, "Well, the plane hasn't arrived yet." He pulled the shotgun out of the back seat.

"Nix," said Kennedy.

"But you said bring a gun."

"Forget it, Tucks. This is no grandstand play. Just walk with me and act disinterested."

They went through the swing-door into the waiting room and crossed to the desk behind which stood Bob Angler. Angler said, "Hello, gang. They're standing over in the corner."

"Thanks," said Tucker.

Neither Joel Webb nor Inez Canfield moved when they saw Kennedy coming towards them. Webb's eyes darkened and his lean jaw tightened up. The girl took hold of his arm. Kennedy and Tucker came up to them and Kennedy, taking his gun from his inside pocket and putting it into his overcoat pocket, said:

"Let's go."

Webb muttered angrily, "Now look here—"

"I'm looking, sweetheart—right at you. We've got a car outside. You and the girl get moving."

"Now listen—"

The schoolmasterly looking Tucker said from beneath his derby, "Can it, bozo. Ankle out. This is no celebrity interview."

The girl's eyes were wide with fright. There was something sinister about Kennedy's emaciated, lacerated face, and about his quiet, dreamy voice. She tugged at Webb's arm. Scowling, he started walking with her. Kennedy walked at his elbow. Tucker walked at the girl's elbow. Outside, Kennedy said to the girl:

"You ride in front." And to Webb: "You and me in back. Get in."

The sedan picked up speed on the cement highway. "Where are we going?" Tucker asked.

"Nine-ten Waterford," said Kennedy.

The girl looked around, startled.

Kennedy nodded. "Yes, Inez—back home. Gradually I'm going to get all you people in one spot. This has got so far that it's a circus, with me the head clown. Now somebody else is going to be the clown. Step on it, Tucks. The boy friend here is getting restless and if he doesn't sit still I'm going to shoot out a rib."

"Shoot between the ribs," Tucker recommended. "It goes farther. So I hear, anyhow."

Webb suddenly shouted, "You can't arrest us! You guys aren't cops!"

"He's just thought of something," Kennedy sighed; and then he snapped, "Sit still! Is a bullet in the gut worth arguing about whether we can arrest you or not?"

The girl said, "Don't, Joel. Don't."

Webb folded his arms and towered in savage silence, his teeth digging into his lower lip. The sedan rolled through the outskirts of the city, hit Southern Road and followed it to South Waterford. Eleven blocks farther on it pulled up in front of 910 Waterford and Kennedy said:

"Now wait. There's not going to be any confusion here. Tucks, you go in with the girl first and go right up to four-eight. Wait outside four-eight. I'll be up in a minute with Webb."

Tucker got out, gripped the girl by the arm and entered the apartment house. A minute later Kennedy backed out, said, "Okey, brother," and Webb followed.

Webb sneered. "Pretty cagey, aren't you?"

"Just careful, for once in my life. If you try to make a break for it now, the girl won't be with you. Move along."

When they reached the lobby the elevator pointer was stopped at the fourth floor. Kennedy buttoned it down, told Webb to open it, and then stepped in close behind him. When they got off at the fourth floor Tucker and Inez were standing halfway down the hall.

"Open it," said Kennedy.

Her lips were shaking, there was terror in her eyes. With fumbling fingers she took a key from her purse, clattered it into the keyhole, turned it. Her face was dead-white. Tucker took hold of the knob and pushed the door open. Kennedy pulled his gun out of his pocket and said:

"In, Webby."

Tucker hustled the girl in and then Kennedy prodded Webb in with the gun. He saw the girl stop, put her hands to her cheeks, sway. She uttered not a sound but he could see her back grow rigid. It was Tucker who said:

"Blow me down! Will you look at this!"

Emmy lay on the floor, disheveled, part of her dress torn. Kennedy began to see that the room was in a greater state of chaos than when he had left it. Webb turned and looked at Kennedy furiously, as though Kennedy were the cause of it. The girl dropped to a chair and began shaking violently, though she made no sound. Regret seemed not a part of her emotions: there was tragedy in her dark eyes, and fear, too.

Tucker's eyes grew round. He said, "They strangled the old dame and then breezed!"

"She's strangled, all right," mused Kennedy. "Just as Marty Sullivan was strangled." His voice dropped lower as he turned to the girl: "What were you looking for in the *Carioca*—back in Sullivan's office?"

Webb broke in— "She was—"

"Clam yourself," Kennedy told him dryly. "I'm talking to the girl. Come on, Inez, up and out with it."

Her fists were clenched, her lips pressed tightly together. She shook her head. Kennedy strolled over and stood back of her, his gun trained on Webb.

He was still tranquil: "Come on, Inez, spout."

"I'll tell you!" Webb rapped out. Kennedy smiled. "Make it good this time."

Webb's jaw jutted. "I was in Sullivan's office the night of the raid. I was waiting there for him to come back to the office. I was sitting there smoking a cigarette when I saw a light on his desk blink. That meant trouble out front. The hat-check girl must have flashed it when you came in."

"How do you know the light meant trouble?"

"I'd been in the office before, once, when a fight started in the lobby and the light flashed. The night of the raid I was sitting there, smoking, as I said, when the light flashed. I got up and ran out of the office and when I saw what was going on I beat it out the back way. I left my cigarette case behind. When you saw Inez there, she was looking for it."

"Why didn't you go back after it?"

"She wouldn't let me. Besides, she had a key to the back door and wouldn't give it to me."

"And why were you worried about the cigarette case?"

Webb looked suddenly confused.

Kennedy said, "Now did you do this? When you saw the trouble light flash, did you leave the office, go down that narrow hallway to the little door that leads into the dining-room? Did you reach in through that door and choke Sullivan to death before the lights went on? Did you then run out back, go to the alley in the rear and catch the fan dancer—Inez here—as she came out of her dressing-room window?"

The girl cried out, "No, no!"

"Now I'm talking to Webby," Kennedy said.

Webb's voice sounded clotted: "Why should I kill Sullivan?"

"Why were you in his office? Why, why, why—there's a lot of whys floating around. Maybe this. Sullivan was the only one, so far as we knew then, that knew the identity of his fan dancer. You knew that if the cops nailed him ten to one her identity would come out. You didn't want that. Why? Well, you love her. You don't want her name dragged in the mud. You choke Sullivan to keep the secret. You skin out the back way, taking the girl with you. Then you remember that you left your cigarette case behind."

The girl got to her feet, her lips shaking, her fists clenched. "It's a lie—a lie—a lie!" she choked. "He was there—he did leave his cigarette case there—he did help me out the back window—but he didn't kill Sullivan!"

"How do you know? You were backstage."

"I know! I know, I tell you!"

Kennedy smiled ruefully. "Then you know who did kill him?"

She choked, tightened her lips. Her eyes sprang wide open with shock and her hand flew to her face.

Kennedy said to Tucker, "Okey, Tucks. She knows. Phone Headquarters and tell them to send over somebody."

TUCKER walked across the room to the phone but he never reached it. The closet door opened and Jaeger stood there with a big gun in his hand. His shirt was torn, there were scratches on his face, his hair was matted. He looked big and gross and pasty.

"Stay away from that phone," he muttered thickly. His eyes were haggard.

Kennedy aimed, pulled his trigger. Nothing happened. He tried twice more.

"Drop it," said Jaeger.

"I may as well."

Jaeger said to the girl and Webb, "You two go. Go on."

The girl stared at him as though he were a ghost.

Jaeger muttered bitterly, "Take her, Webb. Take her out."

Webb's face was lined, grim. He crossed the room, took Inez by the hand and went with her to the door. They left. Jaeger remained, leaning in the closet doorway, his breathing slow and thick. "Wait," he said. "Just wait." And when five minutes had passed, he moved from the closet, crossed the room to the corridor door and said, "If you come after me, it's the works." He opened the door, backed out, closed the door.

Kennedy pointed. "You stay here. Call the office about this dead one. Her name's Emmy Canfield. The other one's her daughter. Then call the police."

He scooped up the automatic he had dropped, yanked out the magazine. It was empty. "That tramp Paderoofski," he said, and ran into the bedroom. He went out by way of the window and down the fire-escape to the courtyard. When he reached the front, he saw Jaeger jogging along a block away. Kennedy looked at the car, wondering about the chances of driving it and trying to run Jaeger down. He jumped in—but of course Tucker had the key. He jumped out again, took the old shotgun with him and started off up the street.

Jaeger saw him and fired but the bullet passed somewhere overhead. Kennedy ran on, hugging the housewalls. He could hear Jaeger's big feet clubbing the pavement, see his big ungainly body lunging on through the darkness. A second shot was closer: it scarred the sidewalk beneath Kennedy's feet. Kennedy jumped. He licked his lip and wondered whether he ought to stop but while he was wondering about it he kept on running.

He saw Jaeger turn again and plant himself in the middle of the sidewalk. Kennedy dropped behind an iron lamp standard as Jaeger cut loose. Four explosions banged in the street and lead whanged against the iron lamp standard. Kennedy was grateful for being skinny as a rail. He saw Jaeger reloading. Jumping up, he ran towards the man, hefting the shotgun as a club, hoping to reach Jaeger before he could reload. But the distance was too great to strike him with it. Kennedy saw him snap shut the gun.

Kennedy was fifteen feet from him in the open; there was nothing to hide behind. He waved his shotgun, yelled, "Stop or I'll shoot!" and made a pretense of aiming the gun. He even went so far as to press the trigger. The shotgun banged and the recoil knocked him to the sidewalk. As he scrambled to his feet, he saw Jaeger lying on the corner. Kennedy picked up the shotgun, went forward, aiming.

He said, "Don't move, Jaeger."

"You got me," Jaeger panted. "In the leg, high up. I can't move and I'm bleeding. Listen, leave Inez alone. She didn't have nothing to do with it. It was me killed Emmy. 'Cause why? Well, I'm a fine-looking guy to be nuts about Inez, but I am. She ain't that way about me, but you can't blame her for that. Her and Webb are nuts about each other. I knew I'd let Emmy have it some day.

"Look, Kennedy. She ain't that gal's mother. She never was. She's the one made Inez do that fan dance. When Inez'd fight against it, the old lady would threaten her with a knife. She had Inez scared to death. I seen she was scared to death. You see, Marty wasn't the only one knew who the fan dancer was. I did, too. Inez thought she was her mother, but she wasn't. I found that out. I found out that her mother died twenty-one years ago, out in Tulsa, and left her with Emmy, who ran a boarding house. I just found it out the day the cops raided the *Carioca*.

"I'd been begging Marty to cut out the fan dance. He used to just laugh. And when I got this news, I went up to him and told him. He says, 'Sure, I know that. Do you know who her father is?' I said I didn't and he said, 'Dan Osborne. But Dan doesn't know. If he closes me up, I'll spring it on him then.' That kind of floored me. He laughed. He thought it'd be a great joke. Then when the raid came— Look, I knew Inez didn't care a rap for me, but—well, I didn't want to see her scandalized. When the raid came—I seen it through the door—I seen MacBride come in—why, I just went in that hallway, stepped through that little door and let Marty have it."

"Why'd you give it to Emmy?"

"She suspected I'd killed Marty. She came to my place and told me so—that was when you got there and she chucked you down the stairs. Well, I told her I knew Inez wasn't her kid. I told her if she'd squeal on me I'd tell what I knew. So that was a bargain. But I got drunk. I thought o' the times she'd threatened Inez and got sore enough to kill her then. I went up there first and seen her coming to on the floor—that was after she had the fight with you. I heard you in the other room and took her out, figuring to take her to my place and beat hell out of her.

"But downstairs, I saw Inez running away. I ran after her and she said she was going to meet Webb and they were going to run away and get married. That kind of socked me, though I half expected it. I let her go. Then I lost sight of Emmy. I came back later and found her. She said Inez had gone away and she was going to turn me up because I'd always taken Inez' side against her. Then I choked her to death."

He rolled over and a cigar fell out of his pocket. Kennedy picked it up. It was triangular in shape.

"You smoke these?"

"Dan Osborne gave me a couple. He was around asking me questions and he gave me a couple."

"Does he know about Inez?"

"No."

"I'll get an ambulance."

"No, no," begged Jaeger. "Let me pass out here. I tried to kill you in front of *Enrico's,* Kennedy. You knew too much. I tried it again here. I killed Marty. I killed Emmy. I don't want an ambulance."

Kennedy stared at him, said, "Well, it'll take a while for one to get here."

THE NIGHT wind was strong, it whistled past the high casement windows. Osborne watched the Night Express come up to the East-marsh Bridge, string across it. He pulled on his cigar.

"I never thought Marty was a rat like that," he said. "He always used to kid me, ride me, but I never thought he'd do a thing like that. When he kept telling me that if I closed him up I'd rue the day, I don't know, I just thought it was bluff. He was always full of bluff. But now I can remember his evil grin—I didn't think it was particularly evil then. But I know it was, now. He hated my guts. He hated me in his smiling, droll way when I went over on the side of the law. Kidded me about it. Razzed me. But I always gave him a break. I should have killed him."

Kennedy said from the depths of the divan, "I sure had you picked as a major suspect for a long time. I guess I wasn't big-hearted enough to believe that you'd pull punches with Marty just for old times' sake. I really thought he had something on you."

"I know you did." Osborne's eyes dreamed. "You see, the child must have been born after my wife left me. I never knew about it. She ran away with some musician. I suppose I was to blame, a bit. I buried myself in work so."

Kennedy stood up, yawned. He said, "Well, MacBride goes back to work tomorrow. Same job. He doesn't know it yet, so I think I'll go find him and razz him a while, because tomorrow I won't be able to."

Osborne was wrapped in thought. "Did Inez say she would come here?" he asked.

"Yes. She and Webb never did leave the apartment house. They went down as far as the lobby and then Inez wouldn't go any further. I found them there when I ran back, after I shot Jaeger."

Osborne sat down, saying, "I won't know how to act. How do you act, Kennedy, when you meet a daughter you've never seen?"

Kennedy was on his way to the door. "I never was a father, Dan. I wouldn't know. So long. I'm going around to *Enrico's* and take a punch at Paderoofski."

When he drifted into *Enrico's* fifteen minutes later Enrico himself was behind the bar. At sight of Kennedy he held his head in his hands.

Kennedy said, "Come on—tell Paderoofski to get out from under the bar."

Enrico threw his hands in the air. "But ain't you heard!" he exclaimed. He groaned, "Poor Paderoofski!"

Kennedy looked puzzled. "Huh?"

"Look, Kennedy, sir. After Paderoofski gives you the gun he remembers it ain't loaded with no bullets. He cries out. He runs to the street and yells, but you drive off. He yells some more. He pulls his hair. He jumps. He prays. Then—yes, then poor Paderoofski has nervous collapse. I send him to the husspital in an ambulance. In an ambulance to the husspital goes poor Paderoofski with big nervous collapse! Is that not sad, Kennedy, sir?... Please, quick, go to the husspital so Paderoofski shouldn't beat up no more doctors. Four already he's beat up, not counting three orderlies. Quick, before the husspital she's a wreck!"

No Hard Feelings

Skipper MacBride drives a killer to cover and Kennedy points him.

Chapter I

THE TRAIN slouched in through the outer yards of Richmond City and Kennedy hopped it at Tower B. It was a fine night, mellow with stars. The air was mild, it was moistened just enough by a lazy east breeze. Kennedy swung up to the observation platform, crumpled his hat beneath his coat, under his armpit, and drifted into the lounge car. It was bright and cheerful with lights. The porter was gathering up magazines.

Kennedy found the Pullman conductor in the smoking compartment of the third car from the rear. The conductor was busy getting his papers in order and did not look up. Kennedy said:

"Are we on time?"

"On the nose," the conductor said.

"Where can I find George Torgensen?"

The conductor said, without looking up, "Drawing Room A, next car ahead."

Kennedy went through the narrow corridor into the vestibule, crossed the shifting apron to the next vestibule and entered a car named Xanthus. He rippled his knuckles down the door of Drawing Room A and when a voice said, "Come in," he opened the door and was thrown in by a lurch of the car. He reeled around, got the door shut, was thrown a second time and landed on a narrow green settee.

"Haven't got my sea legs," he said, with a dusty smile. "Glad to make your acquaintance, Mr. Torgensen."

"What've you got to be glad about?"

"My name is Kennedy."

"Am I supposed to be glad to meet you?"

They looked at each other for half a minute. Torgensen began to smile. He was a short, round, moon-faced man. His hands were short

and chubby and very well taken care of. The beginnings of his smile made his face look rosy, jolly, and presently he began to shake with noiseless laughter. He had his derby on and a pair of lightweight gray gloves lay on his left knee. His bags had been taken out.

"Okey, boy," he said good-temperedly. "I was only kidding. What's on your mind?"

"I'm from the press—"

"Sure. Coppers and newspapermen—I can tell 'em in the dark."

"Do you think you're going to like Richmond City?"

"I can learn to like any place."

"What do you think of Fitz Mularkey going idealistic?"

Torgensen said, "I haven't thought about it. Fitz has always been a funny guy. But a white guy, from his big feet right up to his big head— and there's a big heart in between the two. Fitz wants to get out. That's his business. He wants to sell his empire to me and that's his business and mine. I know a good buy when I see it. Fitz and me are old buddies."

Kennedy nodded. "Do you know that quite a number of guys in this town have overbid you?"

Torgensen waved his hand. "I didn't bid, boy. Fitz

came to Boston and said, 'George, I'm bailing out. I'm going to get hooked with a good gal, I'm going in partners with a real estate broker and I'm going to live like a human being. You can dig in on the old gravy for a million flat. Five hundred thousand down and the rest in five years.' So I didn't bid. I understand he got an offer of a million and two hundred grand, and several others. But we're old buddies, boy."

"Can I print what you've just said?"

"Print it? Hell, yes! And you can print more. You can tell the town that George Torgensen comes to it with his feet washed. I'm going to run the Eastmarsh Track, the Town Arena, and the *Million Club* the way Fitz ran 'em—on the level." He picked up his gloves and leaned forward. "And that's the reason, boy, that Fitz is selling to me. He could have sold to any number of punks, at more than I'm giving him—but he wants to leave his babies in good hands. He wants to live like what he calls a human being. That's his business. Me, well—I like it like I am, a little rough, a little tough, and a little nasty. But"— he pointed and looked along his level finger with a sharp, squinted eye—"on the level." Then he stood up. "Well, here we are."

Kennedy stood up too. He smiled. "You sound like good oats, Mr. Torgensen."

"Hell, I'm just a plain guy trying to make a living. Come around and see me sometime. I'm stopping at the *Bushwick.*"

The train had stopped.

Torgensen said, "Come on, I'll drop you off," and stepped out into the corridor. On the platform, he walked fast, with a brisk snap to his short legs, and he had an air of self-sufficiency. Kennedy, round-shouldered, hollow-chested, tagged along at his elbow. The reporter looked as if he had slept in his suit, and his hat was on backwards, the brim up in front, down in back. They went through the milling crowd in the waiting room, the redcap ahead of them lugging three heavy bags.

There was a cobbled space outside, dim-lit, where a line of cabs stood waiting. The Negro stowed the bags in the first one and Torgensen stood cupping his hands around a match and lighting a cigar. Then he tipped the Negro and when Kennedy said, "Beauty before age," went into the cab.

Kennedy was raising his foot, to follow, when the two explosions whacked out and streamed into one blast of thunder. The taxi driver went down behind his wheel. Torgensen poised in the doorway of the cab, then fell backward, crumpling. Kennedy was starting for the other side of the cab but Torgensen's chunky body hit him. He stopped, to catch the man. Caught him but was unable to master his balance enough to hold him. Both went down, Kennedy on the bottom. With Torgensen on his chest and the cobbles against his back, Kennedy said, "Ooch!"

Then Torgensen rolled off. Kennedy rolled too and found himself facing the man. Torgensen was in pain. His mouth was crooked, his eyes full of wonder and sadness and something between pain and anger. His lips bubbled. Kennedy thought a bitter smile came to the chunky man's lips. He heard Torgensen say almost wistfully, "Ain't this something, boy...?"

The taxi driver was yelling, "The shot come through the other side of the cab! The other side... through... it come!"

Torgensen said, "H'm," reflectively, and a sigh bubbled out.

Legs moved about Kennedy. Big, black, polished shoes. He looked up and saw a red face coming down towards him. Above the face a visored cap with a shield on it. The cop grabbed hold of Kennedy.

"Not me," Kennedy said. "Him. He's the guy's shot."

Someone was shouting, "Ambulance! Ambulance! Somebuddy get an ambulance!"

"Through the other side," the driver insisted. "The window. Right through the window."

The cop, kneeling, said, "This man's dead. Yop. Feel here. Look at his face. Look at his eyes. I seen a man once...."

Kennedy was on his feet.

The cop grabbed him, snapped, "Was he a friend of yours?"

"Well, he would have been, I think."

"Listen, this ain't no time for funny-bones. Who is he?"

"George Torgensen."

The policeman thought hard. "Tiny Torgensen?" he asked.

"Something like that."

"Um," the cop said, staring down at Torgensen. "Fitz Mularkey ain't going to be crazy about this. I only read in the papers today that Fitz Mularkey says Tiny Torgensen—"

"I know he's dead," Kennedy said in a quiet, confidential voice, "but just for the sake of appearances, officer, you ought to call an ambulance."

The taxi driver was hopping about and telling everybody how Torgensen was shot. A beggar wearing dark glasses and a sign that read *I Am Blind,* was not begging. More cops came on the run. Torgensen looked for all the world like a man asleep. The night train was whistling out of the yards.

Kennedy shrugged his way through the fast gathering crowd, gained the edge and slouched away.

Chapter II

THEY said of the *Million Club* that you could let your sixteen-year-old daughter go there and she'd be safer than in church. Fitz Mularkey was that kind of idealist. He'd always had a lot of respect for women. He employed six men for the special purpose of seeing that drunks got home safely. Everyone in his employ saw to it that a drunk was safe while on the premises. Fitz Mularkey was forty-four. That is an unusual age for a man to be still an idealist.

He liked blue. The hangings in the *Million Club* were blue and the indirect lighting had a bluish tinge. The high stools in front of the bar had blue plush seats. Mularkey was sitting on one of them drinking a glass of seltzer when Dolly Ireland came up to the bar and said:

"So this is the night, eh, Fitz?"

"This is it. You're looking swell, Doll."

"Don't it make you kind of sad leaving"—she smiled around—"all this?"

He didn't have to look around to check up. He chuckled and shook his head. "Not a bit, Dolly. The game's getting full of crackpots and tin-horns. I'm fed up, lady. I want to live like a human being. I'm tired of grifters and drunks and guys trying to sell me white elephants. I want a real home and a real business, a business I can be proud of."

"Gee, Fitz, you ought to be pretty proud of this."

"I ain't. That's it. I ain't. I want kids and a nice wife and regular hours— Say, you never met Marcia, did you?"

"You never brought her around."

He looked a little sheepish. He shrugged. "She don't go for these kind of places. Hey, have a drink."

"I'm on my way inside, Fitz."

"Oh, sure, I forgot."

She put her hand on his sandy, flat-boned wrist. "I thought you might be sliding out early. I just wanted to wish you luck, Fitz—all the good things; you know, the things you want. You're a grand guy, no kidding, and I'm all for you."

He had slate-blue eyes that could look murderous or full of happiness. They looked happy now. He said awkwardly, "Thanks, Dolly. You know—well, a lot of people think I'm going high hat. I ain't,

Dolly. I just want—I just want—"

She gave a low, warm laugh. "I know, Fitz. I know just how you feel." She dropped her voice, looked grave. "What are you doing about Steamboat?"

Mularkey looked unhappy. He said in a low, husky voice, "I'm fixing it so he'll get an income for life—three hundred bucks a month. Dolly, I had to cut away from Steamboat. I know he's been what they call my man Friday for years, but you just can't break Steamboat o' the habit o' packing a gun. And the life I'm going to lead, why, hell, Dolly, I don't need that."

"He's pretty sore, Fitz."

"I know he is. He'll get over it. He ain't really sore—not at me, Dolly. He's just sore because he thinks I'm leaving a good thing. He don't understand."

She patted his arm. "Well, I've got to get back to my party, Fitz."

"Gee, you look swell, Dolly."

He stood spread-legged and his eyes admired her as she walked out of the bar. Then he put a cigar in his mouth, did not light it, and strode into the lobby. His sandy hair was crisp, tight against his scalp. His long face was slabsided, rough around the jaw. He had square shoulders and long straight legs. His stare was a little chill when he was wound up in thought, but otherwise it was twinkling, good-natured. You knew that he was tough but you knew also that he had spent a lot of time smoothing down the rough edges.

Tom Carney, his manager, came up and said, "Fitz, maybe you'll slam me for this."

Mularkey grinned. "Maybe. Why?"

"Steamboat. I wouldn't let him in."

"Go on."

"Well, he was cockeyed drunk and noisy. I took his gun away from him and sent Eddie and Boze to take him home."

Mularkey brooded. "Poor Steamboat."

"Yeah, I know, but—"

"Sure, Tommy, sure. That's okey."

The front door opened and MacBride came in, showing behind him for an instant the doorman, the marquee and a street lamp. The doorman pulled the door shut and Mularkey dropped an aside to Tom Carney:

"The skipper looks—"

"Yeah," nodded Carney.

MacBride came right up to them and said, "See you alone, Fitz." His dark eyes had a slap in them and you could tell that he had hurried.

Mularkey said, "Sure—over here," and led the way into a small triangular room. It contained a desk on which there were a telephone and a form-sheet for taking reservations. There were two armchairs studded with antique nails. A lamp with a green glass shade diffused quiet light.

Mularkey was offhand, genial— "Sit down, Steve."

MacBride seemed not to have heard. He stood looking at the green lamp as though he liked it and were considering buying one some day. His eyes were bright, dark, contracted. Mularkey was waiting for him to sit before he himself should take a seat. But the skipper did not sit down; instead, he said:

"About how many guys wanted to buy you out, Fitz, when you said you were chucking all this?"

Mularkey sat on the corner of the desk. "Oh, about four or five."

"Made some hard feelings, eh? I mean, going out of town for your buyer."

"Hell, no; no hard feelings."

"Who're the four or five?"

Mularkey gave him a brief squint, then looked at the ceiling. "Well, Guy Shaster and Will Pope came to me together. Then there was Brad Hooper. Then Pickney Sax. Four. That's all. Four."

"And no hard feelings, eh?"

"What makes you think there was any?"

"Torgensen. Torgensen was killed. Yeah. Tonight. About half an hour ago. About a quarter past eight."

Mularkey pushed himself up off the desk, cupped his right elbow in his left palm and used his right thumb to scratch his chin. He strolled around the room, each step slow, timed. The carpet was thick and his footfalls made no sound. He said from one of the corners:

"Where?"

"Front of Union Station."

Mularkey made another slow circuit of the room, still scratching his chin. He sat down, took his unlit cigar from his mouth, looked at it, put it back between his lips again. He said very thoughtfully:

"So there were hard feelings, huh?"

MacBride put his palms flat on the desk and leaned on his straight, braced arms. His face was wooden.

"I'm going to say a few words to you, Fitz," he said, "and I want you to listen. You've been here in Richmond City a dozen years. I've been a cop over twenty. You've kept your nose clean ever since you been here. How, in the business you're in, hell knows. But you've kept it clean. You're all set to bail out of it clean. You're going into what we call legitimate business. I'm all for you. I like to see a guy do that. A lot of people think I like to see guys tossed in the can all the time. That's crap. Now I know you and Torgensen were old buddies. I was glad when I heard you were selling out to Torgensen. I've got his record and it's clean. Now some mugg's knocked him off. I know how you feel about that and that's what I mean. I mean, Fitz, keep your nose clean. I like you, I've liked you ever since you came here, but the minute you take a sock at anybody with a gun—even if they did kill Torgensen—it'll be murder and you know my answer to murder."

Mularkey was remembering— "Little Tiny… he never toted a gun or a bodyguard around with him. He always used to say guns and bodyguards are what get guys killed."

MacBride leaned across the desk. "You heard what I said, Fitz, didn't you?"

"Yeah, sure. Sure, Steve."

MacBride fixed a hard dark stare on him. Mularkey looked up; then he rose and tucked down the lapels of his vest. He said, "There's only one thing stopping me from getting my nose dirty, Steve. I'm going to marry Marcia Friel. I think Tiny'd understand that." His jaw tightened. "He's got to. I'm too nuts about Marcia to ball things up by killing anybody."

MacBride gripped his arm. "That's sweet music, Fitz." He added, "I could have saved my speech."

"You could've saved it all right."

Mularkey tossed away his unlit cigar.

"Orchids to her," MacBride said.

"That's an idea," Mularkey said, and phoned and ordered.

Chapter III

THE SKIPPER got back to his office at a quarter to ten. A couple of flies were roosting on his desk and he got his fly-swatter down from a hook in the closet and nailed them. He noticed that someone had left his window open without putting in the small rectangular screen he used at night. He figured it was Abraham, the porter, and made a note of it. He turned to spit and found that his spittoon was gone. He knew it was Abraham. He looked irritated for a minute, but he was too absorbed with other things to remain irritated long. Stuffing his pipe, he paced the floor. Lighting up, he still paced. On his tenth trip past his desk he slapped open the annunciator and said:

"Send up Lieutenant Blaufuss."

In two minutes Blaufuss, head of the Flying Squad, stuck his long nose through the doorway and said, "You looking for me?"

"In, Leon," MacBride beckoned. He had not stopped pacing, nor did he now. Ribbons of tobacco smoke trailed behind him, overlapped him on the turns. "Leon...."

The skipper went to the closet again and got his fly-swatter. "Leon, what do you know about Pickney Sax, Guy Shaster, Will Pope, and Brad Hooper?" He nailed a fly on top of the telephone.

"Jeese, d'you want me to sit here all night?"

"Know plenty about 'em, huh?"

"More than I know about my in-laws."

"Okey, Leon. Now...." He stopped and aimed his pipe-stem at the lieutenant. "I want their inside men—all of them. I don't want Sax, Pope, Shaster, or Hooper. I want their inside men. All of them. And I want their women. Not their wives, understand—but their women."

"Brad Hooper has none."

"Okey, the other three, then."

"Any charge?"

"No. I'll book 'em en route."

Blaufuss pointed. "There's a fly—right there—on the—"

MacBride smacked it.

Blaufuss said, "Anything else?"

MacBride shook his head and Blaufuss went out. The door had

hardly closed when it opened again and Kennedy came in tapping a yawn. He moved haphazardly across the office, set two chairs opposite each other; sat down in one, put his feet on the other and drawing a sporting sheet from his pocket, proceeded to read it. The skipper had taken to pacing again and was going up and down at a great rate. After a couple of minutes Kennedy said:

"Please stop it, my friend. It makes me nervous."

MacBride stopped and held up four fingers of his right hand. "Four guys, Kennedy. Four. Four guys wanted to buy out Fitz. He turned 'em down."

Kennedy said, "My, my, here's a horse I should have bet on."

"Fitz leans to his old pal Tiny Torgensen. Torgensen's killed as he comes out of Union Station. Four guys. One of them did it. One of them got Torgensen before the deal was closed. Fitz is bound to sell. He wants to get out. He *will* sell."

Kennedy said, "I was going to bet on this horse, but I let Paderoofski talk me out of it. He talked me into betting on Full House because he said he had a dream in which he was playing poker and he dreamt he had a Full House. And here Stumble Bum, a twenty-to-one shot—"

Exasperated, MacBride spat. He spat where he was used to finding his spittoon. It wasn't there, and with a growl he called the central-room desk and bawled, "Tell Abraham to bring a mop and my spittoon back.... No, not a cop—a mop!"

He hung up violently and glared at Kennedy. "You know what I'm doing?" he demanded.

Kennedy looked up at him, shrugged. "Standing there working up a sweat."

MacBride was not to be sidetracked. "I'm rounding up the pulse men and the good-time dames of Pope, Sax, Shaster and Hooper. I suppose *you* thought I'd round up the head men themselves." He swatted another fly by way of emphasis.

Kennedy yawned. "Well, it's all right, Stevie. Gathering in all those guys is good display psychology. Keeps your cops busy and makes news for the papers. But"—he rubbed his eyes—"I don't think you're going to find anything."

The skipper cut him with a caustic stare. "Oh, no? And why not?"

"Well, you can't charge these guys with anything that'll hold. You can only hold 'em overnight. You'll drag in, all told, about twenty guys and three or four dames. You'll have to do some shellacking. If you worked on each guy three hours, which is a very short time, it would take you sixty hours to get through all of them—which is longer than you can hold 'em."

"That's just paper figuring."

Kennedy took off a shoe in order to scratch the arch of his foot. He pointed lazily with the shoe. "Here's some more paper figuring. Guy Shaster and Will Pope teamed up trying to buy out Fitz. Pickney Sax tried it alone. So did Brad Hooper. There you have three bidders, each with enough dough to buy him out. Why should one bidder knock off Tiny Torgensen and take a chance, if Fitz does sell to one of them, of Fitz selling to one of the others? I know that all these guys have settled more than one argument with a gun, but here's a long chance, too long to play on. These guys are not hop-heads, they're business men. A murder has to get them something definite before they pull it."

The skipper planted his fists on his hips, screwed down one eye and flexed his lips. "Go ahead with some more paper work."

Kennedy put his shoe back on, took his time about lacing it up. He became absorbed in a spot on his coat and tried to remove it by scraping with his thumbnail.

MacBride laughed raucously. "You're just one of these destructive critics. You tell a guy everything he does is lousy but you can't build up anything yourself."

Kennedy smiled gently. "Potato, you're doing swell. Your display work is the tops and—"

"Listen, pot-head, I don't need display work. I didn't send my men out because I figured they needed some road-work. I sent 'em out because I—because I—" He made a crooked, irritable face and then barked, "I wish the hell you'd stop doing paper work on me! It gets me all jammed up!"

Kennedy sighed, "Ever hear of Steamboat Hodge?"

"Don't ask foolish questions."

"All right. Paper work. Steamboat's been around Fitz for ten years. He's been Fitz's constant shadow, his old dog Rover. He doesn't want Fitz to bail out of the business because when Fitz bails out Steamboat's usefulness is done. Maybe Steamboat figured that if Torgensen was out of the way Fitz, feeling the way he does about his business, wouldn't sell to any of these shady big shots in town."

MacBride shot back at him, "If he felt that way about it, why didn't he take a crack at Marcia Friel?"

"Like Fitz, maybe, he thinks a woman's a wonderful thing. For the past week Steamboat's been slamming around town stewed to the ears. You hear it in all the bars. The guy was breaking up."

MacBride stared down his bony nose. His lips moved tautly against each other. He looked upset, harassed, and finally he ripped out, "Damn you, Kennedy!" He crossed the office and got his hat. "Come on," he growled, digging his heels towards the door.

The big Buick was being washed and the skipper said to Gahagan, "Boy, you sure pick a swell time to wash it."

Gahagan pointed with the hose and almost doused MacBride. MacBride jumped out of the way and Gahagan said:

"On'y this afternoon you told me to wash it tonight."

"How did I know I was going to be busy?"

"Well, how did I?"

MacBride colored and went across the basement garage to his own flivver coupé. Kennedy climbed in beside him and the skipper pressed the starter and kept pressing it.

"Try turning on the switch," Kennedy recommended.

MacBride turned on the switch and the motor started. He whipped the car out of the garage, clicked into high and drove down the center of the street. A truck came booming up from the opposite direction and its driver leaned out and yelled, "Get over where you belong, you mugg!"

The skipper shouted back, "Yeah!" and pulled over so far that he almost hit a car parked at the curb.

Kennedy said, "Maybe we should have waited till Gahagan got the Buick washed."

"This car's been steering funny of late."

"I can understand that. It might be a good idea, if you're going to drive all over the street, to put your lights on."

MacBride scowled and turned on his lights.

WHEN he walked into the *Million Club,* Tom Carney said, "Round trip, eh, Cap'n?"

MacBride blew his nose loudly. "Steamboat around?"

Carney's smile faded out. "No."

"Fitz?"

Carney shook his head without saying anything.

MacBride put away his handkerchief. "Where is he?"

"I think he went home."

"Steamboat still bunking with him?"

Carney shook his head very slowly. "No. Steamboat got temperamental and moved to diggings of his own, I don't know where."

"Thanks, Tom," MacBride said, and fanned out.

Kennedy was behind the wheel.

"Move over," the skipper said.

"If I move over, I move out. I'm going to see what's wrong with this steering gear."

MacBride grunted, gave him a suspicious look and climbed in. "Fitz's place."

Kennedy drove out Webster Avenue, tooling the car neatly through traffic and with little effort. He pulled up in front of an ivy-covered apartment house, set the emergency brake and switching off the ignition, said:

"I guess the steering gear's a little better."

"Sometimes it is and sometimes it isn't. That's what's funny about it. Do you know offhand what Fitz's apartment is?"

"Six-o-six, unless he's changed."

"Well, we'll go right up anyhow."

A gray enameled elevator hoisted them silently to the sixth floor and cushioned to a jarless stop. MacBride strode out and was halfway down the hall when Kennedy whistled and pointed in the other direction. MacBride pivoted and went after him and they arrived in front of 606 together.

Mularkey himself opened the door, holding an unlit cigar between two fingers. His sandy eyebrows made a hardly perceptible movement and a smile came a second later to his eyes, slanted down across one slablike cheek to the corner of his mouth.

"Come in, come in," he said. "I want you to meet Marcia Friel...."

He had spent a lot of money on his apartment, some of it not wisely. But you could not expect a one-time dock-walloper to be expert at decorating. He'd mixed antiques with ultra-modern nightmares.

Marcia Friel was wearing a three-cornered hat and a lightweight coat of some dark, crinkly material, draped under the arms and with a loose scrollwork collar. She was tall, with black hair and very fair skin. Her face was triangular, intelligent, and she had an air which she wore easily and naturally. A young, slender man was standing near her. He held a pair of gloves in one hand, a dark Homburg in the other.

"Marcia," said Mularkey, "this is my old friend Captain Steve MacBride… and this is Kennedy; I've known him a long time too. Boys, this is Marcia Friel."

She dipped her chin, her brows. "I'm so glad to know you both. I have heard about you."

"I guess we've heard about you too," the skipper said, with an approving nod towards Mularkey.

"And this," said Mularkey, "is Marcia's brother Lewis. We're going in the real estate game together."

Lewis Friel wore good clothes well. His brown hair was knotty, with a short part on the left. His brown eyes were candid. He came across the room with trim, elastic tread, his hand held out before him, a small amused smile on his lips.

"Fitz has talked enough about you," he said. "It's tough there had to be a murder in order to meet you."

Mularkey explained to MacBride, "I had 'em stop by, Steve. It kind of shook me up, after I got to thinking about it."

Marcia's eyes clouded. "Mr. Torgensen was, you know," she said to Kennedy, "a very old friend of Fitz's."

Mularkey looked moody, a little broken up. "I think I'm all right now, though."

Marcia Friel made a gesture of patting his arm. He turned to drop a smile on her—it was full of thanks and adoration and at the same time a little embarrassed.

The skipper said, "Fitz, can I see you alone?"

"Sure. Excuse us, Marcia… Lewis."

There was a small study off the gallery. It was lined with books, all finely bound.

"Some library," MacBride said.

Mularkey brightened a bit. "Like it? I hired a guy to pick those books. I don't read myself."

"I don't either, much, but I like to see 'em around."

"Me too," Mularkey nodded.

Both stood looking at the books for a minute and then the skipper said:

"Steamboat around?"

Mularkey looked more steadily at the books. "Steamboat claimed I was getting too high hat." He chuckled. "He shifted to other quarters."

"Where?"

"Yeah," Mularkey slowly reminisced, "Steamboat's very touchy. He said this place was getting like a museum or something—no place for a decent man to live in."

"Quite a guy, Steamboat," MacBride said.

"Yeah, quite a guy, Steve."

"Where'd you say he moved, Fitz?"

Mularkey looked at him. "Want to see him?"

"Yeah, I'd like to."

Mularkey picked up the phone. "I'll ring him and tell him to come over."

He rang but there was no answer and he hung up. "No answer," he said.

"Where's he living?"

Mularkey sighed, went slowly around to the other side of the desk, pulled a small book out of a drawer, looked in it, then tossed it back into the drawer. "Over at sixty-five Lyons Street. It's a rooming-house. He's in room fifteen." He looked at his unlit cigar. "What's the matter?"

"Oh, nothing, Fitz. Just checking up."

When they returned to the living-room Marcia gave them a troubled look. Mularkey, seeing it, touched her on the shoulder reassuringly, said, "The skipper and me always have our little secrets."

Lewis Friel, lighting a cigarette, gave him a minute's careful scrutiny, and then his sister turning to MacBride, said:

"You will talk to Fitz, won't you, Captain? You will stop him from doing anything foolish?"

Mularkey laughed outright. "Listen to Marcia!"

Lewis Friel made a troubled movement of his head. "Nevertheless, Fitz, she's right."

MacBride said, "Fitz has given me his word. He knows better than break it."

"Sure," said Mularkey. "Sure." The second "sure" seemed to tail off just a trifle and for a brief instant a chill blue light waved through Mularkey's eyes.

MacBride and Kennedy went downstairs and Kennedy, having the ignition key, got in behind the wheel. MacBride was clouded in thought.

" 'D you see that look in Fitz's eyes?"

Kennedy started up the motor. "The gal looks cream enough to keep his coffee from going bitter."

"Kennedy, she's the one thing that stands between Fitz and a gun. If what you think about Steamboat's true—and if Steamboat gets crocked and decides to turn native and clout that gal with lead...."

"I catch on. It means the end of Fitz."

MacBride nodded gloomily. Then he said, "Go to sixty-five Lyons Street."

Chapter IV

LYONS STREET is a narrow defile on the southern fringe of the city. Many of the buildings there have been condemned and the city hopes to condemn all of them some day and build a park and playground. But a few houses are still occupied. One of these is 65.

Kennedy, climbing out of the coupé, said, "Steamboat must certainly have wanted to be alone. A lot of men do that. When things go wrong, they hide away alone and brood. That's bad. They get complexes."

"The room's fifteen," MacBride said, hiking across the broken sidewalk.

The glass-paneled door with the faded 65 on it was not locked. MacBride opened it and Kennedy followed him into a barnlike corridor where a light with a broken glass shade stuck out of the wall. Somebody in a rearward room was coughing.

"Fifteen ought to be upstairs somewhere," the skipper said.

He climbed, his hard-heeled cop's shoes slugging the carpetless steps. They found 15 on the third floor, front. It was locked and after knocking several times and getting no answer, MacBride used a master key. The break was simple, for it was a makeshift lock. He spanned the room with his flashlight's beam, spotted a light cord and yanked on the light. It was a bare, downtrodden room, with two front windows. There was a patchwork quilt on the bed and a shuffled rag rug on the floor. A big suitcase, open, lay on the floor. It contained clean clothes. A heap of soiled clothing lay in a corner. Nothing had been hung up in the closet.

"He's just marking time here," Kennedy said.

"I wonder when he was in here last."

Kennedy dawdled over to the bureau and looked at a glass half filled with water. "Not very long ago."

"Huh?"

"Drops of water on the outside of the glass, where he slopped it over."

"Sweat, maybe."

"Sweat beads. This is water."

MacBride nodded. "I guess you're right." He picked up the stub of a cigar. "Yes, you're right. The end of this cigar's still wet. Did Steamboat smoke cigars?"

"Always. I saw him without one one day and didn't recognize him. What's this?"

Kennedy picked up a writing pad and carried it over beneath the light. He slanted it in various directions, then said, "He wrote with a pencil, a hard one, and he pressed hard. Here's the impression he left—part of it."

"What's it say?"

"Hard to tell. He presses hard on some letters and soft on others. But I can make this much out: " 'If you go through with it—' and then I can't make the next words out. But here, a little later on: 'Fitz don't know what he's doing—' and then it fades again. Look—now listen to this: '—try to muscle in and I'll—' and that fades and then two lines down I see this: '—even if he calls you his best friend.'" He handed the pad over. "Take it along. It might help."

"*Might* help?"

"You could never hang a guy on that."

MacBride snorted. "But I can hang a lot on him."

"Maybe."

MacBride grumbled, "You make me sick! You get me all steamed up on a thing and then you chuck cold water on me!" He went to the wall and lifted the telephone receiver. He called Headquarters and said, "Moriarity or Cohen get back yet?... Well, send Cohen over to sixty-five Lyons Street, room fifteen. Tell him to snap on it.... Sure it's MacBride."

He hung up as Kennedy said, "Listen."

MacBride turned his head and heard footsteps climbing the staircase. He pulled his gun and went over to face the door and as it opened he cocked the trigger and said:

"Put 'em—"

He lowered the gun.

Mularkey leaned in the doorway with his big hands sunk in his coat pockets. He didn't smile. He looked weary and his voice when he spoke was low and bore a note of resentment.

"I took it into my head," he said, "to come over and see what all this stuff is about Steamboat."

"Nothing, Fitz. I'm just—"

"Just checking up. Ditch that, Steve. You can hide what's on your mind about as well as I can hide a day-old beard. You don't have to kid me."

MacBride shrugged and said, "Why don't you go home and take a sleep, Fitz? You're taking all this too hard."

"I'll sleep when I feel like it and I don't feel like it. You're not checking up. You're looking for Steamboat."

"You're getting tough, Fitz."

"I'm getting sore."

Kennedy said, "Don't get sore, my friend."

"You mind your own business. When I want a chirp out of you, I'll say so."

MacBride shook his head. "That's no way to talk, Fitz. If you wasn't all upset, you wouldn't talk that way. You're just stepping on your friends' toes right now."

"I want to know what you got on Steamboat."

"Nothing."

"You're a liar. I can tell when you're checking up and I can tell when you've got your nose close to the ground. If you got anything on Steamboat, I want to know it. You have—and you're a liar if you say you haven't."

There was dull red color pushing through the skin on the skipper's neck. He said very slowly, "I got nothing on Steamboat."

Mularkey was looking at him with the chill blue stare.

The skipper repeated—"Nothing."

Mularkey dropped his eyes. He pushed out his lower lip, drew it back in again. He frowned, shook his head. He looked disgusted and badgered. After a long minute he turned without a word and went away, his steps slow and heavy as he descended the staircase. Kennedy, looking out the window, saw him walk slowly away down the street, disappear.

Kennedy turned, saying, "There's a man that's slowly turning into a stick of dynamite."

MacBride was staring morosely at the door. He said in a preoccupied voice, "Any guy but him that talked to me that way, I'd kick his teeth out."

Cohen arrived.

"Stay here, Ike," the skipper said, still preoccupied. "When Steamboat Hodge comes in, pick him up. Come on, Kennedy."

Chapter V

STEAMBOAT did not show up at the Lyons Street place. Cohen hung around until midnight. He was relieved by another man, who was relieved by another at eight in the morning.

The skipper arrived in the Headquarters garage at eight-thirty with a dented mudguard. He had clipped a traffic blinker on his way from home. His shoes were polished, he wore a freshly pressed blue serge suit. He had shaved and his face was ruddy, bony, with highlights on his cheekbones.

"Somebuddy bump you?" asked the garage watchman.

"Yeah. Run around to Louie's and tell him to straighten it out."

"Hoke, Cap."

MacBride reached the central room with his coat tail bobbing. Bettdecken, on desk duty, looked over the top of a detective story magazine.

"Any news from the Lyons Street place?" MacBride asked.

"Nope. That is, whosis—what's-his-name—you know—"

"Steamboat."

"Yowss. Him. He ain't showed up. Gigliano's on duty there now. Gig says the place is a dump."

"What else?"

"Well, Blaufuss and his Flying Squad was out practically all night.

He rounded up a lot of potatoes. Twenty-three guys and seven dames in the holdover. He ain't sure about the dames. He brung the seven in just to be sure. Oh, yeah. Pickney Sax come in about ten minutes ago. He was the one give me this magazine."

"Where is he?"

"Somewheres. Maybe he's out back playing cards with the crew. Somewheres. I dunno. Say, what's a locust, like in this book?"

"I think it's police slang for a nightstick."

MacBride went up to his office, flat-handed the door open and saw Pickney Sax sitting in the desk chair with one leg over a corner of the desk and the other over an arm of the chair. He was reading a detective story magazine.

"You read too, eh?" MacBride jibed.

Sax said, "Yeah. Want one?" and drew another out of one of his pockets, tossed it on the desk. "I always carry three or four around with me. When I get sick of reading 'em, I cut paper dolls."

"From cutting throats to cutting paper dolls, huh?"

"Never cut a throat in my life. Sight of blood makes me whoops."

He was the thinnest man MacBride had even seen. He looked as if he had been put together with laths and putty. His clothes cost plenty of money but didn't prevent his looking like a scarecrow. He slouched and was careless of his linen and his hair was a mustard-colored thatch, his nose looked like a rudder put over to swing a boat hard to starboard. His voice was laconic and always sounded as if he had a cold.

"What got you up so early?" the skipper asked.

"I ain't been to bed yet."

"Want to see me?"

"Yeah." Sax closed the magazine. "Yeah, I want to see you. Five of my boys were picked up last night by a gang of your stooges. And a gal I know. The boys would like to see a football game today and the gal would like to get her hair waved this morning."

"That's interesting."

"Nuts, there's nothing interesting about it I can see. What are you holding 'em for?"

"A fella was killed last night."

"Sure a fella was killed last night. A fella from Boston. A little big fella. Tiny Torgensen. I did it. So what?"

"You worried?"

"Yah, sure I'm worried. Lookit me. Ha! Lookit me puss hang down to me toes with worry!" He stood up, gaunt, gangling, and said with ripping sarcasm, "You and your crummy ideas!"

MacBride sat down and said, "Beat it. They'll get out at noon."

Sax slammed his fist down on the desk and roared, "They'll get out now! *Now!*"

MacBride stood up and kicked his chair back at the same time. His fist traveled two feet, crashed. Sax slammed to the floor. MacBride sat down again and said:

"Now beat it."

Sax scrambled to his feet, fell on the desk and snarled, "Why the hell would I knock off Torgensen when any big shot you can name in this lousy burg could outbid me on Mularkey's deal? What about Steamboat? Twenty minutes after Torgensen was killed last night I was walking past the *Million House*. I seen Steamboat in the doorway there tussling with a couple o' Fitz's boys. They took away his gun. I seen them take away his gun. Mularkey knows who knocked off Torgensen. So does Dolly Ireland."

"Cut. Well, what about Dolly Ireland?"

Sax swaggered to the door, swaggered back again and cackled, "What about Dolly Ireland!" He leaned forward, propped a gaunt forefinger on the desk. "I know a guy, Skipper, I know a guy—a blind guy—only he ain't blind. A moocher. He seen Dolly Ireland and Steamboat walk past Union Station fifteen minutes before Torgensen was killed. Figure it, figure it out. You're smart. Figure it out. Sure! Steamboat loses a soft berth if Fitz bails out of the old game. Dolly Ireland's crazy about Fitz but he's going high hat with a swell dame. Figure it out, Skipper. I ain't making no charges. I ain't saying anything. I'm just telling you what I seen and what I heard!"

He snatched up his two detective story magazines and banged out.

The office became very silent and into the silence, after a minute, the skipper said, "H'm," and reached for the phone. He called the *Free Press* office and asked for Kennedy. It was Kennedy's day off.

The skipper took his hat and went downstairs to the garage. Gahagan put on his coat and started up the Buick.

"Kennedy's place in Hallam Street," MacBride said.

He sat in back, bounced slightly as Gahagan went over the rounded apron leading to the street.

Gahagan said, "It's a fine day. It's the kind of day I like. I like this here time of year. I like—"

"Shut up. I'm trying to think."

"Take my wife, now—"

"You got her, you keep her. And shut up."

Gahagan sighed, wagged his head and grooved the car through the bright, mellow morning. Hallam Street was in a quiet, unpretentious part of town, and the rooming-house where Kennedy lived was like many other rooming-houses in Hallam Street. The street had a washed look, like those Pennsylvania Dutch towns.

MacBride went in and rapped at Kennedy's door. Entering the room, he saw Kennedy sitting on the bed in his pajamas, with an ice-bag on his head, and staring reflectively at a huge Saint Bernard dog.

MacBride said, "I never knew you owned a dog."

"Neither did I," Kennedy said.

"Where'd you get him?"

"I don't know. I woke up and there he was."

The dog looked gravely at MacBride.

"He's big enough," MacBride said.

"Every time he puts his paws on my chest he knocks me down. He's knocked me down six times this morning. Well-meaning chap, though. I wish I knew how I came to possess him. It reminds me of the time I woke up one morning and found a donkey in my room. Animals must like me."

"Well, when you get tight—"

"Kind of pet him, Steve, so I can get dressed."

MacBride sat down and stroked the dog and Kennedy rose and began to fumble into his clothing.

"Know anything about Dolly Ireland, Kennedy?"

"Who? Dolly Ireland? Sure. I think she's a dress model these days. Fitz used to run around a lot with her. You'd see them at all the places. They looked swell together. Dolly's one of these girls—well, you know, she walks right up to you, sticks out her hand and says, 'Hi, boy.' I always thought she was pretty regular, though I saw her get mad once and crown a guy with a bottle."

"Was Fitz and her, you know, ever that way?"

"You mean *that* way? Well, it's hard to say. They were together a lot, but it always looked like a sister and brother act to me. I wish I knew how I got that dog."

"Where does Dolly work?"

"Over on Central Avenue. Maffee's."

MacBride stood up and the dog reared and pushed him down onto the bed. The skipper grinned, cuffed the dog and said, "Some dog, Kennedy."

"They carry brandy around in the Alps."

Chapter VI

Mac**BRIDE** went to Maffee's on Central Avenue and was told that Dolly Ireland had not come in. They gave him her address and he had Gahagan drive him to 598 Moor Street. It was a five-storied walk-up and he found Dolly Ireland's name alongside a door on the third floor. When she opened the door he could smell coffee making.

"I'm MacBride from Headquarters," he said.

"Yes?"

"Talk to you," he said, inviting himself in with a gesture.

She was dressed in a white shirtwaist and a snug skirt of speckled gray flannel. Her yellow hair was long, it was pulled tight around the back of her neck and rolled in a bun on her left ear. Her face was a little bony, with wide, sensuous, attractive lips, and her eyes were very blue.

"Sure," she said, motioning him in. "I'm just making breakfast."

"Hate to interrupt," he said, going in and sitting down when she nodded to an armchair.

A tea-wagon was set for one.

"Have some coffee?" she asked.

"Smells good. Yeah."

She poured out two cups and nibbled on a piece of toast.

He said, "Murder's pretty serious, ain't it, Miss Ireland?"

"You ought to know, Captain; you handle enough of it."

"Yeah. What were you doing down around Union Station last night, about eight, with Steamboat Hodge?"

She looked at him, gave a startled smile. "Boy, you get around, don't you?"

"I hear things."

"Well, there's a dress shop in the station run by a friend of mine, Nora Burns, and I stopped by to tell her that Maffee had a few samples she ought to buy. I was on my way to the *Million Club*. When I left the station, it was by the north door, I ran into Steamboat. Steamboat always goes down to the station to buy his old home-town newspaper. He was born and brought up in Detroit, you know. Well, he was pretty drunk. I took him by the arm and walked him past the station. I remember he stopped to give a blind man a quarter and he said, 'Buddy, it's tough you're blind, because you can't see a looker here—a real gal—Miss Dolly Ireland.' I shushed him and we walked on for about three blocks, but he said he had a date some place and I shoved him in a cab and then took one myself."

MacBride looked into his coffee and said, "H'm." Then he said, swirling the coffee around, "I got to ask personal questions sometimes. I got to ask you were you ever in love with Fitz?"

She smiled ruefully. "That *is* personal."

"Yeah, I know."

She sighed. "Fitz is one of those men—one of those grand men. But I don't know, we just seemed to eat and drink and dance a bit and kid around. Being around Fitz was always comfortable."

"That's a part-way answer, ain't it?"

She smiled ruefully again. "Yes, I guess it is. Fitz used to look at the moon with me a lot but I was never up there in the moon. It was just as well. We always had good times. He's getting what he's always wanted and I'm mighty glad."

"You don't look sore."

"Why should I? I'm no sorehead. Why be sore when a grand guy like Fitz makes the grade?"

MacBride finished his cup of coffee. "Where's Steamboat?"

"The last I saw of Steamboat was when I put him in that cab I told you about." She suddenly looked at MacBride with very level eyes. "I saw Fitz late last night. He didn't look good. What's up?"

"I don't know. There's a chance Steamboat knocked off Tiny Torgensen."

She put out a hand. "My God, don't let Fitz know that! All Fitz has done for Steamboat, if he found out Steamboat killed Torgensen—"

"I know, I know," MacBride muttered. "That's why I'm trying to find Steamboat. I think Fitz suspects."

Her face had gone white. "Poor Fitz! Poor Fitz!"

When MacBride walked out on the sidewalk Gahagan was beating himself on the chest with his fists and saying, "Ah, wotta day, wotta day! I feel like a million bucks. I could write a pome, I could. A pome I could write."

MacBride, not paying any attention, stood for a minute nibbling his lip and staring narrow-eyed into space. Gahagan kept on pounding himself on the chest, and finally MacBride looked at him, made a sour face and said:

"What the hell are you doing?"

Gahagan threw up his arms, shrugged and climbed disconsolately in behind the wheel.

At Headquarters Marcia Friel was waiting with her brother. Her face looked a little drawn. "Captain…" she said.

The skipper was rapt in thought and a kind of hard, bony dignity. He pulled himself out of it. "Yes, Miss Friel."

Lewis Friel said, "It's about Fitz."

"I saw him this morning," Marcia said. "I think he was out all night. He wouldn't admit it, but I think he was. Can't you do something? Can't you go to him and talk to him? Can't you advise him to sell his business to anyone who wants to buy it? I know it was admirable of him to want to sell only to Torgensen, but now that Torgensen's dead, why, what does it matter? If he got out of the business now, it might help him a lot."

Lewis Friel's brows were knotted seriously. He said suddenly, "I'm afraid, even, that he might not sell at all now, and if he doesn't, I'm out of luck. I've got this real-estate business all set up, I put a lot of money into it, and if Fitz backs out, I'm sunk."

Marcia said, "Oh, forget about your business, Lewis. We've got to think about Fitz first. I don't know… somehow"—she shuddered—"I'm afraid for him. That look in his eyes."

MacBride muttered, "I'll have another talk with him today."

He went up to his office and spent an hour on routine matters. At noon he released everybody in the holdover. He tried to get hold of Mularkey and phoned three places but could not locate him. He phoned Steamboat's place in Lyons Street and the man on duty there had nothing to report. At twelve-thirty Moriarity blew in and said:

"What's wrong with Kennedy?"

"Well, what is?"

"It's his day off and he won't take a drink. He's busier than a guy juggling eight balls. Running around town, turning down drinks."

"Probably looking for Steamboat."

"I asked him and he said no."

"Well, that's Kennedy for you. He gets tired of ideas quick. Soon as he gets me tied up in an idea, he drops it and goes looking for another one. I think he does it just to annoy me."

At three o'clock Bettdecken phoned from the central-room desk and said, "I hear a guy's been killed down in the *Shane Hotel.* I thought maybe you'd wanna know."

Chapter VII

*T*HE SHANE was a second-class hotel out on Wolff Avenue. It was pretty crowded. It was always pretty crowded, for it was hard by the wholesale houses. MacBride weaved through the people in the lobby and went up to the desk showing his badge.

"Where's the trouble?" he asked the clerk.

"Ten-twelve."

The skipper went up in a noisy, crowded elevator, got out at the tenth floor and went down a narrow corridor checking off door numbers. He opened 1012 and a cop turned and looked at him and then touched his cap indifferently.

It was a single room with a metal bed painted brown and with a grain, to look like wood. Two precinct detectives, Klein and Marsotto, were standing with their hands on their hips. A man from the coroner's office was rolling down his sleeves. There were three uniformed cops besides the one standing at the door. The dead man lay on the floor with his head smashed.

MacBride said, "That's Steamboat Hodge."

Marsotto turned. "Yeah. That's what I told Klein. He was registered as J. Martin, though."

"He was hiding out," MacBride said.

"That's what I thought."

"What time did it happen?"

"Well," said Marsotto, "a guy in the room below heard a racket up here at a quarter to three. He phoned the desk and told 'em to send somebody up and quiet it, account of he had a headache. About five minutes later they sent a guy up and he found this. When he arrived, that chair was overturned, that bureau was knocked cockeyed, and there was blood in the bathroom where somebody'd washed."

MacBride asked, "What was he hit with?"

Marsotto pointed. "That pinch bottle there. It was washed when the guy washed his hands and I'll bet you don't find any fingerprints on it."

"Anything else I ought to know?"

"Well, the clerk said that at about half-past one this guy came down to the desk and asked for an envelope, a thick one, they were safe-keeping for him." He pointed. "There's the envelope but there ain't nothing in it. Whatever was in it, it was snatched."

"Anything else?"

"Yeah. One of the elevator lads said that about the time it happened he took on a guy here. The guy's hat was dented in and he was drying his hands on his handkerchief. The guy was tall, with kind of long flat cheeks and sandy hair." He glanced at MacBride. "It sounds like Fitz Mularkey. We ain't touched anything here, there might be prints. Rugge is on his way over here now."

"Find a gun?"

"Yeah. Steamboat's old double-action Colt with his initials carved in the bone handle. I'm holding that for Rugge too. It was halfway across the room from Steamboat, by the bureau. The way it looks, well, fingerprints have been rubbed from everything. You can tell on the bed there and on the basin in the bathroom and the mirror—all around here."

MacBride was laconic: "Well, you don't need me here. I'll go over and see Fitz."

He went downstairs and walked into the hotel bar and had a beer. He sipped thoughtfully of the beer, his face expressionless as a slab of wood. Usually he drank beer down with a couple of swallows. This time he took it like wine. He paid up and brooded his way through the lobby and out to the street where the Buick was parked. Gahagan was posing for a picture which a couple of young girls, obviously tourists, were taking.

"I wisht I had me medals along," Gahagan was telling them.

"What medals?" MacBride asked.

Gahagan made a petulant face and shoved in behind the wheel. MacBride climbed in back. "Fitz's place," he said.

"The *Million Club?*"

"No. Where he lives. Wait. Go to the *Million Club* first."

There was an early cocktail crowd at the *Million Club* when Mac-Bride got there. He found Tom Carney in the bar and said:

"I hear a couple of your boys took a gun away from Steamboat last night." He added, "Don't try to think up any fast ones."

Carney laughed shortly, a little puzzled. "Well, sure. Yeah. We took a gun away from him. He didn't have it out. We just took it away from him and sent him on his way."

"What'd you do with it?"

"Stuck it in the safe."

"Get it."

"Sure. Come along."

They went into the office and MacBride stood dour-faced while Carney took a key and opened the wall safe. The gun was not there. Carney turned from the safe shaking his head in puzzlement.

MacBride growled. "Who else has a key to it?"

"Hell, only Fitz."

"That's enough."

Outside, he said to Gahagan, "Now go to Fitz's place where he lives."

Going up in the elevator, the skipper seemed to sag a bit. There was a look around his mouth as though a bitter taste were in it. His face appeared to grow more haggard as the elevator climbed and he rubbed his hands against his thighs because his palms were sweaty. He looked leaner, thinner, as he walked down the corridor, and his head was forward, his jaw hanging, and his shoulders appeared lifeless. There was not about him that usual snap and self-certainty when he reached the door to the apartment. He hesitated. Indecision, hardly ever a part of him, crinkled across his face and down his body. He licked his lips. He put his finger on the bell-button, hesitated, then poked it hard. His hand went toward his gun but he shook his head and took his hand away again. He straightened his shoulders, cleared his throat. He ground every hint of emotion out of his face.

A houseman opened the door.

MacBride thrust him aside, walked down the entrance hall and out into the center of the living-room, where he stopped, for no one was in the room. The houseman came in timidly.

"Where's Mr. Mularkey?" the skipper asked.

"I think—" The houseman looked aloft towards the gallery.

MacBride went up.

Mularkey was in his den at the end of the gallery. He sat in the big desk chair, his hat, bashed in, on his head and his gloved hands resting palms down on the desk. He gave MacBride a brief, uninterested, absent-minded glance, and then returned his stare to the surface of the desk.

The skipper said, "I've come to get you, Fitz."

"Yeah," Mularkey muttered.

His fancy books, which he never read, circled him and added a strange dignity to the utter silence. He took a fresh cigar from his pocket, put it between his lips but did not light it. He leaned forward, putting his elbows on the desk, rubbing his gloved hands slowly together.

"Why'd you do it, Fitz?" the skipper asked.

Mularkey kept rubbing his hands slowly together, staring at the cased books which he never read. "He killed Tiny."

"You promised me—"

"H'm. He threatened to kill Marcia. He told me he'd kill Marcia."

Into the minute's silence that followed MacBride said, "Why didn't you phone me and let me take him?"

"I d' know," Mularkey murmured. "I d' know."

MacBride dropped into a chair as though someone had smacked him across the back of the knees. His face was heavy, bitter, disgusted.

"That's all right, Steve," Mularkey said slowly.

MacBride said, "It's tough, Fitz, that you won't be able to plead self-defense."

Mularkey looked at him.

"I know," MacBride said, "that Steamboat's gun was taken away from him last night and put in your safe. You took it out." He added, "You took it over to his hotel and left it there."

Mularkey leaned back. "You're right. You can't blame me for trying."

MacBride said, "What did you take out of that envelope?"

"What envelope?"

"There was an envelope that Steamboat got out of the hotel safe before you got there. The clerk said it felt pretty thick. The envelope was empty when the precinct men got there."

Mularkey looked confused, his eyes flicking many times at the skipper. Then he shrugged. "Hell, I don't know. I don't know anything about that."

MacBride went on: "Another thing. You took a lot of care about wiping away fingerprints, which seems funny when you had no intention, as far as I can make out, of trying to scram."

Mularkey looked morose. "Hell, when I got back here I thought, what's the use?"

"Did you ever hear of Dolly Ireland crowning a guy with a bottle once?"

"Dolly?... No. Why?"

"I don't know. Except that Steamboat was crowned with a bottle."

Mularkey put a chill look on him, then smiled. "It was the only thing handy I could crown him with. I know you're trying hard as hell to give me a break, Steve, and thanks. I could've forgiven Steamboat about Tiny, maybe. It was when he said he'd kill Marcia that I saw red."

MacBride was looking hard at him, thinking hard. The skipper said, "It means the chair, Fitz. You went there deliberately to kill Steamboat. It means weeks and months of trial and then more weeks in the death house. It means...."

Mularkey frowned and rubbed his jaw with his thumbnail. Then he stood up and tossed away his unlit cigar. He casually opened his desk drawer and pulled out a gun and said:

"I just pulled a gun on you."

"Yeah, I see."

"Okey, Steve. I pulled a gun on a cop. Pull your own and let me have it. I can take the chair but I can't be pestered by a long-drawn-out trial."

"Put the gun away."

"Do what I tell you."

"Put it away."

"If you don't, I'm going to slam out of here and in an hour you'll have every cop in town after me—so do as I tell you."

MacBride pulled his gun and it banged in his hand. Mularkey's gun fell to the floor and he looked down stupidly at his bloody right hand. He said almost sorrowfully:

"You only got me in the hand."

"Yeah. Where did you think I'd get you?"

Mularkey grimaced. MacBride crossed the room looking for the slug that had glanced off Mularkey's hand. He saw a tear along the backs of three books, high up.

"Get one of those books, Steve."

MacBride had to get up on his toes, and as he was toppling one of the books out, Mularkey scooped up his gun in his left hand and jammed it against MacBride's back.

"Drop your gun, Steve."

"You go on being funny, huh?"

"Drop it. I'd hate like hell to drill you, pal, but I'm a desperate man."

MacBride dropped his gun. Mularkey shoved him roughly forward and was able to pick up the discarded gun with his bloody right hand.

He said, "I'll leave it with the elevator boy."

MacBride said in a thick, emotional voice, "The next time I see you, Fitz, it'll probably be on a slab in the morgue."

"I just can't stand a long trial," Mularkey said.

He backed out of the den, disappeared at a run. The skipper did not start after him. He took out his battered briar and his worn tobacco pouch and loaded the bowl to a little less than flush. He lit up slowly, then blew out the latch and walked down to the living-room. In the elevator, he said to the boy:

"Did Mr. Mularkey leave me something?"

"He left a gun for Captain MacBride."

"Thanks."

Chapter VIII

WHEN MacBride entered the small lobby of the apartment house where Dolly Ireland lived, the janitor was polishing the brass top of the newel post. The skipper had forgotten the number of her apartment. He said to the janitor:

"What's Miss Ireland's apartment?"

"Thirty-two."

MacBride drummed up the staircase, heard the janitor say: "But she ain't in."

The skipper came down again.

"When'd she leave?"

The janitor made a gesture of taking his hat off but didn't. "Oh, half an hour ago. I carried her bag out and got her a cab."

"Bag, huh?" the skipper muttered to himself.

"Yop. Went to Union Station."

"What'd her bag look like?"

"Black. I guess patent leather. *D.I.* on it, so it was hers."

MacBride strode out to the Buick and said, "Burn it to Union Station, Gahagan. Siren and all."

That was right up Gahagan's alley. He opened the car wide and broadcast with the siren. People, cars swept out of his way. He waved to cops he knew.

"Never mind waving!" MacBride shouted. "When you do seventy, keep both hands on the wheel!"

Gahagan arrived in front of Union Station with the siren scream-ing and instantly cops came running from all directions. MacBride hopped off and pounded his heels into the waiting room. The clock above the information booth said 4:52. MacBride went on to the train gates. Two boards were up showing trains scheduled to leave at 5:30 and 5:55. He went back into the waiting room. Nowhere did he see Dolly Ireland. Of the man in the information booth he asked:

"What was the last train to leave here and where was it bound?"

"The last was the Twilight Flyer, for Boston. It pulled out at four-forty."

"What was the one before that?"

"A local for New York. She pulled out at three-fifty."

The skipper checked up with the porters. One said he had carried a black patent leather suitcase for a woman boarding the Twilight Flyer. MacBride banged into a phone booth, called Headquarters. He consulted a time table, held it to the light while he said into the transmitter:

"Call the state police barracks at Bencroft and tell 'em to board the Twilight Flyer, due there in twenty minutes. Tell 'em to take off a Dolly Ireland. She's traveling with a black patent leather suitcase with the letters *D.I.* on it. She's a tall, good-looking blonde about twenty-eight. Ask 'em to run her back here in a car to Headquarters—quick."

He hung up and sailed out of the station; said to the dozen cops gathered round the Buick, "Okey, boys; it's nothing," and climbed in. "Headquarters, Gahagan."

"Siren and all?"

"No. You've had your fun."

The skipper strode into Headquarters with his shoulders squared, his arms swinging, the cuffs of his trousers slapping his ankles.

Bettdecken said, "I hear Mularkey was the bad boy o' the Steamboat killing. You sent out an alarm for him yet?"

"No."

"Gonna?"

"No."

MacBride went to his office and crammed his pipe and pulled hard on it. He had held off the general alarm for Mularkey because he had an idea Mularkey was determined to be taken only after a gunfight. The skipper was sure of this. But he wasn't so sure that Mularkey had told the truth. He went back mentally to the scene of the crime, the words of the precinct man on the case. He made notes, put down a lot of numbers, scratched his head and shook it and sucked on his pipe and when it was empty loaded it again.

At 5:25 the Bencroft barracks called. Dolly Ireland had been taken off the train and was being rushed back to Richmond City by automobile. The skipper hung up, rose and took a satisfied punch at the air. The door opened and Kennedy drifted in, saying:

"So Steamboat got it, eh?"

"Plenty."

"I told you you were wasting your time rounding up all those heels."

MacBride grinned ferociously. "Oh, yeah? Well, don't kid yourself, baby. I rounded 'em up and Pickney Sax got sore and came here and we had an argument and out of that argument I learned things. I learned that not only was Steamboat around Union Station when Torgensen was killed, but Dolly Ireland was there too. I pull boners sometimes. Okey, I do. But sometimes a boner turns over and you learn things." He flexed his shoulders, smacked his hands together and said, "You just sit here, Kennedy." He opened a drawer, pulled out a bottle. "Nuzzle this bottle and hang around and see what Daddy MacBride will have to show you."

Kennedy took a drink, looked at it. "So now you think Dolly Ireland is mixed up in it."

"I wouldn't tell you a thing, boy. You just sit and wait."

Kennedy smiled. "Okey, big fella. Your liquor's good, the chair is comfortable and I don't mind your company too much."

The skipper sat down to a mass of desk work. "And shut up. I got to get caught up here."

At half-past six Kennedy was in a mellow alcoholic fog and Mac-Bride was putting aside his last paper. The phone rang and the skipper scooped it up, said, "Yup.... You bet. Right away."

Two minutes later the door opened and a state police sergeant carrying a black patent leather suitcase, came in with Dolly Ireland.

"Thanks, Sergeant," MacBride said.

"Don't mention it."

"Wait downstairs, will you?"

"Sure thing."

Kennedy, looking a little befuddled, put his sixth drink aside and passed his fingers across his face. Dolly Ireland stood where the sergeant had left her, just inside the door. Her face was flushed, her eyes were alive with uncertainty, but her lips were set.

MacBride was dour. "Sit down," he said.

She sat down, inhaled and then let her breath out slowly.

"Why'd you beat it?" asked MacBride, watching her narrowly.

"I didn't beat it," she said.

"Just went away, huh?"

She nodded. "Just went away. Took a little trip—or started to."

"When did you decide to take the trip?"

She shrugged. "On the spur of the moment."

"After Steamboat was killed?"

Her eyes snapped upward. They widened. They stared first at Kennedy, then at MacBride. Confusion left its red trail down across her cheeks and round her neck. Her lips stumbled and her hands trembled.

MacBride said, "Were you afraid that Steamboat, going around drunk the way he was, would pop off about you and him getting together to kill Tiny Torgensen?"

Her confusion kept her speechless.

"Did you," MacBride asked, "put Steamboat up to kill Torgensen?"

She flared, "No!"

"You killed Steamboat with a bottle, didn't you?"

She grimaced.

MacBride pointed. "You killed Steamboat with a bottle and Fitz took the blame for it!"

"What is this, what is this?" she said brokenly.

MacBride was stern. "Things don't hang together. Fitz confessed to killing Steamboat. But listen to this. At the scene of the crime, Steamboat's room in the *Hotel Shane*, a lot of care was taken to wipe away all fingerprints. It takes time to do that, to go over everything carefully. I judge it would take at least ten minutes and very likely more. A guy in a room under Steamboat's heard sounds of a fight and called the desk to send up somebody to stop it. Five minutes later the desk sent up a guy. The guy found Steamboat dead."

MacBride paused. His eyes got hard.

"Now Fitz had to finish his fight and wipe out all those prints in five minutes. And if he did that—just suppose, for the sake of argument, he did—why should he leave the hotel with his hat bashed in and wiping his hands dry on his handkerchief? Fitz didn't kill Steamboat. You did and Fitz covered you. Now listen to me, lady. Something was stolen when Steamboat was killed. Something out of an envelope. Fitz didn't know that. He looked surprised when I told him."

The skipper stood up and said, "Open your bag."

"No."

"Okey, I'll open it."

She cried, "You leave it alone!"

Kennedy stood up and crossed to her. "Come on, Dolly. Give *me* the key."

She stared up at him with a stricken look.

His eyes were lazy, without expression. He held his hand out and after a minute she gave him a key. He knelt and opened the suitcase and MacBride leaned over the spittoon to knock out his pipe. Kennedy slipped a small photograph swiftly up his sleeve and MacBride came over from the spittoon and got down on his knees. The skipper ransacked the suitcase while Kennedy knelt, watching him absently. MacBride found nothing of interest.

He stood up and looked down slyly at Dolly Ireland. She was crying. He grunted, said, "That won't get you anything here."

Kennedy tapped a yawn. "What time did you say Steamboat was murdered?"

"About a quarter to three," MacBride growled.

"Well," said Kennedy, "that's funny. I was with Dolly from half-past one till three o'clock."

MacBride spun, stabbed him with a dark stare.

"At the *English Chop House,* eating," Kennedy added, "in case you want to check up."

The door opened and Haims, the ballistics expert, stood in the doorway holding Steamboat's bone-handled revolver. He said, "This ain't the gun that killed Torgensen."

MacBride muttered, "Did you check up carefully?"

"I didn't have to. This is a forty-five. Torgensen was killed with a thirty-eight."

MacBride's eyes glittered, his lips snapped shut. He turned on the annunciator, rapped into it, "Pick up Pickney Sax!"

Kennedy was saying, "Haims, try this one," as he withdrew from his inside pocket a .38 short-barreled revolver.

MacBride clipped, "Where'd you get that?"

"Never mind until we get Haims' report. What you ought to do now, Skipper, is find Fitz. Have you tried Marcia Friel's place?"

"Do you mean to tell me Fitz knocked off Tiny?" MacBride demanded.

"I'm not telling you anything. But it might be a good idea to get hold of him." He turned to Haims, saying, "When you check up on that gun, if I'm not here, phone Western four-one."

Chapter IX

MARCIA FRIEL'S living-room was long, narrow, with casement windows overlooking Western Drive and the park. She made no attempt to hide a troubled curiosity when MacBride and Kennedy walked in on her. Kennedy dawdled but the skipper moved with vigor and his eyes snapped darkly around the living-room. Lewis Friel shut off a radio to which he had been listening and reached down to squirt charged water into a half-consumed highball.

MacBride said outright, "I'm looking for Fitz."

Marcia looked at her brother and Lewis Friel tasted his drink and said, "Haven't seen him since this morning. You remember we told you about that. I haven't, anyhow. Maybe Marcia has."

"No," she said thoughtfully; and to MacBride, "but what's the matter, what's wrong?"

"Steamboat Hodge was killed, murdered, at a quarter to three today."

Lewis Friel said, "Oh-oh," and set down his glass very carefully.

Marcia Friel began to shake. "But Fitz didn't do it! He promised me—"

"He told me he did," MacBride said.

Lewis Friel looked puzzled. "But if he told you—I mean I thought you were looking for him."

"I am," grunted the skipper. "He got away."

Marcia sat down, unnerved. "Is this a blow," she murmured.

Lewis Friel seemed exasperated. "Damn Fitz!" he exclaimed. "I told him, I begged him to let the police handle everything. He's crazy. He's—oh, I don't know—he's crazy. He must be!"

"Be quiet, Lewis," Marcia said.

"Oh, yes, be quiet!" he flung back at her. "I spend weeks and months arranging for our business deal—corporation papers and everything— fees—day and night work— I'm no millionaire. I can't afford—"

"Do be quiet," Marcia said in a muffled voice.

MacBride said, "Is Fitz here?"

Marcia started. "No—no." She looked around the room. She looked at Lewis. "Here? No, I haven't seen him since early this morning."

Kennedy had wandered to the far end of the room and was standing in front of a console scattered with cigarette boxes, glasses and several decanters of liquor. He turned and cut aimlessly across the room and sat down.

MacBride said, "I'll have to look."

"Oh, don't be foolish," Lewis Friel said. "Fitz is not here."

The skipper was stubborn. He visited the dining-room, the kitchen, two bathrooms and two bedrooms. Returning to the living-room, he said:

"Has he been here since noon?"

Marcia was on the point of tears. "Oh, no—no!" she cried.

"I want the truth," the skipper blared, pointing. "You're close to him, both of you, and I want the truth. I want to know where he is. I want to get him personally. If I don't, if I have to send out a general alarm for him, he'll be killed. He threatened to shoot it out and he will—and he'll be riddled!"

Lewis Friel ground fist into palm and said, "The fool, the fool! The utter fool!"

Kennedy said, "Could I, by the way, have a drink?"

Marcia rose out of pure nervousness and said, "I'll get it for you."

"Just straight, please."

She crossed the room to the console, picked up a glass and one of the decanters. Then suddenly she dropped both, staggered, and caught hold of the edge of the table. The decanter hit the floor, its glass stopper popped out and its contents flowed out. Lewis Friel strode across the room, his eyes dark with concern, and took hold of her.

"Marcia!" he said.

"Have her lay down," the skipper said. "This business probably got her down. Come on, Kennedy; let's blow."

Marcia suddenly screamed hysterically. Lewis put his hand over her mouth and cried, "Marcia, get hold of yourself!"

But she screamed again, half laughing, through his fingers. MacBride crossed to her saying, "Come, now, Miss Friel. I didn't mean to upset you...." He took hold of her arm and shook her and it was at about this time that Mularkey came into the room with his left hand in his pocket and in his right hand a gun.

"Quit it, Steve," he growled.

MacBride turned on his heel and looked at him, unbuttoning his coat as he did so.

"Watch your hand, Steve," Mularkey said wearily. He looked worn and haggard and the fine dignity with which he used to carry himself was gone. He looked like a sick man, his face drained and its muscles sagging. Only in his eyes was there life—a chill blue glare, unwavering.

He demanded, "Why didn't you turn in a general alarm on me? I gave you the chance. I tell you I won't be taken alive!" His breath pounded hoarsely. "You don't have to go soft about old friendships. I'm not asking for a break."

Marcia had covered her face with her hands.

Mularkey ground on, "You can't pick on Marcia. I won't let you do it. Marcia, go in your bedroom. Lewis, you take her in and close the door. Take her in, I tell you!"

From the depths of the chair in which Kennedy lounged he said, "Wait."

Mularkey roared, "Pay no attention to him!"

"Wait," said Kennedy. He rose, looking slightly foggy and unsteady on his feet. "Mr. Friel...."

Lewis Friel looked at him across Marcia's shoulder.

"Now listen, Kennedy," MacBride said, "don't show off."

Ignoring the skipper, Kennedy said, "Mr. Friel—"

The ringing of the telephone bell interrupted him. Lewis Friel went over to answer it. He turned and said to Kennedy:

"It's for you."

Kennedy crossed the room and picked up the instrument. "Yes, this is Kennedy.... I see.... Well, thank you so much, my friend."

He hung up, scratched his head, then said, "Oh, yes... Mr. Friel. When I stopped by your office today for a little chat about your proposed partnership with Fitz, I remarked that you looked like a pretty strong fellow. Then I said that I'd never been able to gain any and that that was funny, because my old man was a big strapping fellow and so was my mother pretty large. You said it was not unusual in your case, though you didn't think you were particularly heavy—not as heavy as your late father, who you said was over six feet. Do you remember that?"

Friel chuckled. "Why, of course."

"Kennedy," barked Mularkey, "you keep your mouth shut and—"

"Miss Friel," said Kennedy, "in that little chat we had today when we met on the corner of Belmont and Grove I said jokingly that I'd like to take you dancing sometime but that I was too short. Offhand I asked you if you took after your father or mother. You said your mother. You said your father was short."

Mularkey came towards him threateningly, while still keeping an eye on MacBride.

Kennedy held his ground and said quietly to Mularkey, "He said his father was tall and she said her father was short. So what? So they aren't sister and brother. Steamboat's .45 never killed Torgensen. Torgensen was killed by a .38. That phone call I just had was from Headquarters. They've got the gun over there. I found it in a dump heap across the way from the station. Haims at Headquarters says it checks with slugs found in Torgensen. A dealer down in Beaumont Street told me he sold it to Lewis Friel."

Friel shouted, "That's a lie!"

"You can't prove it's a lie."

"Oh, can't I?" snapped Friel. He pulled a gun from his pocket and said, "There's my gun and I'll face that dealer and make him prove he sold me the gun you're talking about."

Kennedy said, "Steve, take a look at his gun."

MacBride strode across towards Friel. Something snapped in Friel's eyes and he jumped back. "Hold on there!" he said.

MacBride scowled. "Don't point that gun at me."

"I'm pointing it at you."

Marcia said, "I've got 'em from this side, Lewis."

Kennedy turned. Marcia Friel was holding a very small automatic.

Lewis Friel said to Kennedy. "You almost trapped me, smart boy."

"What do you mean, almost?" Kennedy drawled.

Mularkey was now the most dazed man in the room. His mouth hung open and his eyes gaped, the gun in his hand drooped.

"Nobody moves," Lewis Friel said; and to Marcia, "Get your hat and coat and my hat and that cash out of the bureau. Pick up all pictures, too."

She moved with alacrity, going into the bedroom and returning in a moment with her hat and coat on. She gave Lewis his hat, said:

"All right, I have the money."

Friel said: "Drop your gun, Fitz."

Mularkey dropped it, still in a daze.

"If you make one pass at yours, MacBride," Friel said, "I'll drill you. That goes for you too, Kennedy."

MacBride's face was wooden. "Get going," he muttered.

"We intend to. Come on, Marcia."

They backed up swiftly to the far end of the room, glanced at the door through which they must go into the foyer. The skipper stood motionless, his hands raised, his right hand dropping imperceptibly, the fingers already formed to grip a gun's butt. The girl and the man must have realized that their greatest danger lay at the doorway. MacBride realized this too. His eyes were sharp and hard and narrowed down.

Mularkey came out of his daze. It seemed as though all at once he put two and two together. Chagrin, humiliation, an awful sadness— all these grew up and out of his eyes. He swallowed hard. He looked at MacBride. He was so near that he could see the slight lowering of the skipper's right hand, the tilt of his shoulder, the hawklike expression on his face.

A great dignity came back to Mularkey. He laughed. It was a rich, round laugh, and it boomed in the room. He swept down towards the gun which he had discarded. It was practical suicide. Lewis Friel fired and Mularkey laughed as he was hit and tried in a vague, fuddled way to get his fingers around the gun. The skipper's body seemed to weave and out of its weaving came his gun. The gun cleared and exploded simultaneously.

Lewis Friel jerked against the wall. Marcia fired. Cold-faced, hot-eyed, she held her gun up and fired again. The second one stabbed MacBride in the leg. She held her gun trained on him for a third shot. There was a twitch on his lip as he fired and a gagged feeling in his throat as he saw her drop her gun.

Mularkey was down on his hands and knees and sagging lower. He was laughing quietly, reflectively, and still trying to pick up the gun. Kennedy, who was unarmed, took it away from him. Ducked as two explosions banged in the room. One of those was MacBride's. Lewis Friel's smoking gun came up again. MacBride pressed his own trigger. It clicked. Kennedy fired and Lewis Friel turned away and fell through the doorway into the foyer. They could still see his feet. The feet did not move.

The skipper stood licking his dry lips. He moved his leg and felt the warm blood trickling. He limped across to where Mularkey was now sitting on the floor. Kennedy was telephoning for an ambulance. MacBride sat down on the floor beside Mularkey.

"How you feeling, Fitz?"

"I dunno," Mularkey said. A dreamy smile was on his face. "Funny, ain't it? Funny...." He laughed brokenly. "When I was feeling mixed up and lousy all day today, I kinda felt like seeing Dolly Ireland. Funny, huh?"

Chapter X

MacBRIDE, lying in a hospital bed, said, "Talk to me, Kennedy."

"Well," said Kennedy, "they weren't brother and sister. She was going to marry Fitz for his dough. Lewis was going to manage the dough. She talked plenty in order to clear herself of the murder of Steamboat. Lewis killed Steamboat. It seems Steamboat raided her apartment one night and found some letters buried in an old trunk. Love letters, from Lewis to Marcia while she was in Boston, before she came here. In one of them Lewis wrote of meeting Fitz and about Fitz yearning to meet a real high-class gal. Lewis suggested that she come down and pose as his sister. Well, Steamboat wrote her a letter the other day—we saw part of it in the impressions on that pad we found in Steamboat's room. He gave her hell and, the part we didn't see, he told her he had no intention of telling Fitz if she'd clear out. She phoned him and told him she'd like to see him.

"Well, he wouldn't go to her place and she wouldn't go to his, so he said he'd take a room at the *Shane*. But she didn't go. She sent Lewis. Steamboat was drunk. He told Lewis he had letters that would prove they weren't brother and sister. He waved them at Lewis. Lewis conked him with the bottle and took the letters and ran back to tell Marcia what he'd done. Marcia, to save him, went to Fitz and told Fitz that she'd killed Steamboat because Steamboat had attacked her because she wouldn't promise to leave Fitz. She also told Fitz that Steamboat'd told her he killed Tiny. Fitz sent her home. He reached the hotel an hour after Steamboat had been killed. He wiped everything clean of fingerprints, then smashed some furniture around and walked out, to make it seem, by the noise, that the killing happened an hour later than it actually did."

"Where does Dolly fit in?"

"I'd been wondering about Lewis and Marcia. They didn't look like sister and brother. Just on an off chance I asked first one and then the other about their father. Then I crashed her apartment and found that all her clothes had Boston labels. I swiped a small photograph of her and went to Dolly Ireland. Things began to connect. Torgensen came from Boston. Marcia's clothes came from Boston. I gave Dolly the photograph, which had the photographer's name on it, and told her to go to Boston, to the photographer's, and see what name the picture was registered under. Whatever name she got, she was to go to the names of the dress shops I'd got out of Marcia's clothes and check up there. You crabbed that by having the state cops drag her back."

"Why did Marcia faint that time, or almost?"

"Well, I wasn't sure about anything, so when you had Dolly in the office I opened her bag because I knew she had Marcia's picture in it. I slipped it out. At the apartment, I put it back where I'd stolen it from—on the console. They'd missed it, and then when they saw it again—"

"I catch on. But what about that gun you had Haims examine?"

"I did find it where I said I found it, down near the station. Some jumpy guy must have tossed it away. So when Haims told me over the wire that it didn't check, I told Lewis that it did just as a gag. He pulled his gun and I meant to have you take that and check it."

"So they came from Boston?"

Kennedy nodded. "They both knew Tiny Torgensen and they knew that Torgensen knew them as Frank Lewis and Marcy Corson, a couple of high-class, college-bred confidence workers. They had to kill Torgensen. With over a million at stake, they had to stop him from accidentally meeting them some day."

MacBride sighed. "Poor Fitz... poor old Fitz. He'd have died for that dame."

"Well, now he's living for Dolly Ireland. She's up with him now."

"Great!" grunted MacBride.

Kennedy stood up. "Well, I've got to get along."

"Stay sober, boy. Well, part sober anyhow.... Say, did you ever find out how you got that Saint Bernard?"

"Oh, sure. I traded a sheep dog for it."

"Sheep dog? Where'd you get the sheep dog?"

"That's something I haven't been able to check up on."

Crack Down

If anything gets Skipper MacBride seeing red it is to have someone give him a run-around.

Chapter I

THE DINNER hour at *Enrico's* in Flamingo Street was always a good one. The rectangular dining-room was busy, noisy with conversation and the clatter of crockery, the clank of knives and forks and spoons; the whir and clangor of the enormous polished cash register. It was rich with the smell of spiced foods, steaming soups, hot coffee. It was a plain place meant for eating and Enrico himself, short, plump, well-groomed, handled the cash and kept a warm eye on the patrons, a sharp eye on the black-coated waiters.

Steam and frost rimed the front windows that night in February when the door opened and Nick Danizak came in with Abel Springer, the criminal lawyer. Danizak was young, slender, wrapped in a blue chinchilla-cloth overcoat, belted, and with a flaring collar turned up to his ears. Over his left eye drooped the brim of a dark blue fedora. His face was thin, smooth, with a blade of a chin. His skin was tight, swart, with a grayish pallor underlying it. He had half-open expressionless black eyes. His underlip was thick, his upper nothing more than a penciled line. His nostrils moved at the rich odors of hot food and he murmured, "H'm."

Enrico dropped his brown-moss eyes; his whole face seemed to tighten with disapproval. Springer gave a dry short laugh. "Hiyuh, Enrico."

Enrico was polite. "Hello, Meester Springer."

Danizak stood running his half-open eyes the length and the breadth of the restaurant. He saw a beckoning finger rise from a table far in the rear.

"Come on," he said to Springer. His upper lip remained motionless when he spoke; only his lower moved.

Springer was gay, cocky; there was a brazen, good-humored leer on his dry, crackly face. He was much shorter than Danizak, skinny and pinch-shouldered. As they moved down the dining-room and

Danizak took off his hat and overcoat, small exclamatory sounds rose from scattered diners. Danizak looked straight ahead. When he reached the rearmost table he said, "Hello, guys," and hung up his things on a hook on the wall.

The two men at the table stood up. They were not beauties. The bigger of the two was the biggest man in the place and he had a face that looked as if a horse had stepped on it. But Pig Iron had never been near a horse in his life: a cop's night-stick had caught him one night. He stuck out a huge paw.

"Greetin's, Nick," he croaked.

"Yeah, greetin's, Nick," said Belly Skoba, thrusting out a round, pudgy hand.

Danizak gave each a hand briefly as he sat down and Springer,

having hung up his hat and coat, sat down too, chafing his spidery hands, winking, saying:

"Don't I get congratulated, too?"

"Jeese," said fat Belly Skoba, "you was great, counselor!"

Springer bowed mockingly. "That's better." He spread his fingers towards Danizak, said, "Boys, I give you Nick Danizak. I give you him back. I plucked him from the hot squat and I give him back to you. The State is chagrined. But we, we are infinitely happy, we are—"

"All right, all right," muttered Danizak. "Suppose we eat instead. I been sitting for days and weeks listening to you and that loud-mouthed District Attorney use a lot o' big words. I want a double Martini and then I want chow. And I can do without anybody talking for weeks to come. Hey, you with the false teeth," he said to a waiter, "how about some service?"

The waiter said, "Keep your shirt on."

A girl got up from a nearby table and came over. Her eyes were wide, there was a fluttery, dizzy smile on her face. "Are—are you Mr. Nick Danizak?" she gulped.

He gave her an upward uninterested look. "Yeah."

She gushed, "Well, Mr. Danizak, I was so interested in the trial, I *so* hoped you would be set free, I was *so* thrilled a couple of hours ago when I heard on the radio the jury said not guilty." She fidgeted with a small leather-bound book. "Mr. Danizak, will you give me your autograph?"

Danizak moved his half-open eyes to Springer. Springer made a slight negative movement of his head, then said, "Mr. Danizak would like to, madam, but as his attorney I don't think he should. Mr. Danizak is very tired and... thank you so much, but...."

She blushed. "Oh—well, of course, yes...." And fluttered back to her table.

The waiter came over and grunted, "Well?"

Danizak and Springer ordered.

Belly Skoba sighed. "How the dames fall for you, Nick!"

"Dames is all right," said Pig Iron hoarsely. "It sure was a dame that saved Nick from gettin' his slats fried on the—"

"Cut it," Danizak clipped.

"Jeese, Nick, I was just—what I was sayin'—"

Danizak looked at him. "Cut it."

Moriarity, sitting at a table with Kennedy of the *Free Press,* said, "Well, there he is, Kennedy. We get him and a lame-brained jury lets him go. MacBride's boiling so hard that if you put a hat on his head it'd bubble off."

Kennedy hiccoughed.

"Hahn?" said Moriarity.

"Nothing."

Moriarity leaned on his elbows above his cup of black coffee. His pale blue eyes glinted across the table at which the four men sat. Kennedy put a glass of brandy to his lips, sucked at it. His sleepy, washed-out eyes floated from Springer to Danizak. He put the brandy down and sipped some coffee.

He said, "It was the woman's word against the State's circumstantial evidence."

"Yeah," growled Moriarity. He chuckled ironically, "Yeah. I get it. Nick is just an injured young boy scout. Like those other two muggs with him there. Pig Iron Brenner and Belly Skoba." He made a low rasping sound. "The skipper's pinched Danizak four times in the past two years—but he's still free. Look at him sitting over there in a restaurant with honest people—"

"You're getting like MacBride," Kennedy drawled. "Selma Jellif saved him this time. Sometime he won't be so lucky—"

"Hey, look!"

Moriarity nodded to a man who had just entered *Enrico's*. The man was tall, lean, round-shouldered. He was young. His face was long, pale, with big glassy eyes and a loose, floppy mouth.

Kennedy murmured, "M'm'm. Selma Jellif's husband."

Jellif shoveled his hands in his overcoat pockets, craned his long neck. Presently one big eye cramped to a squint, the other remained balefully open. He took his hands out of his pockets, hunched his shoulders and strode recklessly among the tables towards the rear. He reached the table where the four men sat and Danizak leaned back in his chair and looked up at him.

Jellif said in a constricted voice, "Get up, Danizak."

"Sit down, sit down," said Danizak. "Have a drink."

Jellif's voice was loud. "Get up." It was so loud that people in the dining-room began looking towards the table beside which Jellif stood.

Danizak dropped a breadstick he had been eating, pushed back his chair and stood up. His eyes were half-open but not drowsy. He hooked his thumbs in his lower vest pockets. Jellif said, "You lousy bum!" and swung at him. Danizak ducked and shifted on his feet and Jellif crashed to the floor with the chair on which Danizak had sat. But Jellif scrambled to his feet, upsetting another table.

Pig Iron stood up slowly and Danizak said across to him, "You sit down." Pig Iron pulled at his ear and sat down and Jellif pivoted, spat out an oath and took another wild swing under which Danizak, not moving his hands, weaved. Springer yelled:

"Cut it out, you fool!"

Three waiters ganged on Jellif and he tussled with them and shouted, "Leggo! Lemme at this bum! Him and my wife—" He heaved and twisted while Danizak stood dark and close-faced and motionless. Some people got up from a table and moved out of the way. Enrico stood watching his three waiters at work. He was angry, exasperated. He did not like fights in his restaurant.

Moriarity rose, took his shield out of his pocket and walked over and held it up for the struggling Jellif to see. Moriarity said, "How would you like to get pinched, buddy?"

Jellif glared at him.

Moriarity turned to Danizak, "Want to make any charges?"

"The guy's screwy," Danizak said. "Just chuck him out."

Moriarity put his shield back into his pocket and said to Jellif, "Take the air, buddy."

"All right, I'll go," panted Jellif, his eyes bulging at Danizak. "But you ain't seen the last of me, Danizak. You ain't seen the last of me by a long shot."

Moriarity said to the three waiters, "Rush him out, boys. I hate to exercise after a big meal."

The three waiters manhandled Jellif to the front of the dining-room. Enrico opened the door and the waiters heaved Jellif out. Enrico closed the door, brushed his hands and went behind his cash counter. He was breathing angrily through his nose.

Danizak sat down, picked up the breadstick and nibbled on it. Springer broke a roll. Pig Iron and Belly Skoba looked down at the table. Nobody said anything.

Moriarity rejoined Kennedy and said, "Jellif was sore all right."

"So would you be sore, my friend, if your wife two-timed on you the way Selma Jellif did. She saved Danizak's life but lost her reputation—and probably her husband—doing it."

Moriarity squinted towards Danizak, muttered absently, "And for a rat like that," and wagged his head, unable to understand.

Chapter II

HACKINSON, the District Attorney, dropped to the big easy chair near the casement window of his living-room and took a swig at the hot Tom and Jerry. He was in pajamas and robe and he looked worn out, fagged. There were dark shadows beneath his eyes and the tug of strain had left its mark around his mouth. He sighed back into the generous depth of the chair, said:

"Well, it was a tough one to lose—but we can't win all of them."

MacBride was standing at the casement window watching the lights of the city winking in the cold clear night. There was a rebellious tight warp to his mouth. He growled, "The only way you can get a guy convicted nowadays is show a jury a movie of the guy actually committing the crime." He made a scornful rasping sound in his throat.

Hackinson said, "I had him, I had him till Selma Jellif turned up as a surprise witness. I had him placed near the scene of the crime by three witnesses. I had him hooked up with a long distance call to Cleveland the night before Rutter was killed. I had a witness who saw a green Olds coupé—Danizak's was a green Olds—parked a block from the scene of the crime five minutes before the shots were heard by Patrolman Boroski and when Boroski rounded that corner two minutes later there was no green coupé there. I had the glove that Boroski found in the gutter: we couldn't prove it was Danizak's but it fitted his hand perfectly. I had witnesses to show that up to three years ago Danizak and Rutter had been pals in petty jobs; they broke and Rutter left Richmond City. I tell you, Steve, I had him on the skids until the woman turned up. She swung the jury."

MacBride gave a harsh short laugh. "Yeah, it fitted in. It fitted in sweet. Danizak never offered an alibi. Then when the woman turns up and says she was with him that night in his apartment—then Springer shows the jury what a man of honor Danizak is. 'Nicholas Danizak didn't tell, gentlemen, because he wished to preserve a woman's good name.' There you have it, the whole works."

Hackinson nodded, took a drink. "You know, Steve, we never did find out a substantial motive for that crime."

"Bah! Guys like that don't need motives."

"I know, but Rutter flew here for some reason. He flew here in a hurry, to meet somebody, or to turn a bit of business."

MacBride said, "To meet Danizak. We traced the long distance call from Rutter's place in Cleveland to Danizak's apartment. It might have been business—but whatever it was—"

"Danizak admitted the phone call, you remember."

MacBride scowled. "Yeah. A social call, he said." The skipper sighed, went across the room and picked up his hat and overcoat. "It was the fourth time I pinched Danizak. And he's free again." He chuckled caustically. "Last month a little Dutchman finds three nickels in a telephone-booth box. He picks 'em out, the same as you or me—and a company dick nabs him and the poor little guy gets thirty days. God, there's something wrong these days!" He looked at his old, heavy gold watch. "Well, it's past eleven, Hack. I got to beat it. The wife's sick in bed with a cold, my daughter's away, and I got to take the dog out."

Hackinson stood up. "I hope she gets better in a hurry, old boy."

"Yeah. I'll make her a hot toddy when I get home."

Hackinson smiled, dropped a hand on the skipper's shoulder. "I'm sorry we didn't get a conviction, Steve. I tried my best."

"Hell—sure you did, Hack. It's the system. That guy'll go on and on—a theft here, a killing there. Some day he'll go down. But in the meantime he goes on and he might kill a good man some day but we got to wait, watch—we got to get him red-handed."

Hackinson grinned. "And meantime we've got to take it and like it."

"I take it, kid, but I'll never like it. I'm a sorehead. I hate rats and Danizak's a rat, only he's the kind of a rat you ain't allowed to kill. Night, Hack."

Chapter III

AT **MIDNIGHT** the patrol flivver came up to the bleak, windy darkness of Division Square and turned down into Silver Street. It was a narrow street, long and steep, that dropped from Division Square down to River Road and the docks and freight yards. The name had come to it by way of one-time Alderman Nathan Silver, through whose efforts the street had been paved. Textile mills and a couple of shoe factories walled it in, and there were some warehouses and a few open lots.

The police flivver was a roadster and it was cold. Tolfson, the cop at the wheel, was shivering, and his partner Riorty was drumming his thick heels on the floorboards. Riorty said:

"We c'n stop down at the lunch wagon."

"Yeah."

"Maxie keeps a bottle under the counter and we can spike a cup o' coffee. I'm froze."

"I ain't berlin' myself."

"Jeese, I wish I was on the theater detail. One o' them burlesque houses, f'r instance. Long shows. I'm froze. Didja see that we just passed?"

"What?"

Riorty looked around. "I dunno. Looked like it might be a drunk."

"I didn't see nothin'."

"In the short grass back there along the curb."

Tolfson said, "Maybe you was just imaginin'."

"Yeah, maybe I was. It mighta been a log."

The flivver creaked and rattled down the grade.

"How," Tolfson said, "could a log get there?"

Riorty looked around again. He shrugged. "Maybe we ought to take a look. You think we ought to?"

"What do you think?" Tolfson asked.

"Jeese, I'm froze."

Tolfson pulled up in the middle of the street, looked back. "I guess we better take a look. If it's a drunk we can lug him right down the lunch wagon."

"I guess you're right. Let's."

Tolfson turned around in the middle of the street, climbed the hill in second and pulled up against the curb on his left. Riorty, complaining about how the cold got at his bones, climbed out, passed in front of the headlights, a bulky short man, and stepped into the short grass. He leaned over, then turned his red face toward the car and said:

"Hey, it's a dame."

Tolfson said, "It's what I claim, I claimed it long ago—they shouldn't let women in bars. If I ever seen my wife in a bar I'd clout her across the ear and—"

Riorty was shaking his head. "This dame ain't drunk, I don't think, bo." He took off his leather glove and knelt down. He turned his head towards Tolfson. "My hands are so cold, hell, I can't feel nothin'. You feel."

Tolfson removed his gloves and got down on the other side of the body. He held the woman's wrist. "Mine, too. I can't even feel I'm holdin' nothin'. Get the flashlight."

Riorty rose, went heavily to the car and returned snapping on a flashlight. He stood on heavy legs, the wind moving the skirt of his overcoat, and sprayed the light down on the body. Tolfson looked at the eyes, moving the lids with his cold forefinger.

"She looks dead," he said.

"That's what she looks to me. You can usually tell by the eyes."

"Yeah. But I wish I could feel somethin', a pulse or somethin'."

Riorty said, "Listen, we better run her to a horsepittle. The South Side Memorial. It ain't only about ten blocks."

"Right."

"Come on. You take her legs and I'll— Hey, give a look at this," Riorty said suddenly. "Hey, this dame's been—"

"Now ain't that somethin'," Tolfson said, bending and touching the soggy cloth on the left side of the woman's coat. "I might not know right away a stiff when I see one but I sure know blood when I see it."

"Boy, it's lucky we turned around!"

"Yeah. Would we ha' got hell from the sarge!"

Chapter IV

THE *HOTEL TRIGG* was a six-storied red brick structure on the farther reaches of Webster Avenue. It was second-class, clean and unpretentious. Its lobby windows were huge squares of plate glass, always darkly gleaming, and on either side of the entryway was a brass name plate. There was a small coffee shop in the basement, reached by way of an areaway. The single elevator was an old brass cage and its shaftway was brass grillwork. MacBride entered it at half-past nine in the morning, followed by Detective Ike Cohen.

The cold winter morning had lacerated the skipper's bony face, reddened his nose, his cheeks, and the knob of his chin. He wore mittens of wool, which his wife had knitted, and beneath the collar of his dark gray overcoat was a woolen scarf which she had knitted also. His black shoes, twice resoled, shone beneath the cuffs of his blue serge trousers. He had about him a neat, scrubbed, soap-and-water look. When he got off at the top floor he said:

"This way, Ike."

They walked down a wide dim corridor on worn dull red carpet. At the end of the corridor was a window overlooking a parking lot and a sweep of rooftops. To the right of the window was a door. The skipper hit it with his gloved knuckles and in a moment Dave Trigg, dressed in pajamas and a blue flannel robe, opened it and said:

"Right in, Steve."

Trigg owned the hotel and lived in two rooms. He was a big man in his late forties; not fat, but big all around. His face was large, heavy at the jaw, clear-skinned, with a wide flexible mouth and light blue eyes. His hair was the color of cornsilk, a little thin on top, and his head rather set down between his husky shoulders. He tapped a newspaper he had been holding when he opened the door, tossed it to a table and said:

"Imagine that."

MacBride could see the column head: *Selma Jellif Found Dead.* He nodded grimly and taking off his mittens said:

"That's what I came here about, Dave."

Trigg sat down before a small table littered with a breakfast only partly consumed. He buttered a piece of toast. "What do you expect to find here?" he asked offhand.

The skipper said, "The Jellif girl worked for you down at the cash desk in your coffee shop. Since she came through with that alibi that saved Danizak she has lived in a room here."

"Yeah," said Trigg, crackling toast between strong hard teeth. "There was no living with her husband and she asked me if she could stay here. I let her stay here. Her husband kicked her out."

MacBride said, "Did you ever have any idea she was running around with Danizak?"

Trigg stopped chewing and stared straight ahead at a window, his eyes wide open, ruminative. "No," he said after a moment. "No, I never did." He leaned back and gave the skipper a long steady stare. For a brief instant a hurt expression moved in his eyes. He said, "You know, I was the guy that advised her to go to bat for Danizak."

Ike Cohen said, "Advice to the lovelorn, huh?"

"This ain't funny," Trigg told him. "I don't know why Selma came to me. Maybe because she's worked for me three years and because— well, you never know about women. She came to me looking sick and choked up and told me she guessed she was leaving. I asked her why, naturally. Then she told me how she was at Danizak's apartment the night he was supposed to have killed Rutter. She said she couldn't hold off any longer account of she loved him. I asked her why she waited so long. She said she was afraid of what her husband might do. I said, well, if she felt that way about Danizak there was only one thing to do."

The skipper said, "How well do you know the husband?"

One of Trigg's eyes remained open, the other squinted. "I hate his guts. He used to park himself down in the coffee shop and watch Selma like a hawk. If she smiled at a guy, he'd go up to her after the guy left and bawl her out. I had to put him out more than once. He never worked if he could help it. She brought in the money. I don't know how she stood it as long as she did." He took a drink of coffee, said, "Any dope yet on how she was killed?"

"We can't find Jellif, if that's any dope."

Trigg scowled hard at MacBride and then the scowl vanished and his eyes swung to the window, stared at it. He crunched toast absent-mindedly between his teeth while MacBride was saying:

"Moriarity and Kennedy were in *Enrico's* last night when Jellif came in and took a swing at Danizak. So far, that's the last check we got on him. I was over to the place where Jellif lives but he wasn't in and he hadn't been in all night. I came over here to take a look at the room Selma stayed in."

Trigg was still staring at the window. He started, said, "Oh, yeah. Sure. Want to look at it right now?"

"Yup."

Trigg got up and went over to the telephone, called the desk. He said, "Charley, send someone up to open three-eleven. Captain Mac-Bride wants to take a look-see." He hung up, saying to the skipper, "You can walk down to three just in time to meet the lad with the key."

MacBride said, "Thanks, Dave. Come on, Ike," and stretched his legs across to the door. Cohen followed him into the corridor and Trigg remained standing in the doorway; he called after them:

"Let me know if you find anything."

It was an old-fashioned stairway, wide, with heavy dark banisters. As MacBride and Cohen reached the third-floor corridor a colored bellhop came out of the elevator jangling a key.

"That for three-eleven?" MacBride said.

"Yes, suh. You Cap'n MacBride?"

"Yeah."

The bellhop led them down the corridor, opened the door of 311 and stepped aside. The skipper went in first and Cohen followed and the skipper stood in the middle of the room, his hands in his overcoat pockets, his dark eyes striking bluntly at odds and ends of the room. It was a large room with a single large window. The woodwork was heavy, dark, and the bed was brass. Up one step was a bathroom that looked as if it might once have been a closet.

There was a wall telephone. The bed had not been slept in. A nightgown lay across a Morris chair and in front of the chair was a pair of worn mules. A couple of dresses hung in a closet. A pair of sick stockings hung on the towel rack in the bathroom. There were several toilet articles—some powder, rouge, a lipstick, a bottle of mouthwash. In a bureau drawer a few pieces of lingerie, handkerchiefs. The skipper made his rounds swiftly, methodically, never retracing his movements. He turned suddenly, looked at Cohen, then at the bellhop, who stood respectfully in the doorway. The skipper said to Cohen:

"You just been smoking?"

"Me? Nope."

"You?" the skipper said to the bellhop.

"No, suh. Ah don't smoke."

MacBride sniffed. "There's smoke in here—cigarette smoke."

"What I was thinking," Cohen said. "Smells like—"

"Them Cuban or Spanish cigarettes like," the skipper said. "Sweet, kind of."

"Yeah, that kind," Cohen nodded. He suddenly crossed the room to the window, touched his finger to the sill, held up the finger. "Ash." He opened the window and looked down to a cement footpath that ran between the building and the cinder parking lot. He turned and said, "I'll be back," and lined out through the door.

The negro said, "Don't see how nobuddy would be in here."

MacBride paid no attention to him. A wary look had come into the skipper's eyes and now they cruised the room again—not swiftly and bluntly as they had done before, but more slowly now, taking object by object until at last they settled on the phone. He approached the instrument slowly, raised his hand toward it but closed his fingers, shook his head. Then he separated his forefinger from the fist his hand had made and ran it around inside the phone's mouthpiece. He rubbed his forefinger against his thumb, used a small pocketflash to spray light into the black mouthpiece.

IKE COHEN breezed in holding up a half-smoked slender cigarette. He said, "It was still burning when I got there but it went out before I could get up here. The name's burnt off but you can tell it's one of them Cuban or Spanish butts. It was down on the cement below this window. It must have been tossed out only a couple of minutes ago, and then the window closed."

The skipper said, "Don't touch anything, Ike. You, boy," he said to the negro, "give me that key. And keep your hands off anything in this room. And get out."

"Yes, suh. Sho' 'nough, Cap'n boss."

The bellhop ducked out. The skipper looked darkly, angrily around the room, then said, "Wait here, Ike," and slapped his heels out of the room. He drummed down to the lobby, pushed open the swing-door beside the desk and shoved into the little cubby where the hotel switchboard was located. A girl with shingled copper hair looked up.

MacBride said, "D' you put a call through to three-eleven in the last ten minutes?"

"No."

"Well, any time this morning?"

"No."

He fished his badge out of his vest pocket and let her take a look at it. She looked at it, raised her eyes and said:

"Well?"

He slipped the badge back into his pocket, said, "All right. Did you put a call *out* of three-eleven to anywhere?"

She gave him a droll half smile. "What are you doing, trying to kid me? According to the morning paper, three-eleven's a pretty dead woman."

He gave her a long, narrowed scrutiny. There was a flash on the board and she said, "Excuse me," and plugged in. Then she turned her eyes upward again, said, "What else?"

"Okey," he muttered and turned and shouldered out. He went around to the elevator and said, "Top floor." And when he reached the top floor he strode down the corridor to Trigg's apartment, knocked.

Trigg opened the door. He was dressed now in trousers and shirt and had his tie partly tied. "Oh. Find anything?"

The skipper pushed into the apartment and said, "Who's the girl at the switchboard?"

"Martha Rains?"

"That her name?"

"Yeah."

"What do you know about her?"

Trigg bent a grave, curious stare on the skipper. His voice was a little puzzled when he said, "Nothing much, except that she's worked here a couple of years—been on time, no complaints." He grinned. "Unless you've got a complaint."

MacBride shrugged. "There was somebody in three-eleven just

before we got in."

Trigg stopped working with his tie, dug another deeply curious look at the skipper.

MacBride said, "We smelled cigarette smoke, there was ash on the sill, and Ike found a smoldering butt on the walk below the window. I found moisture in the mouthpiece of the phone in the room, like somebody's talked into it and his breath left the moisture there." His tone was in no way accusatory, it merely stated facts, doggedly.

Trigg, still eyeing him curiously, got his knot tied and snugged up into the crotch of his crisp white collar. "Did you ask Martha Rains?"

The skipper nodded. "She said no. No call in or out."

Trigg went across the room and picked up the telephone. He said, "Martha, come up. Turn the board over to Charley." He put the instrument down slowly, stood drawing his lower lip in under his upper and frowning heavily at the table.

In a couple of minutes there was a knock on the door and he called out, "Come in." Martha Rains was a tall girl in her late twenties. She had long, tapering legs, narrow hips, and a good-looking aquiline face. Her manner was casual, matter-of-fact.

Trigg looked steadily at her. "Captain MacBride thinks there might have been a call through to three-eleven."

"That's what he told me," she said.

"Was there?" asked Trigg.

"I told him there wasn't."

Trigg was cold-mannered. "You know, I suppose."

"I ought to."

"This is a serious business," Trigg told her.

"All right, say it is," she said dryly. "The answer is: there was no call—in or out."

Trigg frowned, shrugged. He pulled at his lip and took a turn up and down the room. He stopped and shrugged again. "I dunno, Steve. You heard what she said...." He spread his arms, then dropped them.

MacBride tilted his chin toward the woman. "You can go."

She was brief: "Thanks." She turned and opened the door and went out, closing it quietly.

Trigg stood nibbling at his lip and pondering. He said, "I wonder what the hell anybody would want in her room."

"Somebody wanted something out of her room. The precinct guys that went over the hospital last night when she was lugged in missed a trick. When they turned over her purse to me this morning there wasn't a hotel key in it. When I came in downstairs I asked the guy at the desk if she'd left it before she went out. He said no. So she had it with her when she was knocked off. And it was taken."

Trigg stared at him, shook his head, said, "I guess I'm kind of dull-witted, Steve. I can't figure it."

MacBride barked out a short laugh. "Hell! Can I?" Then he dropped his voice: "I want to use your phone. I want to get a fingerprint man over. Nobody's to go in three-eleven."

A knock sounded on the door and Trigg went over and opened it. Garfield, the house officer, was mopping his forehead. "Anything I can do? I just got in. Charley said— Oh, hello; Cap'n MacBride. I just heard you found something."

"They been kidding you," the skipper growled, and hung up.

Garfield was a small fat man dressed in drab gray clothes. He had a round brown face, choppy black hair and wore horn-rimmed glasses. He looked like a neighborhood grocer.

He said eagerly, "But if I can help you, Cap'n—"

"You can help, fella, by not turning detective. In other words, stay out of three-eleven."

Garfield's eyes and mouth got very round. "Oh," he said vaguely, as though he did not quite understand. Then he hastened to say, "Oh, sure. Anything you say, Cap'n. You know me—always coöperate with the police."

MacBride said, "Atta boy," with hard jocularity; said, "Okey," to Trigg, and hoofed out jabbing a cigar between his teeth.

Chapter V

HE WAS sitting at his desk, his elbows in a mass of papers, his voice ripping into the telephone, when Kennedy dawdled in at twenty past one. Over his shoulder Kennedy carried a duck. The duck was dead and the price tag was still attached to it. He plopped the duck down on the skipper's desk, yawned, scratched his ear. The skipper hung up and stood up all at once, and carrying on, picked up the duck and flung across the room. He sat down, said curtly:

"Get that out of here. Better yet, you get out too."

"I won it," said Kennedy, expiring into a chair. "From my old friend and confidant Paderoofski, head barman at *Enrico's*. I bet him I could put an egg in a glass, big end down, and then without touching the egg or the glass turn the egg upside down, so that the little end would be down. Paderoofski had just won the duck from a friend of his named Bonofrio on a bet as to who could sneeze first. Bonofrio had won the duck from a friend of *his* last night on a bet as to who—"

"My God," groaned MacBride.

"Would you like to bet on my egg trick?"

"I bet," ground out MacBride, "that I can chuck you out of here before you can say Jack Robinson."

"Jack Robinson," said Kennedy.

Moriarity came in with his coat tails flying and said, "Hey, what do you think, Cap'n? I just come from that lunch wagon down the foot of Silver Street. I been dusting that neighborhood all around where the Jellif woman was found, and so naturally I dropped in the lunch wagon there. The night man was there. He wasn't on duty, he was just there, and he told me that at about half-past eleven last night he stuck his head out the window to get a look at the clock in the River Terminal tower. His was stopped. And he told me that as he looked out that window he seen a car come hell-bent down Silver and make a swing into River Road and howl off. He didn't think anything about it then except he remembered the license number; he remembered saying to himself, 'Box cars.' You know, two sixes."

"What was the initial?"

Moriarity shrugged. "He can't remember that. It was just the number combination he remembered, account of—"

"I know—dice."

"Yeah. But the car he thinks was a five-passenger convertible, some dark color with a light canvas top."

MacBride said, "Get in touch with the Motor Vehicle Bureau. You'll have to get all the letter combinations that go with sixty-six. See if you turn up somebody we know. No, no—don't use my phone. I want this wire clear. Go to another."

Moriarity said, "Sure," and dived out.

The phone rang and MacBride picked it up, barked, "Yeah?" And then, "No!" He slammed home the receiver, snarled, "Would I be interested in a pair of waterproof zipper spats!"

Kennedy pulled a flask out of his inside overcoat pocket and took a mouthful "Want a snort?" he asked.

"No."

"Swell."

"I thought I told you to get out of here. The way you guys float in here and hang around you'd think my office was a kind of social club or something. What do you want here anyhow?"

Kennedy capped the flask and said tranquilly, "News for the late edition."

"There ain't any news. I got ten Bureau men out looking for Jellif. I got the hotel room in the *Trigg* where Selma Jellif stayed sealed up. Obermeier got some prints and is working on 'em now. I sent Ike Cohen to get Nick Danizak over here. I got Barney Loftis planted in Jellif's room in the rooming-house in Swann Street. And I don't know who killed Selma Jellif."

"You don't think it was her husband?"

MacBride snapped impatiently. "Of course I think it was her husband, but I don't know. I've *got* to think it was her husband. He took a swing at Danizak; he threatened Danizak in public; he was goofy jealous of his wife; he ain't where he lives. I'd be a lulu to say, no, I don't think it was her husband."

Kennedy drawled, "As far as you've figured out, Stevie, she was shot and then tossed from a car. Jellif didn't own a car."

"You're splitting hairs now, kid," the skipper objected.

"Well, it helps pass the time. What kind of bullet killed her?"

"A .32. Two shots, both in the same place."

Obermeier came in with his spectacles pushed up on his forehead and laid a sheet of paper on the desk, "I got the prints of the maid that cleaned the Jellif woman's room. I got the Jellif woman's prints. I got Ike Cohen's. I got only a smear off the window. Off that telephone receiver in her room I got something funny. They ain't regular prints, Cap. You can see them there. I tell you what they are. They were fresh when I got 'em and they're the inside edges of somebody's first and second fingers. Whoever took that receiver off the hook, took it off between his first and second fingers—like taking something between a crotch, for instance. The marks coming down from the knuckle are a little higher on the right side of the receiver than they are on the left, which is why I say it was taken between the first and second fingers. If the receiver was taken, for instance, been the second and third fingers, the marks would be higher on the left." He added, "You don't see everybody holding a receiver that way—I mean between the fingers."

"That's an idea," the skipper nodded. "Thanks, pal."

Obermeier went out and MacBride stood up, palmed the back of his neck, rubbed briskly up and down and said, "I'm going to have another go at Martha Rains—the one I told you about at the hotel this morning." He put on his woolen scarf, lapped it across his chest, then shouldered into his overcoat and slapped on his hat. On his way out he picked up the duck, which looked as if it had been kicked around quite a bit, and took it down to the central room. He gave it to Otto Bettdecken, who was at the desk.

"I hope you like duck," he said.

"My kid always wanted a duck, but it was a live one he wanted."

"Stuff it and put wheels on it."

Kennedy appeared buttoning up his threadbare topcoat. "What did you do with that duck?" he asked.

"I gave it to Otto. He likes duck."

"Personal," said Bettdecken, "I like partridge."

Moriarity came scooting out of an arterial corridor. "Cap!"

"Yeah?"

"Hang on to something, palsy-walsy—"

"Don't call me palsy-walsy."

"Well, anyhow, hang on to something, 'cause this might knock you down. There's an R-Sixty-six registered in this city. A five-passenger Buick convertible, black paint job. Guess who's name it's registered in."

"Can't."

"Come on, guess."

"Don't be a damned fool, Mory! I'm busy!"

Moriarity put his hands on his hips, tipped himself back on his heels and said, "Abel Springer."

MacBride scoffed, "Yeah, him—the slickest criminal lawyer in the state—he'd be just the one to—"

"Nuts! It's the only sixty-six pad in this city; in this part of the state!"

MacBride pursed his lips, bent a speculative stare on Moriarity and then blew his nose. He said, "Thanks, kid," and swung off towards the basement stairway.

Gahagan, his chauffeur, was just affixing a sticker to the rear window of the big sedan. The sticker read, *Vote for Voltman.*

"Take that off." MacBride grunted.

"But—"

"Take it off. The next thing I know you'll be using this car for display advertising."

"But Danny Voltman's my wife's uncle."

"Take it off. Get in behind the wheel and drive to three-o-nine Bank Street…. Listen, Kennedy, don't be following me around. You're worse than a summer cold."

"I'm not following you around, tomato. I simply happen to be going to the same place you're going."

"You ain't simple and you don't just happen."

"He's really a fine, upstanding gent," said Gahagan, getting in behind the wheel.

"He's a damned drunk," said MacBride.

Gahagan resented that. "He ain't ever took a drink in his life. You ain't got no cause to slander my wife's uncle."

"Listen to me, Gahagan…."

THE SEDAN rolled out into the bright cold day. A lean, hard-striding wind met it, strummed and whanged in the radiator shutters. They wheeled past a traffic cop whose face was beet-red with the cold, whose breath smoked whitely round his head. A newsboy stood on a corner with a sheaf of papers under his arm, his hands in his pockets, his feet drumming the pavement. Steam twisted from the whistle of a peanut-vendor's cart. Women walked tautly in furs through the wind, sometimes turning and taking a few steps backward. A car was stalled, with steam blasting from its radiator. The traffic thickened. Gahagan snaked the car expertly. In Bank Street, a narrow canyon of office buildings, he pulled up beside an iron lamppost.

MacBride ducked out of the sedan, stamped his foot in order to get his trouser-cuff down, and held on to his hat as the wind yanked violently at it. Kennedy came huddled miserably in his inadequate topcoat, his teeth chattering. They entered 309 together, MacBride growling:

"It's a wonder you wouldn't buy some warm clothes instead of boozing all the time."

"They make me itch."

"Would you rather itch or die?"

"I know what it is to itch."

They got into an elevator and rode it to the third floor, Kennedy still shivering and MacBride eyeing him with exasperation. At the end of the third-floor corridor was a frosted-glass door inscribed, Abel Springer, Counselor at Law. MacBride straight-armed the door open and a flat-haired brunette took a cigarette out of her mouth and said:

"Yes?"

"Mr. Springer," MacBride said, swinging past her and heading for a solid door.

"Hey, Mr. Springer's busy—"

"So am I, miss."

He opened the inner door and Abe Springer, sitting on his desk, with his arms folded and his legs swinging, gave an upward annoyed look. He said in a thin, undisturbed voice:

"Oh, it's you. I thought it was a truck coming in. I'm busy. Park outside a while."

"Yeah, sure," the skipper said in a brief, sardonic voice, entering the office.

A chestnut-haired girl with a nice pair of legs was sitting in an armchair taking a drag at a cigarette. She wore a short fur coat, a dress of dark green flannel with a belt and a harp-shaped buckle. Her skin was fair, clear, her lips reddened darkly by rouge. She had sulky, sultry brown eyes, a rather heavy nose. She was a big girl, but built right.

MacBride planted himself and said, "I want to see you alone, Abe."

"Sure. When I'm ready. I'm busy now."

"Tell the lady to excuse you."

Springer stopped swinging his legs. "I see people by appointment only—and that goes for cops too."

"Not this cop, buddy."

The girl stood up slowly. "I'll toddle," she said. "This gent looks as if he never goes in reverse. Be seeing you, Abe."

"You spoil him," Springer said, sighing.

The girl folded a newspaper, thrust it beneath her arm and sauntered towards the door.

MacBride turned to Kennedy, who was leaning in the doorway, and said, "You get out, too, Kennedy. Wait outside for me."

Kennedy shrugged and turned away. When the girl had passed through the doorway MacBride closed the door. He turned and gave Springer a blunt look and said:

"Your car was seen in Silver Street last night about the time Selma Jellif was dumped out."

Springer got off the desk, drifted across to a water cooler and drew a glass of water. He drank it down, taking his time, then wiped his hands, his lips on a handkerchief and smiled. "So that's what's worrying you, eh?"

"I'm not worried."

Springer winked at him. "I am, I suppose." He chuckled dryly, sat down at his desk, leaned back and gave the skipper a long, mocking look. He seemed to be enjoying himself immensely.

"So my car was in Silver Street last night. Well, well, well. That's very interesting, isn't it?"

MacBride went over to the desk, stood beside it, with his fists resting on it. "Listen, baby, don't start to get funny. You can pull your act in a courtroom and roll the guests in the aisle—but we ain't in a courtroom now. A gal was knocked off last night. She was dumped in Silver Street and your car was seen in Silver Street around that time. I want to see the car."

Springer built a steeple with his hands and looked coyly around it at MacBride. "Can't be done. Sorry."

MacBride's voice was hoarse: "I'm telling you, honeybunch, don't get funny. I want to see the car."

Springer grinned. "No can do."

MacBride's thumb went up. "Get your coat and hat, wise guy."

"Nothing doing," Springer said, putting his hands behind his head, tipping his chair back. "You can't see it, my boy."

"I said get your hat and coat." The skipper took a step, gripped Springer by the arm, hoisted him out of the chair and planted him on his feet. "The funnier you get the harder the smash in the puss I'll give you."

Springer's thin lips quivered. "Take your hands off me, cop!" he spat out. "Pull up once in a while and use your head! I've been razzing you, cop! Why don't you check up once in a while?"

"Lazy, baby—"

"You listen to me, cop! My car was stolen last night! I reported it missing, by phone, to your Stolen Cars Bureau at eleven o'clock last night! I made the phone call from the *Press Club* and if you want to know where I was from then to one, ask the steward at the *Press Club!* And take your paw off me and get the hell out of here before I have you tossed out on your pants!"

MacBride was grave. He released Springer, picked up the phone and called Headquarters. To the Headquarters operator he said, "Give me Dill…. Hello, Dill. MacBride. Check up and see if Abel Springer reported his car stolen last night at eleven. License R-Sixty-six." He waited, stared blankly into space. After a couple of moments he said, "Yup?… Okey."

He hung up and his face grew red. He jabbed a look at the attorney, said nothing, turned on his heel and banged out. He could hear Springer's raucous laughter. It made his face redder. Down in the street, he headed straight for the sedan. There was a *Vote for Voltman* sticker on the iron lamppost there. The skipper's eyes steeled on Gahagan. Gahagan cleared his throat. MacBride ripped the sticker off the post and entered the sedan, banging the door behind him.

He sailed into Police Headquarters, went down a corridor to the Stolen Cars Bureau, found Dill at a desk with a card index. MacBride bit off:

"Who was on duty here last night?"

"Blakeney."

"Was that data sent out on the teletype, the radio?"

Dill looked uneasy. "It ain't marked here. I guess—"

"You guess Blakeney forgot or was drunk, or tired!" MacBride leveled a finger. "Get it out now. When Blakeney comes on duty, he sees me. I'll toss that sloppy bum back in harness and shove him so far out in the sticks he'll need a map to find his way back."

"Jeese, Cap'n, anybody can make a slip."

"This ain't the first time Blakeney's made a slip. If that data'd been shot out the minute it was received that it might have been picked up and a man might not have been murdered! That's what kind of a slip it was!"

Chapter VI

DANIZAK was sitting in the office when the skipper walked in as said, "Took you long enough to get over."

Danizak shrugged. "You got no lease on my time, MacBride. I came over when I felt like it." His voice was flat, casual, and the expression on his face was equally flat, equally casual. He sat on a straight-backed chair, his knees and ankles together, his overcoat neatly folded over the back of another chair and his fedora perched on top of it.

The skipper hung up his things, got a battered briar out of his desk and pushed coarse tobacco into the bowl. Meanwhile he kept a cold scrutiny fixed on Danizak. The slender young man showed no uneasiness; in fact, he paid no attention to MacBride. The skipper lit up, sat down and said:

"What do you think about the killing of Selma Jellif?"

Danizak looked at his fingernails. "Tough."

"That all?"

Danizak looked at the palm of his right hand. "What else?"

"Oh, when a gal busts up her home in order to save a guy, you'd just think the guy might take it to heart a bit when she's knocked off."

Danizak folded his arms. "What should I do, weep on your shoulder?" He frowned. "Listen, MacBride. You been against me for a long time. That gal did what she did because she wanted to. I didn't want her to. She was nuts about me but I wasn't nuts about her. If I was nuts about her I'd ha' come through with that alibi. I didn't come through with that alibi because I didn't want to have nothing to thank her for."

"You'd have taken the chair, eh?"

"I'd have taken a chance on the chair, yeah. She was a white kid, game a mile long, and it's tough she had to feel the way she did about me."

"After you were released, did you meet her?"

"No."

"Why not?"

Danizak frowned. "I wanted to duck her. I didn't want to have to tell her that I couldn't go for her."

"You didn't even want to thank her, eh?"

"Yeah, I wanted to thank her, but I wanted to have time to figure out how."

"You know Springer's car was stolen last night, don't you?"

"No. It must have been after I ate dinner with him at *Enrico's*."

"You ain't seen him since then?"

"No. We had dinner and he dropped me off at the place where I live."

"You mean he dropped off you and Pig Iron and Belly Skoba."

"Sure. I ain't taking no chances on Jellif taking a shot at me." He nodded to the window. "Pig Iron and Belly are across the street now."

MacBride squinted. "You kind of got an idea Jellif might do that, huh?"

"Yeah, kinda."

MacBride tamped his pipe. "You can go. Only don't go far. Don't go out o' the city limits."

"I guess I can go where I like."

"Try it. I want you to stay in this city till this murder's cleared up. Nobody's accusing you of anything, but I want you to stay here. Is that plain?"

Danizak gave him a cold unemotional stare. "I figured on taking a train South tonight. I got reservations."

"Cancel 'em."

Danizak stood up slowly, took his time getting into his overcoat; stared moodily at the floor while he buttoned up. He put on his hat and while adjusting it to the angle he liked, said, "You still got a grudge against me, eh?"

"I got a grudge against all heels. You're a heel. The fact you got free don't change things at all. You ain't hard, Nick. You're just cold. I'm hard. There's a difference. You ain't tough. There's just something you ain't got that most guys have. I'm tough. I'm ten times tougher than you. When I first picked you up—it wasn't a pinch—four years ago, I think I picked you up for beating an old man. I gave you a talking to, but I knew then just by looking at you, mugg, that my talk wasn't going to do any good. I preached. Yeah, I always do, and sometimes it works and sometimes it don't—but I get a great kick out of it when it works. I'm not preaching now to you. That's all through. You'll get in a stink again sometime—and watch me crack down on you."

Danizak was pulling on his gloves. "Through?"

"Yeah."

Danizak strolled out whistling a popular air.

The skipper stared hard at the closed door. Then he wagged his lean head, knocked out his pipe and attacked some paper work. He had his desk pretty well cleaned when, half an hour later, Kennedy meandered in tapping a yawn. He went across and pressed backwards against a radiator, his face pinched by the cold outdoors, his fingers red and shriveled looking.

MacBride, writing a notation on a bulletin, said absently, "No loitering."

"I hear," said Kennedy, "your act with Springer didn't come off so well."

"Says who?"

"Springer. I phoned him about half an hour ago to see if he had a statement. That was some looker he had in his office when you steamrollered in. How'd you like to call on her?"

"Them days is gone forever."

"You wouldn't like to call on her even if she came from, say, Cleveland?"

"I wouldn't like to call on her even if—" He stopped, twisted his neck and spiked Kennedy with a sharp look. "What's that about Cleveland?"

"She comes from Cleveland, tomato. You may recall, and ten to one you don't, that as she left Springer's office she folded a newspaper and put it under her arm. I saw it was a Cleveland paper. I thought I'd follow her but when I got downstairs she was in a cab and off, there wasn't another in sight, so I lost her. But you can't buy Cleveland papers all over town. There are only two places that specialize in out-of-town newspapers: one is the stand in Union Station, the other is in the lobby of the *Metropolitan Hotel.*

"I went down to Union Station and asked the guy that runs the stand there if a gal of her description stopped for a Cleveland paper every day. He said no. So I went to the *Metropolitan* and the guy there said yes; he said he had it reserved daily for her and that her name was Nance Shannigan. I asked him if he knew where she lived and he said no. I asked him how long she'd been getting the paper and he said ten days. He said she usually stops by for the paper about four in the afternoon. I just thought I'd tell you. Unimportant, but—well,

Rutter, who flew from Cleveland and was shot down dead last November.... I was just killing a little time."

The skipper was hawk-eyed. "Nance Shannigan," he mused.

"Another little item, Skip, Paderoofski, the head barman at *Enrico's*, is a good friend of mine. He speaks dago and he speaks spic. Ah!—and he speaks English. But he speaks spic, that's what I'm getting at. You and Ike Cohen were all worked up about that cigarette butt Ike found outside Selma's hotel window, and about the smell of smoke in the room. You both decided the butt was Cuban or Spanish. So, killing time in *Enrico's* I got Paderoofski to call up the *Trigg Hotel* and in his best broken English to inquire about rooms and rates. Paderoofski's English is not merely broken, it's shattered, busted. But I told him to mix it up worse than he usually does and then to ask the operator at the hotel if somebody there spoke Spanish. Well, somebody on the staff speaks Spanish. A guy. Paderoofski spoke Spanish and was told what the rates were. I had told him to ask the name of whoever spoke Spanish, but the guy at the other end just told my stooge that anyone at the hotel would take care of him, and hung up. Nothing important. I just thought I'd tell you, just in case you had nothing to do and wanted to—"

"Lay off, boy," the skipper broke in slowly. "You're the tops, Kennedy." He flexed his shoulders inside his coat, pushed his palms hard against the surface of the desk. "There's going to be a crack down on somebody around town and I'm—" He cut himself short, stood up and said, "I'd like to use Paderoofski but it wouldn't be baseball. He might get hurt. There's a guy in the third precinct speaks Spanish. Louie Barba. I'll get him. We'll dress him up like a spic that's just landed, get him a suitcase and have him go over to the *Trigg*. You want to be a pal, Kennedy?"

"If it doesn't cost anything, okey."

"Hang around the *Metropolitan*, try to spot the Shannigan woman and follow her. Barba's on desk duty. I'll run right over to the station house and—" He snapped across to the clothes rack, poked into his overcoat, put on his woolen scarf, his mittens, his hat; took a look at Kennedy and then pulled his scarf off. "Here, you wear this before you freeze to death."

"I'll itch."

"Don't argue, damn it!" the skipper said and wrapped the scarf around Kennedy's neck.

HE HIKED out of the office, ran hard-heeled down the stairs to the main floor, then punched open a metal swing-door and strode down a cement ramp into the basement garage.

"Gahagan!" he bawled. He reached the sedan, pulled open the door, glanced impatiently around the garage. He stuck his hand into the car and let the siren rip. Gahagan came galloping out of a doorway and struggling into his overcoat and the skipper said, "The third-precinct house, stick in the mud."

"I was sewing a button on my pants."

"Get in, get in."

Gahagan jumped in behind the wheel. The skipper started to get in, then cursed, reached over the back seat and hauled the duck out of the rear of the car. He swung it and let it sail and it plopped against the wall. Then he climbed in, saying desperately:

"I'm not going to say anything about it."

Gahagan wheeled the car out, explaining, "I traded it from Bett-decken for a love-story magazine."

MacBride said nothing about it. Gahagan gunned the car up the street, whipped it around the rotary traffic circle on Main and lined out Main at fifty-five. Main, east, slashed through a rundown part of the city; second-hand stores, dime museums, cheap haberdashers, beaneries, rakish tenement houses, gaunt rooming-houses, pool-halls, Greek restaurants; noisy, dirty, down at the heel.

"Cut through Lester Street," MacBride said.

Three blocks farther on Gahagan unleashed the siren, snapped between two trucks, scared the daylights out of a jay walker, and whipped into Lester Street. He slapped the throttle down, boomed past the huge metal car barns. Four blocks beyond he had to brake down; there were six or seven cars muddled in the street and a crowd shifting.

"Take it easy," MacBride said. "There's something going on here. Pull up, better."

Gahagan braked to a stop and the skipper swung out, slammed the door shut and chopped with his shoulders through the crowd. Voices sputtered, droned, clicked all around him. Eyes rolled. Heads bent towards one another. There was the sound of someone battering on wood, and when MacBride had slammed through the crowd he saw a uniformed policeman driving his shoulder against the door of a two-storied, ramshackle frame house. The skipper recognized the cop: Adam

Krantz, white-haired, hound-dog jowled, up for retirement that year. An old-timer who usually walked school kids across bad crossings.

"What's up, Adam?"

Krantz turned. "Oh, Cap'n MacBride. That Jellif fella. I seen his face stickin' out o' the top window. Sure it's his. He was askin' a news kid to chuck him up a paper."

"Which window?"

"The one right over this door."

"Who owns this house? Who lives in it?"

"Nobody, far as I know."

MacBride said, "Look out, Adam."

The skipper stepped back, took a running jump at the door and heard it crackle. He stepped back again. Gahagan came over and said:

"Let's both try."

"Okey, let's."

They both rammed the door, popped one of its wooden panels. MacBride ripped the wood away, reached in through the gash, found a bolt and drew it. He pushed the door open, turned to say:

"You guys stay here. Adam, clear this crowd away. Gahagan, you stand by the curb. If Jellif comes out instead of me, let him have it."

"No, sir! I'm going in with you!"

"Gahagan, I'm not going to have you getting under my feet. Do as I tell you!"

He stepped into the hallway, pulled his gun, cocked the hammer and went up the dim staircase at a run. At the head of the stairs he crouched, listened. His gun was level, its cocked hammer on a line with the buttonhole of his right lapel. His left arm was bowed out from his side, the fingers splayed and clawed a bit. He went forward, walking on the balls of his feet, his body twisted at the waist so that his right shoulder acted as a prow for his body. A man going sidewise into gunfire offers half the target of a man going square on.

It was no job to figure which room was above the hall door. MacBride tried the doorknob. The door was locked and he said in a low, clear voice:

"Jellif, come out."

He heard sound—the movement of a foot or of a body against some object. And he could hear, faintly, the strident murmur of the crowd in the street; it was chilling, expectant, touched with hysteria.

"Come out, Jellif. It's the cops."

This time he heard, unmistakably, the scuff of feet on the floor, the jarring of a piece of furniture. He heard Adam Krantz' loud old voice driving the people away from the front of the house.

"I'm coming in, Jellif."

He stepped back, fired twice at the lock. He raised his foot and drove it against the lock, sent the door on a swinging crash against the inner wall; whipped his body to one side, had his trigger half-squeezed when he saw Jellif totter in the midst of an explosion. Jellif's own gun-muzzle pressed against Jellif's own body. The skipper let his hammer down. He saw Jellif cringe and bend over like a man with a violent stomach-ache. MacBride went towards him. Jellif's knees flopped and he went down in a kind of boneless huddle, knelt for an instant and then fell quietly forward on his face.

Gahagan appeared in the doorway, his gun drawn.

MacBride said dully, indifferently, "Put it away," He bent down and rolled Jellif over. "Call an ambulance, Gahagan."

Gahagan ran out.

Jellif lay groaning.

MacBride picked up the gun that Jellif had dropped, hefted it, emptied it, juggled the bullets in his hand, frowning.

Krantz puffed into the room. "God, Cap'n, I'm glad it wasn't you! He is Jellif, ain't he? He is the guy that knocked off his wife."

The skipper was in a brown study. He muttered, "It is Jellif, Adam." He hefted the gun again, looked at it. "I don't know about the other."

Chapter VII

KENNEDY was slouched behind a newspaper in the lobby of the *Hotel Cosmopolitan* when MacBride strode in at twenty to four. The skipper sat down beside him, nibbled the end off a cigar, and said:

"We got Jellif."

"Swell. I won't have to hang around then."

MacBride shook his head while lighting up. "I don't know, Kennedy. We took him to the hospital. He was unconscious and he ain't out of it yet. House in Lester Street. I crashed it to turn the heat on him but he turned the heat on himself. He had a .32—Selma was killed with a .32—but she was killed with metal-point bullets. The slugs in the gun I found on Jellif weren't metal-point."

"Hell, he could have bought some new ones."

The skipper nodded. "You're right." He puffed for a minute on his cigar, his eyes cramped with thought. Then he said, "Anyhow, tail the woman, kid. I'm going over to the *Trigg* now."

He rose and his knees fanned the skirt of his overcoat on the way out. The sedan was parked at the curb, its motor running and Gahagan at the wheel. In the rear sat Officer Louie Barba dressed as an immigrant.

"Scat, Gahagan," said MacBride.

Gahagan threw into gear and hauled away from the *Metropolitan*. It was a fifteen-minute ride to the *Trigg* and Gahagan parked a block away. MacBride said to Barba:

"Get it straight now. You go in and talk broken English to the clerk—so broken that he won't understand you. You say, 'Spik Spanish, spik Spanish,' over and over. You want a front room. If the guy who speaks Spanish turns up, you ask him his name so you can get him again, you say, if the other guys don't understand you. You go to the room they give you, write the guy's name on a hunk of paper, spot me, and pitch it out the window. Stay in the room till you hear from me."

"Right," said Barba. He carried a suitcase out of the sedan and walked up the street, entered the hotel.

MacBride got out, stood for a couple of minutes with his foot on the running-board, then crossed the street and idled along. He stopped and leaned outside a cigar store and watched the front of the hotel. It was ten minutes before he saw a window open. Barba spotted him and tossed something and MacBride was on his way across. He picked up a rumpled piece of paper, opened it, looked at it, then crammed it into his pocket and dug his heels toward the *Trigg* entrance. The elevator was parked at the lobby floor and he took it up to the sixth, got out and strode down the corridor. He knocked on Trigg's door and in a minute Trigg, holding a batch of papers in one hand and a pencil in the other, opened it.

"Oh, hello, Skipper."

"Hello," said MacBride, pushing in. "Get Martha Rains up here and Garfield your house dick."

Trigg put his papers and pencil down on a desk and said, "Huh, what's up?"

"Get 'em."

Trigg shrugged, made a phone call. MacBride went to a window and stood there drawing on his cigar, taking slow drags and oozing the smoke out of one side of his mouth.

"Drink?" asked Trigg genially.

"No. I been going light on it."

Trigg poured one for himself, drained it with his big eyes fixed speculatively on MacBride's back. He said, "Mind telling me what's the matter?"

"I don't know what's the matter," the skipper said, still staring out the window.

Trigg shrugged and fooled around pointlessly with the papers on his desk. When a knock sounded he called, "Come in," and Martha Rains and Garfield entered.

MacBride walked across the room and without saying a word began slapping Garfield's pockets. From one of his coat pockets he drew a packet of cigarettes; tossed it, caught it and closed his hand over it. His eyes wore a glitter.

"Like Cuban butts, eh, Garfield?"

Garfield's glasses moved on his fat nose. "Yeah—sure. I—"

"Speak Spanish?"

Garfield looked puzzled, upset. "Yeah—a little."

"You were in Selma Jellif's room a couple of minutes before me and Ike Cohen went in there this morning."

Garfield seemed to rebound. "I wasn't!"

MacBride pointed. "Call the desk."

Garfield said, "Huh?"

"Phone the desk."

Wide-eyed, Garfield crossed the room and picked up the telephone. He picked up the receiver between the first and second fingers of his right hand.

"Okey, forget it," MacBride said.

Confused, Garfield fumbled the receiver back on to the hook.

MacBride turned on Martha Rains. "All right, sister. Now you. You rang Selma's room and told Garfield to clear out."

She was cool.

"Did I?"

"You did."

She smiled. "You must know more about my business than I do. Tell me some more." Her eyes, cool, unwavering, ridiculed him.

Trigg sat back in a big chair, lit a cigarette and looked at Martha Rains, at Garfield, at MacBride. He looked heavy and physically tranquil in the big chair.

Garfield, after his first wave of confusion, began to puff up with indignation. "This here is ridiculous!" he spluttered through moist lips. He waved a short fat arm. "It's an outrage!"

MacBride looked at Trigg. "What have you got to say?"

Trigg said good-naturedly. "I was keeping my mouth shut. I thought the argument was between you and them. If you want me to butt in, Cap, I got to say, well"—he chuckled apologetically—"I got to say your argument sounds screwy."

"Yeah?" MacBride growled. "There was somebody in that room before Ike and me got there. There was cigarette smoke in the room and it was the kind of smell comes from these butts I just took out of Garfield's pocket. Somebody was in the room and they were warned to get out. They were warned by phone. The only line into that room is through the switchboard."

Trigg sighed and shrugged. "You got me, Skipper. You accuse these people of things you can't prove. That's why I say your argument's screwy. Martha's been here over two years and Gar's been here five. You don't expect me to chuck all that service aside just because you're hell-bent for a pinch. You asked me what I had to say, and there it is."

MacBride put his fists into his overcoat pockets. "Did you see Selma Jellif after Danizak was released?"

"No."

"It's damned funny that nobody saw her. I had Danizak over to Headquarters before and he didn't see her, either. He was all ready to grab a train South."

Trigg squinted. "What's he in such a sweat to get out of town for?"

"Like all these punks, I guess he thinks he needs a rest. I got Jellif—"

Trigg opened his eyes.

"Yeah," said MacBride. "He's in the hospital. Tried to commit suicide when I cornered him."

Trigg stood up, spread his arms. "Then why in God's name are you worrying about who killed Selma?"

"Fella, this thing goes back. It goes back to November when Rutter was killed in Wellman Street. I collared Danizak for that job but a foxy shyster and a gal's alibi cleared him. But it still goes back. The Jellif woman's death is somewhere mixed up in it. It looks like Jellif killed her because she was his wife and she fell for Danizak. That's what it looks like. Except for a little difference in bullets. I might be even wrong on that. When they get the bullets out of Jellif they can check on the rifling with the bullets they took out of his wife. But I ain't waiting for that. Danizak's packed to go South. All right. I told him not to. If he does I'll haul him back and frame him into the can until I can clear this thing up." He looked at Garfield. "And you," he said, "so you won't be insulted again, come along with me."

Garfield pursed his lips and his bug eyes popped. "Now you look here, Captain MacBride—"

"I'm looking right at you, Garfield. We've got some prints we took off the receiver in Selma's room. Come over and see. The prints were made by a guy who has a habit of picking up a telephone receiver between his first two fingers—like you did when I told you to call the desk."

Garfield's whole body became agitated. "I never heard such nonsense in all my life!"

Trigg sounded reasonable: "Don't you think this is going a bit far, Skipper?"

"Yeah. Sure. It's a general crackdown."

Trigg said, "Better go, then," to Garfield. He smiled, added, "Humor the old boy."

MacBride's grin was tight, mirthless. "Yeah, humor me, Garfield."

Garfield blurted, "Suppose my prints were on the phone! I got the run of the hotel. I might have been in that room days ago."

"You might have been in it a couple of minutes before I went in, too. Stop beefing. Let's go."

Chapter VIII

THE SKIPPER turned Garfield over to Obermeier, said, "Try the insides of his fingers, just for fun. Phone me if you get something." He went up to his office, sat down with his hat and overcoat on and drummed his fingers on the desk. There was a batch of papers on his desk but he was in no mood to tackle them. He stuffed his pipe and then, caught up on a line of thought, forgot to light.

Moriarity came in saying, "I checked up on Danizak. He bought four tickets for Palm Beach. A drawing-room for two and a section for two. They ain't been canceled yet and the train pulls out in an hour."

"Four," MacBride said. "H'm. I thought he had only two bodyguards."

"He has. Maybe Springer's taking a trip with him."

MacBride shook his head. "Springer wouldn't be sap enough to travel South with three gangsters."

"Any news on the car yet?"

"No. The boys have been fanning all the garages but no soap yet. If we found that car, Mory, we'd know a little more. I've been hightailing around like I knew a lot, but as a matter of fact I don't know anything—except that everything is cockeyed." He phoned the hospital where Jellif had been taken, talked for a couple of minutes, hung up. "Jellif's still unconscious. They got the bullets out and are sending 'em over."

"Hell," said Moriarity, "don't you think Jellif did it?"

MacBride made a fist. "Boy, I want to think Jellif did it but—but—" He stood up and walked around the room, chuckled grimly. "I just can't get it out of my nut that it goes deeper, and back—back to November when Rutter was killed. Why was he killed? Why did he fly here? Who was he coming to see?" He clasped his hands behind his back, flexed his arms against his sides. "Mory," he muttered, "I'm a stubborn guy. A fat-head, maybe—"

The phone rang and he blew out a breath, said, "Ah, well," and scooped up the instrument. "Yeah?... Hi, boy.... When?... Right.... Where?... Yeah, I think I know it. I'll be over in a shake." He clipped in the receiver, said, "Come on, Mory. Kennedy thinks he's putting two and two together."

They trooped down the corridor in step and Moriarity laughed.

"What's funny?" MacBride asked.

"I just thought of something. Gahagan. Gahagan sold the duck to the dago street cleaner that works this street. For two bits."

"The robber."

"No. The street cleaner really thought he got a break. It seems he got mad at Gahagan because Gahagan was always pasting stickers on the guy's pushcart; so Gahagan said he was sorry and to show what a white guy he was he'd sell a good duck for a quarter to him."

They reached the bottom of the staircase, took the ramp into the garage, MacBride saying, "The only reason that guy's on the Force is because he can drive like a bat out of hell.... Hey, horse trader," he yelled at Gahagan, "we'd like to go to the corner of Middleford and Sixteenth. Do you mind?"

"Delighted, so to speak," said Gahagan.

"Step on, pal-o."

No matter how fast he drove—thirty or seventy an hour—Gahagan did it negligently and seemed to be thinking of other things besides the business at hand. He drove, it seemed, with his fingertips; it was only an illusion, for his whole body was behind and part of the wheel. He could make time. He was a kind of marksman, able, without slowing down, to gun the big sedan between two other cars with only an inch to spare on either side. Driving was his business. He had been a flop as a traffic cop, a patrolman, a Headquarters clerk, and a plain-clothesman. MacBride had given him a chance to drive. And though Gahagan still had a few loose ideas about traffic laws, and was far from a mental giant, his driving was superb.

He pulled up at the corner of Middleford and Sixteenth exactly six minutes after he had looped out of the Headquarters garage: five miles, most of it through traffic. Yawning, he said, "Should I shut the motor off or what?"

"Wait'll I see."

Kennedy came weaving across the sidewalk and Moriarity said under his breath, "Kennedy looks a little crocked."

MacBride was cranking down the window.

"Good time," said Kennedy, and hiccoughed.

MacBride said, "Well?"

"Better leave the car here. It isn't far."

"Come on, Mory," the skipper said. "Wait here, Gahagan."

"Hic-*uck*," hiccoughed Kennedy. The muffler MacBride had given him was still around his neck, one end trailing over his left shoulder. "Up Sixteenth a bit," he said, starting off. "I followed her right from the *Metropolitan*."

It was a fairly decent street flanked by some brownstone fronts, a few small apartment houses, occasional bake-shops or grocery stores, a filling station, a small fenced park. Kennedy stopped in front of a narrow, two-storied stone house with a semi-circular glass vestibule up a flight of four stone steps. There was a sign—gold letters on black—that said *Floor to Let*.

"The upstairs floor is the one to let," Kennedy drawled sleepily.

MacBride was scowling. "Hey—this is where Danizak lives!"

"Isn't that a coincidence!" said Kennedy, climbing the stone steps.

Moriarity and MacBride hopped up on either side of him and for a second all three became jammed in the vestibule doorway. It was MacBride who wedged through, tried the inner door, then pushed the lower of two buttons.

Pig Iron Brenner opened the door and said, "What do youse want?" And then, "Oh, jeese, I didn't rec'nize youse. Ha! Ain't that funny! I didn't—"

"Move," said MacBride, pushing past him.

Pig Iron began to look slow-wittedly upset.

Kennedy got in Moriarity's way, so Moriarity shoved him into the small square entrance hall, followed, and booted the door shut.

A circular stairway led upstairs. To the right was a door, half open. A face appeared there, then a body: Danizak.

"Come for tea?" he asked, unsmiling.

MacBride was on his way to the door. Danizak didn't move.

"Move," said the skipper.

"What's the matter with you guys, you hard up for something to do?"

Moriarity straight-armed him back into the room, said: "Go ahead, Cap."

Danizak, regaining his balance with the effortless ease of a cat, stood lean and dark and supple; trimly dressed—linen, tie, suit all merging nicely in color. His rather large lower lip was motionless, a little wet, shiny.

Nance Shannigan sat in a green barrel-back chair, her legs crossed, a buckle gleaming on the pump of the top foot. She had her hat on; also her fur coat, which was thrown back. Her sultry eyes stared and said nothing, nor did her drooping, surly, sensual lips move. She looked, if anything, bored.

Belly Skoba, sitting on a reversed chair, was making an elaborate show of cleaning his fingernails with a huge jack-knife.

On the floor were three suitcases, two gladstones, two smaller bags. Over the suitcases were thrown a couple of topcoats.

MacBRIDE said, "Going places?"

"Yeah," said Danizak.

"I told you—"

"I know what you told me," Danizak cut in leisurely. "But I'm going places. South."

"Yeah," horned in Pig Iron hoarsely. "We're just gittin' fed up on this here now lousy stinkin' cold weather. I been wantin' to see a palm tree since I was a kid. Jeese, now, it's funny—times I kin go along f'r mont's, years, likin' the winter, and then sudden-like, I dunno, I git a oige—"

Moriarity said, "You touch me—honest you do."

MacBride was digging his stare into Danizak. "Don't think because you got clear of that last rap that you can high-hand your way around this town, baby. I told you not to leave and I meant it."

"Huh," grunted the girl.

MacBride crossed the room, put his hands on his hips, and looked down at her. "Ever know Tod Rutter?"

"No."

"When you came from Cleveland, where'd you put up in this town?"

"A hotel."

"What hotel?"

She leaned back. "Why?"

"I just want to know, so I can check up and see what hotel you stopped at."

Her upward stare at him was humid.

Danizak strolled over and said, "Skipper, you can't read the riot act around here."

"At this minute," MacBride said, "I'm not talking to you."

"You're in my flat and you're talking to a friend of mine. It's the same thing. You tried to hang a job on me. You didn't hang it. Twelve men cleared me. You hate hell out of me, and that's all right but you can't smear yourself around my place here."

Pig Iron honked, "Atta boy, Nick! Atta old kid!"

"Button your lip," Moriarity said.

"Ha!" laughed Pig Iron.

Moriarity back-handed him across the mouth.

Belly Skoba said, "You hit my pal, you gotta hit me."

Moriarity kicked Belly Skoba in the shins.

"Tsk, tsk," said Kennedy.

MacBride, paying no attention to the by-play, was saying to Danizak, "This woman comes from Cleveland. She was in Springer's office today. She's here now."

"What the hell of it?" the girl demanded. She took a hard angry walk to the end of the room, her plump hips bouncing, her heavy silk skirt slapping at her calves. She swiveled and slapped her thigh and demanded again, "What the hell of it?"

MacBride's face was getting wooden. "Do you by any chance live here?"

"Listen to him!" she laughed.

"You going South with Nick?" he asked.

"I'm going to go nuts any minute if you don't stop trying to be so bright."

The skipper turned to Danizak. "We'll see. Open those bags. All of them."

"Don't make me laugh," Danizak said negligently, dropping his eyes and brushing at his coat lapel.

"Open 'em, Mory," the skipper said. "If they're locked, bust 'em open."

Pig Iron towered indignantly. "Dis is against de law!" he bellowed.

Danizak stepped nimbly across the room and got in front of Moriarity. "Copper, if you want to open these bags, get a search warrant."

"And you'll be doing what while I'm getting it?"

"Get it—that's all," Danizak said coldly. "There's no dirt on my nose and you guys can't rough my place up."

"Save it," sighed Moriarity as he bent over and unbuckled a strap on one of the suitcases.

Danizak pushed him half the length of the room.

The girl snapped, "Who the hell started this?"

Moriarity stopped moving backward and as he did he yanked his blackjack. Belly Skoba kicked him in the diaphragm and MacBride went for his gun. Pig Iron's left fist came up and plowed into the skipper's ear while his right sprouted a bulky automatic and his hoarse voice said:

"The idea is, kinda, who's gonna finish this."

Kennedy pulled a half-empty glass flask out of his pocket and broke it over Danizak's head. The whiskey sprayed, slopped down Danizak's face; it burned his eyes and he knuckled them furiously and threw himself blindly across the room, butting furniture, stumbling.

"So you wanna play too," said Belly Skoba, his big feet making the floor shake.

Kennedy kicked a chair that skidded into Belly Skoba and then hopped across the room to a telephone. Belly Skoba picked up the chair and flung it and Kennedy went down with the phone, which fell from his hands and lay disconnected on the floor. Belly Skoba picked it up, said, "Excuse it," into the mouthpiece; hung up and then ripped the phone out. "Smart guy," he said.

Pig Iron was saying dully to MacBride, "Don't pull the smoke, Skipper, or I give it to you—no fooling."

"He won't," said Belly Skoba, coming over and whipping his fist up under the skipper's chin. MacBride's eyes jiggered as his head banged against the wall. Belly Skoba guffawed, "That makes me feel good."

Nance Shannigan screeched, "Look out for the other guy!"

Moriarity, she meant. Mory, pain ripping across his face from the kick to his mid-section, was coming up, pushing himself up with his left hand, his breath retching in his throat, his mouth wide open, crooked with the effort.

Belly Skoba turned. Moriarity fired and the topmost button on Belly Skoba's vest vanished. The fat man's face was suddenly rigid. Moriarity, unable to get himself up, fell flat on his face and sighed and the bullet from Pig Iron's gun licked the cloth on the back of Mory's coat and banged into a radiator. MacBride chopped at Pig Iron's gun, hit Pig Iron's wrist. He got his own gun out as Pig Iron butted him in the chest. Belly Skoba suddenly fell down and drooled and as Pig Iron was shifting his gun from his right to his left hand the skipper stuck his own gun against Pig Iron's ribs and pulled the trigger.

The girl screamed and ran towards the door. Got her hand on the knob. Kennedy, a trickle of blood on his lip, hit her with the disconnected telephone.

Pig Iron's dead weight fell against MacBride. Danizak's eyes were sharp, his nostrils were flickering. He skipped across the room, swept up one of the suitcases, jumped over the girl and yanked open the door. Kennedy started after him, tripped and fell. MacBride was trying to shove off Pig Iron's dead weight. Danizak got through the doorway, into the hall.

Kennedy was getting up. The sound of two shots exploding somewhere beyond the door stopped him halfway to his feet. He cocked his head.

The front door banged.

MacBride got rid of Pig Iron, bounded to the open door and through into the hall. He almost fell over Danizak. Danizak was lying on the floor with a bloody face. The skipper jumped to the hall door, whipped it open, bounced through the vestibule and cleared the steps to the sidewalk.

Half a block away he saw a man running with a suitcase.

"Hey—you—stop!" he roared.

The man kept on running.

MacBride raised his gun, his arm out level from his chin. He pulled the trigger and somewhere a woman screeched and slammed a window shut.

The man up the street let go of the suitcase, threw his arms out and reeled. He sashed into a pole, rebounded into the gutter, half turned around and then buckled and fell down on his back beneath the street light.

MacBride walked, his gun still out, the wind cold against his hot face. He left the sidewalk and proceeded along the gutter and when he reached the prostrate man he bent over. His eyes grew wide and his mouth flew open.

"You—you shoot too—too straight," said Dave Trigg thickly.

Back in the house, Kennedy was helping Moriarity to his feet. Moriarity was a chunky man and Kennedy had quite a time of it, but he managed to get Moriarity into a chair. Then he tottered across the room and sat down himself. He looked around at the unconscious girl, at Pig Iron and Belly Skoba, both lying very still and looking very dead. Kennedy smiled ruefully and his weary, young-old eyes drooped.

He sighed, "Still life…" and wiped the blood from his lips and chuckled, but without humor.

Chapter IX

AT ELEVEN that night MacBride came into his office carrying half a dozen typewritten sheets of paper. He dropped them to the desk, looked across the room at Kennedy, who was huddled beside the radiator, and said:

"I knew it went back—back to November, when Tod Rutter was knocked off." He nodded to the sheets of paper. "There it is, authored by the Shannigan woman, by Trigg, with a few extras by Garfield. Like to hear it?"

"Well, if you can make it brief."

MacBride pointed. "Danizak killed Rutter. By God, I knew he did! Rutter was bringing a hundred and thirty thousand bucks to this city. It was the loot of a dozen small banks in the West and Middle West that were knocked off between four and five years ago. Rutter'd been running around in Cleveland with the guy that collected it but the guy was afraid to spring any of it. Rutter told him he knew a guy here who used to pass hot money for him through a sure-fire way. The guy was Trigg.

"Trigg had us all fooled. He had no record and as far as we knew all he did was run a hotel. Well, there you are. He got rid of hot money through the hotel. He usually passed it out to people who were checking out and going some distance. He even made a custom of the house to cash checks and he got very few bum ones. It was practically sure fire, fool proof. If there was any comeback—and he never had one— he could have said, well, the hot money must have been taken in in the course of business. So Rutter and this guy were to bring the money here. Rutter wrote ahead to Trigg and Trigg answered, yes, he would handle it, for twenty-five percent commission. But the night before they were to leave, Rutter's pal got killed in a taxi smash.

"Rutter'd been living with Nance Shannigan. She wanted to fly here with him but he wouldn't let her. They got in a fight and he told her he was through with her and walked out. She used to pal around with Danizak, she knew he was here, and she phoned him long distance from Rutter's apartment and told him Rutter was headed East with plenty of grand but she didn't know where he was taking it. She told him the plane Rutter was leaving on and said she'd come on later for her cut.

"Selma Jellif just worked for Trigg—she didn't know anything about his underworld activities. She was sick of her husband and wanted to get away. She had a kind of wild desire to go to South America and kept telling Trigg about it. She hated Jellif but he wouldn't leave her. So Trigg got a bright idea. He wasn't sure that Danizak had knocked off Rutter and he knew he couldn't find out with Danizak in jail and headed for the chair. He took Selma aside one day and said, 'Look here. You want to shake your husband. You're nuts about going to South America. There's a guy up for murder—you been reading the papers—this guy Danizak. He's got no alibi. Go to his lawyer and tell his lawyer you'll alibi for him for—well, for whatever amount you think you want. Try it. See what happens. If it works, you'll be rid of your husband and you'll probably get plenty of dough.' Well, she was a loose dame but she had no police record.

"Springer took her proposition to Danizak. The chair was staring Danizak in the face. He took her up and agreed to the fifteen thousand she asked for. Springer coached her for two weeks before she finally stood up that day in the courtroom and made history. It was simple. We couldn't pin a record on her. She worked for a living, got a small salary, had met Danizak at the cash counter in the coffee shop and fallen for him.

"Danizak went free. That's what Trigg wanted—he wanted to have Danizak out of jail so he could find out if Danizak had the dough that Rutter brought East. As soon as the trial was over Selma got her cut. She took the money back to her hotel room and hid it—hung it in the flush-bowl in the toilet. She was scared, nervous. At ten o'clock last night she went to Springer's apartment and asked him if he thought it would be all right if she left right away for South America. He told her it would be better if she left with Danizak for Florida and then gradually moved on from there alone.

"When she left his apartment she ran into Nance Shannigan. Leave it to one woman to distrust another. Shannigan was jumpy too. She doubted that Selma'd done what she did just because she had a wild desire to be rid of her husband and go to South America. She had a hunch, just like a woman, that somebody might have put the idea in Selma's head. At any rate, she wanted the truth—so she could know where she and the others stood. Springer's car was parked out front, the key was in it, and she forced Selma in and drove off with her. Then she began to ask questions. Selma was pretty shaken up and soon she got out of control and yelled at Nance to stop the car. Nance, just to scare her, pulled a gun—she had no intention of shooting Selma—she just wanted to scare the truth out of her. But Selma got frightened and began to strike her and the gun went off twice—once by accident and the second time on reflex. Nance was plenty scared. After she dumped Selma out she ran the car down to River Road, found a deserted spot and let it shoot off into the river. She didn't tell the other guys what she'd done. So Selma was dead.

"When Trigg heard of her death he sent Garfield to her room and had him frisk it. Garfield found the pay-off money. Fifteen grand, all of them western bank-notes. Trigg felt good. He had an idea she'd crossed up with one of the gang and that one of them might come back to pick up the dough. So he planted Garfield in the room to wait and see. He was the guy that phoned Garfield to duck out when me and Ike started down.

"Jellif didn't kill anybody. He was going to kill Danizak and figured he'd have to get tanked up to do it. He got so tanked up that he passed out and woke up in a deserted stable on the South Side. When he saw the papers about Selma's death—when he couldn't remember where he'd been or what he'd done—he lost his nerve, got the bug in his nut that he'd killed her and tried to hide out. He ain't a bad guy. A sap, but not a bad guy. He was never very strong and couldn't hold hard jobs and the way his wife kited around just drove the poor guy ga-ga. He'll live and I figure maybe I can get him a job somewhere."

"I wonder why Trigg, after all that careful work, decided to crash Danizak's place."

MacBride said, "I remember I told Trigg that Danizak had his bags packed for a trip South. He just wanted to checkmate Danizak. There was enough dough involved to make it worth the chance. Ninety-eight grand in that suitcase he took away from Danizak when he shot him down in the hallway."

Kennedy stood up, stretched. "Nice, nice people."

"Rats."

"Rats, lice and—you make the history, tomato."

MacBride chuckled roughly. "I make a salary, Kennedy. That's good enough for me."

Kennedy put on his hat, fumbled into his topcoat and yawned on his way to the door. "A drink—and so to bed."

MacBride, rising, said, "Wait" He stalked across the room. "No—turn around—your back to me. That's right." He peeled a square of paper off the back of Kennedy's coat, saying, "This."

Kennedy turned about, looked at it "Vote for Voltman? Never, never!"

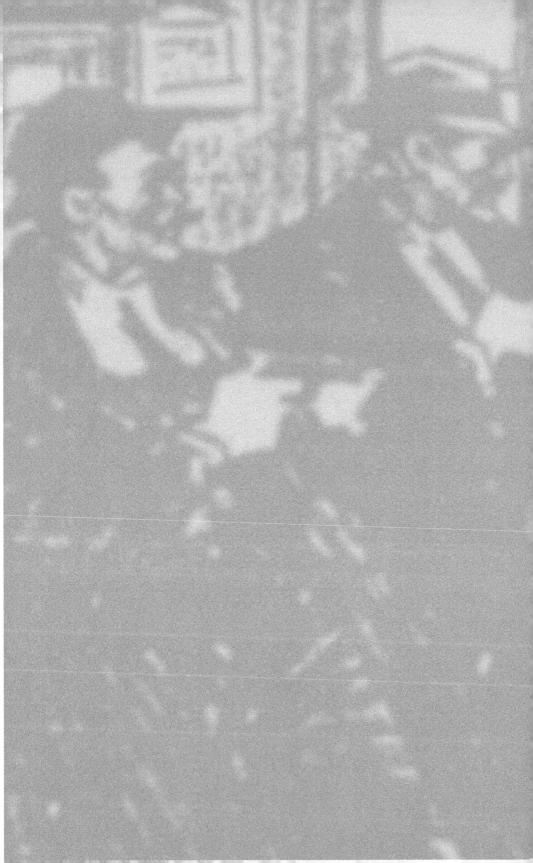

Hard to Take

And when MacBride and Kennedy are through it isn't any easier.

Chapter I

THE CAB swung down into Dominick Street at eleven, leaning hard on the turn and toppling Kennedy against the side of the seat. He woke up, pushed himself leisurely to an upright position, and yawned. The jolt had knocked his limp fedora over on one side of his head, exposing a slab of dry pale hair. He did not bother to straighten his hat but sat drowsily watching the lights roll past.

There were not many lights in Dominick Street—an all-night delicatessen, a couple of lunch-rooms, a pool-hall, intermittent bars, and the scattered windows of run-down flats. At the foot of the grade the cab pulled up before two plate-glass windows that were painted black halfway up. Over the door between the windows hung a wooden sign lighted from above by a metal-shaded electric bulb.

The driver said, "Well, here's the *Idle Hour.*"

"So it is," said Kennedy, and got out. "Hang around," he added. The wind against his back had an edge and he huddled in his threadbare topcoat as he crossed the sidewalk. On the single wooden step in front of the *Idle Hour* was a rubber mat with ten-inch white letters saying *Welcome.* Kennedy pushed open the door.

The old upright had a couple of sour keys and the bag-eyed fat man playing it managed to hit them frequently. Two men were playing pool in the harsh white downpour of two one-hundred watt bulbs. Five men sat in at a stud game while three others looked on. Tobacco smoke hung layer on layer in the low-ceilinged room. No one paid any attention to the man playing the piano. In the rear of the room was a two-banistered staircase that led upstairs and as Kennedy reached it a gaunt man with a derby on the back of his head got up out of a worn leather chair and, folding a newspaper, said:

"Looking for somebody, Kennedy?"

"Hello, Stamps. Yes. Mike upstairs?"

Stamps Kruger shook his gaunt head. "Uh-huh. Ain't been in tonight. What's new?"

"The Mayor called up fifteen minutes ago. It's all over."

"Which way?"

"There's going to be a fine new recreation center in the Third Ward."

One of Kruger's big eyes remained wide open, the other closed down to a tight squint. His nose, which slashed his face sharply down the middle, twitched. He grunted, "Have a drink," and led the way into a small back room. He pulled a couple of bottles of beer out of an old wooden icebox, uncapped them, handed one to Kennedy. He was still squinting with one eye, boring Kennedy with the other. "It sounds like a fluke," he said.

"It's no fluke," Kennedy said amiably. "This square block, right here, will be razed. Every building. The Municipal Reconstruction Committee will reimburse Mike. It was in the cards, Stamps. The City Engineer's staff condemned the buildings and it remained only for Brick O'Connor to give his okey and the Mayor to sign the order."

Kruger's voice was low, angry. "You seen O'Connor yet?"

"No. I want to see what Mike has to say."

Kruger drained his bottle of beer, thumped down the empty bottle and let his hand remain on it while he stared hard at the wall. He shook his head, as if unable to figure things out. Then he growled:

"Mike's probably home."

"I'll go there," Kennedy said. "Thanks for the beer."

"I'll go along."

Kruger opened a closet door, pulled out a black overcoat and shrugged into it. A deep angry puzzled frown had fastened on his

gaunt face. He said, more to himself than to Kennedy:

"Mike'll have plenty to say. Let's go."

He tipped his derby down over his left eyebrow and strode savagely out to the sidewalk. Kennedy meandered along in his wake, said, "Go to 340 South Dublin," to the taxi driver and climbed in. Kruger followed and bounced on the seat as the cab jerked away from the curb.

He ripped out, "You know who's really behind this, don't you?"

"Your guess is as good as mine, Stamps."

"I don't mean the Mayor or the City Engineer or Brick O'Connor. I mean the lug that started it, the lug that started it a year ago, before that even."

Kennedy shrugged. "You guys had it coming, fella. You can't run fast houses high, wide and handsome and get away with it. You can't run gambling joints where guys get clipped every now and then. There's a law about those things. When the cops find six hot cars over a period of two months in one of your garages—" He shrugged again, sighed. "Why go on? They'd close your joints one week and they'd be open again the next. So finally they said, 'Well, we'll condemn the property, raze it, and use it for the new community center.' No kidding, Stamps—you lads had it coming to you. Sure, I know who really started it." He chuckled. "Mike isn't the first guy that didn't take MacBride seriously. There's just two pigeon holes in the skipper's desk. One is marked lawful and the other lawless. You know which one Mike's been in for years."

Kruger leaned back, stuck a cigar between his teeth and lit it. His eyes glinted in the match's flame.

"On the top of that," Kennedy added. "Mike had an idea he could buy Brick O'Connor."

Kruger looked at him sharply, his lips tightening on the cigar. He suddenly pulled the cigar from his mouth, as though to say something. But he said nothing.

"Huh?" said Kennedy.

Kruger looked away, put the cigar carefully back between his teeth and merely said, "H'm." He folded his arms and with a stony-eyed stare watched the street lights swing past.

Chapter II

GAHAGAN, police chauffeur, was sitting on a three-legged stool in the basement garage at headquarters. Above him was a Western Union clock that showed the time to be twenty minutes shy of midnight. Gahagan was reading a book entitled *Hypnotism Simplified* and the painful effort of concentration was stamped on his large, ruddy face. So intent was he that he was unaware of the arrival beside him of MacBride, Moriarity and Cohen. MacBride, smoking a pipe, wore the expression of a pained but compassionate father toward a backward son. Moriarity lifted his foot and hit the cement floor with a resounding smack.

Gahagan jumped up and squared off in a fighting pose. Then he relaxed, looked sheepish.

MacBride said laconically, "Okey. If it's not asking too much, we'd like to be driven to 340 South Dublin Street."

Gahagan grunted, stamped across to the big police Buick, got his overcoat from the front seat and put it on. He shoved in behind the wheel and the skipper sat down beside him. Moriarity and Cohen got in back. Gahagan grooved the car deftly out of the garage and was doing fifty at the next block.

Moriarity said, "I wonder if O'Connor knows yet."

"Not unless they told him," MacBride replied, making a half turn and draping his left arm over the back of the seat. "This is going to raise a stink somewhere."

"It would have anyway," Cohen put in. "When the Mayor signed on the dotted line—"

"H'm," mused the skipper. "There were a lot of guys figured that Brick O'Connor might put up the stop signal, account of Mike Devlin's power in the Third Ward. But O'Connor came through. Well, if we've got to have a city political boss, it's just as well we got O'Connor." He dropped his voice, muttered, "I told Mike Devlin two years ago that I'd break his vice hold in the Third Ward, no matter if he did have a couple of magistrates greased. Well, it happened."

Moriarity said, "There's still Kruger."

"He's finished too," the skipper said shortly.

The sedan ripped through the night, the wind whanging in its radiator shutters, whistling past the windows. Gahagan drove with a seeming negligence—but he drove, MacBride would have admitted, like an angel. He ate up Division Road, cut through South Park, hit South Dublin Street near the overpass. The three hundred block contained remodeled houses of two or three stories. Number 340 was two-storied, with a new brick front, a street-level vestibule. There was a fat uniformed cop out front fanning his arms to keep warm. Gahagan pulled up, shut off the ignition, and tapped a yawn.

MacBride was the first out and the uniformed cop said, "Hi, Cap'n."

"Hello, Blumenfeld. How's the kid doing?"

"Lots better, last time I phoned, Cap'n. She ain't been coughin' half as much."

"Swell, boy—swell! Who's inside?"

"Nordecker from the precinct. He was just comin' by."

The skipper went into the vestibule, pushed open the inner door and entered a small, oblong entry hall. At the left were French doors, open; beyond, a large, well-furnished living-room. Kennedy was stretched out in a club chair with his feet planted on a leather ottoman.

"So glad you were able to come," he said drowsily.

Detective Nordecker, from the local precinct, was just hanging up the telephone. He said, "Hello, Cap'n. I just phoned the medical office."

"Hello, Bennie," the skipper said.

Stamps Kruger came sullenly out of the dining-room, his gaunt bald head shining. The skin of his face was uniformly yellow and his wide mouth was bent downward at the corners. He said with heavy sarcasm:

"Well, well, now that the brains of the Bureau has turned up—"

"Before you start," said Moriarity, arriving casually in the room, "that's enough."

Nordecker nodded towards the dining-room, said, "In there."

MacBride crossed the living-room and, stopping in the dining-room doorway, put his hands on his hips. He frowned, flexed his lips, shook his hard-boned head briefly. Mike Devlin lay on the floor beside an overturned chair. There was a dark blotch on the otherwise smooth white surface of his dress shirt. The toes of his patent leather low shoes shone in the light from the center chandelier. He was a slender corpse, oval-faced, fiftyish. The hair on his narrow head was tangled. His hands, narrow, long-fingered, lay peacefully on the carpet alongside his body.

Kennedy, at MacBride's elbow, said, "When I heard the Mayor had signed the condemnation order, I dropped around the *Idle Hour* to get a statement from Mike. He wasn't there. Stamps and I came over here. All the shades were drawn but the lights were on and the radio was playing loud. We knocked and knocked. Stamps had a key and we came in. And there lay Mike. I turned the radio off. It'd been playing a long time, apparently—was so hot you could hardly touch it."

MacBride was bending over the body, his hands braced on his knees. "The guy who did it knew how to shoot. Smack in the heart."

Nordecker came in holding a gun in a handkerchief. "This is the rod. A .32 auto." He nodded to the dining-room table, covered with bills, receipts. "Mike must have been going over his accounts."

MacBride said, "How do you know it's the rod?"

"I don't. I'm guessing. It was laying on the floor over here."

MacBride grunted. He straightened up and said, "If it was left behind, probably there's no prints on it—but keep it clean anyhow." To Kennedy: "What time did you and Kruger come in here?"

"About twenty after eleven. Maybe twenty-five."

The skipper turned back to Nordecker. "Did you ask around next door if they heard any shots?"

"I sent Blumenfeld. He said no."

MacBRIDE walked around the room and stopped at the farther end to say, "Devlin must have gone out to a dress-up dinner or something. Maybe when he came back, the killer was already planted in here."

"Maybe he didn't even go out," Kennedy said.

"Oh, I suppose he'd get all dolled up just to look at himself in a mirror."

Kennedy shook his tousled head mildly. He ambled across the room and picked up an empty cardboard shoe-box from beside a waste-paper basket. "A shoe-box," he explained sleepily. "Now take a look at the dogs on Mike's feet."

MacBride had to come back across the room to do it. He nodded. "You're right. These shoes he's wearing have never walked on anything but carpets. He got dressed to go out—and then didn't go out. Hey, ain't he got any servants?"

"A housekeeper," said Kennedy. "She went off today at noon. She goes off Thursdays at noon."

MacBride pivoted. "What do you know about this, Kruger?" he grunted.

Kruger was standing in the doorway with his hands sunk in his hip pockets, his stomach thrust forward, his chest sunken. "About as much as you do—nothing," his surly, antagonistic voice said. "Or maybe," he added sarcastically, "you know more."

Moriarity walked across the room and faced him. "You wouldn't be playing guessing games, would you?"

"Was I talking to you?"

"You are now."

MacBride said, "Forget it, Mory. Go phone the fingerprint bureau to send a man over. Kennedy, you phone your paper yet?"

"One minute after we found the body."

Ike Cohen appeared, yelled, "Hey, Cap. Come here a minute and take a look."

"Where?"

"This way. The bathroom."

The skipper drummed his heels after Cohen, followed him upstairs and into a bathroom with a black tile floor. Cohen pointed, saying, "The shower curtain's wet. There's Mike's dirty underclothes hanging on the hook. He took a shower, say, before dressing. Then he doused himself with powder. There's a lot of it on the floor. Look out—don't step in too far. Take a look at the floor—at the powder there."

"This, you mean?"

"Yeah—the mark left by a woman's shoe—small and pointed. Which means that between the time Mike took a bath and now there was a woman in the house."

MacBride said, "Okey, Ike. Out." And when Cohen had stepped out the skipper took the key from the inside of the door, inserted it in the outside and locked up. He slipped the key into his pocket and went downstairs.

Brick O'Connor, political head without portfolio of Richmond City, was standing in the dining-room looking down at Mike Devlin's body.

"Hello, Stephen," he said offhand.

"Where'd you come from?"

"I was home. Kennedy's editor phoned me. I thought I'd drop around. Who polished off Mike?"

"That's going to be something interesting to find out."

O'Connor was a broad man of medium height with a fine head of dull red hair. A raglan overcoat of soft brown wool was wrapped round his body and a tan silk scarf was knotted loosely at his throat. He had an iron jaw, imperturbable blue eyes and a heavy ease of manner.

He said heavily, "I figured Mike 'd come to an end like this some day, but I didn't figure it'd happen so soon."

"Especially," said Stamps Kruger, with a glitter in his eye, "so soon after you gave the Mayor the high-sign to sign that order practically kicking Mike out of the Third Ward."

O'Connor turned slowly, gave Kruger a grave stare, then said to MacBride, "Any leads?"

"Hell, we just got here. Ike found a woman's shoe print in some powder on the bathroom floor, upstairs. By the way, what woman was Mike running around with, Kruger?"

Kruger laughed. "Ha! Right away there's a woman in it!"

"Well, who was he running around with?"

"I dunno. A jane named Daisy Swartz, I think."

"Where's she live?"

"I think at the *Eldorado* but I ain't sure."

Kennedy said, "By the way, when did you last see Mike today?"

Kruger turned sharply and scowled. "About noon—why? I ran into him at the *Ship Grill*, eating."

"Where were you from, say, five this afternoon till the time I dropped in at the *Idle Hour?*"

"There, there," growled Kruger. "At the *Idle Hour*."

"Upstairs or down?"

"Sometimes I was up in the office and sometimes I was down."

"And when you were up, was there anyone with you?"

Kruger put his head over on one side and squinted truculently with one eye. "Say, are you trying to kid me, half-pint?"

"Skip it, if you want to," Kennedy said indifferently.

"I don't have to skip it! I ate dinner downstairs in the *Idle Hour*, had it sent over from the *Cozy Corner Café*, and then account of I always sleep after I eat, I went upstairs for a sleep." He towered, his face dark with anger. "By God, some wise guys around this town that hated Mike might have framed him into getting himself killed, but I'm left—damn it, I'm left!—and nobody's going to tack up a frame around me. Mike was killed because he wouldn't get in line—he was a tough baby and the only way to stop a tough baby is to kill him!" He spun and glared at Brick O'Connor. "Maybe you figured that out too, *Mis*ter O'Connor!"

MacBride said, "Go ahead, Brick, it's okey by me if you take a poke at him."

O'Connor dug his hands deep into his overcoat pockets, shook his head. "Let him rave," he said dryly.

Kennedy picked up a torn, empty envelope from the litter on the table, folded it in half, and then once again, and tucked it away in his vest pocket. He said:

"Well, one thing we know—he always sleeps after he eats. Do you still collect stamps?"

Kruger brawled, "Yeah—and I got the best collection in town."

"Swell!" smiled Kennedy.

Chapter III

THE SKIPPER walked into his office at eight next morning, tossed the city's two morning newspapers on his desk and hung up his hat and overcoat. Though he had had only five hours sleep he looked fresh, scrubbed, and the cold morning wind had beaten strong color into his face. He sat down at his desk and spread out the newspapers, scowled at the headlines while he crammed rough-cut tobacco into his charred old brier. Side by side were the stories of Mike Devlin's murder, the Mayor's statement concerning the Dominick Street community center. There was an editorial on the strange coincidence that Mike Devlin should have died on the night that his property was officially condemned.

The *Express* said in part, "It was Captain Stephen J. MacBride who two years ago first started the reform rumbling that today ends in the condemnation of the Dominick Street property and the strange death of Michael Devlin. Is it possible that the captain, stormy petrel of many a vice crusade, may find his a hollow victory?"

MacBride grunted, clicked his pipe-stem between his hard teeth. He read every word in both papers, sat back, finished his pipe with his eyes fastened unremittingly on the wall.

At nine o'clock Moriarity opened the door and said, "Hey, Cap, I got the Swartz woman outside. Want to see her now?"

"Yeah. Shoot her in, Mory."

Daisy Swartz was small, well-built. Her hair was flat and yellow and dropped to her ears and the ends were frizzed. She wore a small blue hat cocked over on one side. Her eyes were too large for her face and she had a small, puckered, spoiled mouth. She moved into the office with a mouse-like quietness and stopped just inside the door.

"Sit down," MacBride said, creaking back in his chair and hooking a heel on an opened lower desk drawer.

She took a seat and folded her hands in her lap. She had not looked at MacBride upon entering, nor did she look at him now. Her fingernails were lacquered red and there was a vague, waxlike prettiness about her face.

"We're trying," MacBride said, "to find out who killed Mike Devlin."

She nodded without looking up and the skipper spent a minute studying her blank, pretty face. He leaned forward, wrinkling his forehead, and said:

"Is there anything you know that might help us?"

She shook her head slowly. "No."

"When did you last see Mike?"

"Night before last."

"Did he say anything, either then or any other time, that showed he was afraid of being killed?"

"No."

"Where were you last night?"

"Home."

"All night?"

"Yes. I had a date with Mike, he reserved a table at the *Palais Royale* for nine. He was going to pick me up at the *Eldorado* at eight-thirty. When he didn't show up at half-past nine I phoned him." She paused.

"Did you get him?"

She nodded while keeping her eyes fixed on the floor. "Yes. He said unexpected business turned up and he wouldn't be able to meet me."

"Is that all he said?"

"Yes."

"Then what did you do?"

"I read a while and then went to bed."

MacBride leaned back. "Now is there anything else? Be sure. Think hard. Is there anything Mike said on the phone, or when you last saw him, or at any other time, that might help us?"

She remained silent for a minute, then shook her head and said, "No."

He leaned forward again. "Mike, for instance, never said anything about Kruger, about being afraid of him?"

"No."

"When you were dressed last night, waiting for Mike, what kind of slippers did you wear?"

Her eyes raised, then lowered. "Blue ones. I had on a blue dress."

He stood up. "That's all." He pressed a button and Moriarity came in. "Mory," he said, "take Miss Swartz back to her apartment and when you get there have her give you her blue evening slippers."

A cloud passed downward across her face and vanished and left her face blank again.

"I catch on," Moriarity said.

MacBride said, "Miss Swartz, you're not to leave the city."

She nodded, waited.

MacBride moved a finger. "Okey, Mory, take her home."

She passed through the doorway and Moriarity came over to the desk and said, "I tried to check up on her movements last night at the *Eldorado,* but they got no lobby man there and you work the elevator yourself."

MacBride was sitting down. "Okey. Check up on the slippers and see if they fit that print in the bathroom."

Moriarity went out and through the doorway MacBride caught a glimpse of Daisy Swartz powdering her nose. Then the door closed behind Moriarity, shut her from view.

THE skipper squinted at the door for a long time, polishing the bowl of his pipe against the side of his nose until the door opened and Kennedy drifted in saying:

"Did Daisy make the gun go root-a-toot-toot?"

MacBride clasped his hands behind his head. "They had a date last night for the *Palais Royale* and he was to pick her up at half-past eight. When he didn't, she phoned him—at half-past nine and he said he was busy, he wouldn't be able to keep the date. So we know he was alive at nine-thirty. Baumlein placed the death roughly between nine-thirty and ten-thirty."

"Any prints on the gun?"

"Only smudges. Nothing worth a damn."

"How do you know she actually phoned him at nine-thirty?"

"I think she was telling that much truth. However...." He called the Headquarters chief operator and told him to check on calls out of Western 909 last night.

Kennedy, still only half-awake, slid on to a chair and said, "If Mike was killed between half-past nine and half-past ten, then the Mayor made the phone call to the newspapers that the condemnation order was okeyed...." He paused, shrugged. "He made that phone call *after* Mike Devlin was dead."

MacBride's face turned wooden. "What the hell are you trying to rig up?"

"Oh, nothing, nothing. The sequence of events simply happens to be very interesting. I've seen too many political regimes come and go to be shocked at the idea of murder among the powers that be. You've seen the same. Mike Devlin was a nasty actor, he had several magistrates soaped, he was always a tough loser. He might have contested that condemnation order—he might even have won and thereby have made Brick O'Connor lose face as overlord of Richmond City's political machine—"

MacBride made a grunted sound. "Brick O'Connor's always been untouchable."

"There's always the hundredth chance," mused Kennedy; he added with a gray little chuckle, "Don't get me wrong, old tomato. I'm not trying to pin anything on anybody. I've no ax to grind. But the possibilities are amazing. You've got to admit that Devlin practically ran the Third Ward and that O'Connor played ball for several years by keeping his hands off, turning his head the other way. No crime in that. That's politics. But then you began to hit Dominick Street, you chucked case after case into court and it was promptly chucked out again.

"But you kept it up and finally the *Free Press* began to get behind you, people, the law-abiding people of the Third Ward woke up, and O'Connor realized that something had to be done. So did the Mayor, but the Mayor had to have O'Connor's okey. If I had about three drinks under my belt, I'd be more eloquent—but there's the gist of it. The condemnation order is passed—and before Mike Devlin can make a statement or a reprisal, he's found dead. Hell, maybe there's no connection at all. But it's a swell idea to fool around with."

MacBride was scowling. "You can make anything sound plausible, Kennedy, but I think you're screwy about Brick O'Connor."

"Do you know," said Kennedy, "that Brick O'Connor is almost flat broke?"

"No."

"He had practically all his dough tied up in Middle-East Utilities. Last month he sold two paintings that he'd picked up when he was in the fat cash—sold 'em for four thousand dollars, half of what he paid for them."

The phone rang and MacBride picked it up. "Yeah?... Oh, you, Pfluger... What?... Well, you dumb-ox, what'd you let her do that for?... Ah, excuses, excuses! You make me sick!" He banged the receiver into the hook and rasped, "Pfluger, that guy I stationed at Devlin's house, let the housekeeper come in and clean up. She opens the bathroom door with a key of her own and mops up the floor—and that shoe print! By God, if you don't do a thing yourself in this lousy police department—"

Bogardus looked in. "Cap'n, there's a man out here wants to see you. He says his name's Pringle and it's in connection with the Devlin case."

"I'll take a chance, Bogey—send him in."

Pringle was a slender, middle-aged man, with thin white hair and parchment skin. He was conservatively dressed and carried gloves and a walking stick. Entering, he dipped his head gravely and said:

"You are Captain MacBride?"

"I am. Sit down, sir."

"Thank you. I am Henry Pringle, secretary of the Merchants Bank and Trust Company. Yes, ah—reading in this morning's newspaper of the death of Michael Devlin, I thought I would come round and tell you something that perhaps you do not know, inasmuch as I saw no mention of it in the newspaper. Michael Devlin was a client of our bank. You knew that?"

"No, I didn't."

"Well, of course, this may be of no value whatever, but at half-past two yesterday afternoon Michael Devlin drew twenty-five thousand dollars from his account—in cash—and took it home with him. I personally placed it in one of our green envelopes."

"That's something!" grunted the skipper.

Kennedy said, "Mr. Pringle, how do you know he took it home?"

"I seem to have a horror of anybody carrying so much money on his person, so I sent one of our bank guards with him. A man named Thomas Blount. Blount escorted him home. As an added precaution, I took down the numbers of the bills. Here is the list."

MacBride stood up to receive the list and said in a voice of genuine approval, "Mr. Pringle, as an old cop I got to congratulate you on your foresight."

"Ever since our payroll was stolen four years ago, I've been very conscious of the dangers of transporting cash."

The skipper's eyes were shining. "Thanks a million, Mr. Pringle."

"Don't mention it. Duty, sir, is duty."

He dipped his head once towards MacBride, once towards Kennedy and walked out.

The skipper sat down, rubbed his jaw, bent his brows deeply. "So there was money involved too… murder and robbery."

"They often," said Kennedy, "go hand in hand—like ham and eggs."

Chapter IV

THE MORNING was bright, windy. Pale cloud fragments traveled fast above the city and at some of the street intersections small whirlpools of wind spun scraps of paper. The sound of street car bells was sharp, distinct. A traffic cop's whistle could be heard for blocks.

Gahagan pulled up before a two-storied white frame house on Webster Drive and MacBride got out, grabbed hold of his hat as the wind pounced on it. The wind rippled his trouser-legs as he warped up the cement walk between neat rows of blue spruce.

Brick O'Connor kept a cook and a houseman. The houseman was pretty old, but rugged. His name was Bachman and for years, up until the time his eyes had gone back on him, he had been a chauffeur for several mayors. He opened the door and said:

"Mornin', Cap'n."

"Hello, Joe. Mr. O'Connor in?"

As the skipper entered the square entry hall Blanche O'Connor reached the foot of the center stairway. Seeing him, she stopped with her hand on the round newel post. She was a handsome woman of about forty with dark brown hair flecked with slivers of gray. She had, MacBride thought, tragic eyes—large and soft and deep. She was Brick O'Connor's wife—she had been his wife now for over twenty years.

The skipper said, "Good morning, Mrs. O'Connor. I was just wondering if Brick was in—"

"Yes, I'm in," O'Connor said, coming up from the rear of the lower hall. His voice was heavy, smooth, rounded. "Come in the living-room, Steve. Blanche, you'll excuse us, honey?"

She nodded. There was mild confusion in her eyes and she remained standing by the newel post as O'Connor took the skipper into the large, restful living-room. Bachman closed the front door very quietly, as though not to disturb anyone.

A youth of about twenty got up from a divan, shoved back his cornsilk hair and tossed a newspaper aside. He was wasp-waisted and his chin dropped inward from his mouth.

The skipper said, "You're Ned, ain't you? Well, boy, I guess I haven't seen you in four or five years."

"Hello," Ned said, sloping casually out of the room.

When he had disappeared Brick O'Connor said, "Well, Steve, what are you looking dark about?"

"Me dark?" chuckled MacBride.

They sat down on a window seat and O'Connor said, "Pretty, the morning papers, huh?"

"I got something prettier."

O'Connor leaned back. "Yeah?"

"Mike drew twenty-five grand out of the bank just before closing time yesterday."

Brick O'Connor stared straight ahead for a long time. "So maybe he was murdered for his dough."

"Logically, yes. I'm thinking of something else. It's tough that that condemnation order had to be delivered to the press the same night he was killed. It's tougher, Brick, that he had to draw out twenty-five grand only a few hours before both those things happened."

O'Connor nodded slowly. "I see."

"His woman phoned him at half-past nine and he was still alive. We checked on her call. It's okey. She said he told her he was taken up by business and wouldn't be able to keep a date with her at the *Palais Royale*. Outside of that, we've been unable to check on her movements. Devlin's housekeeper, due to a fat-head of a cop I had stationed there this morning, mopped up that shoe print in the powder on the bathroom floor."

"You really think there's a woman mixed up in it?"

MacBride wrinkled his nose, flexed his lips. "Brick, did Mike try to bribe you?"

"Whether he did or not, he didn't succeed."

"I hear you're pretty broke."

O'Connor scowled. "Where'd you hear that?"

"Well, I heard it. Skip it."

O'Connor shrugged. "Pretty broke since Middle-East Utilities blew up. But I can still buy hash."

The skipper stood up, walked the length of the room and returned with his eyes glued on the polished toes of his shoes. "You weren't over to Mike's anytime last night, were you?"

"When there was any business between Mike and me, he came to me." O'Connor stood up, his large jaw hard, his nape straight. "I went over late because the press phoned me and told me he was dead."

"Home all evening, eh?"

"No. I spoke at the Safety League Dinner at the *Capitol* and left with Billy Humphrey at about ten-thirty. He dropped me off here, oh, about twenty minutes later. I was having a nightcap when the phone call came in. Blanche was in bed with a headache." His tone, heavy, suave, was touched slightly with irritation.

MacBride stood up and said, "Don't get sore, Brick. I just want things straight in my mind. Everybody knows that it was up to you whether the Mayor signed that order or not. Everybody knows that Devlin ran the Third Ward—but that you had the power to trump him any time you wanted to. It's just all these things happening at once, loose strings that a lot of wise guys are going to try to tie together—"

"Including yourself."

MacBride shrugged. "It's habit with me." He dropped his voice: "And remember, Kennedy's on this case for the *Free Press*. He'll kid you, drink your liquor, crack jokes with you, seem to fall asleep in your company, but he's nobody's fool. Drunk or sober, he's a smart fella."

O'Connor held out his hands. "See those hands? They're clean, boy—clean as a whistle."

"Brick, will you tell me one thing? Will you tell me why the Mayor phoned to the press at that hour last night instead of shooting the order through in a regular day's business?"

O'Connor frowned. "Yeah, sure. It was a kind of trick on my part. The Mayor meant well, but he was afraid of the Third Ward. He was at the Safety League dinner, everybody wanted to know how I stood on the issue, and I got up and said I stood for immediate condemnation of the Dominick Street property. The Mayor was in a spot. He had to stand up and say he agreed with me. Then he phoned."

"Okey," MacBride said, and scooped up his hat. "They were questions I had to ask, Brick. I'd have to ask 'em of my own brother. I got a one-track mind."

O'Connor's chuckle was hearty now. "I'd hate to have pulled a crime, Steve—and have you on my trail," he said as they walked across the living-room.

THERE was a slight thump, a slight sigh. O'Connor quickened his pace and reached the entry hall and MacBride was at his heels. O'Connor's wife sat on the floor, dazedly rubbing a hand across her forehead.

"Gosh, Blanche!" O'Connor said, lifting her to her feet.

She murmured, "Coming down the stairs… a dizzy spell."

"I told you you should have stayed in bed this morning."

She smiled wanly. "I'm sorry, Brick."

"Come on, I'll carry you up."

"No, no; I can make it."

O'Connor said over his shoulder, "Excuse me, Steve."

Ned O'Connor was standing at the head of the staircase. He called down, "What's up?"

O'Connor, making no reply, was already helping his wife up the stairs.

Bachman, the old houseman, came hurrying from the rear of the hallway. His husky voice asked, "What's wrong, what's wrong?"

"Nothing, Joe," O'Connor said.

MacBride put on his hat and did not wait for Bachman to open the door. The skipper reached the sedan with his eyes narrowed and staring straight before him.

"Say, what do you think, huh?" Gahagan asked.

MacBride, preoccupied, stared at Gahagan as though he were a bare wall. Then he pulled open the rear door, climbed in, slammed it shut.

"Honest," said Gahagan, "I ain't kidding."

"Shut up and roll this buggy to Headquarters."

Gahagan smacked his foot down angrily on the starter, slapped into gear and swung the car away from the curb with a violent twist of the wheel.

MacBride yelled, "What's the matter, are you trying to turn us upside down?"

Gahagan, saying "Nuts!" under his breath, straightened out and did a sweet job of driving all the way to Headquarters. He shot the car neatly into the Headquarters garage, shut off the ignition and set the brake at the same time, opened the door and slouched out. Mac-Bride got out at the same time and Gahagan gave him a one-eyed sour look.

The skipper said, "Well, what's eating you?"

"Ah, what's eating me!" Gahagan bawled, striking himself on the chest with both fists. "I try to tell you something when you come out o' Mr. O'Connor's place, and whaddeya do?"

"Well, what'd I do?"

"Told me to shut up!"

"All right. So what were you going to say? Make it good, because I'm tired of your screwy ideas."

Gahagan, still looking injured, said, "Well, about five minutes before you came out, a taxi drives up and out gets Stamps Kruger, looking tough, with his derby planted over one eye. He's heading for the O'Connor house, but seeing me, he turns and gets back in the cab and drives off."

"M'm."

"So I get out and stand in the street watching him and as I'm doing this, memorizing the license number, just in case, another cab goes by and damned if Kennedy ain't in it!"

"Where'd he go?"

"How do I know? Kruger's cab turns right about four blocks on, and so does Kennedy's. And if I was asked, I'd say he was tailing Kruger."

MacBride laid a hand on Gahagan's shoulder. "Okey, boy, okey. I was just thinking back there when I came out of O'Connor's. By the way, what was that license number?"

"Why sure, it was—" Gahagan stopped, reddened, began to look very uncomfortable. "Jeese, it seems it's slipped me mind."

The skipper said, "Ah, well," sadly to himself and rapped his heels towards the stairway. Reaching the central room, he ran into Ike Cohen, who said:

"Well, it's a dead end on that .32, Cap. It was one of the guns that Patrolman Beckholtz swiped out of the Fourth Precinct arsenal five years ago and sold around anonymous. You remember that—it came out after Beckholtz was shot and killed in the election riots that year."

"I remember," MacBride nodded. "Well, we're getting nowhere fast, Ike. Did you go to the *Palais Royale*, like I told you?"

"Yup. Mike had a table reserved okey and didn't show up. But there was a guy there looking for him. This guy showed up at about eight-thirty in the bar. At ten he went into the dining-room and asked the headwaiter if Mike Devlin had showed up. Mike hadn't, of course. The guy left about fifteen minutes later."

"Do they know him?"

"Nope. I got the headwaiter downstairs now looking through the Rogues' Gallery. He can't remember whether the guy was dark-haired or light or what kind of a suit he had on. I don't even know if he'd recognize a picture if he saw it. But there was a guy looking for Mike at the *Palais Royale*."

The front door opened and Kennedy wandered in, went across to a steam radiator and warmed his hands. The skipper crossed over to him and said:

"What's this I hear about you tailing Kruger?"

"Oh, it was just an idea. He just went 'round and 'round. Out to O'Connor's house, where he changed his mind about going in, and then back to the *Idle Hour*. Would you like to pinch Kruger?"

"Why should I?"

"Just another idea." He drew from his pocket a torn, empty envelope folded twice. Unfolding it, he took out an air mail stamp. He said, "Kruger said he didn't see Devlin all day yesterday. He said especially he didn't see him last night. Kruger, old tomato, lied."

"That's very nice. Tell me some more."

"You see this envelope? I snitched it off Devlin's table while all you cops were horsing around. Why did I snitch it? Because I noticed that it had a special delivery stamp on it, canceled, and that it had had another stamp—removed. I noticed that the receiving post office stamped it at 6:30 p.m. last night—the night of the murder. I since found out that it was delivered at seven-fifteen. Kruger collects stamps. A stamp had been cut off the envelope. This morning I got Kruger to show me his stamp collection. I swiped his last entry—this air mail stamp. It fits perfectly. It must have been removed from this letter after seven-fifteen on the night of the murder. Which means, Skipperino, that our dear old philatelist—"

"Kennedy, if I didn't think it was bad for you, I'd buy you a bottle of whiskey."

"Let it be bad for me."

"No, Kennedy, I refuse to do you any harm."

"You wouldn't," said Kennedy, "be Scotch on your father's side, would you?"

Chapter V

IT **WAS** noon at the *Idle Hour*. A dozen men were in the place, lounging around or eating sandwiches and drinking beer. One man was practicing billiard shots. The bag-eyed fat man who had been playing the piano the night before merely sat now on the piano stool, dreamily eating a banana. The large room was drab, it still smelled of last night's tobacco smoke and spilled beer. At sound of a car stopping out front, several men raised their heads; none bothered to get up.

MacBride came in, slammed the door shut and said to the nearest man, "Where's Kruger?"

This man had his mouth full of food, so he pointed at the ceiling.

The skipper strode between the pool tables, hammered his hard-soled shoes up the staircase and, reaching the top, saw through an open doorway Kruger sitting at a roll-top desk and eating. MacBride went in and said:

"Almost finished?"

Kruger's yellowish face twisted. "I got dessert yet."

"You can pass up the dessert."

"Oh, I never passed up dessert in my life."

"Well," the skipper said, feeling his oats, "there's always a first time."

Kruger leaned back in his chair. He said in a sardonic voice, "Somebody around here's trying to be cute."

"Yeah, you. Put your hat and coat on. You haven't seen Headquarters since we repainted it. You must come over."

"Oh, so I'm the one that's cute?"

"Maybe not. Maybe not as cute as you think. Anyhow, the hat, the coat; and the police department will provide the transportation."

Kruger stood up, his fists clenching, a storm-cloud sweeping down across his gaunt sour face. "Come out of your dance, Skipper!" he growled. "There's no copper putting the sign on me."

MacBride crossed casually to him, suddenly grabbed him by the arm and piled him out through the doorway into the upper hall. Kruger landed on his back and with a clatter of elbows and heels. MacBride walked out and watched him get up.

"Go on downstairs," the skipper said.

"By God, if you think you can come in here and—"

MacBride took a step and a swing and Kruger went down the staircase on his back, turned over and hit the floor below flat on his face. The skipper took his time walking down the staircase and, reaching the bottom, said in a loud voice:

"If anybody knows where Kruger's overcoat is, get it for him." And to Kruger, "Get up, and stop clowning."

Kruger got up, rubbed a hand across his mouth and said sarcastically, "Okey, Skipper. I'll go." He leered, crossed the room and took down his hat and overcoat. "Don't get excited, boys," he said to the men sitting around the room. "I'm going over and look at a new paint job. Maybe somebody's going to get painted. Smeared, I mean."

MacBride marched him out to the sedan, said, "Get in," and followed him. As Gahagan drove off, Kruger looked the skipper up and down with a contemptuous glance. Then he spat on the floor.

"If you got to spit," MacBride said, "roll down the window and spit out it."

Kruger prepared to spit a second time on the floor and MacBride held up his fist, saying, "Go ahead, go ahead, if you want to eat nothing but soft grub till you get new teeth."

Kruger snorted and sat back, folding his arms. "You ain't worrying me," he said. "You and your whole stinking police department ain't worrying me. Yah!"

MacBride was busy stuffing his pipe. He lit up and watched the buildings sweep past. And when they drove into the Headquarters garage he climbed out and said:

"All right, let's go."

Kruger swaggered along beside him and when they reached the skipper's office Kennedy was dozing comfortably in one of the chairs. He woke up, stretched.

"Well, if it isn't Stamps himself. I didn't know you and MacBride ran around together."

Kruger said, "I'm just seeing the seamy side o' life."

"And plenty seamy," MacBride nodded, granite faced. "Kruger, did you know Mike drew twenty-five grand out of the bank yesterday?"

"How'n hell should I know? I ain't his bookkeeper."

"You said you weren't over to his house last evening or night. You said the last time you saw him yesterday was noon at the *Ship Grill.* That right?"

"I said it, didn't I? Then it's right."

MacBride pointed to the envelope and the stamp lying on his desk. "Recognize that stamp?"

Kruger looked. He scowled darkly. "Say, who the hell lifted that stamp outta my book?" He swiveled and glared at Kennedy, who was dreamily paring his fingernails. "You!" he shouted. "That stamp was in there when you looked at my album!"

"Soft pedal," MacBride said. "That stamp was also in Mike's house last night—and it wasn't in Mike's house before a quarter after seven— and it wasn't there when you and Kennedy walked in. In other words, it got into your album between a quarter past seven and the time you and Kennedy found Mike dead. I suppose it just got up and walked over to the *Idle Hour* and hopped into your album."

"Listen," roared Kruger. "I want that there stamp! It's a first issue and it'll be worth dough some day. Listen, you guys ain't got no right to swipe stamps outta my album!"

MacBride was unmoved. He said, "Tell us how it got from Mike's place into your album."

"Oh, so you in your dazzlin' bright way figured that maybe I went over and knocked Mike off, huh? So you figure I went over and knocked him off and got the stamp then, huh? And I suppose I'm walking around now with twenty-five thousand bucks in my pants? Ha, you guys make me laugh! Ha, ha!" He paused, bent his brows and ripped out savagely, "Listen. I stood enough from you wise babies. I want that stamp back!"

"How did you get it?" MacBride asked.

"Oh, nuts. Happy Jack brought it over. The fat guy that pastes the piano at the *Idle Hour.* He took Mike around a couple bottles o' rye and Mike give him the stamp to give to me."

MacBride picked up the phone, called the desk and said, "Send a man over to the *Idle Hour* and have him pick up Happy Jack. Right away, Otto."

Twenty minutes later Happy Jack entered the office wearing a shy, bashful look.

MacBride said, "What did you do after, say, five o'clock last night?"

"Who, me?"

"Yeah... you."

"Well, lemme think. Oh, I know. I was over the dentist at five—Dr. Leopold there, in Fife Street. I guess I was there till maybe half-past. I had a tooth yanked out. This one here. See? Then I had a bowl o' vegetable soup at the *Cozy Corner*, that musta been around six, account of I walked from the doc's. Then I went over to the *Idle Hour* and played piano a while and around seven or so the phone rang and I answered. Mr. Devlin asked me to bring him over a couple bottles rye from the private stock upstairs. So I did that. I took the bottles over and came right back to the *Idle Hour*."

"What 'd Devlin give you?"

"Oh, a buck, for makin' the trip."

"What else?"

"Huh?"

"What did he give you besides the buck?"

"Jeese, ain't a buck enough?... Oh, wait. Somethin' for Stamps here. Yeah, a stamp. He said, 'Here, give Stamps this for his collection.'"

"Was Devlin alone?"

"Yop. I guess so. I didn't see nobody else."

"So what now, Skipper?" Kruger laughed.

MacBride said, "What were you doing around Brick O'Connor's place this morning?"

"Is there any law against me calling on Brick O'Connor?"

"No. But why didn't you go in?"

Kruger thrust out his jaw, screwed up his nose. "Because I seen your bus outside and I figured you was in O'Connor's house and I'd never got a word in edgewise." He hitched violently at his belt. "And the next time you haul me over here, Skipper, be sure you know what you're doing. If you think I'm finished in this town—or in the Third Ward—you're screwloose! Come on, Happy, let's get out o' this dump." He swaggered to the door, pulled it open; then stopped and yelled, "Hey, that stamp—gimme that stamp!"

MacBride said, "There it is—take it, fella."

Kruger snatched it off the desk "You bet I'll take it!" he snarled.

MacBride had gone to the window and stood there looking into the street, rubbing his jaw.

Kruger slammed the door hard on the way out and Kennedy said, "Well, old tomato, that idea of mine wasn't so good—but at the time, it seemed swell."

IKE COHEN came in and said, "Nix. That guy from the *Palais Royale* didn't find anything in the Rogues' Gallery. He got cross-eyed looking. But he suddenly remembered that the guy stopped and talked to another guy in the lobby—like they met by accident. Just for a minute. You know, hello, good-bye. Now *that* guy was a fellow named Lester Dewald—a young broker—"

"Sure, the Dewald family," put in Kennedy. "One of our best families."

MacBride said, "Go down to Dewald's office, Ike, and ask him to mention everybody he talked with at the *Palais Royale* last night. Mike had a date there with Daisy Swartz—but ten to one he had a date with this unknown guy too, on the side."

Cohen on the way out bumped into Moriarity. When they broke and Cohen went on his way, Moriarity leaned in the doorway and said, "Well, that powder was mopped up, as you probably know. So there was no soap there. But I took the blue slippers around to Greenbaugh to see if there was any powder on the soles at all. He put 'em to the test and, brother, there was no powder on the soles at all. I think you got that gal wrong."

Kennedy moaned, "Don't say that, Mory. Don't break our hearts entirely."

"She's just a persecuted woman," said Moriarity.

Kennedy said, "Not too persecuted. She had a key to Mike's house."

"Who says so?" MacBride barked.

"The late Mr. Devlin's ancient housekeeper. I happened to drop by this morning and ask her. There were four keys. Mike had one, the housekeeper had one, Kruger had one, and little Daisy had one. Kruger says he was upstairs in the office over the *Idle Hour* part of last night. Who knows? There's a back way out. He could have got over to Devlin's and back in from thirty to forty minutes. Daisy says she was home in her apartment all night. Who knows? The housekeeper told me that from six to eleven-thirty she was at a church dance. She was. I checked with Father McGlynn on that."

Moriarity demanded, "What the hell motive would Daisy Swartz have for knocking off Mike. She was in the sugar. She was his gal."

Kennedy was tranquil. "I'm not saying she knocked him off. I'm not saying anybody knocked him off." He looked at his watch, said, "I want to make a phone call. The office." He got up out of the chair, lay across the desk and called the *Free Press* office, saying, "Give me

Hendricks." And then, "This you, Tod?... This is Kennedy. Get any dope yet on what I asked you?... Swell.... Well, I thought so, but I wasn't sure." He listened for a full minute, nodding, smiling dreamily. Then he said, "Thanks a million, kid," and hung up.

Still lying on the desk, he said, "That was Tod Hendricks. He used to be a night police reporter, oh, about three years ago. And a regular pub-crawler. Knew all the hot spots. This Daisy Swartz came to town just about three years ago. From Akron. Turned up one day with Kruger, who brought her from Akron. Was his gal, my good fellows— until about a year and a half ago, when she blossomed out in the fancier joints with Mike Devlin. Motives don't always mean a hell of a lot, Mory, but since you brought it up, maybe Kruger had a motive for knocking off his boss Mike Devlin."

MacBride put on his hat and overcoat. "Just for fun, I'm going to have another talk with Daisy. You stay here, Mory. If Ike shows up, or calls, tell him to phone me at her apartment. Otto has the number."

He banged out of the office, went down to the garage and found Gahagan standing before Abraham, the negro porter, who was seated. Gahagan was making motions with his hands and saying solemnly, "Sleep... sleep... sleep."

"Gahagan!" barked the skipper.

"Yes, sir!"

"What the hell are you up to now?"

Gahagan, blushing, picked up his book entitled *Hypnotism Simplified* and trudged across to the sedan. The negro said after him, "Ah ain't a good subject, Mist' Gahagan, account of Ah can sleep anytime wit'out bein' hypnotized to it."

MacBride said sternly, "Go to Maitland Street, Gahagan, number two-o-nine, and don't spare the horses."

Kennedy came toddling up saying, "Wait for baby."

"Gahagan," MacBride told him, "is studying hypnotism. It seems to me that if more people in this police department studied police work instead of screwy books, leg shows, and how to get leaves of absence with pay, we might get somewhere."

Gahagan muttered. "Just because you been having bum luck is no reason you gotta take it out on me! Ah, like me old man said, I shoulda joined the Navy and seen the world."

"It was certainly a bad break for me, when you didn't take your old man's advice. Now get going. And cut out giving me a lot of back talk.

If I don't wear a uniform around here, I get no respect at all."

A police flivver bounced into the garage, slowed to a stop. Cohen jumped out and came over on the run. The skipper rolled down the sedan window and Cohen handed him a slip of paper, saying:

"Here's every guy Dewald said he talked to at the *Palais Royale* last night."

MacBride squinted at a list of fourteen names. Then he scowled, bit his lip. He said, "Kennedy, get out. I'm going somewhere alone."

"Being stingy, huh? All right, all right," Kennedy replied amiably and got out. "I'll likely meet you at the *Idle Hour,* anyhow."

"Roll, Gahagan," the skipper said. And when the sedan had cleared the garage— "Brick O'Connor's house."

Chapter VI

WHEN Gahagan pulled up in front of O'Connor's house Mac-Bride did not snap out of the car with his usual briskness. He got out slowly, took his time closing the door, and walked slowly up the cement footway. Bachman let him in and closed the door softly and MacBride stood with his hat in his hand, chewing on a corner of his mouth.

"Ned in?" he asked.

There were footsteps and Blanche O'Connor came out of the living-room, moved her head slightly in a gesture of greeting and said in a hushed voice, "Captain MacBride."

"Yes—I'm kind of back again, Mrs. O'Connor."

"Brick," she said, "is not in—just now."

"I was looking for Ned," MacBride said.

She started and a faint flush of color lapped across her cheeks.

"It's nothing much," the skipper found himself saying. He was standing ramrod straight, his spare-boned head erect. "He might be able to give me a little information that might help."

Blanche O'Connor turned and said, "Ned," into the living-room. And then— "Come in, Captain."

He would have much preferred her being elsewhere.

Ned was standing by the piano, his back against it, his elbows lolling on it. MacBride, going right up to him, said, "Hello, Ned. You were at the *Palais Royale* last night, weren't you?"

"Me?" Ned drawled.

"You ran into Lester Dewald there—remember?"

Ned's eyes slid down the skipper's chest. "Oh, sure. I dropped in there, I guess. Yes, I did, as a matter of fact. I remember. Les Dewald was there."

"Did you just—um—drop in, or were you looking for somebody?"

"Oh, I just dropped in. You know, how you drop in a place."

"And when you left, where'd you go?"

"Oh, I spent about an hour watching 'em roller-skate at the Embassy Rink."

"Alone, were you?"

"Yes. Alone."

"Did you meet anyone there you knew?"

"Uh-huh." Ned shook his head. "No, I didn't." He strolled away from the piano, sat down on the divan and took a cigarette out of a humidor.

MacBride said, "About what time did you leave the *Palais Royale?*"

Ned was lighting up. "Ten, I guess. Maybe a little later."

"Do you remember asking the headwaiter something?"

Ned almost dropped both match and cigarette. Blanche O'Connor laid a quivering hand on MacBride's arm. He turned and looked at her. Her lips were pressed tightly together but trembling and even the light in her eyes seemed to quiver. Her voice was low, throaty, congested:

"What's wrong—Captain MacBride?"

"Nothing—probably. But things can look queer at times." He turned to the youth, who was now sucking rapidly, nervously at his cigarette. "Ned, why were you looking for Mike Devlin?"

Ned cleared his throat "Well—I heard he hung out around there a lot, and—well—I don't know—I just wanted to see him. I'd heard so much about him."

"That's no reason," the skipper said gravely.

Ned jumped up and ran his hand through his hair. "I tell you, that's all it was!"

"Didn't you have a little date there with him?"

Ned stopped and clenched his fists, his eyes jigging. "No! No, I didn't have a date with him. Why should I? Gosh, can't a fellow—"

"Ned," said Blanche O'Connor in a low tragic voice. "Ned, be quiet.

Sit down." Her hands were locked in front of her, the knuckles white. She turned her sad eyes on the skipper and said in the same low voice, "If you think anything of Brick, and I believe you think a lot of him—if you think anything of him, don't tell him that Ned was looking for Mike Devlin."

MacBride looked down at his toes, kept his lips clamped tight.

Blanche O'Connor said, "Ned's been in a little trouble. I tell you this because I feel I have to. Brick doesn't know. For God's sake, don't tell him. A little trouble—nothing terribly serious but—well, in the light of recent events, serious enough. You must realize that Ned's only a boy—you must have had your fling too, when you were a boy. Well, Ned went to a gambling casino one night. They knew who he was, and let him play. He misunderstood the value of the markers and before the night was out he owed nineteen thousand dollars.

"Well, they let him go. But they told him to get the money—or they'd go to his father. Brick's stern about that sort of thing. Besides, he hasn't got the money. I went to the casino and begged them not to tell Brick, that Ned would get the money—I'd get it for him. They said they'd wait a little longer. My father's in the hospital in Seattle. He'd let me have the money, but he's so ill now I daren't ask him. I must wait till he's well. But the man at the casino began to get ugly.

"Then about a week ago Ned received a telephone call from Mike Devlin. Devlin wanted to see him. Ned kept the appointment and Devlin was very fatherly. He said he'd heard Ned was in a little trouble. Ned admitted it. Then Devlin offered to lend him the money. Ned didn't accept then—he said he'd think it over. And then the man at the gambling casino got uglier. Ned phoned Devlin. Devlin told him to meet him last night at the *Palais Royale* and he'd have the money. So—Ned went there. But Devlin didn't show up. That's all—only please, I beg you, don't tell Brick."

MacBride's face was furrowed with wrinkles. He said, "What casino was it?"

She bit her lip. "I had to swear to the man I wouldn't tell. I—I can't tell you, Captain."

"You've got to tell me."

"Please—I can't."

He was dogged. "You've got to! That's an old trick—not making the value of the markers plain! It's a clip-joint stunt!"

She grimaced. "I'm sorry—I can't tell you."

"That's it—I don't want you to be sorry. This is no debt of honor! I've been trying for years to stamp out these joints. I've got to know, Mrs. O'Connor. I'm a friend of Brick's and I hope I'm a friend of yours—but we can't be sentimental about this. Link by link we make a chain—and this may be a link in the chain that'll lead to the solution of who killed Devlin."

Her face was rigid, her neck red. "I can't—tell you. Don't you realize—under the circumstances—I can't tell you?"

The skipper looked at the youth. Ned dropped his eyes and seemed to shrink. The skipper blew out an exasperated breath, slapped himself on the back of the neck, rubbed his nape briskly as he took a turn up and down the room. He suddenly barked, "I got to go out and think." Without another word he strode long-legged from the living-room, slammed out the front door and climbed into the sedan. "Drive around, Gahagan."

"Around where?"

"Just around."

"Oh, willy-nilly, you mean. I get it."

The skipper slouched in a corner of the seat, his jaw down between his shoulders, mixed anger and unhappiness in his face. He had a horrible feeling that he had opened a door through which it would not be pleasant to pass. Ned O'Connor could not prove where he was during the hour after he had left the *Palais Royale.* Brick would have to know—it would have to come out eventually. Blanche O'Connor was trying her best to protect the boy and at the same time to save Brick a lot of humiliation. But it would have to come out; in the end, it would have to come out.

Now the skipper began to reflect on other things. He remembered how insolent Stamps Kruger had been, how apparently certain Kruger had been that nothing could touch him. And suddenly he remembered what Kruger had said at the *Idle Hour:* "Maybe somebody's going to get painted. Smeared, I mean." The skipper sat erect on the seat. Was it possible that Kruger knew about Ned's gambling debt? Was it possible that Ned owed the debt to one of Mike Devlin's blind gaming casinos?

"Gahagan, go to two-o-nine Maitland Street."

Chapter VII

DAISY SWARTZ let the skipper in her third-floor apartment and closed the door casually behind him. She spent a moment plucking a flake of tobacco from her lip, then took a drag on the cigarette and let the smoke dribble from her nostrils. She wore a brown soft suit and brown oxfords and her face, anaemic and yet sensual, was as expressionless as ever. MacBride felt peculiarly uncomfortable in her presence without knowing why.

He said outright, "Exactly when did you throw Stamps Kruger over and take up with his boss, Mike Devlin?"

She gave him a slow, blank look and sat down. "Oh, about a year and a half ago, I guess."

"Why'd you throw Stamps over?"

She made a slight movement of her left shoulder. "I don't know. It just happened. Mike was a good dancer."

"And he had more money, huh?"

"I fell for him, that's all."

MacBride said, "Stamps is a pretty hot-headed guy. He goes off the handle pretty frequently. Have you ever thought that Stamps might have knocked off Mike?"

She frowned. "No."

"Mike was quite a stepper. How'd you manage to keep him a one-woman man for a year and a half?"

Her eyes clouded for an instant, her lips tightened; but then she shrugged and was herself again—blank-faced, a little listless, remote.

He said, "You have a key to Mike's house."

Her eyes slid slowly across his face. "Yes, I have a key." Her eyes dropped and stared blankly at the carpet.

"You don't seem very upset over Mike's death."

"I guess I don't show my feelings."

MacBride said, "Put a hat on and let's go places."

"Where?"

"The *Idle Hour.*"

She regarded him with her large, vacant eyes. Then without a word she rose and went into her bedroom and through the doorway he could see her putting on a hat. She also slung a fur neckpiece round her shoulders and came back into the living-room pulling on gloves. She appeared undisturbed.

MacBride took her down to the sedan, handed her in and said to Gahagan, "The *Idle Hour*."

They rode in silence. The skipper chewed on a dead cigar and looked straight ahead, his eyelids shuttered, his bony hands cupped on his knees. Daisy stared absently out the window, her hands motionless in her lap, the corners of her mouth drooping. When they drew up in front of the *Idle Hour* the skipper got out, held the door open and watched her descend to the sidewalk. She made an idle, unimportant adjustment of her hat as they crossed the sidewalk. Pool balls clicked as they entered and the men playing or standing around looked up. A few exchanged puzzled glances.

MacBride did not see Kruger, so he took hold of Daisy's arm and walked her up the staircase. The office was empty. The skipper went out to the head of the staircase and yelled down: "Where's Kruger?"

Happy Jack came halfway up, said. "He ain't in."

"Well, where is he?"

"Jeese, I don't know. He went out about an hour ago."

"I'll wait," said MacBride.

He returned to the office and found Daisy reading a moving picture magazine. She was chewing gum now. He sat down and lit his cigar and squinted at her, shook his head, sighed and drew deeply on his cigar.

Twenty minutes later there were footsteps on the stairs. Kruger came to the doorway, stared bold-eyed at MacBride, gave a short hard laugh and swaggered in, saying:

"What's this office getting to be, a hang-out for the police department?"

MacBride said, "I was thinking of picking you up and tossing you in the can."

"On what?"

"Suspicion."

Kruger grinned. "That's a laugh."

"You can't account for every minute of last night, Kruger. This gal used to be your gal until Mike swiped her from under your nose."

Kruger was still grinning. "Yeah? Now ain't you just the great old finder-outer."

"In fact," went on MacBride, "I'm going to pick both of you up—you and Daisy. You both have keys to Mike's house."

"Yeah? So has his housekeeper. Why don't you pick her up?"

"She has an iron-bound alibi. You haven't. Daisy hasn't. Twenty-five thousand dollars was stolen when Mike was murdered. You and Daisy were close to him—you knew a lot of his business. Who else would have known—but the bank—that Mike drew out twenty-five grand?"

Kruger's grin was endless. "Maybe that's what we're getting to, baby." He looked at his watch. "In fact, I'm glad you're here. I'm expecting some people any minute." He put his watch back into his pocket, smacked his hands together and swaggered across the room. He poured himself a drink of rye, downed it, rasped his throat with evident pleasure and smacked his hands together again. "And you, Skipper, and some other guys around this burg are going to find it hard to take."

Daisy turned the pages of her magazine without batting an eye. Kruger raised an ear, then stalked out into the hall and called down the stairway, "Okey, come on up."

MacBride rose, a deep frown in his eyes, and went over and stood with his back to the window. His frown deepened and was touched with wonder when he saw Brick O'Connor, Blanche O'Connor and their son Ned walk into the office.

Brick's face was heavy, grave, and he looked puzzled. He said, "Hello, Steve."

"Hello, Brick," said MacBride.

Kruger beamed maliciously. "Well, folks, sit down and make yourself comfortable."

Blanche and Ned took seats but Brick remained standing. He scowled at Kruger and said, "I hope you're in your right mind."

"Oh, I'm in my right mind, all right," Kruger chuckled. "Plenty." He spread his legs, placed his hands on his hips and said, "I'm in my right mind so much that it's gonna be kind of painful to you people. You were wise to bring the family around when I told you to."

O'Connor said, "I figured you wouldn't have made a threat unless you had something. Well, what is it?"

Kruger's eyes darkened malevolently. "O'Connor, when Mike died I took over the running of the *Idle Hour,* Incorporated, and all its holdings in the Third Ward. I want a clean bill of health. You can't condemn this property, you can't kick me out."

"The order's been given," O'Connor muttered.

"It's gotta be killed—kicked over the fence. It's gotta!"

O'Connor's jaw was grim. "It's a crooked ace, Kruger—but let me see it."

"It ain't a crooked ace, O'Connor, and if I was a real dirty guy I'd have showed it some place else." He drew from his pocket a small silver case, flat, and about three inches square. Engraved on its surface were the letters B.D.O. He held it out in his palm. "Recognize it?"

BRICK leaned forward and a look of shock struck down across his face. He raised his eyes slowly, turned and looked at his wife. Blanche O'Connor met his stare with glazed, unseeing eyes. He spun and snapped at Kruger:

"Where'd you get that?"

Kruger smiled. "I found it in Mike Devlin's house last night when I went there with Kennedy."

"You lousy pup!" snarled O'Connor, taking a step.

Kruger nodded to the doorway, where Happy Jack and another man stood leaning indolently. Kruger said, "Just witnesses. Meet Happy Jack and Kingpin, two boys around the place."

Brick O'Connor's face was dull red.

His wife said, "Don't, Brick. Be careful. I was at Devlin's house last night."

He turned. "Why, Blanche? Why, in God's name?"

"She did it account of me, Pop," Ned choked. "She went there account of me. Tell him, Mom."

She swallowed. Her head was lowered, her hands fought each other in her lap. "I—I went there to prevent Devlin from lending Ned some money. Ned was in a bad jam. He owed a gambling debt. They were threatening to tell you. Devlin offered to lend him the money."

O'Connor demanded, "How did Devlin know?"

"I don't know. He phoned Ned one day and asked to see him and Ned went and Devlin said he'd heard he was in a jam. Ned refused the loan, then—but when they kept threatening he got desperate. I heard him phone Devlin. I listened on the extension and heard Devlin tell him to meet him at the *Palais Royale* at half-past nine last night. I tried to stop Ned from going. But he was desperate. So—so I knew Joe Bachman had a gun. He was out of his room and I went in and took it and went to Devlin's. I got there at eight and he was in and I begged him not to give Ned the money. He refused. I drew the gun and said, 'I'm going to keep you here all night, if I have to.'

"So there we sat, at opposite sides of the dining-room table. When the phone rang, at about half-past nine, I told him to answer it and say he was busy. He did, and hung up, and then he tried to duck out of the room—he ran into that bedroom off the living-room but I was after him and made him stop in the middle of it. And then—I can't remember what happened—I must have fainted—I woke up lying on the bed. I—I got up and found—found Devlin lying on the dining-room floor—dead. I—I ran out."

MacBride said, "Did you go up to the bathroom?"

"Bathroom? No—no. Why should I go to the bathroom? I—I wanted to get out. Wait—I did go. Yes. I—I was ill."

Brick O'Connor was licking dry lips. His neck was taut and his hands were opening and closing fitfully. He moved across the room and put his hand on his wife's shoulder, patted it.

She sobbed, "I didn't want Devlin to lend Ned that money. I felt there was something wrong—awfully wrong."

"Don't, honey—don't," O'Connor muttered.

Kruger said, "So there's my ace, O'Connor. Mike's dead and a dead man is a dead man and here is a deal. You gotta revoke that condemnation order. You gotta let me run the Third Ward like I want to run it. From now on, I'm boss in the Third Ward. There's your deal."

O'Connor muttered, "It's hard to take but"—he patted his wife's shoulder again—"there's no alternative."

MacBride said, "Wait." He added, "There's still twenty-five thousand dollars to be accounted for. Did you take that with you, Mrs. O'Connor?

"Take it!" she cried. "No—no!"

MacBride snapped at Ned, "Did you pay back that debt?"

Ned started. "N-no. How could I? I didn't have the money."

"Now listen to me, boy," the skipper said doggedly. "We're all at a bad time right now. I want to know where you made that debt—what the place was. I want to know now. This minute!"

Ned moved uneasily on his chair.

Brick said, "Steve, let us get this other thing—"

"Brick, you keep quiet! You're the political boss of this town but right now I'm a policeman! Ned, I asked you a question. I want an answer."

Ned choked, "It had no name. It was in a place on Luke Street, top floor."

"What address?"

"It was number five-fifty."

"And who'd you give the I.O.U. to?"

Ned squirmed. "Uh—Mister—Kruger."

MacBride spun and flung at Kruger. "So—one of your hot spots, eh? Devlin knew he couldn't do much with an illegal debt so he contrived to make a legal one by offering to lend the kid the dough—then get it back through you, with the kid still owing him the original amount. Sweet!"

Kruger grinned. "What of it? It's done—and now we got something else. We know who killed Mike."

"Do we? And do we know what happened to the twenty-five grand he drew from the bank?"

Brick O'Connor said, "The fact that he drew it from the bank shortly before closing time doesn't mean that it was in his house or on his person last night."

"Brick, you stay out of this argument," MacBride shouted.

"I can't! Damn it, man, I've got my wife to think of! I'd make any deal, no matter how dirty, to save her!"

The skipper leveled his arm at Daisy Swartz and said, "You all seem to forget this young woman. She was Devlin's woman. How about it, Daisy?"

Daisy looked at her hands, frowned. "Fat chance I'd have of getting any say."

"That's a lie! You can have your say now. You can stand up and, in view of what you've heard, charge this woman with the murder of Mike Devlin!"

"Steve!" groaned O'Connor.

But MacBride paid no attention. He said to Daisy Swartz, "Come on, here's your chance. Say it! Say you want to prosecute this woman for the murder of Mike Devlin!"

Daisy Swartz stared blankly at the floor.

"What!" MacBride exclaimed. "You mean to say you're going to let these people get away with it! You mean to say that after your boy friend's been murdered you're going to say nothing!"

Kruger rapped out, "I can take care of her! You just forget all about her."

"Why?" the skipper demanded, swinging round. "Why can you handle her? You couldn't handle her when she threw you over for Mike. How is it you think you can handle her now?"

THE two men standing in the doorway were jostled and Kennedy came into the room saying, "I've been eavesdropping, folks, so before you get around to too much bargaining I thought I'd come in. Yes, yes, the old press—sees all, tells all."

Kruger blurted, "Who let you in?"

"Nobody. I saw all the official cars out front, so I came up the back way."

Brick O'Connor dropped desolately to a chair and his wife covered her face with a handkerchief.

Kennedy said quietly, sleepily, "Mrs. O'Connor...."

"Yes?" she said into her handkerchief.

"Listening in the hall, I gathered that when you shot Mike Devlin it was accidental. That is, he ran into the bedroom, you ran after him and in the excitement, and in your hysteria, you shot him."

"I—I don't know. It could have been any way."

"I'm wondering why the radio was turned on loud, then, when you shot him."

She looked up slowly. "The radio wasn't turned on."

"No?... Was it turned on when you came to?"

She started. "I—I—" She stopped, her eyes widened and her jaw shook. "Yes! Yes, it was! I had a horrible headache and the noise of the radio—"

"It was still turned on," Kennedy mused, "when Stamps and I arrived." He raised his eyes drowsily towards Kruger. "Where'd you find that vanity case, Stamps?"

"In the bedroom."

"The one off the living-room?"

"Sure."

"I was the first one in that bedroom. You're got a bad memory. You never went in that bedroom. You came as far as the doorway, then turned back. I came out. The next man in that bedroom was the precinct detective. Maybe," smiled Kennedy, "you found it, say, in the living-room?"

"Yeah—maybe. I was so excited at the time."

"All right. Mrs. O'Connor says she fainted in the bedroom. Devlin was standing in the middle of the bedroom. He was shot smack through the heart. If she fired as she fainted, how is it he was found in the living-room at the opposite side of the table from that bedroom door?"

Kruger stamped. "How the hell can I figure out your screwy ideas? You're drunk."

"I am. A little. It's easy to figure out. If Mike was shot in the heart while in the bedroom he'd have been found in the bedroom."

Kennedy said to Blanche O'Connor, "Mrs. O'Connor, when you were at Devlin's house did you notice a large green envelope?"

"Yes," she murmured, between sobs. "He took it from his pocket and said. 'Your son gets this tonight. Twenty-five grand—enough to clear up his debts and enough left over to get another start.'"

"Then what did he do with the envelope?"

"He placed it on the table."

Kennedy looked very cheerful. He said, "During the past hour I made two calls. I dropped around at your apartment, Stamps, and I also dropped around at yours, Daisy." He turned to MacBride. "Skipper, I've got the twenty-five grand." He drew from his pocket a large, fat green envelope. He looked at Kruger and said, "Pretty good, eh?"

Daisy Swartz jumped up, picked up her chair and broke the nearest window; MacBride took a long stride towards her. Kruger pulled his gun and said:

"Stop it, Skipper."

MacBride stopped in his tracks. Daisy stopped too and stood poised, her nostrils quivering, the rest of her face blank.

Kruger said to the two men standing in the doorway, "What are you hanging around like a couple of dummies for?"

Happy Jack and Kingpin drew their guns and came into the room.

"This move proves you're dumb, Kruger," MacBride said.

"It's gonna prove I'm quick on the trigger if you don't stop sliding your paw to your gun."

"So you knocked off Mike and swiped his roll, huh? What a pal!"

Kruger's face was dark, gaunt. "Keep your mouth shut."

"Listen," said Brick O'Connor, "let my wife and boy out of here."

"You shut up too," Kruger said. "If you or MacBride or anybody else is fool enough to make a bum move, it's not my fault if your frau gets hurt in the shuffle. Kingpin, take away the skipper's gun."

Kingpin crossed the room and took away the skipper's gun. Happy Jack removed a gun from Brick's hip pocket. The boy Ned was unarmed.

Kruger said dully, "Kingpin, frisk Kennedy too."

Kingpin found no gun on Kennedy.

"Take," said Kruger, "that envelope away from him.... Now give it to me." He grabbed hold of the envelope and thrust it into his pocket. The skin seemed tight-drawn, yellow, on his face, and his lips were thin, dry. "Now get that rope in the closet and tie 'em up. We got to get out of here."

Slowly, inch by inch, the head of Gahagan rose above the sill of the broken window. His eyes were wide, full of amazement. He did not utter a word but raised his gun, leveled it across the windowsill and fired. The explosion roared in the room and Kruger clattered backward, upset a chair and crashed to the floor.

MacBride took a flying leap at Kingpin, who had ducked at sound of the explosion, and smashed with him against the wall. Brick O'Connor was close enough to Happy Jack to take a chance on a swing. He swung and knocked Happy Jack across the desk. He followed him but Happy Jack bounded off the desk, spun with his gun held low. Brick O'Connor struck at his jaw and the gun went off, the bullet buried itself in the floor. MacBride got hold of Kingpin's gun hand, twisted it, kicked Kingpin in the shins. Kingpin's gun went off three times and a shot, ricochetting, nailed Daisy Swartz as she was passing through the doorway. Kennedy, who had reached out to stop her, drew his hand back. He turned and used his meager body weight to shove Blanche O'Connor back into a corner. MacBride's fist rose, landed, dropped Kingpin at his feet. He scooped up Kingpin's gun and whirled with it, cocking the hammer.

O'Connor was standing over Happy Jack, who lay on the floor with a bloody mouth. O'Connor's knuckles were bloody too. He rubbed them in a handkerchief. He turned and looked sadly around the room.

Gahagan was climbing in through the window, saying, "I was dozing out in the car when I heard glass crash, so I got out and took a look around. I seen glass on the grass downstairs and I looked up and seen this window busted. So I got a ladder from the garage out back and clumb up here. Did I do right?"

MacBride said, "We can always expect the unexpected from you,

Gahagan. As it happens, you did right." He looked at Daisy, at Kruger. "Now go call an ambulance."

The skipper dropped down beside Kruger, whose eyes were wild with pain and fright. The skipper said, "You tried hard to be smart, fella. I don't feel proud. You were just dumb. I had a hunch all along—but I couldn't figure it out. You were in it somewhere but I didn't figure you'd murder Mike."

Kruger gagged, shook his head. "I—I didn't knock off Mike. Honest to God I didn't! You can't say I knocked off Mike!"

"A little bird, huh? A little bird did it?"

Kruger grimaced. Fear burned out of his face. "You can't hang that on me! Not on me! She—she did it. She did it!"

"Who?"

Daisy said thickly, "You were always yellow, Stamps. In a tight spot, you were always yellow. A loud mouth and nothing else. Okey, I did it. But you knew I did it and you took the money. You took it away from me—to hide. Hell, you sure made a swell job of hiding it!"

She was lying on her stomach on the floor, her mouth sullen. Her eyes were still blank, far away, and she rambled on as if to herself, "Sure, I did it. I phoned Mike and he said he was busy and I went around to see. I had a key. I let myself in quiet. I saw him standing in the bedroom doorway, with his hair mussed. I saw a woman on the bed. I was jealous—always jealous of him. The gun was on the table. He must have picked it up and put it there. I didn't know. I picked it up and he turned and I reached over and turned on the radio. It got loud. He came up as far as the table and I let him have it and he fell.

"I saw the dough sticking out of the envelope and I picked it up and there was a vanity case laying on the floor and I picked that up. I was going to plug her too, but I seen she was fainted—I seen then she was fainted all along and she wasn't a young doll. Then I figured maybe I made mistake—but there was no time, so I left. I walked into Stamps as I got outside. I had to tell him. He took the dough and the vanity case and said for me not to worry. But I had to promise to be his girl again. I did. It was tough, but I did. I figured he might welch if we got in a jam—but there was nothing I could do."

She put her head down on her arm and cursed quietly.

MacBride stood up, shook himself as though to get rid of an unpleasant sensation. He crossed the room, bent down and pulled the fat green envelope from Kruger's pocket.

"Well, Kennedy," he said, "I ought to ask how you found this money in Kruger's apartment."

Kennedy shrugged. "Old tomato, I wish I could tell you."

"What?"

"I mean, we know the money's in Kruger's apartment, so you just take a squad of men over there and turn it upside down. I've never been in Kruger's apartment."

"Is this another one of your gags?"

"Sort of. That envelope you're holding contains cut-up newspaper. I got the envelope from the bank—it's the same kind of envelope they said they put Mike's money in. I thought it might be a good idea to kid Stamps with it. It was."

Deep Red

*A phone in the night calls
Kennedy to murder.*

Chapter I

THE TELEPHONE BELL made a loose, jangling sound. Kennedy turned over in bed. He gave a throaty, congested sigh and lay with his eyes half open. The bell started again, jangling with a kind of half-hearted persistence. He groped in the darkness, got hold of the instrument and pulled it into bed with him. He said sleepily:

"'Lo."

A man's hoarse, taut voice said, "Kennedy?"

"Ummmm."

"You did me a good turn once, fella. Here's turn-about for you. Go to room four-ten at the *Hotel Pillars*."

"Why?"

"Get it straight. The *Hotel Pillars*. Room four-ten."

A closed connection clicked in Kennedy's ear. Sleep-muddled, he lay with his cheek on the pillow, the phone lying on the pillow also. A bell tolled three times across the darkened city.

"Andover one-one-two-two," he told the operator.

"This is the *Hotel Pillars*."

"Room four-ten," said Kennedy lazily.

The bright, sharp voice cut into his ear: "Room four-ten does not answer, sir. Do you wish to leave a message?"

"No message," he mumbled, and hung up.

He dressed slowly, his pale, thin face filmed with a brandy haze, his eyes only vaguely curious.

DIMLY lighted at this hour, the lobby of the *Pillars* was silent, cave-like. A couple of porters were slushing mops up and down the marble floor. The desk was the only bright oasis of light, and back of it a man was bent over a ledger. Kennedy sloped over to the elevator bank.

Outside one of the three cars a colored boy sat on a marble bench, his arms folded and his chin on his chest.

"Upsydaisy," said Kennedy.

The colored boy unraveled to six feet.

"Yes, suh."

"Four."

The walls of the fourth-floor corridor were tan, the carpet brown. The doors quite matched the carpet and their numbers were streamlined in chromium. Number 410 was midway between the elevators and the fire door. The chromium knocker was shaped like a cat's paw. Kennedy worked it twice. He worked it again, after a minute's wait, and stood back on his heels, yawning and blinking his eyes sleepily. Then he tried the knob, absent-mindedly, not expecting to find it unlocked. But it was.

He bumped the door with his knee and ambled into a narrow entrance hall, whose length stretched six feet away from him and emptied into a living-room. Four wall lights, bracketed in pairs, glowed with an effect of false daylight. The room was large, the furniture was new and modern in design. Every piece looked as though it stood where it was originally placed.

Kennedy poked across the room, his feet cushioning on the carpet, the stillness of the apartment poised above his head. He came to an open doorway and looked into a large bedroom which was also lighted. There were twin beds. One was completely made up, the other was turned down. Neither had been slept on. He could see a bathroom beyond. It was empty when he entered it. Two unsoiled bath towels and five hand towels progressively overlapping one another hung from a porcelain rack. The efficient orderliness of the apartment went well with the absolute silence.

Kennedy returned to the center of the living-room and stood with his hands sunk in his pockets, his wrinkled fedora on the back of his head. On his face was a hazy, puzzled look, and in a vague way he began to wonder if he had dreamed about that telephone call. The fact that most of the lights in the apartment were turned on did not disturb him; people living in hotels often leave lights on. The living-room carpet was a dark mulberry broadloom, and for an absent-minded moment Kennedy studied two lines that traversed it: they were not impressions but disturbances of the nap such as are caused by dragging a weighty object across any new broadloom. By simply rubbing his toe on one line, he erased three inches of it. The lines ran from the center of the living-room to the bedroom door, and were about a foot apart.

The electric clock on the drop-leaf table said half-past three. Kennedy checked it with his own and shrugged to

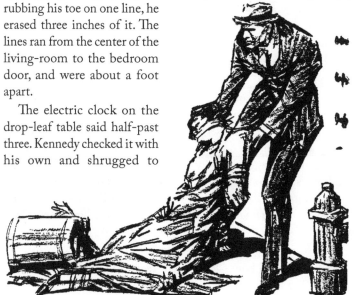

himself. He looked up, looked round the room again. The man standing at the living-room end of the entrance hall might have grown out of the floor, so silent had been his approach. He was a broad man with a very broad, solid-looking stomach and a squat brown face under a thick brown fedora whose crown was without a crease. His right hand was around back, resting on his right hip pocket.

"Good evening," said Kennedy, sleepily amiable.

"It's morning," the brown broad man grunted.

"So it is, so it is. Whom have I the honor—"

"Skip it, punk."

The gun the broad man suddenly held in front of him was heavy, short-barreled. His voice chopped bluntly:

"Get 'em up."

Kennedy, looking bored, sighed and raised his hands. The broad man came over and slapped deftly at his pockets; finding no gun, he stepped back and said:

"Keep 'em up."

Then he went sidewise to the bedroom doorway, glanced into the bedroom and then frowned at Kennedy. "Get over here," he said.

Kennedy crossed the room and the broad man shoved him into the bedroom, gave him another shove that sent him teetering into the bathroom. The fact that no one was in the bathroom seemed to annoy the broad man, and he frowned again.

"Get back in the living-room," he growled.

"Hold my hands up, too?"

"Be funny!"

A flat-handed slap on the back of the neck slanted Kennedy through the living-room doorway, sprawled him onto the soft nap of the mulberry broadloom and sent his hat flopping away in a half circle. He lay with his hands on the carpet. He wasn't hurt, he was merely puzzled and sleepy and mildly exasperated. The fingers of his right hand, pressing into the soft nap, felt moisture; not surface moisture but moisture that had settled down into the basic weave. He turned his hand over. The fingertips were stained—not mulberry. Red. Deep red.

"Get up, you!"

Kennedy toiled bone-weary to his feet and put his hands in his pockets. The blunt-barreled gun came up and pressed against his meager chest. The brown hard eyes of the broad man drilled him.

"Well, spill it, punk."

"Spill what?"

"Where's Senator Shacker?"

Kennedy's eyes opened wide for the first time since the telephone call had roused him.

The broad man stiffened his wrist, snapped, "Come on, bright eyes! Where is he? What the hell you doing in here? Where is he?" He lifted up his left fist, asked, "Or do you want your kisser turned around?"

Kennedy simply turned about, drifted over to the nearest easy chair and let himself down into its generous depths with a tranquil sigh and a wistful, amiable smile.

The broad man seemed to expand in all directions. "By God!" he blurted.

Kennedy held up his index finger, waved it in gentle admonition. "I'm Kennedy," he said, "of the *Free Press.*" He scaled his press card across the floor. "Read it—if you can read, loud mouth."

The broad man bent, scooped it up, read it.

"And don't tell me," Kennedy said, "that you're the butler."

The broad man said in a dull, defiant voice, "I'm Tom Bugle, the house officer here."

Kennedy gazed dreamily at his bloodstained fingertips. "And where, Mr. Bugle, is Senator Shacker?"

Chapter II

THE HEADQUARTERS car was a seven-passenger Packard touring, three years old but sleek and fast and with a nice sound under the hood. At eight in the morning Gahagan bent it smoothly around Center Circle, in Richmond City's mid-town, and then cut down into Andover Street. In the rear MacBride, on the small of his back and with his legs thrust straight out, was on his first pipe of the day. A hard straw hat was tipped over his wiry black brows. He wore a blue serge suit, neatly pressed, black shoes and white socks. The collar and cuffs of his white shirt were slightly starched, and he wore a black bow tie.

He said, "What's the matter with the right-hand side of the street?"

"Nothing," said Gahagan.

"Then get over on it."

Gahagan, muttering under his breath, pulled up in front of the *Hotel Pillars*. The doorman came across the broad sidewalk and opened the rear door of the car. The skipper stepped out, rapped his pipe against the heel of his left hand, blew through it and then slipped it into his breast pocket. He was an angular, tall man, straight-backed, and his bony face was clean-shaven. His heels crossing the marble lobby floor struck clipped, sharp blows, and as he entered the elevator he took off his straw hat and clamped it under his elbow.

The corridor on the fourth floor was silent, as though nothing unusual had occurred. The skipper knocked on 410, dropped his hand to the knob, but before he turned it the door was opened from the inside.

Moriarity said, "Hi, Cap'n."

"Hi, Mory. You were on the twelve-to-eight, huh?"

"Yeah, but I'm hanging around."

"Atta kid. Didn't get the story until I hit the office."

"No reason showed up yet to get you out of bed."

A portable table containing the remains of breakfast dishes stood at one side of the living-room. Kennedy was finishing up coffee and sucking at a cigarette. Mike Borodino, an Assistant District Attorney, was looking darkly indignant about something. He was a slender, strong-looking man with a long nose and a wide, ruthless mouth. Tom Bugle was going around the room making believe he was looking for clues. A news cameraman named Shotz was lounging languidly on the divan. Bevans of the police Scientific Bureau was there. Harcott, the hotel's resident manager, was sitting on a cabinet radiator; he looked very fresh and trim in his morning clothes. There were three uniformed policemen standing around and looking bored stiff. On a straight-backed chair sat a huge man with a meat-cleaver jaw and innocent blue eyes; he was playing with a couple of trick keys, linking them and unlinking them very deftly.

Moriarity said to the skipper, "Only don't step inside that," and pointed to a circle, about five feet in diameter, chalked on the broadloom.

"Why?" asked MacBride.

"There's some blood down in the carpet there. Kennedy found it. He wanted to wait with me and see what turned up."

"Any word of the Senator yet?"

"No. We didn't want to take the chance of getting in wrong with the Senator, and the hotel people didn't want us to either; but when he didn't show up by an hour ago we thought something better be done about it anyway."

MacBride looked at the man who was fiddling with the keys. "Who's that?"

Moriarity shrugged. "He says he's the Senator's chauffeur. Vincent Lanihan. He hit here about ten minutes ago. He said he was to call for the Senator at eight."

"Yuss," said Lanihan gravely. "Eight sharp, at."

MacBride still looked at him. "When was the last time you saw your boss?"

"Ten, it was, last night, about."

"You mean you drove him home—here?"

"Yuss, I mean. I did drove him home here, arriving, so to speak at ten."

"Where'd you drive him from?"

"A house in Charles Street, the number I don't remember, account of the Senator tells me I should drive him to Charles Street, down Charles Street. And when he says, 'Vincent, stop here,' I stop in front of this now house. 'Wait, Vincent,' he says, and I wait, sitting in the car there for an hour reading a book. Then out comes the Senator and away we go, lickety-split."

"How'd he look? Was he upset or anything?"

"Well, excuse me, that I could not say. Except maybe he was a little mad, account of the way he snapped, 'The hotel, Vincent!' like that. And then, when he got out, the way he snapped, 'Eight sharp in the mornin'!' like that."

"Ever take him to that house before?"

"Nope—I mean, no, sir."

"Would you recognize the house?"

"Gee, no, sir. Only I remember I was parked next to a light-pole on the north side o' the street and a block farther on was a crosstown trolley. All them houses look alike."

MacBride said, "Do you know why the Senator came to Richmond City?"

"No, sir."

The skipper raised his voice: "Anybody here know? You, Mr. Harcott?"

The resident manager said, "No. He was traveling incognito as James Welsh. I recognized him and so did Tom Bugle, but we said nothing to the Press. Tom, when he found this door open early this morning, and Mr. Kennedy in here, got excited and mentioned the Senator's name. He thought Mr. Kennedy was a gangster, I guess."

Assistant District Attorney Borodino said, "Maybe he wasn't so wrong at that."

Kennedy put down his coffee cup, looked dreamily at Borodino and smiled.

Borodino did not smile. He snapped, "Yes. I mean you!"

"What's eating you, Mike?" MacBride asked. "What're you sore with Kennedy about?"

"What's eating me! I don't like his tricks, and now he springs one of his fantastic stories about an anonymous telephone call. Some mysterious voice on the wire tells him to go to room four-ten at the *Pillars* and then hangs up. That's what *he* says. *He* says he comes over here, finds the door open, walks in and finds all the lights on and the apartment empty."

MacBride asked, "What's wrong about that?"

Borodino snorted contemptuously. "The only thing that's wrong about that is that he won't tell who phoned him to come over!"

"A voice," said Kennedy dreamily. "A voice on the wire."

"A stool pigeon!" Borodino rapped. "One of your stool pigeons! One of the crowd you consort with in all the bars of this city!"

Kennedy's gentle, tired voice said, "Pfui."

"All I know," Tom Bugle plowed in, "was this here door was locked at two-fifteen when I made my rounds. I know because I try all the knobs. If I find a door ain't locked I got to knock and tell 'em to lock it. Rules of the house. It was locked at two-fifteen and it wasn't locked at three-thirty."

"How'd you happen to come by at three-thirty?"

"The dinge elevator operator said a punky-looking guy got off at the fourth floor. It was him—Kennedy."

"Did anybody see the Senator go out again after he came in at ten?"

"No, no," said Tom Bugle.

"Could he get out without being seen?"

"Maybe, sure. The fire stairway. It comes out in the east wing, where they dim the lights at midnight. Then out by the side door to Wolff Street. All I say is, this door was locked at two-fifteen."

"Were there lights on?"

"You can't tell from the hall."

"Any phone calls or visitors that asked for him?"

"No."

BORODINO shook a finger at Kennedy. "There's the guy that knows more than he's telling."

"Maybe," said Kennedy. "Like this. There's blood soaked in the carpet and as far as I've been able to find out, it's only in one spot. You can still see two lines on the nap of the carpet, as if something'd been dragged across it. All the furniture is in place. Every leg fits every impression in the carpet. So we can take it for granted that no furniture was moved, therefore it wasn't a piece of furniture that made those lines. What else? Maybe a man's heels—the heels of a man who was dragged across the floor. Or maybe his toes.

"Somebody bled in this room—he bled in one spot, inside that circle Mory drew. The bathroom is clean. There are two unsoiled bath towels in there and five unsoiled handtowels. They put six handtowels in these apartments. The maid swore she put six in here. There's no dirty one anywhere. None has been removed, according to the maid. There were six handtowels. When I first looked in the bathroom there were only five—there are still only five."

"Towels! Towels!" scoffed Borodino. "What about the towels?"

"Just that there's a towel missing. There's a towel missing, there's blood on the carpet—and where is Senator Shacker? The beds haven't been slept in. He didn't go to bed last night. I repeat, for the skipper's record, that at about three o'clock this morning I received an anonymous phone call, male voice, telling me to go to room four-ten at the *Pillars*. The guy said I'd done him a good turn once. I guess he figured he was giving me a news break. In my usual state of semi-sobriety, I came over here."

Borodino smiled maliciously. "Tell me, Kennedy—if a stool gave you a tip and you knew his name, would you divulge it?"

"Probably not."

Borodino spun and said to MacBride, "See?"

The skipper crossed the room and looked gravely at Kennedy. "Listen, Kennedy—"

"Stop before you start, Stevie," Kennedy smiled. "I told you I don't know who made the phone call. If I knew, I wouldn't be hanging around here taking 'em below the belt from the dago Adonis of the District Attorney's office."

Borodino said, "I'm a dago and proud of it."

"You mean you're an Adonis and proud of it."

Borodino came across the room dangerously, his fist clenched.

Kennedy's smile was whimsical. "Go ahead, sweetheart, hit me. A child could knock me down."

"Cut it out, Mike," the skipper said uneasily, turning to face Borodino. "Bickering this way ain't getting nobody nowhere."

"I hate a guy I can't believe," rasped Borodino. "I can't believe that guy. He's a liar from the word go, and he's too damned smart to be alive. He's on intimate terms with more crooks than—"

"You, for instance," Kennedy smiled. "Just a few more than you, Mr. Borodino. About two, say—"

"You," said the skipper, "shut up, too. If I don't step in here, this belly-achin'll go on all day. Now shut up, both of you. And you with the keys," he added, pointing to Vincent Lanihan, "stop doing that. Make up your mind whether you want the keys hooked or unhooked. Mory, I suppose you asked around if anybody heard any noise in here?"

"Sure, long ago. No soap, Cap'n."

MacBride crossed to the telephone, picked it up and stood back on his heels. He called Headquarters. "Otto, this is Steve.... We got to send out a general alarm for State Senator Moss Shacker. He disappeared from his apartment at the *Pillars Hotel* some time after two-fifteen this morning and— Wait a minute.... No, I said wait a minute. Well, forget it. Skip it. No general alarm. No alarm at all."

He hung up and said, "Hello, Senator."

"Looks like open house," said Moss Shacker, scaling his lightweight gray fedora on to a table. He had a V-shaped grin that showed two gold eyeteeth and his face was long, dun-colored, with a long, narrow jaw. His ears stood out from his head. He had a pair of gray, easy-going, mocking, inscrutable eyes. His clothes were loose and ill-fitting on his gaunt, slatted frame, and his hard white collar was two sizes too large for his long heron's neck. He looked, at a glance, like a country yokel, but anybody who knew anything about him knew he was far from being a yokel.

The skipper said, "You gave us a scare."

"Yeah?" Shacker said, chuckling in a rusty voice. He stuck a cheap cheroot between his teeth and lit up. "Try to travel incog—and this is what happens. Where's all the cameras?"

Shotz stood up with his news camera.

Shacker waved him down. "Don't be cute, boy. Well"—he put his hands in his hip pockets, grinned around the room—"what's the occasion, gentlemen?" He waved at Borodino. "Hello, Mike. Hell, I didn't see you at first. You're getting to look like one of them gigolos."

Borodino smiled with his even white teeth. "Greetings, Senator Shacker."

"Huh, Mike. Well, well; you're on the job, too. Stick around, boy, and you'll be Attorney General some day. How are those sisters of yours? Boy, usen't they be hot babies!"

Borodino smiled stiffly. "They're swell."

"Great. Glad to hear it." He looked around the room again. "Come on, come on. Hey, Captain—what're you looking stony-pussed about?"

MacBride said, "I was just about to send out a general alarm for you. Your bed wasn't slept in. You weren't in here since around two this morning. We figured you might have been snatched."

Shacker guffawed. "Snatched! Ho-ho! Me snatched! There's a rich one for you!" His face came together suddenly, pleasantly, and he winked. "Just a scare, I guess—just a scare. You can go right along about your business, Captain. I took a walk. I like to take walks late at night. Think things out. Sometimes I walk all night. All right, gentlemen," he said sharply. "I'm a busy man. You'll have to excuse me."

MacBride nodded to the chalked circle. "We got scared, I guess, because there's blood on the carpet."

Shacker rubbed his nose. He grinned slowly. "Oh, sure. I tripped and got a bloody nose." He wiggled his nose. "I got plenty nose to get bloody, huh?"

MacBride frowned thoughtfully. "Funny thing, though. Kennedy here says some guy phoned him at three this morning and told him to take a look at this room."

"Who's Kennedy?" Shacker scowled.

Kennedy raised his hand.

Shacker said, "What's your business?"

"I'm an unimportant newspaperman. The *Free Press.*"

Shacker's lips became deeply V-shaped in a grin. "Oh. So somebody's been kidding the press too. Ho-ho! That's a good one! Hey, Mike, ain't that a good one?" he roared at Borodino.

Borodino dropped his eyelids and smiled. "Swell," he said in a very quiet voice.

"Hey, you, Kennedy," Shacker said in a loud, good-natured tone, "who was this practical joker?"

Kennedy grinned.

"It was anonymous," MacBride put in. "A guy just phoned him, Kennedy said, and then hung up."

Shacker slapped his thigh. "Boy, I'd give a hundred bucks to find out who kidded the press that way!"

"You're on," came Kennedy's quiet, whimsical voice. Sly amusement floated tranquilly through his eyes. "I'll find the lad that made the call. I can use a hundred bucks. Are you on the level or is this a gag?"

Shacker's eyes danced in their sockets and his coarse voice boomed uproariously. "Hell, man, when I say a thing I mean it!"

Borodino smiled bitterly. "I said all along Kennedy knew who made that phone call."

Kennedy chuckled and ran his hand through his hair, mussing it up some more, "What are you beefing about, Mike? There's no crime—there's no criminal charge against anybody. The Senator just banged his nose and took a walk. But anyhow, Mike, to make you feel better, I don't know who made the call." He smiled gently. "But I'll find out." He looked at Shacker. "Have the hundred bucks in tens, Senator."

Shacker heaved with laughter.

GAHAGAN grooved the Packard around Civic Square and lined out leisurely for Police Headquarters. Moriarity sat beside him, and in the rear were Kennedy and the skipper. Kennedy was 'way down in the seat, his eyes half shut, a lock of hair protruding haphazardly from beneath his hat and bobbing over his left eyebrow.

MacBride said angrily, "I don't see why the hell you had to pick on Mike Borodino."

"He picked on me first."

"Bah! You know Mike! He just goes off the handle.... Besides, you were a nasty guy cracking about him knowing a lot of crooks. You know damned well the tough time he has living down that family of his—those tramp sisters of his and—"

"How about the crack Shacker made about them being hot babies?"

The skipper snorted. "Shacker's a kidder. He's sort of an uncle to Mike."

"Oh, I know, I know," sing-songed Kennedy good-naturedly. "Mike's ambitious, he's come up from the gutter, and there's a good chance of his being attorney general some day. Only he's a bit of a fool. He's tied up with Shacker. And Shacker's a dangerous man. He's kidded his way pretty long, he's romped his way through the state and county, laughing off all kinds of charges and getting away with it. It's women mostly with Shacker. Some day some woman will upset his apple cart and I shouldn't be surprised to find Mike under it. I remember once, while I was in my cups, I told Mike that." He smiled. "Some guys hate you when you tell 'em the truth. So you don't think there's anything to that blood spot on the carpet?"

The skipper said, "As things stand, no. If Shacker was out all night with a gal—well, my job ain't scandal-mongering. Show me a crime, or evidence of a crime, and I'll go to town. This is just a fluke. Forget it, Kennedy."

"A hundred bucks is a hundred bucks," grinned Kennedy.

Chapter III

AT NOON Kennedy stood on the corner of Grover and Charles. He was leaning indolently against a telephone pole and taking slow, ruminative puffs on a cigarette. A block up Charles he saw a trolley car cross the street and vanish down Simmonds. It was in this block, on the right side of the street, that Vincent Lanihan was supposed to have parked for an hour.

Kennedy took a stroll up Charles and looked the houses over. There were four rooming-houses in a row, with a small restaurant at one end of the row and a delicatessen at the other. It wasn't a pretty street.

Kennedy sauntered up and down the block several times, killing time because his plans were vague. On the third trip he realized he was being followed. This didn't occur to him instantly; the fact had worked gradually on his consciousness and now he knew that the man had ridden out on the streetcar with him and that he had casually posted himself at various parts of this block during Kennedy's survey of it.

Entering the first house, Kennedy closed the glass door behind him and stood in the gloom gazing out through the grayish curtain. The man sauntered by without looking up. Kennedy waited five minutes and then went out. The man was leaning in a barbershop doorway across the street. Kennedy entered the next rooming-house, stood in the hallway behind a door identical with the other, and waited there five minutes. The man remained leaning in the barbershop doorway. He was a young man, no taller than Kennedy but better dressed and possessing a wiry build. He looked like a dozen other men you might pass in the street.

Kennedy walked out, this time giving a purposeful air to the manner in which he approached the next rooming-house. He actually ran up the four stone steps to the vestibule, a rare procedure for so low-powered a person. Ducking into the hallway, he closed the door and squinted through the curtain. A moment later the man strolled by, looked up: his face was thin, pink-cheeked, expressionless. Kennedy waited. The man went past again, in the opposite direction, and again looked up. In the next ten minutes he passed half a dozen times. On the seventh trip, he stopped. He stopped out front and gazed quizzically up the steps. He looked up the face of the three-storied building and nibbled on his lip.

Presently he started to climb the stone steps. Kennedy tiptoed to the back of the hall and ducked into the dark well of the staircase. He heard the door open, then close quietly. He smiled impishly to himself. Footsteps climbed the staircase slowly and with a minimum of sound. He heard them proceed along the upper corridor and then climb the top staircase, and after that there was no sound at all.

Kennedy took off his shoes, and holding one in each hand climbed the lower staircase noiselessly as a cat. Pausing at the head of it, he listened for a moment and then went on. He took the steps of the top staircase one at a time and very cautiously; and three-fourths of the way up he was able to peer over the edge of the upper corridor and see the man standing motionless and in a listening attitude in front of the middle door. He saw the man try the knob, turn it slowly to its full circuit, and, when the door did not open, let it back again carefully. He saw the man raise his hand and knock; once, then twice in rapid succession, then once again. The door opened silently and the man walked in and the door closed.

Retreating a couple of steps, Kennedy squatted and reflected. Then he went all the way down to the lower hall and put his shoes on.

Instead of walking down the front steps, he went over the side of the stoop, close to the building, so that he would not be seen from an upper window. He walked along close to the building and entered the delicatessen store, making a bell jingle on the door. He remained by the door and was able to see up the street. Over his shoulder he said:

"Make me a Swiss on rye, plenty mustard."

ABOUT twenty minutes later he saw the slender wiry man appear on the sidewalk, look up and down, and then cross to the barbershop. In about three minutes he came out of the barbershop and stood on the curb looking south. A few minutes later a taxi drew up in front of the rooming-house and the wiry man walked out into the street and said something to the driver; then stepped back, looked up at the face of the rooming-house and made a motion with his finger. He climbed into the cab but the cab did not shove off, it waited.

Meanwhile Kennedy noted that it was a Citywide Taxi Company cab and wrote down its company number and license number. As he looked up he saw a woman shoving a suitcase into the cab and getting in after it. Her dark blue hat was lopped smartly over one side of her face and all he saw was a bit of her chin. The taxi-cab took off. Roving taxi-cabs never bothered with this street, so it was pointless trying to follow.

He went into the rooming-house instead and climbed to the top floor. The middle door was unlocked, the key sticking in the keyhole. Kennedy wandered into an old-fashioned bed-living-room that was threadbare but clean enough. A day-bed, some over-stuffed furniture, and a sink with running water in one corner. The woman had bailed out. Doubtless she hadn't notified the operator of the rooming-house. Kennedy looked in the bureau drawers, in the closet. There was nothing.

Leaving the room, he locked the door and dropped the key in his pocket.

Ten minutes later he was making his way along crowded State Street in the third-class shopping center. Automobiles were whamming past, loud speakers blared, and there was the roar of the crowd. Kennedy suddenly collided with a man and said:

"Whoops!"

The man snarled, "Why the hell don't you look where you're going?"

"Try doing that yourself, my friend," Kennedy grinned.

The big man squinted one eye malignantly, said, "Oh, a wise guy, eh!" and gave Kennedy a terrific flat-hand against the chest. The reporter's feet left the pavement and he shot over the curb. Brakes screamed and wheels wrenched the macadam. The rear fender of a Lincoln sedan struck Kennedy's shoulder, spun him, skidded him back against the curb. Another car braked sharply two feet from his head, and cries rose from the crowd nearby. A chauffeur got out of the Lincoln and picked him up.

"Lucky I wasn't asleep, fella. You all right?" He hoisted Kennedy to his feet.

A cop came plowing through the crowd; arrived and said, "Huh? What's up?"

Kennedy was looking at the crowd, through it, around it. There was no sign of the man who had hit him.

"I'm okey," he said. "I bumped into a guy and he shoved me."

A woman said indignantly. "It looked to me, really, as if that man really *meant* to get this poor little man run over."

Kennedy's smile was whimsical. "I guess he was just sore, madam."

He went round to *Enrico's* in Flamingo Street.

Paderoofski, the barman, said "Grittings, Meester Kennedy! Howsa avery leetle t'ing?"

"Improving rapidly," Kennedy sighed, "at my expense. Give me a double rye, water on the side. You're looking swell, Paderoofski."

Kennedy muddled through his drink and remembered the man who had struck him. A sandy, lantern-jawed face, fierce pale eyes and a kick in his hand like a mule.

Paderoofski was saying, "Dere wassa fella bost in here last night joosta before I'm close op. He wassa look for you accounta you hang out here so much. I'm tal him you go home an hour ago."

"By the way, what time did I leave here last night?"

"She wassa two in the morn'."

Kennedy blinked. "Who was the guy?"

"Jamminy, dat I'm not know, please, axcuse me. He wassa a leetle guy, he's gotta no hair and he keeps a wan eye closed. Maybe he's a got only wan eye."

"Oh-oh," said Kennedy softly.

"Axcuse it?"

"Did he leave right away?"

"Shoo. He make a telephone call from de boot' and den he's scram."

Kennedy finished his drink. "Paderoofski," he said, "I should like to borrow a gun."

"Whatsa mine she's a yours, Meester Kennedy," replied Paderoofski and laid five guns on the bar.

Kennedy chose a small .32 automatic and from the cash drawer Paderoofski supplied bullets.

"Myself, now," said Paderoofski, "I woulda take da .45."

Kennedy said, "Too heavy. It'd wear me down."

"Ah, but I'm like da way she goes 'boom-boom,' axcuse me."

Chapter IV

HIS NAME was Larry Pazchik. More familiarly, Larry the Blink. The only thing wrong about it was that Kennedy could not remember ever having done him a good turn, or any kind of turn. But Paderoofski's description of him was, in its utter simplicity, perfect. It fitted no one else in Kennedy's long array of good, bad, or indeterminate acquaintants. Lorenz Pazchik originally. Then Larry. Then Larry the Blink.

He was small stuff. No major offense had even landed on him. Only petty stuff—like rolling a lush occasionally, or picking a pocket, or running a creep-joint. Once or twice a stolen car. Minor vice charges and once for running a book. His left eye had been knocked out years ago. In a lush underworld he was rated as small carrion that fed on the niblets. A punk.

Kennedy went to Joe Scappa, a big man with a face like a steak, medium rare.

"Hello, Mr. Kennedy."

"Hello, Joe."

Joe was a money-lender to the small fry in the underworld, who are never more than two jumps ahead of the wolf.

"Where's Larry the Blink?" asked Kennedy.

Joe's smile was broad. "I oughta check up on some of my clients. Funny, I don't know."

"Very funny, Joe. Do I look like a rat?"

"No. And I guess you ain't."

"Then let's begin over again. Where's Larry the Blink?"

"Honest, I don't know."

"If I don't find him, somebody else will. This somebody else is liable to drill his eyeteeth out."

Joe looked pained. "And him owing me ninety-two dollars and sixty-five cents."

Kennedy smiled. "You've got a good memory for figures, Joe."

"Jeese, I gotta!"

"Think hard, now. Think of the figures on the door of the place where I'll find Larry, and in what street."

Joe looked gravely at Kennedy.

Kennedy was tranquil. "A dead guy can't pay off his debts, can he?"

Joe's face was serious, very righteous. "But I gotta rule with myself. I never give out addresses." He got up, reached for a dusty derby and bounced it on his head. He went out of his musty office and down the street.

Kennedy followed. Joe knew that Kennedy followed but he made believe he didn't. Nor was Kennedy indiscreet: he followed leisurely, never getting any closer to Joe than half a block. Three blocks north, then two east, then two north again. It was a battered yellow frame house in Swaggerty Street, with a fruit store downstairs and vague quarters above. There was a hall door at the left. Joe entered and went heavily up the worn stairs and Kennedy entered and hung around below. He heard Joe bang on a door, heard him say, "Me, Joe Scappa!" A door opened and was then slammed shut. Kennedy climbed the stairs and, listening at the end door, heard Joe railing. Then Kennedy went down to the street and smoked, leaning against a fruit rack. In a few minutes Joe came out and passing Kennedy made believe he didn't see him. But he was thrusting bills into his pocket.

Kennedy went upstairs and knocked. There was no answer; he knocked again and he almost felt that on the other side of the door a man's heart was beating furiously. He said:

"Hey, Larry."

A word breathed tautly: "Huh?"

"It's me, Larry. Kennedy."

"What you want?"

"See you."

"I can't. I'm takin' a bath."

"I'll rub your back for you."

"What you want?"

"See you."

There was a pause. "You alone?"

"I'm always alone."

"I mean you alone now?"

"Yes."

Few men were smaller or skinnier than Kennedy. Larry the Blink was. He let Kennedy in and hastily closed and bolted the door.

"One thing I like about you, Larry," Kennedy said drolly. "I don't get a stiff neck looking up at you."

The Blink didn't look as if he felt droll. There wasn't a hair on his oyster-white face and he had a neck that looked all Adam's Apple. Somewhere indefinitely between clothes-hanger shoulders was his chest. He was quick as a bird and his fingers looked like gray twigs and there was no seat in his pants. His one eye was a large, startled, scared question mark. He was shabby but neat. So was his room—and it was boxlike, one-windowed and dim. Craft was in his face, but not intelligence.

Kennedy drawled, "What are you jumpy about, Larry?"

"Me jumpy? Me? Hah, I ain't jumpy. Who, me jumpy? Here, sit down. Sit down, Mr. Kennedy. This one. This chair here."

Kennedy smiled to himself and sat down. Larry sat down too, trying to sprawl at ease but unable to keep still.

Kennedy looked at the door and said, "Who's out in the hall?"

The Blink left the chair as if spring-driven and came down catlike on his toes. His one eye was wide open, terrified. His right hand was in under his left lapel and he faced the door, his lips tight.

A door banged and heavy feet went down the stairs.

THE BLINK relaxed, loosened his lips, cocked his eye and gave a macabre grin. "Nothing," he tossed off carelessly, snapping his fingers.

Kennedy smiled good-temperedly. "So you're not jumpy. Cool as a fish."

The Blink sat, started to toss that off too, but stopped midway. His one eye became very guarded. "By the way," he said slowly, "what you want to see me about?"

"About that phone call you made to me at three this morning."

The Blink splayed his fingers against his meager chest and asked, "Me make a phone call?"

"Listen, Larry, the act is lousy. In fact, it stinks. You were in *Enrico's* at three this morning looking for me. I'd left. You went into the booth in the bar and made a call. The call was to me."

The Blink got the jitters. He didn't really get them at that moment because obviously he'd had them all along; but at that moment they broke out on the surface, like a rash. He jumped up and crackled excitedly:

"I don't know a thing! Not a thing! I ain't said nothin'!" He jumped to the window and stared out petulantly.

Kennedy said, "What about a rooming-house in Charles Street?"

The Blink spun around, his mouth wide open and touched with anguish. "I don't know a thing! I tell you, by God, I don't know a single thing!"

Kennedy stood up languidly and said, "Keep your pants on, Larry. I'm offered a hundred bucks to show who made that phone call last night. I wouldn't spring you in the open for a hundred bucks or two hundred or any amount. But I want to know about the phone call. Who's the gal in Charles Street? Who's the young smooth-faced guy? Who's the big sandy mugg with the white eyes? Why was Shacker in Charles Street last night and what happened in his apartment?"

The Blink moaned. "Now look. Now, Jeese, mister, look. I don't know a thing. I *can't* know a thing." Terror bulged out of his eye and he screeched, "I tell you, I *can't* know a thing!"

Kennedy was unmoved, pleasant voiced. "You didn't phone me to do me a good turn, because I never did you a good turn. You know, as practically everyone knows, that I get oiled up at *Enrico's* almost every night. You got sore about something, you must have been pretty damned sore—because you went to *Enrico's* to tip me off, and when I wasn't there, you phoned. You've got to come clean, Larry."

Terror is a great bulwark against reason. Through wet lips Larry the Blink gritted, "I ain't got nothing to say. I ain't said a thing. I ain't gonna say a thing."

Kennedy eyed him speculatively. "I get it. They're after you. For the tip-off. And they're after me because they figured I'll find you. Who are they?"

"I—don't know a—thing."

Kennedy sighed, shrugged. He said offhand, "Pull that shade up a bit, will you?"

The Blink reached up and gave the shade a yank and while his arm was still raised Kennedy pulled out the borrowed gun and said, "Now keep the hand up, Larry, and raise the other one too."

The Blink's breath made a sucking sound in his teeth and his eye blazed.

Kennedy said: "According to the police, there's no case at all. And naturally. But I was offered a hundred bucks to find out who made the telephone call. I was got out of bed at three on a hangover, I was slapped around by a house dick, and I took a lot of crap from Mike Borodino of the D.A.'s office. All on account of a telephone call. You're going with me and I'm going to collect the hundred bucks. After that, you're going to explain to the cops—MacBride, by the way—why you made the call."

The Blink shrank against the wall.

"Either that," said Kennedy, "or you come clean right here. I don't want you, but if I can't get the others, I'll take what there is—you. You won't need a hat. Get going. Keep your hands up," he warned, crossing the room and taking the heavy gun from beneath Larry's left arm.

The Blink looked swamped. He said hopelessly, "Jeese—this to me—to me."

Kennedy shuttered one eye, said enticingly, "If you had an ounce of sense—you'd talk. Now. Instead of later." He waited patiently for a minute, then said, "No?" And then: "Okey, let's go, Larry."

The Blink moved automatically, almost sobbing to himself. He put his hands in his pockets. Then he actually began bawling and took out one hand and covered his face with it. Kennedy reached out and shoved back the bolt. The Blink's right hand came out of his pocket like a Jack-in-the-Box and Kennedy measured himself on the floor. Brass knuckle-dusters glinted on Larry's hand and there was a trickle of blood on Kennedy's jaw.

Even then, The Blink looked scared. He scurried to pick up his own gun, thrust it into its armpit holster, grabbed his hat and lit out with his coat tails flying.

Kennedy got up a minute later and looked at himself in a mirror tacked to the wall. He held a handkerchief to his chin with one hand and with his other recovered the .32 pistol, then his hat, which Larry on the way out had stepped on. Kennedy didn't notice the dent. He smiled wryly to himself, shrugged and left the room.

When he reached the lower-hall, the front door was open and he saw Larry cringing on the sidewalk between Mike Borodino and Sam Sands, a detective attached to the District Attorney's office.

Borodino was saying, "It's a warrant for your arrest, buddy."

"What—what charge?" croaked The Blink.

"Annoying women on the street."

"I never annoyed a—"

Sands said, "Get in, unkpay," and belted him into the waiting sedan. The Blink scrambled to a seat.

Sands and Borodino followed, and the sedan drove off.

Chapter V

A T THE Welch Street terminal of the Citywide Taxi Company, in the office, Kennedy said to the rotund driver whom the manager had called in:

"That fare you called for in Charles Street around noon today— where'd you take the man and the woman?"

The driver looked at the manager.

The manager said, "Go ahead, Izzy. He's a reporter."

"Well," said the driver, "it's easy. I took 'em to one hundred Mularkey Street."

"Sure of that?"

"Sure I'm sure. A brick house with brass rails."

Kennedy went down to Civic Square and the District Attorney's office. He said to the girl in the reception room:

"I want to see Mr. Borodino."

"I'll see if he's in, Mr. Kennedy." She turned to the switchboard, turned away from it a moment later and said, "He's busy right now. Have a seat."

Kennedy sat down, slid to the small of his back and clasped his hands over his diaphragm. He was a patient man. He waited half an hour. Then he said casually:

"Try again."

The girl tried again, then turned to him and said, "Just a minute."

Five minutes later Borodino came down the corridor and into the reception room. He came swiftly, a busy man, a man of affairs. His brows were bent and his manner indicated that he intended giving Kennedy very little of his time.

He clipped, "Hello, Kennedy. What's on your mind?"

"I hear your office picked up Larry Pazchik."

"Yes."

"What charge?"

"Moral charge."

"Who made the charge?"

Borodino said, "Name withheld."

"Where's Larry now?"

"In custody."

"How's to give me a free pass to see him?"

Borodino shook his head, pursed his lips. He grinned, showing his fine white teeth. "That all?" he asked.

"That's all," Kennedy sighed, getting wearily to his feet.

Borodino turned on his heel and went briskly back to his office.

Down in the street, Kennedy climbed into a cab and said, "Go to one hundred Mularkey Street."

Borodino was rated as one of the most ambitious young men in the D.A.'s office. He had played a lot of politics to get where he was, but he was far from a figurehead. He was able. He was the only one of a brood of eight who amounted to anything. Moss Shacker had given him his start. That was ten years ago, when Shacker was a potent alderman in Richmond City. And though Moss Shacker had romped his way through many a scandal, kidding the press and the public, not even the breath of scandal had ever touched Mike Borodino. One or two of his brothers had crossed the law occasionally, one of his sisters had hit the primrose path and another was a strip dancer in a burlesque show. But Mike, according to the record, was pure grain. A little tough, very caustic, but pure grain—trying desperately to live down the shortcomings of his family.

"This must be it," said the driver.

Kennedy saw a two-storied red brick house with brass handrails out front and brasswork on a heavy vestibule door. He got out, paid up, and heard the taxi swish off. He climbed three stone steps, entered the vestibule and pressed a button. The sound of footsteps came to him and then he saw dark curtains on the glass panel part and his heart skipped a beat as he saw, for one brief instant, the sandy face of the white-eyed man who had punched him into the street.

Instantly the curtains snapped shut. Kennedy was no fool. He did not ring the bell again, he knew how close his head was to the lion's mouth. He also knew that this address was loaded with dynamite and that it was the address he wanted. His main desire at this moment was to get out of the vestibule. Turning, he reached for the vestibule door, opened it. There was a click behind him and a hard voice chopped:

"Hey, you!"

Then strong hands gripped his arms and he was spun around and marched into an oval entrance hall. The main door slammed shut. His pockets were slapped and in one of the pockets was his gun. He tried to get the gun out. The big hand on his wrist tightened and his hand felt numb. He saw the gun drop to the floor. The white-eyed man gave him a shove, picked up the gun and held it.

Kennedy said ruefully, "I guess I walked into something."

The white-eyed man said nothing. He was breathing rapidly, his eyes were very wide open, and he looked as if he didn't know whether he had done right or wrong. But at the same time he was determined to be top dog.

"Inside—that way," he growled.

Kennedy went into a large and sumptuously furnished living-room.

The man said, "Sit down."

Kennedy sat down.

A tall, black-haired woman came in from another room and said, "What's the racket, Hal? I thought—" Seeing Kennedy she stopped, and her eyes squinted curiously. She was in her forties but still good-looking in a hard, brash way. She was very well groomed. She crushed out a cigarette she had been smoking, and giving Hal a brief look, said, "Where'd he come from all at once?"

Hal muttered bitterly, "He's Kennedy."

The woman's eyes flashed with anger and amazement. Color waved in a flame across her cheeks and her lips twitched. She cried in a harsh voice, "Why the hell did you let him in?"

Hal grunted defensively, "I had to! It was—it was nabbing him now or letting him get away. He—he seen me. Damn it," he yelled, "he seen me!"

Her voice dropped and was clipped: "Anybody with him?" Her eyes jumped from left to right and then she strode across the room to a front window.

"I didn't see anyone," Hal growled.

She turned from the window, her breast rising and falling rapidly. "This is sweet!" she panted. "This is damned sweet!"

Hal said, "What could I do? What could I do?"

THERE were other footsteps, swift, light, and a slender man came into the room whistling gaily, and evidently headed for another part of the house. He stopped short when he saw Kennedy, and Kennedy recognized the man who had been shadowing him in Charles Street. The man composed his smooth young face instantly, looked inquiringly from Hal to the woman, said lightly:

"Who's our guest?"

Hal gave him a stony look and the woman stared menacingly at him. The slender young man shrugged nonchalantly and went on his way.

"Wait—come back here," the woman snapped.

The slender man stopped, shrugged again and then leaned indolently against the piano.

The woman turned her angry stare on Kennedy. She put her hands on her hips and said, "Well, maybe you want something?"

Kennedy smiled. "Let's skip that. The red-head hauled me in here. Maybe he wants something."

She said, "You skip it. You rang the bell here."

"Maybe it was a mistake. He seems to think I know him. I never saw him before."

Hal looked uncomfortable. He blurted, "Why'd you ring the bell?"

"I'm canvassing for the newspapers. They want to find out how many people get their news from the radio and how many from the newspapers." He looked very frail and innocent. "Do you depend on the radio for your news or the daily papers?"

Hal growled, "He had a gun," and held the gun up.

Kennedy nodded. "I always carry a gun. When a guy hauls me into his house—kidnaps me—I naturally try to use it." He smiled whimsically at Hal. "Wouldn't you?"

Of one thing Kennedy was certain: this was not the woman the smooth-faced man had taken away in a cab from the house in Charles Street.

The woman said to the smooth-faced man, "You stay in here with him." She started from the room, saying to Hal, "Come on, let's talk this over."

They left the living-room. The smooth-faced man remained leaning against the piano and studied Kennedy with a polite, curious interest. Kennedy paid no attention to him. Disheveled, the reporter sat slumped in his chair and gazed absently at the curtained windows. It was ten minutes before Hal and the woman returned, and as they entered the room the telephone rang.

"I'll get it," the woman growled, picking up the instrument. "Hello," she said. "Sure." She frowned. "Yes.... Hang on. I'll go to the other extension." She turned to the smooth-faced man. "Hold this till I get on the other extension, then hang up." Her eyes were bright, hard, apprehensive as she left the room.

The smooth-faced man picked up the telephone, placed the receiver against his ear. A minute later he hung up and put the telephone down. His eyes glittered. He walked across the room to where Hal was standing and whispered in the big man's ear. Their attention was momentarily diverted. Kennedy stood up, took one soft step and a jump and landed on the telephone. He ripped off the receiver, slapped it to his ear. It was against his ear for perhaps a quarter of a minute. It took Hal and the smooth-faced man about that long to get over their surprise and reach him. He had asked for it, and he knew it.

He went down so easily that they were amazed. He just let himself go, falling with their blows, taking the sting out of them.

"I got him," Hal grunted.

The smooth-faced man said, "Go easy, Hal," and put the telephone together.

Hal stood up with Kennedy. The big man's white eyes blazed and his mouth was contorted with a mixture of fear and fury.

"Easy, Hal," the smooth-faced man said.

Hal lowered his doubled fist. He shoved Kennedy violently on to a divan. Kennedy bounced off the divan and ran the length of the living-room. Hal swore and drew his gun and the smooth-faced man, crying, "Don't, Hal!" in a crackling voice, grabbed hold of Hal's arm.

Kennedy knew it would be tough trying to get through two doors to the street, so when he reached the hall he turned left and scampered up the stairway. The smooth-faced man came after him. At the top of the stairway was a heavy chair. Kennedy slewed it around and sent it down. It crashed into the smooth-faced man and took him all the way down again. Below, the woman was shrill-voiced, angry and terrified. Kennedy stretched for a door, flung it open and jumped into a room. He slammed shut the door, turned the key as Hal's body landed against the outside.

"Open up!" roared Hal.

"Ha," said Kennedy, turning and heading for the windows.

But there was a woman on the bed, bound and gagged. A hat and coat were on a chair beside the bed and he could tell by the hat that it belonged to the woman the smooth-faced man had taxied away from the house in Charles Street. He said to the woman on the bed:

"These yours?"

She nodded. Her hair was a shambles and her eyes were wild in their sockets. He had no time to dispose of the bonds that held her hands and feet, for Hal was driving his weight against the door. Kennedy pulled the woman off the bed. He opened the window. He yanked off the sheets, tied them together, then tied the heavy silk counterpane to them and knotted its end to the bed post. The other end of his improvised line he lashed beneath the woman's arms.

"Try this," he heard the smooth-faced man say.

And Hal said, "Gimme it."

Heavy wood struck the outside of the door. Kennedy saw one of the panels splinter. Straining in every one of his meager muscles, he got the woman's legs over the windowsill. He got the rest of her body up, balanced it for a moment, and then, catching hold of the line, let her out. He braced his feet on the baseboard below the sill and paid the line out, his face red with effort, and little grunts in his throat. When the whole line was paid out, he looked down and saw the woman hanging below, her feet almost touching the ground.

With the sound of splintering wood driving him, he forked the windowsill, lowered himself to his elbows, then grabbed hold of the line and slid down. He used his penknife to cut through the lower end of the line, and the woman dropped limply beside him. Unable to carry her, he dragged her on the ground towards the street. The sound of shattered wood reached him and he struggled frantically to reach the street with the woman.

Then he saw Hal's wild, white-eyed face pop out of the upper story window. He saw Hal thrust out his hand and in his hand was a gun. Hal fired blindly—three times before other arms yanked him out of sight. Two of the bullets had hit the woman—one in the neck, the other in the breast. The third had smacked Kennedy's left hand. A strange fire was in his eyes. At the sidewalk, he let go of the woman's hand. The shots had drawn the attention of several pedestrians, several motorists.

Kennedy yelled, "Get this woman to a hospital!"

Three men jumped and lifted her and carried her in to a sedan that had stopped at the curb. As the sedan drove off, two cops came on the run. A crowd was gathering rapidly. One of the cops brawled:

"Hell, if it ain't Kennedy!"

"Mosbaum, surround that house. A redheaded guy just shot a gal. I sent the gal to the hospital. There's a woman and another lad in the house. They're all tough—the three of them."

"What's it all about?"

"I don't know. Except I found the gal bound and gagged in an upstairs bedroom. I tried to get her out and the red-head went gun crazy."

Mosbaum ran up the steps between the brass rails and banging with his nightstick on the vestibule door, yelled, "Open up! This is the police!"

A bull voice roared, "Yeah? Open it yourself, copper, but don't say I didn't warn you!"

Mosbaum came down the steps and said to the other cop, "Arch, ring for reserves. This is gonna be cute." And to the crowd: "Come on, people, beat it!" He waved his arms. "Clear out! If you don't, you might get hurt! Scram, all o' you!"

Kennedy wrapped his handkerchief around his bloody hand. It wasn't enough, so he pulled out his shirt tail, ripped that off and wound it round the handkerchief.

It was getting twilight. The street lights came on.

Chapter VI

THE BLOCK was roped off. Directly opposite the red brick house with the brass rails a police armored car was standing, its searchlight trained on the vestibule. From four rooftops—front, back, and on either side—searchlights poured their white glare upon 100 Mularkey Street. There was an ambulance at either end of the block, inside the ropes; and inside the ropes there was a police emergency car. Policemen, on the roofs and on the ground, surrounded the house. As yet, not one shot had been fired.

In a commandeered apartment on the fourth floor of the building opposite, MacBride stood smoking a pipe. Lieutenant Heine, in charge of the uniformed men, came in and said:

"I think everything's set."

MacBride was squinting at the red brick house. "I want no grandstand plays," he said. "My aim ain't to annihilate those people in that house, or to risk the lives of the police. I just got word that the woman Kennedy rescued from that house just died at St. Mary's Hospital without regaining consciousness. There's a murderer in that house—but we want him alive, as well as the others, if possible. Go downstairs and stand by."

Down in the street, the silence was immense; but the breeze, blowing the window curtains, brought with it the persistent hum of the crowds gathered at either end of the block. In the apartment, Gahagan, munching peanuts, sat by the telephone. In his eyes was a look of distances, as though his thoughts were far removed from the room and its tragic environs. The phone rang and the skipper, standing by the window, said:

"Get it. It's probably Information with that number."

Gahagan got it and, listening, said to the skipper, "Yop. Garden two-four-three. It's in the name of B. Ella." He spelled it.

"Ring it. No, I'll ring it."

MacBride rang it and a moment later a man's voice grated in the receiver: "Yeah?"

The skipper said, "You're completely surrounded. This is Captain MacBride telling you to come out the front door with your hands up."

"Or what?"

"Or else."

"To hell with you!"

The skipper hung up and said to Gahagan, "That guy ain't brave, he's nuts."

"Uhn," grunted Gahagan through a mouthful of peanuts.

The door opened and Kennedy came in, his left arm in a sling, fresh surgical dressing on his hand. He had taken on half a dozen drinks of whiskey—for medical purposes only—and looked mildly tight.

The skipper said, "I've been looking for you. When I got here you were gone."

"I was bleeding all over the place. I went over to St. Mary's to get the hand dolled up."

MacBride, wooden-faced, had his hands on his hips. "What the hell is this all about?"

Kennedy said, "I found the house in Charles Street where Lanihan drove Shacker last night. I saw a guy shadowing me. I saw him taxi a woman away from the house and I checked up with the driver. They were driven to the house across the street. Bag and baggage. The woman was the one I tried to get out of the place. She was bound hand and foot, and gagged."

"How'd you get in the house across the street?"

"I was dragged in by a redheaded guy. He was the guy who several hours earlier punched me into motor traffic in State Street in an attempt to get me run over. The other guy in the house was the one who took the woman from the Charles Street place. The other woman is still there."

"How'd you get out of the place?"

Kennedy told him about the phone call and about the break he had made. "I figured if I got on the extension, while the woman was talking, I'd learn something."

"So what?"

"All I heard was the woman talking. She was yelling into the phone, asking somebody what she and the others should do after they let me go. Apparently, whoever called told her to let me go. I was smacked down before I heard who was on the other end of the wire."

"You couldn't guess, huh?"

"I could, yes. There was only one I saw before I went to the house across the street. I mean, only one person who might be interested in my movements. Mike Borodino."

MacBride scoffed. "Mike's on the level."

Kennedy shrugged. "Do you know that Larry the Blink was picked up by Mike and Sam Sands on a morals charge today?"

"No. Gottschalk'd handle that for the Bureau."

"All right, then. Mike and Sands picked up Larry the Blink on a warrant for annoying women on the street. I asked Mike who lodged the complaint and he wouldn't tell me. I just found out that there was a complaint made against Larry eight months ago, by a tart, for spite. It was filed but never carried out. Until today. The gal's name was Tootsie Maefink."

The skipper looked puzzled, a little impatient. "And where the hell does Larry figure in this?"

Kennedy grinned. "Larry was the guy made the phone call to me to go to Shacker's apartment at three this morning."

"And you're just telling me this now!"

"I couldn't prove it. Larry'd got cold feet in the meantime and wouldn't talk. He took a sock at me in his room and skipped, and when I pulled myself together and went downstairs, I saw Mike and Sands on the sidewalk collaring him on a warrant. But they didn't see me."

"And what do you figure now?"

"That Mike collared Larry the Blink to keep me from getting at him."

The skipper threw up his hands. "I don't believe it!" he shouted, indignant. "Mike's a sarcastic guy but his record's clean as a whistle."

"Remember," smiled Kennedy, "his early political career was sponsored by Moss Shacker."

MacBride picked up the phone and called Headquarters. "Gimme Gottschalk, Otto," he said. And a minute later, to the vice-squad head: "Hey, Gottshy, this is Steve. What you got on the Larry the Blink pick-up today?" He listened, grunting, stabbing his eyes out the window at the scene below. "Okey, okey, Gottshy. I want him picked up again.... Hell, anything! For questioning."

He hung up and said to Kennedy, "The Blink was released an hour ago on order of Judge Cascarrelli because the dame that made the complaint died four months ago of the flu in the City Hospital."

THE PHONE rang again and the skipper grabbed it. "Oh, hello, Mory.... Sure.... Just a minute." And to Kennedy: "Hey, take this down, will you?" And then back on the phone again: "Shoot, Mory.... Evelyn Taunton, alias Eve Tate, alias The Taunter, alias The Duchess. Age forty-one. Buffalo. Columbus, Ohio. Providence. Boston—Okey, Kennedy—Okey, I got it, Mory."

He clipped the telephone together and said, "That was the gal you rescued. Bridges of the vice squad stopped by the hospital and recognized her, identified her by a scar on her thigh. Evelyn Taunton, and the aliases. She was contact woman for the vice ring in those cities mentioned, in the order I gave 'em to you."

"I've heard of her," Kennedy said. "Reporter, thinking he is rescuing fair damsel from den of thieves—" He stopped short, slapped himself in the face.

"I wonder," MacBride muttered, "if the B. Ella across the street is a man or a woman."

"Is that the name?"

"That's the name the phone's listed under. Garden two-four-three."

"How's it spelled?"

MacBride spelled it.

Kennedy cried, "I got it! B. Ella. *Bella.* Bella Kojecki!"

"It sounds," muttered MacBride, "familiar."

"It ought to," Kennedy chuckled. "She's among the first ten in Attorney General Stratt's list of vice queens. It's got to be Bella Kojecki, because that way it adds up. Evelyn Taunton living in a hall bedroom in Charles Street and Bella Kojecki living in splendor in Mularkey Street!"

"Is there a picture anywhere of the Kojecki woman?"

"No. I—"

A shot thundered in the street. The skipper swung on his heel, strode to a window and thrust his head out. There were low voices below in the gloom back of the armored car's searchlight. Dim figures moved about. MacBride yelled down:

"Heine?"

"Yeah?"

"Who did that?"

"It come from the house."

"Anybody hurt?"

"Grotz got scratched in the arm. It ain't much."

The skipper barked, "Bust the attic windows."

He leaned on the windowsill. A blast of interlocked shots cut loose and in an instant there was no longer any glass in the attic windows for the searchlight to shine upon. The figures below, grouped behind the armored car, remained motionless. The murmur of the crowd down the street rose to a hum.

From an upper window in 100 Mularkey a submachine-gun ripped loose for half a minute, the slugs whacking the armored car. Then there was silence again.

MacBride took his hat off, said, "Those babies are asking for something," and put it right back on again.

There was a loud knock on the door and Gahagan strolled over and opened it. Moss Shacker rocked in, and behind him came Mike Borodino. The Senator said in his bluff, heavy voice:

"Hello, MacBride. The news came over the ticker while I was sitting in Mike's office and I thought I'd come over and see you work. And, Mr. Kennedy! Well, well—always where action's the hottest. I'm still waiting to lose that bet. A hundred bucks! Ho-ho!" He rocked across to the window, squinted out. "That's the house, eh? What do you intend to do, blow it up?"

"Wait 'em out," said MacBride. "Dead men don't talk, and there ought to be some good talk come out of that house. Kennedy has an idea Bella Kojecki's in there, the vice queen."

Shacker reared around and guffawed. "By George, the way our Mr. Kennedy pulls 'em out of the air!" He threw up his hand and turned to MacBride. "Come on, Skipper, how about some action? Let's see your big artillery tear into the place."

"Stay away from the windows, Senator," the skipper said. "Those guys across the street might be wild shots."

Borodino hadn't yet said anything. His hands were in his pockets and a very snappy dark blue fedora was raked across one ear. His dark face was set, expressionless. His attitude was that of a man listening very intently, not to anything in the room, but to things outside. He gave the impression of being on his toes, without, actually, being on his toes. In the expressionless set of his face there was something vaguely tragic. But his voice, when he spoke at last, was brisk, tart, forceful:

"What's the layout, MacBride?"

"Two men and a woman in the house. One sub gun that we know of." The skipper was grimly keeping his eyes off Shacker. "I phoned them and told 'em to come out with their hands up, and the guy on the phone told me to go to hell."

Moss Shacker exploded: "And you take a crack like that! By God, if I were in charge of your men I'd blow the place off the street and everybody in it! Trouble these days, you all coddle the criminal too much!"

MacBride looked at the window. "I'm not thinking so much about the ones in the house. I got some good men downstairs. Most of them married and with kids."

"What are cops for?" demanded Shacker. "What do the citizens of this great, this glorious city pay taxes for? For protection against criminals! For—"

THE SUBMACHINE-GUN cut loose again. Borodino began pacing up and down the room, his arms pressed against his sides, his hands dug into his pockets. His lips were pressed in a tight line against his teeth.

The thunder of guns below in the street joined with the sound of the submachine-gun, and the sound of breaking glass threaded through it.

"That's more like it!" yelled Shacker. "Give it to 'em, coppers! Let 'em have it!"

MacBride thrust him away from the window. There was moisture on Shacker's big, loose lips, and a mad, glassy, jubilant fire in his eyes. He was grinning—actually grinning. He roared:

"You've *got* to give it to 'em, Skipper!"

MacBride snapped, "Don't tell me my business—and stay away from the windows!"

Through it all, unobserved, Kennedy was quietly using the telephone. Presently he lowered it, still unconnected, and said:

"Excuse me, excuse me. It's for you, Senator."

Shacker rocked across the room, grabbed the instrument and yelled, "Hello.... This is Senator Shacker." He frowned. His big eyebrows warped down over his nose and a shocked look tore down across his face. He sucked in a breath and hung up.

But Kennedy was at his elbow. The reporter grabbed up the instrument and slapped the receiver to his ear as he jumped back against the wall. The firing had stopped. The room and the street were dead quiet again, except for the distant humming of the crowd and the scratching of a voice in the telephone.

Shacker, his face red and bloated, was glaring transfixed at Kennedy.

Kennedy said to him, "Bella Kojecki thinks you're still on the phone. She says for God's sake do something, call off the cops, get them out—"

"Liar!" roared Shacker. "A frame-up if ever there was one!"

Kennedy hung up, saying, "She stopped talking."

Shacker raised his arms and roared at MacBride. "You heard that! You heard the way this low-down newspaperman tried to frame me! Did you hear anyone on the phone ask for me? No! Did he? No! I tell you, sir, it's your sworn duty to take that house—take it by storm! I demand it, as a citizen and member of the state senate—"

"Quit it," said Borodino in a flat voice.

Shacker whirled to stare at him.

Borodino said to MacBride, "You got the phone number of that house across the street?"

"Yes. Garden two-four-three."

Borodino, his face stiff, his eyes two dead coals in his head, crossed to the telephone and called Garden 243. He said, "Miss Kojecki, this is Assistant District Attorney Borodino speaking. I strongly advise you to stop shooting, to lay down those guns, to turn on all the lights in the house and then come out the front door, all of you, with your hands raised. Your house is completely surrounded. It can be shot to pieces, blown up, or you can be smoked out, at any time the police choose. Besides, Moss Shacker is in custody and you can expect no help from that quarter, from any quarter. Your turning on the lights will be the signal that you intend giving up."

He closed the connection and put the telephone down slowly and stared at it.

Shacker, his eyes bulging, was too stricken to move.

Without raising his eyes, without lifting his voice, Borodino said, "MacBride, arrest this man. For one thing, malfeasance. He came to Richmond City to buy off, quiet, or dispose of, one Evelyn Taunton, until recently contact woman of the vice ring of which Shacker is cognizant, from which he has garnered sums amounting to twenty- or twenty-five thousand dollars a year.

"The Taunton woman was kicked out when she cheated on the intake. She was replaced by the Kojecki woman, a favorite of the Senator's. The Taunton woman threatened to expose the Senator. She demanded to see him. He came down and saw her last night. With her in her room was Larry the Blink, a harmless, small-time punk. He got out when the Senator came in. The Senator and the Taunton woman talked for an hour. She wanted to be put back. He said he couldn't reinstate her. He offered a sum of money which she refused. Angry, the Senator left.

"The Blink came back. The Taunton woman was boiling for revenge. She planned this: She was to go to the Senator's apartment late at night, last night, and while she was there The Blink was to tip off a newspaperman. But things went wrong. The woman wasn't in the apartment five minutes when she pulled a knife, after the Senator threatened to throw her out. He was in an undershirt and got slashed on the stomach, and as she cut him he smacked her down and himself tripped and fell down, getting blood on the carpet. It wasn't a bad cut, and he took a towel and padded it on the cut and got dressed. When he came back in the living-room, the Taunton woman had gone, scared stiff. He went to 100 Mularkey where Bella Kojecki, formerly a nurse, cleansed and bandaged his wound. It's still bandaged, of course.

"The punk Larry got the jitters and hid out. The others were afraid either he or the Taunton woman would spill their grudge. The Senator, of course, was the most scared of all. Alfred Gibling was sent to pacify the woman and entice her, under promise of settlement, to another meeting with the Senator. He took her to 100 Mularkey, where she was bound and gagged.

"The red-head, O'Rourke, was all for nailing Larry the Blink and, being afraid of Kennedy, knowing Kennedy had a hunch, he was also after Kennedy. I arrested Larry on a trumped-up charge to keep O'Rourke from getting him. I warned the Senator that under no circumstances must anyone die. When Kennedy left my office this afternoon, I sent Sam Sands to tail him. Sam came back and said Kennedy'd gone into 100 Mularkey. I phoned Shacker and told him that if anything happened to Kennedy, he knew where he stood. Shacker called the Kojecki woman and told her to get rid of Kennedy, let him go. But again, things went wrong. And the Taunton woman was killed.

"Therefore, you must arrest this man Senator Moss Shacker, in view of the fact that—"

"Why, you dirty, lying, ungrateful pup!" exploded Shacker.

He flung himself ragefully upon Borodino. Borodino did not try to defend himself. His face was tense, his dark eyes intent on space, on thoughts which perhaps no one in that room could possibly share. The headlong rush, the swinging fist of Shacker, sent the Italian flying across the room, crashing into a corner. MacBride stepped in Shacker's way.

"Cut it," he said.

"Why, that—that dirty—that double-crossing dirty—"

"Pull up. You're under arrest."

Shacker stopped short, his lips dripping, his breath pounding his chest up and down. "Arrest! Ha! Me—*me* under arrest!" He pointed to Borodino. "That guy's nuts! Why, damn it, he can't tell a story like that on the stand! *He'd incriminate himself!*"

Borodino got up and in a choked, taut voice said, "Exactly. It's what I intend to do. I thank you for a lot, Moss—for picking me up as a bright lad just out of school. I've covered you a lot since. I couldn't do it any longer. It gagged me. I've been loyal to you, Moss, but the trouble was I didn't know how to draw the line between loyalty and common sense." His eyes were wet. "The complete gag was here tonight when you wanted the cops to assassinate the three in the house across the street—so they couldn't talk against you. *You* figured you knew where loyalty and common sense divided. And so did I. I just found out tonight. My tough brothers and sisters'll give me the birdie—and my old lady'll cry. Thanks for that too, Moss."

He whipped out his gun, trained it on Shacker. "Don't anybody move," he said in a low deadly voice. "Now I'll repay you, Moss."

Stacker's lips flapped. His eyes bulged and he dropped to his knees. "For God's sake, Mike, d-don't shoot me! D-don't, Mike! I—I'll take all the blame. All it, Mike! Only don't—"

Borodino laughed and tossed the gun in the air, caught it and slipped it back into his pocket. "I just wanted to see if you were yellow too, Moss."

There was a commotion in the street. Kennedy looked down and saw Bella and Hal and the smooth-faced man coming down the steps of the house, their hands raised, their faces white in the glare of the searchlight.

He said, "Maybe that was a good idea of mine—phoning Bella and then telling the Senator there was a call for him."

"You always were just a little too smart," Borodino said bitterly.

Kennedy smiled ruefully. "Believe it or not, Mike, I hope the judge gives you a break."

The phone rang and MacBride picked it up, spoke for a minute and then hung up. "They picked up Larry the Blink. At the railroad station. He was going places. They got the tip off a loan shark named Joe Scappa. The Blink was skipping town owing Scappa twelve dollars and sixty-five cents, and Scappa was sore."

Frederick Nebel Reaches the Screen

ED HULSE

ALTHOUGH Dashiell Hammett and Raymond Chandler are the two writers most frequently identified with *Black Mask* under the editorship of Joseph T. "Cap" Shaw, a far more prolific (and only slightly less talented) contributor was Frederick Lewis Nebel (1903-1967). Between March 1926 and August 1936, Nebel's byline appeared in the magazine some 66 times. Thirty-seven of his *Mask* yarns featured the team of MacBride and Kennedy—police captain and reporter, respectively—and provided the inspiration for a popular series of "B" movies in the Thirties.

When first encountered in "Raw Law" (September 1928, the initial installment in a five-story arc billed under the collective title, "The Crimes of Richmond City"), Captain Stephen J. McBride is a ruddy-faced, chisel-jawed, hard-bodied man of 40; a fervent and unyielding defender of the law, keenly aware of the milieu in which he functions but disdainful of any tactic that smacks of corruption or political expediency. Unlike most fictional detectives, MacBride is a family man: He lives with his wife and teenage daughter in a suburban bungalow far from the tenderloin district in which many of his cases unfold.

Kennedy is a reporter for the *Free Press*. Unlike MacBride, he's frail and stoop-shouldered, with pale hair and skin. He always looks tired or hung over and usually is both, especially in the later stories. Glib and sarcastic, he frequently chides MacBride for banging his head against a stone wall but secretly admires the tough cop (whom he calls "Skipper") for his honesty and courage.

MacBride and Kennedy squabble constantly, but their loyalty to each other knows no bounds. When Steve is framed and threatened with disgrace, the wisecracking reporter works tirelessly behind the scenes to secure evidence that will clear him. And when Kennedy takes a beating from gangsters, the Skipper tracks down his assailants and gives them a taste of their own medicine.

In the earlier stories, Kennedy is more of a sidekick than the unofficial partner he eventually became; by the mid Thirties he's accompanying MacBride to crime scenes and helping the Skipper interrogate suspects. In several tales, he actually does most of the detective work.

"No Hard Feelings" (February 1936), thirty-fourth of the series and one featuring Kennedy in his expanded role, begins with the reporter interviewing well-known sportsman George "Tiny" Torgensen, who has just agreed to purchase the gaming interests of erstwhile tough guy Fitz Mularkey, whose Million Club is a popular Richmond City night spot. While entering a cab with Kennedy outside Union Station, Torgensen is shot and killed by an unknown assailant. The Skipper, who knows Fitz well and considers him a straight shooter, investigates the murder with his newshound pal in tow.

Mularkey has planned to dispose of his night club and gambling empire to marry Boston society girl Marcia Friel, and then to go into a "legit" business with her brother Lewis. It doesn't take long for MacBride to find out that Fitz's plan didn't set well with several close associates: his right-hand man, Steamboat Hodge; Million Club manager Tom Carney; and fashion model Dolly Ireland, the gambler's former girl friend. Moreover, several prominent figures in Richmond City's underworld have been trying to buy out Mularkey themselves. To them, the scrupulously honest Torgensen was not only an interloper, but also a significant threat to their intended takeover of Fitz's enterprise.

Suspicion falls first on Hodge, who stood to lose his job when Mularkey sold out and married Marcia Friel. Upon learning this, a seething Fitz goes after his formerly loyal employee, ignoring MacBride's warning to let the police handle matters. Dolly Ireland is also implicated when it's discovered that she and Steamboat were seen together near Union Station just before Torgensen's shooting. When Steamboat turns up dead, the Skipper reluctantly vows to bring the gambler to justice.

Hodge is cleared when a ballistics test proves that his gun was not the murder weapon. If Fitz bumped Steamboat, he got the wrong man. Kennedy determines that the gambler is probably hiding at Marcia Friel's apartment and urges the Skipper to go there immediately. Sure enough, Mularkey is with Marcia and Lewis Friel.

Just as MacBride is about to make the pinch, Kennedy makes an astounding accusation: The Friels aren't brother and sister. In separate interviews with Marcia and Lewis, the reporter has unearthed contradictory facts about their family and background. It turns out they are sweethearts and con artists from Boston, where they knew Tiny Torgensen and learned about his planned purchase of Mularkey's business. They planned to get hold of Fitz's money after he'd married Marcia, and killed Torgensen because he could have identified them and put the kibosh on their scheme.

The ever-loyal Steamboat, to the end protective of his boss, had broken into Marcia's apartment and found a love letter written to her by Lewis. Armed with this evidence, he confronted Lewis with exposure—but made the mistake of doing so while drunk, enabling Marcia's "brother" to get the drop on him. A chastened Fitz sets up housekeeping with Dolly and Kennedy returns to the drinking that was interrupted by detective work.

Warner Brothers, which had previously produced film adaptations of stories by *Black Mask* regulars Dashiell Hammett and Raoul Whitfield, purchased the screen rights to "No Hard Feelings" in mid-1936.

Torchy (Glenda Farrell) and Steve (Barton MacLane)
question Dolly Ireland (Wini Shaw).

Farrell and MacLane clowning in this publicity photo.

Of all the Hollywood studios, Warners was best equipped to translate *Mask's* terse, hard-boiled fiction style to the silver screen. In the early Thirties, under the stewardship of then-production chief Darryl F. Zanuck, Warners specialized in fast-moving films set in an urban milieu. Rapid pacing, crisp dialogue, and violent action were the hallmarks of Warners' crime films, which were leaner and tougher than those of other companies.

(Previously, Nebel had made one other sale to Hollywood. Fox Film Corporation in late 1933 purchased screen rights to *Sleepers East*, a complicated, multi-character novel published earlier that year in hard covers. Never published in the pulps, it nonetheless had a melodramatic flavor and took place on board a passenger train. The rapidly produced movie version, starring Preston Foster and Wynne Gibson, was released in April 1934 but aroused little critical or commercial interest and quickly vanished.)

"No Hard Feelings" was entrusted to Bryan Foy, scion of a venerable show-business family (he was one of the "Seven Little Foys") and supervisor of the studio's "B" unit. He delegated scripting chores to relative newcomers Kenneth Gamet and Don Ryan, who were assisted (without screen credit) by Harold Buckley, William Jacobs, and Ben Kohn. It's difficult to imagine that five writers were needed to complete the assignment, given that the final script follows Nebel's story faithfully, even to many of the dialogue exchanges.

The few alterations to "No Hard Feelings" were minor. Structurally, pulp and film versions were identical. The story's Steamboat Hodge became Chuck Cannon in the movie, possibly because Foy and/or the scripters figured that the name "Steamboat" carried insufficient menace. Nebel's other character names remained intact. Dolly Ireland's profession was changed from fashion model to chanteuse, most likely to accommodate the casting of Warners contract player Wini Shaw, best known up to that point as the vocalist who performed "Lullaby of Broadway" in *Gold Diggers of 1935.*

There was, however, one major departure from Nebel's story. The character of Kennedy was replaced by a female reporter named Torchy Blane. She performed exactly the same narrative function as her male counterpart, even to making critical last-minute deductions that enabled the Skipper to apprehend the real culprits.

The role of Torchy was given to another contract player, Glenda Farrell, who had essayed similar roles in several earlier Warners films, most notably in 1933's *Mystery of the Wax Museum.* Reasonably attractive but no glamour-puss, Farrell was not the type to play romantic leads. Her dynamic acting style—which combined staccato dialogue delivery with expressive body language and rapid movements—was perfectly suited to the type of movie in which Warner Brothers specialized.

Yet another Warners contractee, Barton MacLane, took the role of Steve McBride—who, in his journey from pulp page to silver screen, lost the "a" in his surname and was demoted from captain to lieutenant. Being a bit on the thuggish side in appearance and vocal quality, MacLane wasn't a perfect match for Nebel's Skipper, but he'd already had experience playing tough police detectives in Warners movies, including two Perry Masons and *Jailbreak* (1936), which he made just before going into production on *Smart Blonde*. His McBride was stubborn and pugnacious, if not quite as smart as Nebel's character; this allowed Torchy to take center stage when it came to making deductions.

Frank McDonald's direction was lean and muscular. Like most of the studio's megaphone-wielders, he eschewed elaborate staging and fancy camera moves, instead offering a straightforward treatment of the material that allowed for brisk pacing and continuous forward motion. Ironically, the fidelity to Nebel's original worked against the film in the minds of some critics, who objected to what they saw as an over-reliance on dialogue and a stinting on physical action.

Variety reviewer "Shan," opining in that showbiz journal's idiosyncratic fashion, had this to say: "Picture is fairly well paced with an amount of flip talk, but no [production] mountings to mention.... Outdoor stuff is practically nil for interest and the interiors are not much more than this. There's more chatter than action and, as is usual in such tales, the murderers are nabbed by deduction rather than by filmed action."

Harrison's Reports rendered this judgment: "Passable murder mystery melodrama. It should find favor mostly with patrons who enjoy figuring out solutions, for murderer's identity is not divulged until the end. The story is pretty weak and is developed mostly by dialogue instead of action; for this reason it occasionally becomes tiresome. There is nothing novel in the plot or the way it is developed. The romantic interest is dragged in, in an unbelievable way."

(Director Howard Hawks, never bashful about taking credit for good ideas, often claimed it was his idea to change the sex of the demon reporter in *His Girl Friday* (1940), Hollywood's second adaptation of a celebrated Broadway play, Ben Hecht and Charles MacArthur's *The Front Page*. Making "Hildy Johnson" a female—played by Rosalind Russell—enhanced the tension between reporter and editor, the latter played as charming but unscrupulous by Cary Grant. Ever the blowhard, Hawks in later years boasted that this innovative concept bettered a property that, it should be said, scarcely needed bettering. Unfortunately, nobody ever bothered to confront him with the inconvenient truth—namely, that lowly "B"-movie producer Bryan Foy had beaten him to the sex-change idea. Operating in Tinseltown's upper echelon, Hawks *might* not have been familiar with, or paid much attention to, Warners' low-budget productions. But as someone

Glenda Farrell

who screened movies constantly, he very well may have seen *Smart Blonde* or one of its sequels and been influenced by Glenda Farrell's portrayal of a cynical, fast-talking "sob sister.")

Smart Blonde was released to theaters in January of 1937, and its success led to a sequel released five months later. But instead of adapting another Kennedy-MacBride story, *Fly Away Baby* used as its inspiration the around-the-world airplane journey of real-life reporter Dorothy Kilgallen, undertaken as a publicity stunt. The Warner Brothers scriptwriters dramatized this incident and grafted onto it a murder mystery and international-smuggling plot. The team of Farrell and MacLane once again proved pleasing to audiences, ensuring continuation of the series.

Though popular with moviegoers, the Torchy Blane films were undeniably modest offerings—that is to say, they were simply "units" in the studio's yearly production slate, made inexpensively and designed to fill out the bottom half of a double feature. The plots generally involved murders but every now and then MacBride and company investigated less lethal crimes. Comedy relief became more prevalent, with the Skipper's driver Gahagan (played by Tom Kennedy) being allotted generous amounts of footage for his inane antics.

Seven more Torchys followed *Fly Away Baby*, although Farrell and MacLane bowed out of the series after *Torchy Runs for Mayor* (1939). The final entry, *Torchy Blane Playing With Dynamite* (also 1939), starred Jane Wyman, a Warners contract player who'd played a hat-check girl in *Smart Blonde*. None of the films after the first used a Nebel story as source material, although *Torchy Blane in Chinatown* (1939) used as its basis "The Purple Cipher," a 1919 pulp story by Murray Leinster previously filmed twice.

Publication History

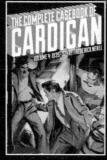

BLACK MASK

The Richmond City Free Press

BLACK MASK

All the Stories from 1928 to 1936

THE COMPLETE CASES OF MacBRIDE & KENNEDY

IN FOUR VOLUMES

BY FREDERICK NEBEL

Crimes of Richmond City

CAPTAIN STEVE MacBRIDE was a tall square-shouldered man of forty more or less hard-bitten

Dog Eat Dog

WHEN CAPTAIN MacBRIDE was suddenly transferred from the Second Precinct to the Fifth, an undercurrent of whispered speculations trickled through the Department, buzzed in newspaper circles, and traveled along the underworld grapevine.

It was a significant move, for MacBride, besides being the youngest captain in the Department—he was barely forty—was known throughout Richmond City as a holy terror against the criminal element. He was a lank, rangy man, with a square jaw and windy blue eyes. He was brusque, talked straight from the shoulder, and was hard-

INTRODUCTION BY DAVID LEWIS

Coming This Fall From Altus Press

The Law Laughs Last

TOUGH precinct was the Second of Richmond City, lying in the backyard of the theatrical district and on the frontier of the railroad yards.

A hard-boiled precinct, touching the fringe of crookdom's elite on the north—the con men, the night-club barons; and on the south, the dim-lit, crooked alleys traversed by the bum, the lush-worker and poolroom gangster. On the north were the playhouses, the white way, high-toned apartments, opulent hotels, high hats, evening gowns. On the south, tenements, warehouses, cobblestones, squalor, and the railroad yards. The toughest precinct in all Richmond City.

Law Without Law

KENNEDY chuckled. "So you're back in the Second, Mac."

"See me here, don't you?"

"Ay, verily!"

The old station-house, blown up during the last election, had been rebuilt, and the office in which Captain Stephen MacBride sat and Kennedy, the insatiable news-hound, stood, smelled of new paint and plaster. Something of the old atmosphere was lost—that atmosphere which it had taken long years to create: dust, age-colored walls decorated with news clippings, "wanted" bulletins, likenesses of known criminals.

Two days ago MacBride had been

New Guns For Old

POLICE Captain Steve MacBride was on leave. He had it coming to him. As one of the main factors in the scouring of Richmond City's corrupt municipal government, he was due some little respite from the shield and the gun. With the passing of a self-seeking Mayor

CPSIA information can be obtained
at www.ICGtesting.com
Printed in the USA
BVHW021236150223
R14653600001B/R146536PG658034BVX00029B/29

9 781618 271310